Books by Susannah Stacey

Hunter's Quarry
Body of Opinion
Bone Idle
Dead Serious
Goodbye, Nanny Gray
A Knife at the Opera
The Late Lady
Grave Responsibility

Published by POCKET BOOKS

HUNTER'S QUARRY

A Superintendent Bone Mystery

SUSANNAH STACEY

POCKET BOOKS
New York London Toronto Sydney Tokyo Singapore

This book is a work of fiction. Names, characters, places and incidents are products of the author's imagination or are used fictitiously. Any resemblance to actual events or locales or persons, living or dead, is entirely coincidental.

An *Original* Publication of POCKET BOOKS

POCKET BOOKS, a division of Simon & Schuster Inc.
1230 Avenue of the Americas, New York, NY 10020

ISBN: 0-671-00119-1

First Pocket Books printing November 1998

10 9 8 7 6 5 4 3 2 1

POCKET and colophon are registered trademarks of Simon & Schuster Inc.

Cover art by Jeff Fitz-Maurice

Printed in the U.S.A.

Chapter

1

·········

The figure appeared while she was in the kitchen, brewing coffee. She could hear Jem and his friends in the sitting room making a fuss of the kittens, but simultaneously she heard water lapping as if a thirsty animal drank nearby. The figure said nothing, did nothing, for the time it took the coffee grounds to slide off the teaspoon as she gazed, and then it was gone.

Emily shook her head a little, to clear her vision, and put the mug on the tray with the others. The water sound had faded to a murmur in her ears, very like the tinnitus she had occasionally, which her doctor kindly told her was only to be expected at her age. She even clattered the teaspoons against the sugar bowl as if to exorcise the lingering presence in the room, the feeling of terrible sadness, of something unspoken that struggled to be said.

She filled the mugs and stirred the coffee. It was a long time since she had seen anything so baffling, so upsetting. As she carried the tray through, lifting a kitten deftly out of the way with a gentle foot under its stomach while she balanced briefly on the other foot—a pity Dr. Bellrose couldn't see her do *that* at her age—she wondered if she'd been looking at any article in the papers about Egypt recently. It might account for that swathed figure, motionless under its wrappings, but it wouldn't account for its distress.

They didn't bury them alive in ancient Egypt, did they? And surely the mummy wrappings were very organized, less disheveled?

"We think we have the right one. What's this one called?"

The daft object held up for her to name stared at her for a moment with huge, clouded blue eyes, and then twisted both ways in Jem's hand and dropped to the carpet where it shook itself and staggered off to be pounced on by a sibling lying in wait under the coffee table.

"Skywalker is his name at present, from running up curtains and people, he doesn't mind which, but it's only a milk name. You'll probably want to give him another when he comes to you and you get the chance to study him. He's one of Arletty's and I warn you he has her appetite, she eats anything from spiders to sushi and"— Emily, sitting down, fended off the exploring glove of an elegant cat, the Arletty in question, sitting on her chair arm and tapping the plate on the tray—"she licks the chocolate off biscuits."

Arletty, displeased either at being frustrated or at having her habits mentioned, switched her tail which became at once the focus of three pairs of kitten eyes doing their best to take in more reality than they could manage. Skywalker, emerging from the ambush under the table, ran upward on the chintz cover of the chair to reach his mother's tail. Jem and the girl watched, fascinated, as he dabbed at the moving object. Emily dealt out mugs, sugar and biscuits.

"Just how many do you *have?*" The girl, looking round her, might well be confused, for Emily had mustered both available kindles of kittens, and some of the cats sensed food and had come in. The question was almost the first time she had spoken and Emily was encouraging in reply.

"It depends if you count the kittens as part of the wildlife and, when I know I'm going to lose them, I tend to think of them as visitors only." She gestured at a large, slightly disagreeable-looking cat, mostly black but with a white patch over one eye, who sat on the low windowsill gazing aloofly out at the village street. "That's Makepeace. He doesn't really like anyone and he puts up with me only because I feed him. I wouldn't do that," she added to Jem who had got up to offer a bit of biscuit. "He has no feeling whatever for biscuit and might take a bit of your finger by mistake."

Jem drew back in exaggerated caution, making the girl laugh and Makepeace flick an ear. Emily thought, they don't know each other well yet, but Jem ought to do her a power of good. He's a nice-looking boy with a lot of confidence, just the thing to bring her out of that shyness. It can't help her that her complexion's not good, she has to wear braces and there's all that thin, drippy hair. If they're going to be brother and sister, so to speak, Jem might give her some of his confidence. She looked as if she needed it and then . . . people said Emily chose quaint names for her cats but it would be hard to come up with one more calculated to repel than the one this girl's mother had wished on her. Treasure, indeed! Jem had looked very demure when he'd introduced her. "Treasure Schlumberger. She's from the States and staying at Herne Hall with her grandmother who says she can have a kitten if you've one to spare."

The trouble with the girl, of course, was that she looked more Schlumberger than Treasure. Emily introduced another cat, Daisy, who now came in to check on her own kittens; the girl put out a hand with chewed nails to stroke her, and Emily wondered how she got on with a beautiful TV star mother.

Emily took a saucer and poured milk into it, at which signal Arletty left the armchair, avoiding Skywalker in a graceful arc, and waited as the saucer descended. For a moment Emily stopped still as the water lapped in her ears again, but the sound resolved itself into Arletty greedily imbibing before Daisy could get her pretty nose stuck in.

"When is the wedding to be? The village is getting quite excited over it."

Emily had a feeling as she spoke that the question was not welcome. Jem shrugged as if his father's wedding had nothing to do with him. Treasure glowered, as if she wished her mother's wedding would never take place; as far as Emily could remember, this marriage to Ken Cryer would be Zephyr's third, and she wondered which of the first two had been the one to Schlumberger which had produced this awkward child. Treasure, however, was the one who answered.

"Mom keeps changing her mind. She wanted it to be this month but one of her astrologers said it's not lucky. She's discussed it with the caterers all the same."

"Marquee on the lawn." Jem grinned. "Bet it'll rain."

"She wanted to have the real wedding, with a pastor, in the village church, but your father"—Emily caught the slightly hostile emphasis—"said your church is uptight about divorced people marrying in church anyhow, and also if they did get some pastor who'd do it, it'd get swamped by TV and the paparazzi, so she's thinking again."

Emily picked up the saucer the cats had licked clean, and mopped up a trail of milky paw marks from Skywalker's having run across it in pursuit of his mother's tail. She came up flushed with stooping and inquired, "Surely you have to give plenty of notice for weddings? I've heard it's not easy to fit anyone in at short notice. Haven't the banns to be read in the church?"

"Mom will fix it. She'll just turn on the charm and everything will happen the way she wants."

Emily, offering a plate of biscuits with one hand and fending Arletty away with the other, thought the bitterness in Treasure's voice must come from long experience. Adolescence, already a bad time for getting on with parents, loaded the girl with a problem not inflicted on everyone. At least Zephyr wouldn't see this drab child as a future rival, so she might be spared a bit of sniping there; of course it might irritate a lovely woman that her daughter wasn't something to show off. Emily didn't see Zephyr West—no wonder she had called her child Treasure—as a compassionate figure.

"And Dad will turn on *his* charm and cancel everything out." Jem turned from regarding the little front garden and the road, in silent collusion with Makepeace, and Emily wondered if the rivalry between the two was really about which had the more glamorous parent. Ken Cryer was a rock star, not given to snorting cocaine or hurling TV sets from hotel windows, but a quiet, pleasant soul; he might live in the local manor house fitted out with every security device under the sun, and employ what Emily had been pleased to learn were called "heavies," but he was very well liked in the small town. People were proud of their celebrity. How would two of them be coped with? Emily had already gathered, out shopping, that there was a resentment such as Jem was showing, at any possible takeover bid by the newcomer.

As Treasure began to reply—and really Emily had never seen an uglier set of braces in any mouth—the church clock at the corner of the street chimed, a solemn sweet sound that made Treasure look at her watch and jump up.

"Oh my stars! Mom said to be back at noon. That woman is coming to fit me with that horrible dress. Jem, how do we make it in time?"

"No problem. Mel will scoot us back. Only a few miles, and the horrible dress won't dissolve by the time we get there."

"I *wish.*" She explained to Emily, earnestly, "It has frills all over and it's yellow like puke."

Silently, Emily sympathized. If Zephyr West was not actually cruel, dressing a plain girl with a sallow complexion in yellow with frills made her seem so. Treasure was struggling now into a denim jacket, very much more

5

her style. Jem, sallow and angular as she was, looked already her brother, in jeans and identical jacket, although his thick mousy hair contrasted with her straggling dun locks.

He came to plant a kiss on Emily's cheek. "Thanks for the coffee and the cat show. I forgot to say, Buster sends his love. He gets on very well at the Manor but he does miss this place and all his aunties."

"Get your father to let you have another—Celsius and Fahrenheit will be ready to leave when Skywalker does. No, let me or he'll pull the threads." Emily bent to lift Skywalker who had started up the back of Treasure's jeans as she made for the door. The absurdity of her own remark struck her as she considered the carefully ripped and frayed surface from which she was removing the kitten. "It's been very nice seeing you both and I'll let you know when this one," she waggled Skywalker's paw as, firmly gripped, he rolled his head back to look at her upside down, "is ready to leave."

Jem got Treasure out down the brick path with a guiding hand on her back, and her not shrugging him off argued that despite the hostility, they had achieved some accord. Parked illegally on the yellow line outside her hedge, Mel Rees, one of the "heavies" with whom Emily was great friends, stood with the car door already open, glancing, not at his passengers, but all round at anyone who might be observing them, just like a bodyguard in a film. Emily supposed, as she waved goodbye with Skywalker's paw, that there might conceivably be those who wished Ken Cryer and his son harm—although she could not imagine what cause they could have—but surely they would never come to a little place like this in pursuit of any dreadful purpose.

As she watched the car accelerate smoothly down the lane, Emily shook her head to free her ears from the noise of water again. If this went on, she was going to bother Dr. Bellrose till he came up with something useful.

Chapter
2
··········

Edwina would not tell Bone over the telephone why Ken Cryer wanted to see him at the Manor that morning. "Let's say he'd rather discuss it with you himself."

Bone glanced at the work in front of him and put his free hand down hastily as papers blew in the draft from the open door. "Well, Ken isn't going to fret about the unimportant, so I take it this is important—"

Inspector Garron, busily working himself into another ulcer, was bawling someone out in the office. He had left Bone's door open and it now swung against the file cabinet behind, making the lettering *Superintendent R. D. Bone* seem to waver on the glass.

"I'd say it is," Edwina admitted. "Coffee at eleven, then?"

So Bone was drinking good coffee with Ken at the Manor just as Ken's son was at Emily Playfair's cottage only a few miles away. Their surroundings were naturally a little different even though cottage and manor house both belonged to the same end of the fifteenth century. There were beams at the cottage that would brain anyone less short than Emily, while here in the Manor drawing room beams ran across the ceiling at a height to accommodate the six-foot-odd of Ken and the all-but-six-feet of Bone. Ken had never thought that the beams which Victorians loved to stain black really needed to be so somber, but instead of bleaching these back to the pale oak of which purists approved, he had enjoyed having them painted lime green, scrolled with gold. He also enjoyed the expressions on the faces of those who sat on the sofa, glanced up and paused to take in what he had done.

Bone knew and liked this from some time ago, and now let his gaze roam over the room while Ken poured coffee. In the same way that he gave up dark beams for an earlier, medieval tradition, Ken avoided chintz: the sofa where Bone sat was covered in scarlet corduroy, the curtains at the big, many-paned windows hung to the ground in stripes of red, amber and chocolate. He had, however, chosen a dark oak sideboard with the dull gleam of pewter dishes propped on it, rather than any brash chrome, and the cavern of the brick fireplace was heaped with pinecones.

"I haven't had the chance to congratulate you, Ken." Bone, perhaps at the very same time as Emily Playfair, added, "When's the wedding to be?"

Ken came over with his coffee before replying. Bone glanced at the pale, sardonic face, the deep lines that hollowed the cheeks and framed the corners of the mouth, and thought it didn't look as if its owner desired congratulations.

"Brownie? Edwina actually makes these things and serves them up. Mrs. Rudyard doesn't go a bundle on that; I suppose housekeepers weren't designed to get on with secretaries." Ken engulfed one of his secretary's productions with ease; he leaned back in his chair, also a scarlet corduroy. His black jacket, T-shirt and jeans gave him a curious look of a demon enthroned in flames. Bone had seen press photographs about the forthcoming marriage, and mused that Zephyr West had possibly chosen her new partner as an interesting contrast, to set off her own blond beauty. The reason Ken had chosen her

8

was obvious enough, though Bone was still surprised at his deciding to settle at all. He could, within reason, have got any woman he wanted any time in all these years, and Bone had understood from various remarks of his that he hung back from commitment in order not to saddle fourteen-year-old Jem with a stepmother. He seemed to think at this moment that he must answer Bone's question, and paused with his coffee almost at his lips.

"The wedding. Wanted to ask you about that." He drank, as if putting off the matter, and succeeded only in making it seem more portentous. He leaned to put down the mug, meeting Bone's eyes at last. "Problems there, in fact."

Bone drank his coffee in the following silence. He considered prompting Ken with "Problems?" supposing he was not required as a marriage counsel or, rather, a prenuptial consultant. If Ken had cold feet he wouldn't call on Bone to warm them. Ken's next words, however, did not seem relevant to the impending marriage.

"Death threats." Ken waved a hand dismissively. "You know I've had them since forever. Anyone who gets up onstage as a target gets them sooner or later. Any audience will have nutters in it, I don't have to tell you."

Bone, twenty or more years back, had been part of security at a rock concert. He remembered the vast area of waving arms like submarine weed, the incredible noise, the mob hysteria, the certainty that many were drunk or high, and he nodded. Rock stars were a natural target for the unhinged. So why is Ken telling me now?—"But the latest lot are connected with the wedding."

Ken sat up, pointing a brownie at Bone. "Now that's the reason I asked for you. You don't need telling things." The last bit of brownie was posted and he spoke through it, distributing crumbs. "This fan feels I am betraying her personally by marrying and says she'll get me for it."

"Do you know it's a woman?"

Ken raised his eyebrows. "Could be a man, though I'd never have said I'm the type."

"Nutters in every audience? It could as well be a man if the letters aren't specific; he could still think you were betraying him. People need the image they're familiar with."

"But it's not like the old days when you couldn't let on you were married in case the fans went off you. Was it Shaking Stevens had to keep quiet for ages about being respectably linked back in the—was it sixties? Or maybe I'm making the bloke older than he is. No disrespect, Shaking." Ken rubbed his thumb along the deep line by his mouth. "I'm no chicken myself. No one should give a damn whether or not I'm married so long as I'm not in a rest home and can keep on churning out albums for them to buy."

"Yet someone's talking of stopping these albums at the source . . . This is not really my field, you know."

Ken grinned. "Thought you might like a briefing before you're called in to deal with a possible result. Seriously, I've not forgotten how good you were over poor Nanny Gray, whom Jem was so fond of, and I couldn't think of anyone I'd rather have to help me not to figure in your caseload."

"I'm flattered of course, but I'm told your security is excellent. We can try to trace who's sending these threats—people evidently know your address. I'll have to hand the job to one of our experts but I'll keep you informed about it. I imagine you're worried about the actual wedding arrangements."

At that moment Ken held up a long finger and Bone caught the crackle of gravel under car tires on the drive. Ken unfolded to his feet and went to the window, positioning himself behind a long curtain so as not to be seen looking out. A door slammed and he turned to Bone with a face of almost comic despair.

"My fiancée. We'll have to talk about this another time. I was not expecting her—but that's Zephyr."

10

Bone stood up, his natural curiosity sharpened. He was about to see the woman for whom Ken Cryer was going to sacrifice his freedom, so he anticipated something worth looking at.

The front door, like the car door, slammed as if Zephyr appropriately generated her own breeze that blew her through life. There was a skitter of high heels on the worn flags of the hall, the sitting room door was flung wide and Zephyr made her entrance.

For a moment it was bizarre. She was carrying a plant, an explosion of scarlet flowers and glossy dark green leaves obscuring her face so that she could hardly be seen. The plant was in a green and white china cachepot, latticed and scrolled with china leaves and clearly heavy as she had to lean back from the hips to support it at chest level. Ken moved quickly to relieve her of it. "Thank you, darling!" She offered her cheek to be kissed while she directed a dazzling smile at Bone. "I thought, *there.*" She pointed to the top of the grand piano between the windows. "It needs something there, and you can see it while you're composing, my sweet. Doesn't it tone beautifully with the curtains?"

Before Ken, obediently placing the pot on the unadorned piano lid, had a chance to introduce Bone, she advanced, holding out her hand, to say unnecessarily, "I'm Zephyr West."

"Robert Bone." He shook the slender hand, assaulted by musky scent, and gave no clue to his profession in case Ken wanted the subject of his visit kept quiet.

Ken, however, after wiping a hand under the cachepot to ensure no damp would damage the mahogany, turned to add, "He's a policeman, Zeph, as well as an old friend. Thought I'd make some inquiries about security for the wedding—whenever and wherever."

Zephyr laughed, and it was a delicious sound. "You are an old worry box. I keep telling you it'll be fine, the stars are in all the right houses."

"They can be in any house they like," Ken said morosely, "if it has a proper alarm system. What about that old biddy who told you that you have Saturn in Pisces or something and you mustn't swim against the tide, meaning me?"

"Oh *that*." She twined an arm through Ken's and led him to the sofa where she collapsed, drawing him down, her long legs coltishly askew. She put back the hair from his forehead. "If you're the tide, honey, I mean to be *swept along* by you. No, she was just in a mood, muttering like an old witch about my being a fish out of water—I'm a Pisces, you see." She gave the information to Bone as if he would want to rush back and put it on the police computer.

"I wasn't expecting you until much later. Did your mother throw you out?"

Again the laughter, with no air of being artificial or rehearsed but delightful, spontaneous, throaty like the slightly gruff voice which sounded as if shaped by a lifetime of smoking and champagne. She leaned her head on Ken's shoulder and looked up at him. "You always pretend she hates me! But I could see she was becoming a little enervated. She's barely over that bout of flu she wrote me about, and you have to remember it's always stressful with a teenager in the house. My mother"—she gave Bone the full-treatment smile again—"lives at Herne Hall, you know. It's a lovely old mansion right close by." Bone did know, although he did not say so. The police weren't ignorant of who lived in the big houses of the neighborhood. He took "close by" for an American opinion of distance, Herne Hall being quite some way off through country lanes. "Mother just begged to have my little daughter stop with her but kids really drain one, don't they?"

Bone acquiesced, thinking of his own teenage Charlotte who, though far from being a difficult child, had yet the power to rouse in him the most passionate anxiety and protectiveness. He noticed that Zephyr had managed to palm off her exhausting daughter on a grandmother still suffering the aftereffects of flu. He had the impression that Zephyr was living here at the Manor.

12

It was hard, too, not to see this lovey-dovey act with Ken, those elegant long legs sprawled so that Bone could see almost to the top of the thighs under the cream linen mockery of a skirt, while the white silk lapels of the shirt fell provocatively apart even further as she leaned on Ken's chest, as flirtation by proxy. If your profession is to make people in love with you, such attitudes must be second nature. Only recently Bone had met, in the line of business, an English TV actress of considerable beauty and charm; next to Zephyr West she was of subdued sexual wattage, but they had in common this instinct to invite admiration—desire—as though it was as necessary to them as air. Ken, at this moment, was providing the oxygen by stroking the blond hair back from her neck and looking down into Zephyr's face as if only Bone's presence kept him from a violent clinch. Bone could see how his breathing had quickened. However, he merely asked, "What's your mother's opinion of your latest plan?"

"She thinks it's heaven! Herne Hall is *the* place for a romantic wedding, she agrees."

"Herne Hall?" Bone's neutral inquiry drew both pairs of eyes, Ken's cool gray and Zephyr's huge blue gaze. "You're thinking of getting married at Herne Hall." His habit of producing statements that were really questions gave Zephyr's plans a sound of finality she was quick to reject.

"Ah, I could still change my mind! Momma wants for me to have the reception there as her gift to me and I know it'd really disappoint her if I didn't accept now that we've talked of it. Honey," she turned her face up to Ken's again, "there is the cutest place by the lake where we could have the ceremony."

"And security," Bone's voice broke in again. "You've given thought to security."

He did not add, *and death threats?*

13

Chapter
3
·········

"Moods, moods. Who needs moods!"

Kelly, opening and slamming drawers full of clothes, was talking to herself. It was a thing she did often, even if she was not alone. After all, in Kelly, she had the perfect audience, ready to applaud her remarks and, if she answered herself, to be sympathetic. Today there was an undertone of irritation, with everything and everyone, even herself.

"Stupid stupid *stupid.*"

She wrestled with a drawer that refused to slide back, snagging askew and wadding up a sweater as an obstacle. After trying to rattle it free, she finally, in an access of rage, jerked it right out, strewing its contents on the floor, where she kicked them, got her foot entangled in the sweater and nearly fell. She saved herself by grabbing the armchair's back, and paused. The armchair was by her own custom surrendered to Alan, while she sat on the sagging sofa to gaze at him and be ready to jump whenever he wanted anything.

Today she would sit in the armchair and she would smoke.

Alan hated her smoking. When she felt the urge for

a smoke too strong to smother she had to go actually outdoors and smoke in the street because, he said, the smoke got in the curtains and he could smell it as soon as he came in.

Recently, he'd said he could smell it in her hair.

She got the pack from her coat pocket, with her lighter, picked her way through the scattered clothes and crashed back into the armchair. There was utterly no point in doing things gracefully if Alan wasn't there to see.

She leaned back, the smoke sharp in her nostrils, and drew on the cigarette luxuriously, eyes shut. The little bracket clock she had inherited from her grandmother struck ten, tinnily. Alan hated that clock, said it was a nagger he didn't need. Well, it was telling her now that she had an hour before he would arrive. Plenty of time to do what was necessary. She stuck her feet out in front of her and flexed her toes so that the bear claws on the fur slippers raked the air with menace. Alan said that they were silly, but Alan's opinions were not important any more. She was free; free to smoke if she wanted to, to eat biscuits in bed if she felt like it, and live in the crumbs if she so chose. So no more talk of her being a slut, no more complaints that she didn't live up to him. No more any of that. Kelly tightened her lips, flexed the slippers again, stubbed out the butt in the saucer of the potted plant and went to make the coffee.

Alan was punctual to the minute. It was one of the things he hadn't succeeded in being rid of. He wanted to be relaxed, saunter into places late, cool, ready with a sarcastic comeback to any comment, but it wasn't in his nature. He found it physically painful to go against the grain. Other things he had achieved: he looked like someone who could afford to ignore time, he lounged superbly, he drawled to perfection, one would take him for a man who only went to bed if more than one gorgeous girl lured him to it, and only rose from it if people made it well worth his while. The deep lines that scored his face, the hollow cheeks, spoke of past dissipation and all the glamour of sleepless nights and hard-lived days. The way the lock of hair fell over one eye was, of course, carefully contrived after long study of photographs and of himself in a mirror. You had to make the most of a face like that.

He was wearing his black leather jacket, black T-shirt and black leather jeans when he rang her doorbell. It was not for her, this time. He couldn't be bothered to impress her any more. She no longer mattered compared with what was before him. He felt strung up and hoped she wouldn't be tedious. No, he had dressed because of the chance of being recognized on the way. It did happen now and then and there was still a buzz in signing autographs. One thing was on his mind as he stepped back to look up at Kelly's windows: would the clothes he kept here be all right? You couldn't trust Kelly. She was spiteful. That time they'd had strife—those damn biscuits in the bed—he found in the morning she'd cut up his best T-shirt, one she'd given him with his face on the front. He shouldn't have walked out on her the other night and not taken his clothes. They were the very ones she'd urged him to buy and they'd cost a bomb—well worth it, beautiful, made him look a thousand dollars, bronze silk shirt, bronze leather jacket that made the one he now wore look a very poor relation. He hoped to hell she hadn't done anything dodgy to that jacket.

The buzzer went, he spoke into the grating and the door sprang ajar. He loped up the stairs; no need to appear languid when no one was to see him. She was waiting at the top.

Now he was looking at her, seeing her rather than knowing she was there as a utility of his life, he was angry with himself. With his looks he should have done better than that. How had he come to be reduced to this one? She was so exactly what he didn't fancy, over-weight, pasty. He liked long luxuriant curls, she had straggly straight hair the worse for being held back with glittery barrettes from that pale slab of a face. When she smiled, and she used to smile at him a lot, she had dim-

ples that weren't bad, and little creases under the eyes
that once had seemed almost fetching. She was not smiling now. She must hate this breakup. It must really hurt.

"I've got all your stuff. You'd best come and get it."

She wheeled and made for the living room. Following,
he smelled the smoke, and his nostrils contracted. God,
he was right to go. He looked round the room, seeing
it too as though for the first time: the rose-sprigged
wallpaper . . . to be fair, the landlord was responsible
for that, but she had never appeared to care how far out
of character such a background was for him . . . that
grotty sofa she'd sit on, waiting for his wishes, calling
him by that name.

He was not to get the treatment today. Did she think
it was a blow, that he'd mind? "Alan," she shouted from
the bedroom. He stood gazing at the street for the last
time—a street so invested with glamour when their
dream first took off. "*Alan.* You'd best come and see if
I've got everything."

Everything, though, didn't matter that much any more.
He needed only that bronze leather jacket and silk shirt.
It was the latest, most correct thing to wear. She mustn't
realize that. She might already have guessed too much
about what he had in mind. Better pretend the whole
idea was that the journey they'd so often taken together
was this time only for nostalgia and no deadly purpose.

So he fussed a bit, over the clothes. He could play it
down, he was on top of things, pretending, opening the
carriers and poking inside, casually, while she watched,
hands on hips—not a pose that suited her build. Thank
God the bronze shirt, which he shook out, was intact,
hardly even creased, and the bronze jacket perfect, good
as new which, in fact, it was. He glanced up as he was
stroking the sleeves to make sure there were no sly razor
rents, and caught her expression, something very like the
old doting gaze.

"I've made you things, the usual. Coffee the way you
like it, very strong, a new brand, expensive, and your
best sarnies, prawn and mayonnaise."

That had been his favorite sandwich ever since that paragraph in the paper she'd cut out to show him. This reminded him: the scrapbook to which they'd both contributed, which they'd pored over together, she hadn't put in with his belongings. Well, like the ordinary clothes it didn't matter now. Let her brood over it alone. She'd have nothing else left. He could almost be sorry for her. After all, he was getting the blaze of glory, she'd be entirely forgotten. He'd be remembered in all the books.

Unless the press dug up his past life and found out about her; a pity to be linked to her. Put such ideas out of sight. Sordid, to be forgotten. Keep a clear mind for what's ahead. On a practical level, coffee and sandwiches were necessary, he could let her do that and even acknowledge it generously. He gave the smile, the smile he had practiced so long, the smile he knew she found irresistible.

"Thanks. You've always been good at that."

Arrogant nerd, Kelly thought, simpering devoutly. Good at coffee, good at fry-ups, mending, sarnies. That's where he's relegated you to. Good at cleaning up, fetching and carrying, at kiss arse, at playing your game. How much of my game did you ever play? You put the light out when we made love so I was cheated of the face even while I had to go on calling you by the name.

And as for the pretense he was putting up that his plan was abandoned, who did he think he could fool? Did he think she hadn't studied him these last six months, hadn't put him under the microscope? Every gesture, every flicker of the eyelids, she knew by heart. As for that matter so did he. He'd worked on that self-production. So the tension, the rapid glances he shot at her and round the room, the heightened glitter of his eyes, the slight flush in the hollow cheek—purple hearts for sure—weren't lost on her. He would take the journey they'd so often taken, but it was not simply to look at the house and mourn the past. He was all cranked up for something and she hadn't to ask all round to know what.

"I won't put these," she brandished the thermos and

the foil packet of sandwiches, "with your clothes. Do you want another carrier?"

"OK. I've left the car just round the corner."

She knew that meant: I don't have to be seen coping with inappropriate carrier bags for too long. She fetched another, a slim dark green one with gold lettering saying "Harrods," to keep him happy, and she watched benignly while he stowed the provisions away. The thin gold bracelet round his wrist was just right; they'd taken ages finding one that looked identical to the one in the photograph.

She went with him to the top of the stairs, wondering if he'd have a try at a kiss. It was his last chance, but not hers. She'd be kissing the real thing soon enough.

It was an exhilarating idea, and it made her smile again, surprising him.

"Take care," she said, knowing he'd need to.

Chapter
4
·········

"Oh God. Mom's back already." Treasure, peering out as Mel swung the limo round the curve of the drive and the little fountain in the center, shrank back at sight of the scarlet sports car slewed confidently at an angle to the Manor's big oak door, shrank as though her mother's influence could penetrate glass and metal.

"Bet you she's thought up a new place to get married by now. Wonder who's there too?" Jem surveyed the other cars, a neutral gray Escort and a small blue Mondeo sitting apologetically near the side wall apart from the rest. Mel came to open the door and Treasure, pulling at her hair, scrambled out onto the gravel. Jem followed, looking quietly determined. No matter what waited for them indoors, he was not going to be overwhelmed.

The Escort turned out to belong to Superintendent Robert Bone whom Jem knew and liked. He was sitting in the armchair when they came in, a silent observer. The Mondeo suited the woman, in green like a gnome, with a bleached fringe to her eyebrows, who was perched on the edge of a chair sheltering her handbag in her lap with tense hands, looking anxious and, while

Zephyr stood before her scanning sheets of sketches, giving explanations in a high squeak. Ken leaned an arm along the shelf above the great fireplace, mutely withdrawn, like Bone, from what was going on.

The entrance of Jem and Treasure altered the scene at once. Bone smiled, Ken raised a hand in greeting with an affectionate glance at his son, the green woman looked relieved, and Zephyr spun round with infinite grace, drawings spilling from her hands to be retrieved by the green woman and Bone, who saw they were variations on a page's suit.

"Darling! At last! Don't tell me you'd forgotten Mrs. Robson was coming to fit your dress. Poor Mrs. Robson has been sitting patiently for absolute hours . . ."

A series of intimidated squeaks suggested that Mrs. Robson challenged this, but Zephyr was already drawing Treasure forward, putting her hair behind her ears, twitching her T-shirt at the shoulders.

"I'm sorry, Mom, the time just—"

"Honey, there's no time for apologies. Take those clothes off and let Mrs. Robson do what she's come to do. I'm sure she has a whole lot more to do today than hang around waiting for you."

Mrs. Robson's squeaks at this point seemed to convey that had she been kept waiting, which she hadn't, there was nothing she'd rather do than wait on Zephyr and her daughter, but no one paid heed to her. Bone was attempting to leave and Ken to detain him, Jem had gone at once to examine the new object in the room, the abandoned plant in its complicated cachepot on the grand piano, and Treasure was resisting her mother's efforts to pull off her T-shirt.

"Mom! Not with people here!"

But the people rapidly scattered. Ken took Bone off to his study, Jem vanished up the stairs, and Treasure was left alone to the ordeal by pins.

Bone, ensconced this time in a vast brown leather chair with ornate scrolled edges, clearly designed for a very large Victorian magnate, spared a thought for the girl as he waited for Ken to produce, from among the folders on his desk, a death threat or two. Treasure was rather younger than his own daughter Charlotte, but like her in being thin and leggy. Of course if you were leggy like Zephyr it was a different matter. Perhaps one day the girl's legs would have some shape and she could show them off under a pocket handkerchief of a skirt as her mother did. Perhaps the plain face would even develop sculptured cheekbones and a deliciously pointed chin. With those appalling braces off—and surely it would have been possible to get a less obtrusive set?—perhaps she could even smile.

Whatever happened, growing up could only be a blessing. "Here." Ken unearthed the right folder, shook it out over the desk and released scraps of paper that settled or flew, one refuging on Bone's knees. "Take your pick, they're all on the same theme. I'd have junked the lot only Edwina made me keep them." Ken folded into the leather swivel chair and pushed back the lock of hair that kept sliding toward his right eye. "Suppose she thinks that if someone does get me she can hand these to the police as a helpful step."

Bone was examining the paper that had landed on him. It was the usual thing, letters, sometimes whole words, cut from newspapers and magazines and pasted up to make the message. What was perhaps unusual was the regularity of the rows of letters even though they were of different sizes. Someone who minded about the appearance of their work had put these together. Bone speculated: a teacher? a librarian? a graphic artist? He saw a hand with tweezers meticulously placing each letter or word, somebody, perhaps peering through spectacles, bending over the paper. Such a person might be most meticulous over killing, want to get every detail right.

The messages were, as Ken said, much alike. Ken was to die if he went through with the wedding.

"Give up the bitch and you live," put it succinctly. "Put the ring on and you DIE." "Betrayal merits

DEATH," were grace notes on this. Ken watched Bone looking them over.

"I've not shown these to Zeph. Think I should?"

The decision was not one Bone felt he could make. For all he knew, Zephyr West might go plain doolally over these, fling them everywhere and instantly enplane for the States. Yet people in the public eye, as she was, often had to deal with similar things, and she might even see the danger attendant on the wedding as an extra spice no caterer could provide.

"It depends." Bone did not intend to commit himself. "From the security angle it might be a good idea." He tapped the sheets of paper with their relentless message. "What's interesting is that it's you, not she, who is threatened. On the face of it, removing her would solve the problem more efficiently."

Ken frowned. "Suppose you're right. But I don't really get this betrayal line. I was married before. No one created a fuss then."

"Maybe you weren't so famous then. Maybe you've only now acquired this fan who's a nutter."

"Maybe it's a woman who thinks I should be marrying *her*."

"All the more surprising she doesn't talk of removing your fiancée." Bone shook the papers together and tucked them in the folder. "I'd like to show these to a bloke who's an expert in this field, but I don't suppose we can come up with anything helpful. It takes a while to trace magazine typefaces and as for prints, there'll be yours, Edwina's, mine on the edges. And the sender, suppose their prints are on the pages, may not have form."

"No form, no records—and if you do trace the typeface, how on earth do you track down who used those magazines?"

"It can be done." Bone did not say that such trouble was only likely if the threats were successfully carried out. "How did these arrive?"

"By post. Edwina keeps the envelopes, all numbered. She says the postmarks are from all over."

"I'll want those." *All over* could mean "all over Essex, Hampshire, the British Isles."

Ken contemplated the folder. "Bugger. She probably had those in order of arrival too. Still," he cheered up, "as you're taking them away she'll never know."

Bone reflected that Ken either was putting on nonchalance or was more afraid of his secretary than of a mad fan threatening his death. He got up to go. "You'll let me know when the wedding plans are finalized. If it's to be at Herne Hall it will be necessary to discuss security arrangements with Mrs. West. Things will be far more dodgy in a place not already wired up with alarms and cameras the way this place is."

Ken, shrugging, rose too. "You're telling me. Women, Robert, women. Believe me, I'm lucky not to be getting married on the slopes of Everest or in a balloon over Lake Titicaca. Zeph's taken a thing about romantic old England and its glorious countryside so Lake Titicaca's been downgraded to this lake at her mother's. Zeph'll probably have it garlanded in roses before she's done with it."

Bone's inner eye provided him with a brief bizarre vision: a lake covered with floating roses and, breaking the surface, a hand, not carrying Excalibur but aiming a harpoon gun.

"I think I'd better have a talk with Mrs. West."

Chapter
5
....

"I do envy you." Grizel, somehow contriving to look elegant despite a pregnancy of eight-and-a-half months, put down a dish of pears in cinnamon before Bone and maneuvered herself into the kitchen settle to watch him enjoying it.

"Last time I saw Herne Hall," said her husband, taking a generous helping of pears and then cream, "it was moldering rather. Sir Valentine hadn't the dosh to do what it needed."

"From what I've heard, Mrs. West has all the dosh anyone could need. My spies tell me she's expanding the conservatory and thinking about a pool. She's in a wheelchair but perhaps she can swim."

"That would be why a pool, when she has a lake—a lake cute enough for Zephyr West, no less, to be married on its banks, or, for all I know, in a boat on it."

"No!" Grizel's green eyes sparkled. Bone, forgetting even his cinnamon pears, looked at her and thought yet again how wise he was to have married her. That had been a romantic wedding, though not quite on a scale to suit Zephyr West; a fifteenth-century church, with a walk down the village green under the glory of autumn chestnut tress, amber and gold, to a reception in a tiny cottage and its garden . . . "By the lake?" she was saying. "How perfect. You don't mean you saw the fabled Zephyr, did you? At Ken's, was she, this morning?"

"Certainly. She even shook my hand; though I'm afraid I did wash it just now."

"Well? Well? What does she look like?"

"You've seen her on TV."

Grizel reached over, with slight difficulty, and removed his plate of pears. "You've seen the pears too, but you'll have no more till I've heard more. Is she beautiful, or merely photogenic? Is she one of those the camera drools over and who looks nothing much off screen?"

Bone eyed the pears wistfully. "I'd say she's genuinely beautiful, yes. Very slim, legs to her ears, enormous eyes—"

"Color?"

"Oh—I think perhaps blue."

"Oh, you trained policeman, you." She put down the pears and, taking Bone's spoon, gave him more from the dish. She held up the little glass jug of cream. "And what was she wearing?"

"Pale stuff. Beige. Silk shirt and a skirt for voyeurs."

Grizel poured cream. "Men, all alike," she remarked unfairly. "Look at Ken. I never thought he'd bother to marry, especially with Jem hardly in need of a feminine influence in the home anymore; then along comes a film star with a short skirt up to her eyelashes you tell me, and he's all for getting married beside a lake. And men talk of women being changeable."

"Who's being changeable?" His daughter had appeared from the garden, her cat Ziggy in her arms, struggling. "Is Daddy going to divorce you and marry Zephyr West? Oh, Father." Charlotte posed in dramatic protection in front of Grizel. "Father! Let her have the baby before you dump her! Let Ken marry Zephyr first and then divorce her so you can have her next."

"Zephyr West would not touch me with a diamond barge pole—"

"Unfortunately," Grizel put in.

"Unfortunately," Bone agreed. "Though not only do I not want to marry her, I'm not wholly sure that Ken does; though *you*," he pointed at Cha, who let Ziggy catapult to the floor, and curtsied, "will keep that under your hat." Cha carefully assumed an invisible hat. "I've the feeling Ken doesn't know how to get out of this one. She's very high voltage."

"Is she gorgeous?" demanded Charlotte, sliding onto the bench opposite her father and parking elbows on table, chin on fists. "Knock-down gorgeous to die for?"

"Ask *her*." Bone nodded at Grizel, and finished the pears in a stern manner. "The interrogation is over. I've work to do. Incidentally," he added, "you are certainly lucky Zephyr isn't your mother or stepmother. Her daughter is called Treasure and clearly finds her mother even more overwhelming than Ken does."

"Treasure." Charlotte sat bolt upright. *"Daddy,* what a chance you missed. You could have called me Jewel or—how about—" She leaned forward, mouthing the syllables genteelly, "Filigree? Filigree Bone? Of course if you really were called Jewel your surname would have to be something like Blobb or—or Boathook or Binbag."

"Well guessed—" Bone reached to put his plate on the drainboard; as he sat back, ready to get up, Ziggy jumped on the bench at his side, walked onto him and settled, purring, "Because Treasure's surname is in fact Schlumberger."

"Oh excellent!" Cha beat her hands together. Then she stopped. "Poor girl, I don't expect she finds it funny. Okay by itself, I suppose, but not with *Treasure.* Did you see her too, then?"

"She's younger than you. Thirteen, perhaps. Thin, with those metal braces," Bone bared his teeth and made a finger-grid across his mouth, "and not pretty. I think her mother's disappointed in her. She was being fitted for a bridesmaid's frock when I left. They had it spread out—yellow with frills. The last thing to suit her. It seems like spite." Bone remembered Charlotte as bridesmaid, so grown-up, in apricot silk, her hair coiled in a little bun with apricot streamers, at the wedding—was it really less than two years ago . . . ? He had certainly never thought, in the wasteland of their lives after Petra died, that he could ever be happy again. Life had its surprises. Perhaps even Ken Cryer was destined to find joy in his second marriage.

Bone doubted it.

"This wedding by the lake," Grizel asked. "What lake? Windermere?"

Bone laughed. "I'll put it to her. It'd make my life a lot easier, handing the whole palaver to the Cumbrian force."

Cha leaned across to scratch Ziggy under the chin. "It's not your job, surely, to look after a wedding? I mean if the bride kills the groom or vice versa, okay, but surely just weddings aren't your bag?"

Bone had never discussed his cases with his daughter if he could help it, believing she should be protected from the ugly side of his profession. This insouciant declaration amused him. However, he did not intend to speak about the death threats made to Ken; the less said about them the better, and Cha was not to start imagining horrors about someone she knew—and of whom she was a professed fan. He finished his coffee and tried to give Ziggy a hint he wanted to get up by shifting his knees. The perceptive animal responded by curling up tightly and embracing its face with a forearm.

"You make my job sound like a hobby, pet. No, security's not my field but Ken's a friend and he wanted advice about all this. When you decide to marry, choose somewhere peaceful, would you?"

Ignoring a mutter from Grizel of "My hubby the bobby's hobby," Cha picked up Ziggy to let her father move.

28

"I don't see why they're bothered. If they want to keep out masses of people, fans and paparazzi, why not get married somewhere secret where no one can get at them? Anyone can get married anywhere now, so why not—" Cha paused to think and Ziggy's throbbing filled the quiet—"a dungeon or something. That'd be secluded."

" 'The grave's a fine and private place.
But none, I think, do there embrace . . .' "

"—hardly romantic," Grizel put in. She had got to her feet and was running water over dishes in the sink. "I imagine she's after somewhere romantic, not spooky."

"Spoo-ooky." Cha echoed Grizel's Scots. "But it could be Gothic romantic. She could get married in a shroud."

Bone laughed. "You may be overestimating Zephyr West's sense of style. She's after ringlets and ribbons, not dungeons and shrouds. As for having the wedding somewhere nice and private, there's one drawback to that. You may marry where you like, that's true—provided they have a license for it—but you have, by law, to arrange one thing: you know when the priest says, 'If any man knows any just cause or impediment why this man or this woman may not be joined, et cetera?' "

"Of course." One of Cha's favorite videos was still *Four Weddings and a Funeral.* "So?"

"If you hold the wedding secretly in a dungeon it doesn't give a chance to anyone but ghosts to speak." Bone got up to take his coffee cup to the sink. "Access, that's what the law requires. Get married anywhere, provided people can come forward and stop you if they want to."

"How can they stop you at Herne Hall lake?" Cha decanted Ziggy into a chair already occupied by Grizel's cat, The Bruce, causing a friendly tussle. "Can't see old Mrs. West letting in the world and his wife and his little dog to pollute *her* grounds in a hurry. Have you seen the size of the PRIVATE notice at her gate?"

"That," said Bone, taking the drying-up cloth from his wife's hands, "Mrs. West will have to discuss with her daughter. From what I saw of Zephyr, if she wants a lake, she'll get one."

In this, his instinct was to prove correct.

Chapter

6

....

The followers of Capability Brown did not always plant trees of the fast-maturing kind, and the great oaks in the Herne parkland, some leaves already bronze, burnished in the sun of late summer, were presences hardly touched by the centuries. No Herne, however badly he lacked money, had dared to cut them down, and their foliage concealed the house until a well-contrived turn in the drive brought it, at the last moment, into view.

It was changed from when Bone saw it last. Sir Valentine Herne, the last of his line, had never possessed sufficient means for its maintenance. Missing tiles had left sad gaps in the roof, the pillars of the Georgian porch needed painting, plasterwork had crumbled, the bricks needed pointing. All this neglect was of the past. The roof shone intact in the sun, paintwork and windowglass gleamed together, huge urns of scarlet geraniums and trailing ivy flanked the porch whose columns were immaculately white. No Herne lived here now but their absence seemed to have given the Hall a new lease on life, and Bone rejoiced at the sight.

"Good afternoon, sir. Mrs. West will see you in the drawing room."

Palmerston had been butler to Sir Valentine. Bone was glad to see him still here. It argued well for Mrs. West's good sense that she had kept him on. A well-trained butler had a price above rubies and Bone, who suspected that Palmerston had worked for a pittance in the old days out of loyalty to the family, hoped he was now getting a salary more in keeping with his value. Bone followed him across the hall's black and white marble, reflecting that Palmerston's muted smile as he opened the door had precisely the degree of warmth suitable to their former acquaintance, without familiarity or any compromise of his dignity. As a smile, it was a work of art.

"Superintendent Bone, madam."

Bone, advancing to shake hands, was slightly disconcerted to find Mrs. West in a wheelchair, although he should have expected it. She had a firm, cool handclasp and looked up at him with eyes as blue as her daughter's but with a much keener glance.

"How kind of you to come and see me so soon. Do sit down. I hope you will have some tea with me?"

Bone having expressed himself delighted, Palmerston left them, and Mrs. West settled back in her chair to continue her silent study of Bone. He had taken in an impression of elegance and of a certain quality which, he felt, made her far more formidable than Zephyr with all her deluging charm. Could that quality be intelligence?

It was hard to tell her age. The iron gray hair was cut in a long smooth bob that framed her face, which was exquisitely made-up, the lips a soft pink, the blue eyes shadowed, the lashes just darkened; the artifice did not intrude except to show its skill. Zephyr had inherited her cheekbones from her mother, and if the smooth sculpture of the face was here a little softened with laugh lines, it gained character from them. Long legs too were a family trait, here in sheer black, with black suede pumps on the footrest of the chair, the skirt, Bone was relieved to note, rose no higher than Mrs. West's knees.

Heavy gold hoop earrings showed in the sweep of iron gray hair, and a huge table-cut diamond, dull enough in its gleam to be Georgian like the house, swiveled on one slender finger. A white collar was all that broke the unrelieved black of the fine wool dress. Mrs. West was, Bone had heard, enormously rich, but flamboyance was not her style, although of style itself she had plenty.

"My daughter tells me you're a friend of her fiancé. Do you know Ken well?"

"Not so very well. My wife and I have dined there once or twice. I met him over a case, as it happens, involving this house."

Mrs. West raised her perfectly arched eyebrows.

"I've heard something of that; another's misfortune turned out to be my luck. I'm finding the countryside round here very pleasant and the garden's shaping up nicely. I am unable to walk far, thanks to an arthritic hip, but it's amazing how much energy one saves for more important things by being pushed or driven about. This afternoon one of the gardeners took me down to the lake so that I could see how suitable it would be for the wedding." She paused. "Of course, you have to be aware that Zephyr will very likely change her mind by tomorrow, and you may make plans in vain. I understand you are taking these threats to Ken seriously."

Bone thought: Ken wanted the threats kept secret from Zephyr, but he's evidently confided in her mother. That itself told him more about Mrs. West and made the interview easier.

"It's as well to take such things seriously. One can't always count on people not doing what they say they will. Ken's had trouble with fans before and, of course, his excellent security system will not protect him if the reception is to be held here at Herne Hall."

Mrs. West was about to answer when the door opened to admit Palmerston wheeling before him a chrome trolley furnished with silver teapot, bone china cups, and plates of scones, biscuits and cake. He brought it to rest by the side of the wheelchair.

33

"Shall I pour, madam?"

"Thank you, Palmerston, I will manage."

Palmerston inclined his head and left the room. Bone envisaged a butler's training including this trick of subtracting oneself soundlessly from the scene. The only other butler Bone had known could also have committed a murder with the utmost discretion and have vanished unnoticed—except that like Palmerston, he was a man of the highest integrity and capable, Bone felt, of stopping a murderer in his tracks with a glance of calm disdain. What Macbeth had really needed at Dunsinane was not a porter but a butler, and Duncan need never have been murdered.

"Do you take sugar, Mr. Bone?"

Bone received his tea and accepted a scone, still hot to the fingers and generously buttered. There was a linen table napkin to put across his knee and get butter on. The rich live differently all the time—Bone had been ready to take a paper tissue from his pocket.

He got down at last to the real purpose of this visit, to discover what, if any, security measures were needed and what existed already at the hall. Mrs. West waved a hand in answer to that.

"Palmerston will tell you about it. Of course I had an expert to discuss the alarm system when I decided to take the house. Nowadays, too, I understand you must cement the garden statues to their plinths and then wire them underground to the central alarm if you want to keep anything on the grounds so," she glanced down at the diamond on her hand, "as I have a few things I'd be sorry to lose, I naturally took precautions to see that I don't." She drank tea, looking at Bone over the cup's gilded rim, making him feel he had managed to imply that she lacked sense. Perhaps, given Zephyr's sweetly scatty ways, this was a mistake people were apt to make about her mother.

"But the alarm system would be switched off during the reception."

"The outer doors have their own separate alarms, some would be kept closed."

"Have you any idea as to numbers at the reception, Mrs. West?"

She shook her head, the bell of hair softly swinging. "Ask Zephyr. I'm only here to pay for it. She's in charge of what she wants, whether it's food or people." She smiled suddenly. When she was young, she must have been far more beautiful than Zephyr. There was that enhancement of beauty, a quiet, observant mind. "Her friends, her plans, change from day to day. Most of her friends can drop everything and fly in at a moment's notice. It'll be helicopters-on-the-lawn time."

Bone refrained from contradiction, but if security were to be maintained the last thing to be permitted would be promiscuous landing of helicopters on the lawn. The idea of vetting these friends who changed from day to day was deeply unattractive. More than one might have a grudge against Ken for snatching so glorious a creature from them. Such a woman must have had lovers as well as husbands; perhaps Mrs. West was not the person to ask about that. Mrs. West held out a hand for Bone's cup, and filled it again. "I expect Dwight will want to come, but he at least won't need his helicopter because he's staying in the house at the moment, on a visit to see Treasure." She raised her blue eyes from the cup. "Dwight Schlumberger is my granddaughter's father. Zephyr divorced him several years ago but I am far from sure he's taken that in. Dwight is not a man to relinquish anything easily."

Bone was about to ask more about this tenacious man who might well want Ken out of the way, when the door was thrust open and a large man stood there, mobile phone to his ear, staring at Bone in a hostile rather than a simply inquiring way. Mrs. West once more indicated with a languid hand, "Here is Dwight himself. Come in and be introduced and have some tea."

Dwight spoke in a soft growl into his phone and clicked it shut. Putting it in the pocket of his linen jacket which had a resigned sag, he advanced on Bone without diminishing the intensity of his stare. The eyes were brown, hot and forceful under thick black eyebrows, the hair was thick brown with gray above the ears and there was silver in the close-cut dark beard. Bone judged him to be in his forties or possibly early fifties and, by the heavy droop of shoulders and the slight swell of belly, running a little to seed. His handshake was ferocious, causing Bone effort to maintain a social smile. Doubling over, wringing one's hand and moaning was not going to give a proper impression of the British police.

"Superintendent Bone?" Schlumberger repeated the introduction with a touch of incredulity. "Has something happened to anybody?"

"Sit down, Dwight, and have some tea. Mr. Bone is a friend of Ken's, here to talk over security at the wedding. Treasure's told you Zephyr wants it here, hasn't she?"

Dwight sat down, his weight making the sofa shift under Bone. "Treasure tells me nothing. I never get to see Treasure." He turned the gaze on Bone again. "My own daughter I am making a special visit with and she is never here. What do you think of that?"

Bone thought it better not to reply that it sounded uncommonly as if his daughter wasn't partial to his company. It might not be hard to imagine why Zephyr had divorced this man, harder to guess why she had married him, unless she'd fancied playing kitten to his bear. Perhaps a very great deal of money put a gloss on anything. Dwight had refused tea but was crunching a chocolate biscuit as if it were the bones of a small animal.

He wiped the flecks from his beard. "This wedding, Superintendent, is not going to come off."

Chapter

7

··········

Mrs. West was the first to respond. She laughed. "Dwight—she's not going to change her mind over marrying Ken. She may change her mind as to *where,* but you can't stop the wedding itself. She's going to marry him."

Schlumberger went grim. "She was in love with me."

"She isn't now." Mrs. West crumpled her napkin and tossed it on the trolley, dismissively. "You really will have to accept that. What Zephyr takes a fancy to, she gets. She was like that at three years old, at thirty-three she hasn't changed."

The thick black brows descended. "Thirty-three? She was seventeen when we married. Treasure is thirteen. Zephyr cannot be more than thirty."

Mrs. West's smile, mischievous, made a brief appearance. "Oh, mothers do get these things wrong. And does it matter now? Life moves on." She gestured down at her elegant legs. "If you had told me ten years ago that I'd be like this I never would have believed you. Things happen. People change, and complaining is a waste of time."

"Complaining! I'm not complaining." Schlumberger

planted large hands on his thighs and looked compla-
cent. "There just is not going to be this wedding."

Sooner than ask questions, Bone often found it paid
to wait for people to tell him things. This assertion of
Schlumberger's was, however, pertinent to the reason
for Bone's presence here; he was about to ask why he
was so sure, when Mrs. West, head on one side, raised
a hand. "There. Treasure is back, Dwight. Now you can
hear all her news. I'm sure she'll have a great deal to
tell you."

This did not appear to be the case. Treasure, rushing
into the room, stopped short of seeing who was there.
Her eyes took in Bone, who perhaps seemed to feature
in every room she entered this morning, and moved on
to her father. She had run in with a look of eager anticipation, which quite transformed her and which made a
statement about her relations with her grandmother. It
had faded to an expression of doubt.

"I thought you'd gone."

"Honey." Schlumberger got up and held out a hand,
his growl offended. "Would I go without a proper talk
with you? When I come to look for you you're forever
with the Cryer boy." He went over toward her.

Bone saw how this rankled. You lose your wife to a
rock star and then your daughter is more interested in
the rock star's son than in her own father. Treasure
stood there, mutinous.

Mrs. West beckoned her over. "Did you see a kitten
you liked, darling?"

"A kitten? What d'you want with a kitten, honey? I
said I'd get you a dog, any kind of dog you like. There's
a guy breeds these pointers—he lives around here—they
make great gun dogs."

"I don't want to *shoot* things, Dad. And Gran would
hate to have a big dog bounding about everywhere. I
like cats and I've chosen my kitten." She passed her
father on her way to Mrs. West, whom she kissed. Taking a chocolate biscuit from the trolley, she turned her
back on her father and went on. "It's gorgeous, all gray

and white with such little bones, you'll love it. It's called
Skywalker but Mrs. Playfair says that's only a milk name
and we can change it when it can leave its mother and
come to us. You name a cat when you see what its character is. You should see her cottage, it is just swarming
with cats, all sizes and colors and ages—I did so want
to get five of them." She crouched by her grandmother's
side, talking through biscuit, looking up, and playing
with the ring on Mrs. West's hand. Schlumberger stood
disconsolate in the middle of the room. To Bone, she
was making a blatant play for her father's attention.

"Darling, how lovely. I'm quite glad you didn't get
five, but I look forward to Skywalker. Now, why don't
you take your father and show him—"

The phone in Schlumberger's pocket imperiously demanded attention. An obstinate look made Treasure
suddenly plain again as he whipped out the phone,
flipped it open and raised it to his ear in one practiced
movement.

"Schlumberger . . . yeah . . . It's okay your side? Listen, we have to fix this . . . No, sure I can talk, hold
there . . ." and Schlumberger opened the door on Palmerston, come to collect the trolley. Palmerston stepped
back, and Schlumberger went to talk business in the hall.

Treasure's resigned irritation was patent. Mrs. West,
amused, said, "Darling, I'm still going to ask you to
show something, so don't run away. The staff is busy
and your father hasn't the time, so that leaves you. Mr.
Bone wants to see the lake. Will you take him there?"

Treasure stood up, reluctant but polite. "Sure. This is
because of Mom's ideas, right? She's talking about getting married on a *raft* now because she saw *Funny
Face*—you know, floating away among the trees at the
end. You should have seen Ken when he heard. If she
goes on this way she's going to end up short of a bridegroom. I mean, Dad would have done whatever she
wanted, got married at the top of the Empire State
Building, in the middle of Golden Gate Bridge, hanging

from a trapeze, *whatever,* so long as it cost and he could organize it, he'd go along."

Treasure Schlumberger, Bone thought as he followed her out, was perceptive enough. She and her mother seemed to typify that cliché of looks and brains. Zephyr might be shrewd in getting her own way, but so far he had not thought her perceptive.

Schlumberger still strode up and down the hall talking into his phone, his free hand emphatically gesturing. His eyes followed Treasure as she went past him, and he turned, but did not interrupt his phone talk.

They emerged from the house onto a paved terrace, where urns like those on the porch spilled ivy and scarlet geraniums, and long windows gave onto a view of trees and low Kentish hills further off. At the edge of the trees, on a rise, was a small gazebo in the distance. Treasure headed to the right, and crossed the grass toward a plantation of birch where steps of natural stone led down a slope. Bone, on his previous visits to Herne Hall, had not seen this side of the house and he was impressed by the vast lawns, a great cedar casting its shade, the air of careless grandeur that a garden which melts into landscape can give. The grass was close-cut, the steps had recently been rebedded securely. Money had much to do with these effects.

Treasure gave no sign of being impressed. This was familiar ground and she set off down the steps at a loping trot, calling over her shoulder, "It's down here." She waved an arm at the expanse of grass. "Mom plans on loads of tents back there. And a band, of course. Jem says they should play only Ken's music but Ken says no."

Quite a few things, Bone thought, that Ken would say no to about the wedding, but this objection was valid. A good many of Ken's songs were far from cheerful, probably why they appealed so strongly to the young, and they might strike an inappropriately melancholy note at a wedding. *Crying Shame,* his latest album, for instance, which Bone knew well because Cha had played

it solidly for a week when she first got it, were full of
forlorn entreaty and pain, whether about heartbreak or
drug addiction. Ken never made a secret of his past,
"high as a kite and stoned as St. Stephen," but that was
behind him now. He told the media so, and Bone believed it was true, but did wonder about the heartbreak.
Ken's first wife, who had presented him with Jem, was
an airhead who had secured as much of Ken's money as
his lawyers were forced to allow, and had disappeared
to the Argentine where she was reputedly living on a
ranch and breeding cattle, an unlikely skill for someone
who had rarely been seen outside nightclubs. Bone knew
that Ken had been relieved to see the last of her; heartbreak was problematical in that case at least. He had
declared he would never make the same mistake again.

Was he doing just that now?

"I wish," said Treasure as they descended the steps,
"that Dad was right and there wouldn't be this
wedding."

"You don't want your mother to marry Ken Cryer."
Bone used a statement to ask a question, as was his
habit. They went down a further curving flight of stone
steps among the trees, Treasure skipping at his side. She
turned a surprised face.

"No, Ken's fine. I like Ken and Jem's really cool. I
just don't think she ought to be marrying *him*. And, I
wish she wasn't set on all this fuss, it's so stupid. If she
has to marry why can't it be quietly? Gran's paper always has notices saying this person or that got married
quietly and Gran says it's because one or the other of
them had been married before. *Nobody* wants the stuff
she's planned. That's just like Mom, if she wants something she'll get it no matter if it hurts other people. I
mean, I don't know if you saw my dress but it is *the pits*.
I hate it and she doesn't care. She doesn't listen to anything that isn't what she wants and nothing stops her
once she gets going."

What on earth could the Schlumberger marriage have
been like, Bone wondered, if two such strong wills had

been linked together? Perhaps at seventeen, the age Schlumberger claimed Zephyr had been at their wedding, her will had not been so splendidly developed. Dwight could have enjoyed giving his beautiful young wife anything she hankered for, up to the point where their wills finally clashed. As the divorce had gone through, though Schlumberger evidently refused to accept it, sometimes pretty kittens must have got the better of bears. Meanwhile, a sympathetic silence was the best answer to Treasure's outpourings. She was now, as they descended a shallow grassy slope cast about with silver birches, telling him of her bridesmaid's dress.

"Yucky and in silk that feels like slime and yellow that's my worst color and I'm to have these crappy little yellow flowers—rosebuds and freesias, Mom says— round here," she encircled her head with one hand "and round my wrists. She says I'll look like a fairy but *I* know I'll look like a *dork*. My hair's to be all curled up like bedsprings, I'm going to look just as terrible as anybody can." She stopped abruptly at the foot of the slope and faced Bone. The black brows came down. "I'd sooner *die!*"

For a moment her resemblance to her father was very marked. She wheeled and pointed. "There's the lake. Believe me, I'd sooner jump straight in it than wear all that stuff."

Bone thought that Zephyr's habit of seeing only what she wanted to see was about to be severely tested when her vision of a transformed daughter was met by the truculent reality.

The delicate foliage of silver birches had hidden the extent of the lake, though he had caught the glitter as leaves shifted. The water stretched further than he had thought and now, as a dark cloud drifted overhead, it become gloomy. Woods of chestnut, oak and evergreens came down to the water on the far side, far too much protection for anyone interested in dispatching the bridegroom at this romantic celebration. As for Treasure's little threat to jump in . . .

"Some of these lakes have a nasty habit of being very deep," he said. "You really would be well advised to deal with the problem some other way."

Treasure surveyed him and her flare of resentment at his remark faded as she took in his serious tone.

"So what about the rest of Mom's wonderful idea?"

Bone pointed to a path he could just make out winding among the trees on the shore across the water. "Does that belong to your grandmother's land?"

"Oh no, that's a right of way. Some people from the village use it now and then, though I've never seen any."

Well, there was the necessary public access for the ceremony . . . a jay scolded harshly from the distant trees, as if disturbed.

Bone had the unpleasant sensation of being watched.

43

Chapter
8
··········

Through the binoculars their faces were quite clear, the girl's he knew after a moment, the man's, unknown—a face that gave no clue about him, good-looking in a severe way, a contained face whose eyes surveyed with more than mere curiosity. Probably here to make arrangements for the wedding; there'd been rumors in the village about its being by the lake, which his own observations had made him believe. For his purpose, excellent.

He adjusted the lenses for a sharper view. There was gray in the fair hair; he judged the man to be in his forties but trim enough, he'd come at a smart pace down that slope after Treasure. The man didn't know Treasure well, they stood apart and used polite body language.

Suddenly the man pointed across the water at him. The binoculars shook. He snatched them from his eyes as though not seeing clearly would make him less visible. Then he was angry with himself. The man had not pointed straight at him. He had a perfect right to be on the public path. He was in shadow under trees and behind tall reeds on the shore. The sun wasn't at an angle that could catch the binocular lenses and flash a betraying signal, and even if he was seen, he might be an ordinary bird watcher. He raised the binoculars again. They still talked, casually, before turning and going back up the slope.

No problem, then. He relaxed. Looking round and seeing the low branch of an oak, sturdy and near enough to the ground, he sat on it and went on staring at the lake's shimmer through the shift of leaves but hardly seeing it.

Instead, he was seeing the woman who had stood across there yesterday evening, when he first found this spot. Dusk was falling and at first he had not noticed her. Then tracking the binoculars along the opposite shore, he had the shock: her face came in view.

Disbelieving, although there was no reason she shouldn't be there, he lost the alignment and had to track back. She was looking upward as if for inspiration, so that what light there was showed the lovely face of which he knew every line by heart. Then, too, he had lowered the binoculars, but in order to take in the whole picture.

She had looked like a ghost, in the gray chiffon dress the evening breeze made flow round the long legs like a mist. Dusk had left the gold hair bereft of color and put mysterious shadows in the background as if she might blend into them and disappear. He almost doubted his eyes. Somewhere, an owl hooted. A low breathy call sounded in the woods behind him.

As if it had been a signal, she began to dance. She lifted her arms and slowly twirled, the chiffon floating after her, folding round her body as a lover might. He gazed like a child, his mouth open, but his emotions were not a child's . . . a child could have taken this vision, surely, for the spirit of the lake, risen from the water, floating on its shores like a dream.

The dream ended when she caught her foot on some obstacle, almost stumbled, and swore.

He had smiled then, aware of his heart beating faster.

He was to be the obstacle, the thing that was to turn the romantic dream into a nightmare.

Kelly treated herself to a second Mars bar. It was another freedom to enjoy now that Alan was gone. When he was around he'd been able to make her feel guilty for eating only one—she would begin to undo the wrapping, perhaps in the kitchen very very quietly in the way people do with sweets in the cinema when they know people behind will tap their shoulder and glare and say Sssh!—and she'd hear him in the living room, listening. Really she could. Or if she was unloading the shopping and he happened to be in the kitchen making one of those eternal mugs of coffee, he'd look at the paper bag of Mars bars with those X-ray eyes and she would feel herself visibly getting fatter, ballooning.

In the end, it was irritation at his looking at her in that way, as much as anything, that made her rejoice he had dumped her. The man she truly loved would never look at her like that. *He* saw her the way she was, the way she was intended to be. She ate the last toffee bit of the Mars bar with satisfaction and licked the inside of the wrapper where a chocolate smear lingered. She'd wash her hair tonight, free of Alan's urging her to get it styled. Simplicity was what her true lover liked best, he'd said it again and again—"Come to me the way you are . . ." You can be taken in by the appearance of simplicity, by artfully disordered locks and of course what she could never aspire to, designer outfits in cashmere and silk that cost the earth and looked stark and natural, the clothes rich women negligently throw on or cast down as though they were charity-shop stuff. But true simplicity is of the spirit. Kelly had heard that on a religious broadcast once when she'd tuned in too early for the program she wanted, and it had profoundly impressed her. It was the thing *he* meant.

She had the radio on while she threw the duvet over the bed and puffed it; you never knew, they might have found him already. He might be only on the local news as yet, of course, and not make it even into the tabloids but, given the circumstances, she was pretty sure there'd be quite an agitation over it all. She would give away all that coffee in the cupboard. Alan didn't want it any more and she was actually a tea person. She had a photograph of *him* drinking tea . . . "Put the kettle on, I feel so down, make me tea . . ."

The third Mars bar tasted better still.

At the station, Bone too was indulging himself. His second-in-command, Inspector Locker, had both a large appetite and a sweet tooth so, as mugs of tea or coffee were produced at midmorning when they were completing paperwork on the latest cases, so was a cardboard box, opened by Locker with loving care and harboring Danish pastries.

"Do have one, sir. I've just discovered this shop that does them really well."

Bone recognized that by taking one of the crumbly confections he would be keeping Locker in countenance, a rather sticky countenance already; he chose one extruding the least cream and leaned over his blotter to take a bite at it. Locker, chewing happily, flicked crumbs off a file he had just closed. Bone remarked, as soon as he could speak for fragmented pastry, "You reckon that's finished, Steve?"

"Got him proper," said Locker cheerfully. "Witnesses. Evidence. Forensic. And confession. Short of video of the act I don't see how we could improve on it. Even the CPS can't say there isn't a case."

Bone, only mildly cynical, agreed that the Crown Prosecution Service, known to Locker as Chop Police Sanity, would probably accept this one. He helped down the pastry with a sip of tea that was still too hot, and considered the dreadful simplicity of it all. Many murderers committed the deed on the spur of the moment and then panicked. Danny Brown had thought he knew what he was about. Having long suspected his wife of infidelity, casual promiscuity with anyone who came to the door of their terrace house—milkman, traveling salesman, speculative gardener—he came home one day unexpectedly to find her in bed with what she said was flu but which looked to him like the aftermath of a sexual encounter. There were rumpled sheets and an empty cigarette pack by the bed with crushed stubs. Shame his wife wasn't a smoker, doubly unfortunate that her husband was a builder and had been putting a new window in the lounge.

Unfortunate for him to explain to a jury why he had gone upstairs with a hammer *before* discovering the scene in the bedroom, for a neighbor washing windows at the time had seen him emerge from his van carrying one. Still unfortunate were his efforts to pretend his wife had left him, the miserable journey that night to dump her body in a river that to him seemed distant, the start at redecorating in the bedroom . . . even the washing machine had betrayed him by breaking down; had he known more about laundry he might have avoided this, but instead of a repairman he got the even more efficient services of Forensic who extracted the bloodstained sheets and pillow.

"I'm not complaining, Steve." Bone shook his head at a second pastry, but watched Locker enjoy. "We don't want clever villains who've thought it all out. They're hard work."

Locker thumbed a crumb into his mouth and said, "Pity we can't advertise their failures and make people think first. Don't tell your wife in front of witnesses, like Danny did in front of his mother-in-law, that you'll kill her. That wasn't a good move."

"That reminds me: any more on the death threats to Cryer? You said his secretary rang about a fax?"

"That's right. The sender must have obtained Cryer's fax number—we know you can buy anything, even a star's fax number—and she, Miss Marsh, had a quite nasty surprise yesterday with 'Don't get ready for a wedding, prepare a grave' coming through. She tells me

Cryer wasn't chuffed, either. The fax machine of origin was in a business supply shop."

Bone aligned the edge of his blotter with the edge of his desk, a habit with him when he was trying to put order in his thoughts. "This wedding isn't proving the most popular thing he's ever done. Do we know if these threats only started with the announcement of it?"

"Hard to say. There've been rumors in the music press for weeks. Miss Marsh has the date of the first threat, about a month ago; they've been by letter up to now, posted all over London—a faint clue there. It'd be hard for someone from, say, Leeds, to get them posted so widely. Then, which I don't like," Locker looked vague, but Bone knew him, "there were a couple from near the Manor. One from Saxhurst, in fact."

"That's too close to home. Any ideas?"

Locker grinned, the conjurer about to produce the rabbit. "Funny you should ask, sir. I had Hill inquiring locally there."

"And?"

"We had descriptions of a couple of people who aren't local and who used the fax in this stationer's place, and Mr. Wright said someone had come in with a message he thought was about a wedding. He did notice the man who sent this." He pushed the fax across. "He says it was Ken Cryer."

Chapter
9
·········

"Ken Cryer? Ken Cryer sending himself death threats . . . ?"

Locker sat back, fetching a dangerous creak from his chair. The result of his news pleased him. "He'd seen Ken Cryer before, he'd gone there to order letterhead stationery. Cryer hardly spoke this time—seemed preoccupied—but if it wasn't Cryer he didn't know who else it could be."

Bone stared at his blotter's unhelpful surface. "I didn't think Cryer was acting a part over those death threats but he might be a better actor than I took him for."

Locker shifted, evoking another protest from his chair. "Could he be trying to get out of the wedding for some reason, sir? Not everyone wants to marry, not even a stunner like Zephyr West. He might think it would put her off, him being a possible target for a nutter. Getting in the line of fire at the altar, say."

Bone laughed. "You have not met Zephyr West, Steve. I get the impression that what Zephyr wants, Zephyr gets."

"Wouldn't she be frightened?"

"I fancy that what would frighten her is lack of publicity. Danger would spice the whole thing up." He paused. "But Cryer did say to me he hasn't told her of the death threats, in case it did upset her."

"She'd spill it to the tabloids, from what you say. Right." Locker crumpled the cardboard box that had been home to the Danish pastries, took aim and shied it into the waste bin beside Bone's desk. "So, either the stationer mistook—and Cryer has a face you could call distinctive; or Cryer is telling porkies for a reason we have no clue to. When you went to Herne Hall, what did you think of the wedding idea?"

"I told Henderson at our Security it's a latent disaster. The Chief was on the phone this morning, himself—I think he must be a fan of the radiant Zephyr—inquiring. I told him what I'd told Henderson: the lake site is bang opposite a wooded hillside with a nicely sheltered right of way. Bang opposite, in fact, might be appropriate if the nutter has a gun."

"What had the Chief to say about that?"

"The general drift was, we should pull our fingers out for an event like this, muster up the men to provide the cover. He went vague when I asked about cost. Henderson is going up to Herne Hall to estimate the manpower on his own account. Of course there's an alternative."

"Persuade Miss West to give up the idea?"

"I was going to suggest to the Chief he should go along with a bunch of roses and make her think getting married in a nice, safe, patrollable, searchable village church is the most romantic you can get."

"What do you reckon we can do about it?"

A burst of shouting and a trample of feet downstairs made Bone turn and Locker say, "That'll be Shay bringing in the bloke whose wife rang to say he was beating her up. He knocked the phone from her hand but Emergency had her number and we sent a mobile at the double. Didn't want another Merton."

Another Merton meant to both of them a case last year. Like Danny Brown who had hammered his wife into terminal submission, Kev Merton had believed his

SUSANNAH STACEY

wife to be "monkeying around" as he put it, and had
attempted to break her of the habit by breaking bits of
her from time to time—her nose, one arm, a couple of
ribs that got in the way of his fist as he was lecturing
her. She too had called the police but when a police-
woman arrived, refused to charge her husband even
when removed from his glowering presence. There were
no children so the Social Services would not intervene
and Mrs. Merton had not called again. The next time
the police were summoned to the Merton house was
when a meter reader found the front door open and
Karine Merton sprawled at the foot of the stairs, dead.
He thought she had fallen down them, but it took under
a brace of shakes for the police surgeon to establish that
she had been strangled. Her husband, found at the pub
where he had gone for a steadying drink and possibly to
make himself an alibi, later admitted that he didn't know
what had come over him. He couldn't think how it was
he found himself with his hands round her neck—no
doubt, as Bone remarked, in the process of reasoning
with her.

As the noise was cut off, Bone said, "On the subject
of husbands, I didn't tell you we have an ex belonging
to Zephyr West who doesn't believe she's going to get
married to Cryer. One Dwight Schlumberger—an im-
pressive name—the father of her thirteen-year-old
daughter, and he, according to his ex-mother-in-law,
hasn't taken on board that he *is* an ex, even though there
was a second marriage, very brief, to a TV producer, in
between. Schlumberger's a businessman. I don't know in
what field but I fancy pretty high-powered, gives the
impression he rushes round the world in a frenzy of
wheeling and dealing. It may be he didn't see a lot of her
when they *were* married, for he's over here ostensibly for
a bit of quality time with his daughter. But while I was
there he was mostly on the phone and his daughter
seemed ambivalent about wanting to get close to daddy.
Of course, thirteen is an awkward age."

At thirteen his own daughter Charlotte had been awk-

52

ward enough, but all the energies which might have been devoted to rebelling against her parents had been taken up by the slow battle of recuperation after the car crash that had deprived her of one of them. Bone's sense of closeness to her at that time was so intense that he could feel sorry for Schlumberger, who hardly seemed to know how to relate to his own flesh and blood; but had not been in any doubt about his ex-wife.

"Why does this ex of hers think she won't marry Cryer?"

"He didn't say. Just made a very positive statement."

"You don't think . . . ?" Locker shifted his bulk in wordless interrogation, and Bone with a tight smile shook his head.

"No, I don't think the death threats issue from Schlumberger or that he has a hit man lined up. If he did have, he strikes me as one who would not make damaging predictions in front of witnesses, particularly police officers. Yet I'd like to know why he's so sure."

While Bone and Locker discussed him, Dwight Schlumberger was being given a chance to demonstrate his confidence. Hearing from Mrs. West where the wedding was intended to be, and failing to interest Treasure in a second trip to the spot, he had gone down there alone. He stood, hands in trouser pockets, frowning round at the woods, naturally unaware that he was being watched from across the water. It was now late afternoon. A little wind had woken, ruffling the surface of the lake. Schlumberger gazed at the ripples for a while before stooping to pick up a stone from beside his feet and hurl it with surprising force quite far out. The stone hit the surface with a *cloop!* that echoed in the quiet, succeeded by a rustling of ripples in the reeds all round the shores as if the spirit of the place were offended.

Zephyr, in silver and rose this evening, her hand linked in her fiancé's, looked down at her ex-husband from the top of the slope with a noticeable lack of delight. Ken Cryer's first reaction on seeing a large stranger in these private grounds was chivalrous, trying to put Zephyr behind him. This, as her hand was linked in his, and she would not let go and had no intention of being hustled out of the way, was not a successful maneuver and almost brought them both to their knees on the slope, to roll rather than stroll the rest of the way. They did descend to the shore in disorder and were still recovering when Schlumberger reached them in a couple of quick strides.

"You guys can't agree already? Need a hand, honey?"

Schlumberger was not known to Ken but he was not left in doubt. Zephyr cried, "Dwight! What are you doing over here?"

"Honey, do you forget we have a daughter? Didn't your mother tell you I was visiting with Treasure? It so happened I have a short time to spend in the U.K."

"That's new." Zephyr's voice was tart. As if advertising her new allegiance she wreathed an arm round Ken's waist, leaned on him a little and looked into his eyes. "You'll have guessed this is the man I used to be married to." Turning toward Schlumberger she said in a tone bereft of warmth, "I knew you were around, sure, but what are you doing right here?"

"Trying to get in tune with you, honey. I hear you want a wedding by this lake, I come to check it out. It certainly is romantic, everything you've always wanted: water, great background, woods, the lot. Why don't we have the ceremony real late, hang lanterns in those trees, float candles and flowers on the water, get a band to play over there?" He gestured toward the watcher, whose hands tightened on the binoculars. "What you say, honey? I could fix it all tomorrow if you say the word."

Ken, drawing himself up a little, was starting to speak when Zephyr dropped her arm from his waist, stepped to Schlumberger and, taking his face in her hands, said, "Dwight, you are an angel! It's *perfect!*" and kissed him on the lips.

Schlumberger, by cupping one hand round Zephyr's head and clamping her to him with the other on her rear, converted the kiss into one of more than impetuous gratitude. She struggled, Ken wrenched at Dwight's arm and the embrace ended in Zephyr's falling back against Ken, hands to mouth and hair over her eyes.

"Dwight! What the hell's the *idea?*"

"The idea is, you want a wedding by this lake, I'm giving you a wedding by this lake. Only the one you'll marry is me."

The watcher, who could hear voices but not words, wondered why at this point they were all silent, fixed as in a tableau. Something dramatic had been said. The next sound, perfectly audible over the water, was the sound of a mobile telephone ringing in somebody's pocket.

Chapter
10
·········

"Bloody hell." Ken seized Zephyr by the arm as Schlumberger whipped the phone to his ear and started talking. "Come away. The man's mad."

The tableau for the watcher in the woods dissolved. The man and the woman made their way up the steps among the birches while the one by the water's edge remained, phone to ear, in the gathering dusk, as incongruous in that landscape as the man in "Monty Python" sitting at his desk up to his thighs in the ocean. A bird flew low over the lake as if to study the strange sight, and flapped on into the woods to seek its roost. Time for every creature to think of settling for the night.

Treasure and her grandmother were companionably in the sitting room whose french windows gave onto the garden. Their peace was shattered by loud wrangling voices approaching over the terrace. Mrs. West put down the drink she was holding, Treasure clapped her book shut, threw it on the sofa and, picking up the remote control from the table by her grandmother's chair, turned on the television and made the sound bellow so that Mrs. West put her hands over her ears. Zephyr burst in through the French windows, startled, Ken at her heels.

Treasure dimmed the sound enough to be heard saying, "You better go someplace else, Mom, and have your fight to yourself. Dad'll be here any minute and he'll want a piece of it."

The logic of this clearly struck Zephyr and she towed a frowning Ken after her through the room. In passing, she snatched the remote control from Treasure, switched the TV off and threw the pad on a distant chair. As the door slammed behind them, Treasure retrieved the control and meekly restored it to her grandmother.

"Sorry. But I hate it when Mom quarrels. She did it all the time with Dad. When he was home. And now she's started with Ken even before he marries her." She brightened, swiveling to face her grandmother. "Do you think she won't, after all? She really should not, you know."

Mrs. West sipped her drink, studying the young, hopeful face, wondering if Treasure would grow up to be happy—what chance she had of happiness with the way things were.

"Darling, I thought you liked Ken."

"Sure I do. Ken is OK. But that's not the point."

"What is the point? Do you want her to get back with your father again? I don't think she ever will, you'll have to make up your mind to that."

Treasure wrinkled her nose. "I guess *that* can't happen. Dad's hopeless. He can't stand to let anything go." She stroked her grandmother's hand and put her head on one side. "Gran, could I have a bit of your drink? Just a taste?"

"No, darling. It hasn't a nice taste, one only gets to like it because it gives one a lift. At my age I need a lift. You don't. . . . But you need a bit of fun, not all this glooming over the wedding. Why don't you bring Jem to meet me tomorrow? Palmerston will do us a nice lunch and you can take Jem to see the lake—"

"I *hate* the lake! I wish there were no lakes *anywhere!*"

Mrs. West was deciding not to comment on the effect this would have on tourism in the North Country, when their attention was diverted by the reverberant crash of a door somewhere in the house, then the eruption of Ken from the hall. Mrs. West had never seen him anything but relaxed and sardonic, a cool observer of life's events. She was not prepared for the manic glare he directed toward her, or his general appearance of having been attacked, with his hair on end and his shirt collar pulled awry. He was shrugging his jacket back onto his shoulders.

The apparition was not there to speak. After that moment's glare, Ken seemed to find his bearings, see the way out, and take it, plunging past them out to the terrace in the deepening dusk. Treasure and Mrs. West had time only to glance at each other in surmise when Zephyr came in Ken's wake. She too was disturbed and angry.

"Has he gone?"

Mrs. West indicated the open French windows, which were suddenly filled by the burly form of Dwight Schlumberger. His gaze fixed at once on Zephyr and he advanced into the room.

"You looking for me, honey? I told you, that place is perfect. I can fix everything. I've been on to a guy who can hang lanterns all through those woods. Just give me the day."

Zephyr had been standing, hands fisted by her sides. Her hair was tousled and—there are no other words for it—her bosom was heaving. As Dwight ended, she took a couple of strides across the room and delivered a swinging slap on his cheek that rang like a whip-crack. She then turned on her heel and went back the way she had come. A succession of slamming doors told of her progress. Dwight, stroking his cheek as if at memory of a caress, smiled.

"That's my girl," he said, with satisfaction.

*　　　*　　　*

Kelly put on "Crying for Help" and wandered round the flat listening to it. The message was so plain that she was surprised she hadn't realized the urgency behind it until now. But of course that was before he'd been trapped.

It was a plea she couldn't ignore.

All this time she had been satisfied with second best, a reminder of the real thing. Those games were over. She knew now that she must act fast. As usual, she'd bought most of the newspapers, the tabloids anyway, no point in papers that thought themselves too grand for gossip; still there was no word in any of them about a date. Plenty about how wonderful it was all going to be, how sensational; well, leave that to her, all right. But not a dickybird about the actual day. Surely, if nothing else, the guests would want to know when to turn up. Even the uninvited ones would want to know that.

One part of her was thinking this while another listened acutely to the words of the song:

> I'm tied up, tied down,
> Only you can free me—
> Your touch can free me.

She stopped to stare out of the window but did not see the street. He's desperate. How *is* it I didn't hear it before? He's begging!

She'd made the mistake of telling Alan that she was getting messages in the songs and he'd laughed at her as if she was a nutter. Alan could well say there was no beseeching to be rescued when that song was made because the singer wasn't trapped then; Alan refused to see that she had always been needed. What could he have known of unconditional real love in that artificial world, surrounded by false glamour?

> False images, false faces—
> You don't wear a mask.

He wanted simplicity, a real person to love and understand him. With her he would find what all his life he'd been looking for, someone without artifice. Men didn't know. They fancied that a girl with big hair and endless legs was going to bring happiness. Girls like that only thought of their own bodies, they were built of delusion. You'd think he'd have learned from his first marriage, to that birdbrain! But he wasn't to blame. He could see that this one had a false image, she was torturing him, putting him through all this pain. But soon enough, soon enough he'd find out those cries had been heard by the one who could help him.

When the track ended, Kelly lit a cigarette and crouched before the papers on the sofa once more. There was another item for which she was looking and which she had not found.

Why was there no news of Alan?

Edwina, Ken's secretary, getting together her supper on a tray, about to go off to her bedroom to watch "Roseanne," reviewed the day, the house and her work. She glanced round the kitchen. Did Zephyr have the bottle of Malvern water by her bed? She made so much fuss when she ran out of the stuff a few nights ago, that one might be excused for thinking it was an elixir of youth without which the lovely Zephyr would wilt and crumble. Edwina, loading a bottle of Malvern water from the fridge onto her tray and adjusting the balance with her orange juice, a covered bowl of noodles with chicken and prawns, and a dish of crème caramel, followed this fantasy to the point where Zephyr, wrinkles crawling over her face as in a horror movie, sank to the ground in a welter of chiffon and dust. She'd have to get married in an urn. *I wish!*

Edwina was smiling still when she went into Zephyr's bedroom after dumping her supper tray by her own bed on the way. The noodles might not be exactly hot on her return but Edwina had a good appetite to which her figure bore comfortable witness. She had observed

Zephyr's widening of her wonderful blue eyes when they were introduced, and she was not as grateful as she might have been for the recent kindly offers of diets and dietitians, exercise videos and, as a possible gift if she could get Ken to agree to her temporary absence, liposuction.

Remembering this, Edwina smacked the Malvern bottle down quite hard beside the lamp and the silver-framed photograph of Zephyr, looking about sixteen and dreamily regarding the baby that was going to grow up to be Treasure and wear dental braces. You can't win 'em all, and Edwina was of the opinion that Zephyr would not have cared for a rival to her beauty. She studied the photograph for a moment before putting it down, and then glanced round. Just as she had expected, the luxuriant plant in its green and white trellised cachepot that Zephyr had deposited on Ken's piano earlier in the day was now sitting on the little table in the window, just as the tapestry cushions she had bought and arranged on the scarlet corduroy sofa had winged their way upstairs and were now in a rather dismal row on the chaise longue. There would be questions asked, as there had been about the china figurine with swirling petticoats and the pair of bonbonnieres with their guardian Oriental animals; Edwina would, as usual, be quite unable to answer. She could have said truthfully that she hadn't moved them.

As she turned to go, something caught her eye. The heavy chestnut wardrobe door stood slightly open and a long ragged yellow streamer was fluttering in the breeze from the window open on the warm evening.

Bone was not yet accustomed to sleeping by himself once more. A few weeks ago, Grizel had declared that there was no room in their bed for her, him, and their imminent son. Bone had therefore camped out in the spare room, not yet used for a guest since they bought the cottage nearly a year ago. At that time, Grizel had been in the early stages of pregnancy and they had been looking for a place bigger than either his flat in Tunbridge Wells or her cottage in Adlingsden where they had been happily weekending—somewhere with room for a nursery. The move itself had been a success. His daughter Charlotte adored her room, with its view over the hills from the low window seat where she would sit, gazing for hours on end. However, plans for the nursery were gravely set back when Grizel had lost the baby early in the pregnancy. It had not been a good time, the more distressing because the doctors could find no reasonable cause for it.

Grizel had refused to be downcast, and went ahead with the decoration of the nursery, getting Cha, who was becoming very good at drawing, to invent a frieze of rabbits gamboling in a garden; then later, announcing she was pregnant again, she claimed the rabbits, fertility symbols, had worked their magic. Bone had made enormous efforts not to nag and fuss, noticing how helpful and protective Cha had become; here they were, gloriously well into the ninth month with nothing gone wrong.

Bone, arranging his bedside clock, smiled at it as he set the alarm. A recent present from Grizel, it provided the sounds of either a mountain stream with crickets, or waves on a shore with optional seagulls, to go to sleep to, a recording that could be set to last up to an hour, by which time Bone suspected any insomniac would have sat up and smothered the clock. Until he discovered how to mute the sound, the mountain stream with crickets had been a confused roar punctuated by tiny castanets, like mice dancing flamenco to Brobdignagian applause—not, in Bone's opinion, designed to lull.

Setting the alarm, he expected to wake as usual before it went off. The idea of it was to encourage the reviving consciousness by infiltrating one's dreams with birdsong. To do this, they had naturally chosen the dawn chorus, heedless that this was the time birds really zapped into action, and even with the volume low the decibels were at shock level.

As it happens, he was not woken by birdsong but by the even more shrill telephone.

He rose on one elbow, put on the light, grabbed the handset and hauled it into the warmth of the bed.

"Bone here."

Steve Locker—on duty tonight—said apologetically, "Sorry about the time, sir"—Bone glanced at the clock, which innocently displayed 1:45—"but something's turned up; or rather, hasn't turned up."

"Steve," Bone heard his voice sharpen, "are you messing with my sleep to ask me riddles? Spit it out."

"It's Ken Cryer, sir. He seems to have gone missing."

Chapter

11

·········

The words "Death Threats" lit up like fireworks in Bone's mind and hung there, burning. He sat up, trying to calm himself.

"Gone missing. For how long? Who's reported it?"

"His secretary and his minders."

"His *minders?*" This was serious. If the people whose job it is to stay with a man report him missing, he probably is. "Let's hear, Steve." He pushed the pillows up to lean on and pulled the duvet round him.

"Cryer had last been seen at Herne Hall, where he'd been visiting, along with his fiancée—"

"Has *she* reported him missing?"

"She's not up to reporting anything. It seems she had the mother of a row with Cryer, went up to the room at Herne Hall she uses when she's not at the Manor, took a couple of sleeping pills and can't be roused."

"What did Ken do?"

"He dashed out into the night; into the garden, Mrs. West thought. Mel Rees and Joe Tench were in the kitchen, chatting to Palmerston, and as time went on they thought to check when they'd be wanted to drive Cryer and Miss West back to the Manor. Palmerston went to ask Mrs. West what was planned and she was surprised Ken hadn't collected the minders and gone, as he'd stormed out of the french windows at least an hour before."

"So?"

"They searched the grounds, phoned the Manor to see if he'd taken off on his tod to walk home—not the likeliest chance at six miles in the dark on winding roads— but his secretary checks and there's no sign of him, the security system hasn't recorded his clocking in."

Bone was silent a minute, considering. "He hasn't gone up in a puff of smoke, pantomime style. Sure he hasn't fallen into that wretched lake?"

"Lake? The *wedding* lake?"

"As you say, Steven, the wedding lake. Zephyr's daughter took me to see it and it's quite deep enough for drowning."

"Sir, are you suggesting Cryer's taken his own life?"

"Not seriously. No. I wouldn't say he's at all the type, but a man who doesn't jump can get pushed. On the premises at Herne Hall is Zephyr's ex, remember, Dwight Schlumberger, who has been sunnily convinced all along that the wedding won't take place."

"You think he could have gone after Cryer and ensured it?"

Bone saw again the dark stare under heavy brows, the determined stride. "Mm. Only if he thought nothing could be proved against him. He did not strike me as a man for rash action."

Locker was making muffled sounds at his end of the line, which Bone was fairly sure were the result of trying to eat quietly. "What do you say we should do, sir?"

That was the crunch. Cryer had come to him about death threats. Could he have been abducted from the grounds at Herne Hall? No perimeter wall or tight security, cameras, all the things that made Cryer relatively safe at his own Manor. Someone could have been waiting his chance there all the time.

And if Cryer wasn't in the lake he might have been

bundled into a car and left somewhere as a surprise present for the police. Just over a year ago a woman had driven her husband to a local beauty spot and left him. As he'd been sitting in the passenger seat none of the transient visitors noticed anything funny for a week. Then the flies clustering round the car drew somebody's attention and the man's appearance, by then, brought a phone call to the police and the unsavory job for PC Brooking of opening the car door.

His wife said later that she thought as he'd always preferred the view to her she'd give him the opportunity of a good long look. He still had the knife in his back.

Bone shook his head. Morbid memories wouldn't help here. He glanced at the clock again. "Not a lot we can do, Steve, at this hour. He's a grown man and we're paying his disappearance some attention so soon because he's Ken Cryer. Tomorrow morning we'll start up. It comes to me that Cryer mentioned once he'd taken off into the wide blue yonder when something was bugging him. A song he couldn't write, was it?"

"I was going to say, sir—Mel Rees told me Cryer had done a bunk last year when a record company was harassing him to come up with an album he didn't want to do. They were in a great old tizz, then Cryer rang from Cornwall, said he'd be back when he'd walked off his need to kill his manager."

Bone reached over his shoulder to catch the duvet as it deserted him. This was more cheerful news. Perhaps by morning Locker would ring up to tell of a call from Cryer, who this time from the sound of it might have to walk off a need to kill his bride.

One thing Bone's job did for him was to make him thankful he hadn't the problems whose pitiful consequences provided his work. Picking up often blood-stained pieces of people's relationships, or more properly their failures, certainly made one grateful for one's own family. "Well, that does cool the urgency a little. Phone me as soon as you hear anything, whatever the time."

Ringing off and lying back, he gazed at his clock and wondered if he started up the mountain stream and crickets, really softly, Grizel could possibly hear it. Waves on the shore might be safer. Then he could think of Cryer striding along some beach in Cornwall and debating whether to get married or not. As he turned out the light and closed his eyes, Bone told himself firmly that if Cryer had managed to evade his minders, the odds were he'd evade anyone with more sinister purposes. With luck.

Chapter
12
·········

Bone was up, as he had expected, long before the dawn chorus broke out on his clock. Cha, in the last week of her holidays, seemed to be still in a generous mood and brought first Grizel, and then her father, a cup of tea. Beside his cup, as she put it on his bedside table, was something which made him, coming in from the bathroom, raise his eyebrows.

"A croissant? What have I done to deserve this?" He sat down on his bed and broke the hot pastry in two.

"It's what you're going to do more."

"Going to do?" He stopped eating and looked at her, putting on a suspicious glower. Today Charlotte was wearing her hair loose, the better to hide behind. The black T-shirt, the long black leggings, gave her a funereal, rather pitiable, air. "What's worth a croissant?"

"You *might* get a supper out of it too. Your favorite. Boof Strog. With lots of sour cream."

"Now I'm seriously worried. What's the favor to match that?" He drank tea. Cha pointed a toe as if about to perform some balletic movement. "Well, it's this project. I was supposed to have done it by this term."

Bone got into his shirt. "A project nobody's heard about until now."

"I've been busy." Charlotte was indignant and Bone partly sympathized. She had indeed been busy, chiefly round the house doing things Grizel now found difficult, and going with Grizel to the shops and to the clinic. A camping holiday with her friend Grue and her parents hadn't provided a great deal of fun, either. Phone calls home had told of rain, of being chased by cows, and of a thunderstorm which had struck a tree not far from their tent. Holiday projects had not reached priority status this summer.

"So? Spit it out, pet. I have to get going." He was at the door. No call had come from Locker about Ken Cryer found or not found. "What's the project about?"

"Justice." The word came out in a rush and Cha hooked her hair behind her ears as if she could now come into the open. "So you *see*. It would be excellent if you could take me on a sort of day's work in the life of. You know."

"I certainly do not." Bone's sharpness derived from his strong feelings about keeping the horrible side of his job from his daughter: the gruesome discoveries, the postmortems, all sorts of things inseparable from his work in the homicide section. Just because many of the deaths his people inquired into took place in rural surroundings did not mean they were sanitized by it. "I don't think that's a good idea at all."

"But why? I'm not asking you to take me to see corpses and that. There must be some sort of investigations, finding things out and so on, that I could get an idea of."

"That's more about law than it is about justice."

"What are you two talking about? Isn't either of you coming down to breakfast?"

Grizel's shout up the stairs triggered an answering shout from Bone and made Cha catch him by the arm. "Please? Just one day?"

"Pet, there are a thousand reasons why not. And anyway today is impossible. I've got something really awk-ward on hand. I couldn't take you along."

"But you will think about it?" Her hair fell forward in her vehemence. Bone considered. Perhaps a day in court would do, on some harmless case that wasn't a murder. He could fix that. He smiled, and put her hair behind her ears.

"I'll see. Don't hold your breath. Start writing: what is justice?—not many people think they've got it."

As he went downstairs, a belligerent dawn chorus issued from the clock.

Bone kissed Grizel, posted a piece of toast between his teeth and said through it as she offered to pour him more tea, "Can't stay, love. Missing person."

He finished the toast as he went, driving himself to Herne Hall after making a call on the car phone to check with the station. At least the worst hadn't happened: no one had found Ken Cryer dead.

All the same, as he drove, the window open to pleasantly warm air, his view of the road was patchworked with cut-out letters arranged in neat rows: "Marry the bitch and you die."

Could Cryer have decided it wasn't worth the risk?

Later that morning, Bone was inclined to agree with this.

He paid a short call on Mrs. West. She spoke of Inspector Locker's courtesy but tended to play down the drama of the missing fiancé, with a most discreet suggestion as to her daughter's ability to create crises wherever she went. According to Mrs. West—very elegant that morning in cinnamon brown with a rose quartz crystal gleaming against it on a silver chain—it was all a lovers' tiff and Ken merely needed breathing space. She said nothing of death threats and Bone saw no point in reminding her. That was his worry if it was anyone's.

Dwight Schlumberger appeared suddenly as they were talking, in a crumpled linen jacket that was either the same he wore yesterday or a fresh one which had achieved an accurate degree of crumple. He looked to have had an excellent sleep and be ready for more pleasant surprises. Neither he nor Mrs. West had anything to add to what Locker had heard the previous evening. Dwight did not disagree with the idea of a lovers' tiff. He made a distinction only in considering it final. He was taking the situation as a war of nerves which Cryer had suddenly and conspicuously lost.

Confusingly, Dwight was apparently helping Mrs. West with preparations for the wedding reception. Bone had arrived to find her beside a table covered with lists and Dwight, when he came in, handed her another list with items ticked off, for which she thanked him. So did he believe that Cryer would return, after all?

The one whose opinion was critical to the issue was not available. Zephyr, her mother said, had been very upset indeed when she finally woke from her sleeping pill trance and found that neither had her fiancé been continually phoning to apologize nor had penitential roses been delivered en masse. She had refused to credit any idea of his disappearance and swept Treasure off to the Manor, set on finding out "what had really happened."

"I'm afraid," said Mrs. West, regarding Bone over the top of her reading glasses with blue eyes so like her daughter's, apart from the shrewd intelligence in them, "she thinks there's a conspiracy against her."

Bone shortly discovered what this meant.

Security was working perfectly at the Manor. He stopped his car at the gates where a camera on the wall eerily moved to observe him; he held up his warrant card to it and, after a short pause, the gates obligingly clicked and swung back. He drove through. They shut behind him. Mel Rees waited at the porch door, burly in white T-shirt and jeans, and for a moment until he saw his expression Bone thought he had news of Cryer.

It turned out he was there to deliver a warning.

"Bloody hurricane blowing in there," he remarked, jerking his cropped head toward the open door of the Manor. The mellow golden infill between the fifteenth-century beams was glowing in the morning sunlight which glittered off the many panes in the long windows. Hardly a breeze stirred the climbing roses up the porch.

This porch jutted out, and above its drunkenly skewed beams was Jem Cryer's bedroom and watchtower. The front window stood open. Shouting and a sudden shriek announced the present location of the hurricane.

Bone, not waiting to hear more, went in fast, ran up the broad oak staircase and reached the top in record time. A corridor led ahead and he gained the door of the little gatehouse, which was open but still hardly gave room for another person to crowd inside. The small space already held four people, one gesticulating violently.

"You are a *devil!*" It was Zephyr, shrieking at Jem. He had backed rather dangerously against the open window. Edwina Marsh, Ken's secretary, was cramming her generously sized body away from Zephyr while keeping her eye out for Jem, of whom Bone knew she was fond. Treasure, trying to get something her mother was holding, added her yells to the din.

What Zephyr held seemed to be a tattered yellow banner, long streamers attached to a frill on a coat hanger. Simultaneously, Bone realized what it must be and Zephyr, seeing Jem look past her, wheeled on Bone, brandishing the coat hanger. "You see what's he's done? *Ruined* her dress—cut it to pieces! Wretched sly little skunk! How are we to get another made in time?"

A pointless question, Bone thought, if the bridegroom didn't show up. This was on Zephyr's mind too. She turned on Jem again, whirling the ravished dress overhead and scraping the ceiling. "All of it's your fault! *You* made your father go!"

"Lousy rag!" shrieked Treasure, reaching for it.

"I know you hate me! You're jealous because your father loves me!"

"I look awful in it, awful! And it's NOT golden! It's PISS color."

"You want to destroy my happiness!" As if in demon-

stration Zephyr flailed the coat hanger down on Jem's
arm, upraised for protection, and hit him with an audible
crack. Treasure grabbed and wrested the object from
her, and Zephyr flung herself at Jem and gripped him
by the neck.

Bone started forward but Edwina, nearer, got in his
way. She caught Zephyr by the shoulders and tried to
drag her back, while Treasure hit out at her mother with
the coat hanger, some of the blows connecting with Edwina. Jem, invisible against the window, made choking
sounds.

Bone shoved in without ceremony, pushing Edwina
aside. She fell on the bed and he got Zephyr by the
wrists; their strength was of a kind he had met before.
Hysteria too can move mountains. Drowned in her
musky scent, whipped by swathes of her glossy hair, he
managed to make her hands open. What is "reasonable
force"? he wondered. He was certainly bruising the slender wrists, hanging on as she still struggled to reach Jem;
he wished for a moment he had handcuffs. Zephyr's face
was a snarling mask. He would not have been surprised
if she'd bent and sunk her teeth in his hand.

He wrenched her round away from Jem, and for the
first time she saw who held her wrists, and glared at this
man who had come from nowhere to thwart her. She
blinked. Bone warily relaxed his grip and she snatched
her hands free, grabbed the coat hanger from Treasure
and hurled it, over Jem's head—and he ducked—out of
the window. The clatter of its landing on the flags beneath reached them in the silence.

Bone, chagrined at her slipping his chancery so easily,
was alert to take hold again if she went for Jem, but her
gesture with the ruins of the dress seemed to have satisfied her for the moment.

"You'll pay for this, little toad. Come along, Treasure." Zephyr grabbed her daughter's arm and, pushing
her ahead, left the room, in her passage knocking over
a table which cast a quantity of small objects to the floor.

Jem rushed to pick these up and check on them, holding his throat with one hand.

Edwina and Bone looked at each other. Edwina said, "She's like that. I don't think Ken realizes." She crouched by Jem, helping him to pick up the small ebony and ivory elephants, pink suede Indian horses with sequinned trappings, tiny jade dogs and a dragon of purple glass with glittering fangs. "Are you all right, Jem? I thought she was going to kill you."

Jem looked up from scrutiny of one of the dogs which had a tiny chip off one ear. He spoke hoarsely, "I thought she was going to kill me. She's got hands like a wrestler."

Bone caught sight of a small turquoise cat lying forlornly by Jem's bed and brought it over.

"You wrecked the dress. Did Treasure ask you to?"

Jem accepted the cat and sat back on his heels. He looked up, grinning, and croaked, "No. Pure charity on my part. It was seriously bugging her so I thought she'd be better off without it. Didn't know her mother would throw a loop—" He stopped, put a hand to his throat and coughed.

"You're going to have a very stiff neck," Bone said. Edwina drew Jem to his feet and led him to the window.

"Let me have a proper look at you. . . . That's a nasty bruise coming along. I'm going to give you a cold compress of witch hazel for it and I think a nice cool drink will help a bit. Come along, you can tidy up afterwards."

As she led him past Bone, Jem rolled his eyes and said, "If only Dad had been there to see."

Indeed, had Cryer been there to witness his fiancée attempting to strangle his son, the odds against the wedding might have increased enough to satisfy even Dwight Schlumberger.

Chapter

13

It was a day on which a number of people were innocently happy, unaware that their work might not be required after all. The firm rung earlier by Schlumberger confirmed the booking for the large marquee to be put up on the morning of September the third in the grounds of Herne Hall, in preparation for the wedding reception to be held in the afternoon. The caterers, who had been warmly recommended to Mrs. West by Ken's secretary, submitted the final menu; the correct calculations had been made as to how many canapés would be needed for the glamorous guests invited by Zephyr West and the rather less high-powered—on the whole—but probably just as hungry friends of the bridegroom coming to see him make his big mistake.

Mrs. West had married wisely and, when her husband died, she had enough at her disposal to be as generous as she wished in providing her daughter's wedding reception.

As she chose to ignore that it might not take place, there was no slackening in the buildup. Zephyr's wedding dress, a miracle of white satin embroidered with silver thread and tiny seed pearls, was still having the final touches put to it by its designer and the team working on it. This designer was now visited in London by a furious Zephyr, daughter in tow, and asked to design and have made up a bridemaid's dress to replace the one ruined. Zephyr had no confidence in the capacity of the little local woman she had before thought good enough, to come up with a duplicate in the time without delaying matters by a heart attack.

This time, she specified that both dresses were to remain with the designer until the wedding day. Treasure watched with disgust as, under Zephyr's directions, something hideously similar to the other dress was formed by the designer's felt-tip. She was to be brought tomorrow for a fitting. The designer, knowing what charge she could add to her usual steep rates for doing a rush job, smiled to herself as she finished the sketch with a flourish, frills cascading from hip to hem; she looked up, to receive a very wide and hideous metallic smile from Treasure, who switched it off as abruptly as she had made it.

A swatch of silk chosen by Zephyr was pinned to the sketch; the color, Treasure considered, was an even more revolting yellow than the previous one. The designer, jolted by that smile, thought she herself would have put the girl in a different color entirely, perhaps rose to warm up the sallow complexion. Certainly she would have left off the frills. She already knew, however, that Zephyr had a whim of iron, and she was the customer.

While everything, like Juggernaut, rolled its relentless way to the wedding, Bone was still debating about the absence of the groom.

"If it weren't for the death threats . . ." He aligned his blotter with the edge of the desk, trying to order his thoughts. Locker, sipping boiling coffee on the other side of the desk, nodded.

"If they were to dry up the same time Cryer disappears . . ."

Bone said somberly, "Edwina Marsh says there's been

one a day until recently. The last was 'Get ready to say goodbye forever.' "

"That's what you might say, on cue."

"Too much so. If it got to the papers someone would be bound to suggest he'd got picked up by a UFO."

"What about dragging the lake, sir?"

"It's not been twenty-four hours yet. All the wedding preparations are at full steam; no one who knows about it seems to be taking a vanished groom seriously. His own people are so little disturbed that I pressed again about their knowing where he is; they swear they don't know, but I can't help but doubt them. A lot of the steam—scalding stuff at that—is being provided by the beautiful bride. Apart from preventing her from murdering her future stepson, the police can only stand by and watch."

"The last threat was two days ago, you said, sir? Where was this one posted?"

Bone stirred, and laid his hands flat on the blotter, making a chevron of them. "That's the worst of it, Steve. Edwina says it was not stamped or addressed; it had only Cryer's name on it, and it was in the mailbox at the gate."

Locker put his cup down crookedly in the saucer. "That's not pretty. If the bloke that's offering to kill Cryer is around the neighborhood, and he's disappeared . . ."

"I know. The buck stops here." In the old days he'd known a joker of a Chief Constable who'd illustrated this saying with a print of Landseer's *Stag at Bay* on the wall behind his desk. But it was not enough to flare the nostrils nobly. The decision must be taken: whether to go public on Cryer's disappearance and, by making a fuss, find some traces of what had happened. To do that, he must get the consent of those most concerned. Cryer had cut loose before and turned up safely. Finally, if the worst scenario were being acted out and Cryer had fallen into the hands of the threatener but was still alive, the publicity might force the kidnapper into killing him.

The buck hadn't just stopped. It was pawing the ground.

"I know sometimes the best thing *is* to do nothing. Say you're trying to talk someone down off a ledge. With some you only show yourself and they jump. Others you can talk to and they still jump. Left alone, some think it over and come in of their own accord."

The trouble was that his argument didn't convince him.

While Bone was discussing options with Locker in Tunbridge Wells and Zephyr was in London commissioning her daughter's dress, and others scattered round the country were busy in their preparations for the wedding, there were of course those to whom the occasion meant nothing and who had work of a less frivolous nature to get on with.

Such was John Hunter, who had set aside part of the day for tidying up the quarry on his land, an old marl pit dug out of the hill, which too many people had come to use as a dump. The trouble was, access was easy, over a broken fence which, admittedly, he had allowed to disintegrate. The state of the fence had been taken as an invitation to drag decaying mattresses across it and hurl them down together with pieces of decrepit machinery that had been clogging up the back garden or the yard, in fact anything too large to get into a dustbin, too noxious to be welcome where it was, and costing money to have removed officially.

The quarry was an ancient one, dating from the times when marl and not chemicals was spread on the fields; its shelving walls grew scrubby bushes and a seasonal pond lurked in the bottom, surrounded by nettles. It was never going to attract the homeless as a permanent hangout when it was so far away from dole lines and passersby to beg from. Hunter had reason to believe that in summer the abandoned car seats provided a place more inviting than the bare ground to make what is commonly called love, to judge from the scattering of beer cans and condoms around them. Bonfires had been lit from time to time, for the fun of it, but too much remained. The old fridge would have to go on the trailer but the mattresses, the wooden bed head, the rags, the car seats, the old wardrobe, would all burn now with a judicious application of fuel.

Hunter's intention was to create a more comprehensive and cleansing bonfire, which by clearing the site would no longer encourage people, by its chaos and decay, to deposit everything past practical use.

What he discovered still fitted that qualification. He sat down his petrol can and hauled out his strimmer to clear the nettles and then, by that scavenger's instinct which lurks in human breasts since the first caveman turned up a likely flint, he poked about among the remains he had come to burn. He put aside a wrench that really needed only a bath of oil to be perfectly viable. There was even a quite handsome little box with one hinge missing, which would answer repair and a good wax and polish; the wife would find it handy for bits and pieces. Head down, turning over things with his boot and the end of the strimmer, he had been looking too closely at detail to see what he had come upon. He saw, with sudden hope, the leather jacket. It would hardly be here if it was not damaged, but perhaps it could be repaired. He picked up the sleeve to examine it and dropped it with a yelp when it proved heavy and he saw a hand at the end of it.

Not long after that, yet another phone rang at the station. The call reached Locker, who came immediately to interrupt Bone as he ploughed through some of his paperwork. Bone, looking up as Locker burst in, had all at once a premonition of what he was going to say.

"They've found Cryer, sir."

79

Chapter

14

· · · · · · · · ·

The day had turned warm. Bone, as a PC lifted the tapes for him, felt the damp under his arms and between his shoulder blades as he ducked. The warm breeze had the smell of decay on its breath and, looking round, he wasn't surprised. With Locker stumping after, he trod along the trampled path between nettles and wiry shrubs flowering with rags. A buckled bumper and part of a car radiator powdered with rush had been heaved aside.

The group standing at the edge of the quarry peered past him. Bone guessed that the large florid man unnaturally drained of color was John Hunter who had found the body. He was a burly man, in a checked shirt which brought out the faded beetroot of his cheeks; he stood in a collapsed fashion with hunched shoulders and hanging arms, that argued he would have been glad to sit down if there'd been anything more handy than a grotty car seat, and if he didn't want to look gutless for being shaken at holding a corpse by the arm.

Bone, forced to wait until the last of the flash photos, the Polaroids, and the measurements had been taken, was keeping a tight rein on his own feelings. It would not do to show dismay before his team. The litany of

self-justifying continued in his head but yet he did not
believe he could be accused of acting unprofessionally.
Cryer had not been gone for the statutory twenty-four
hours that would qualify him as officially missing. Yet
Bone had been aware of the death threats; if heads had
to roll, it would be his in the basket.

And Ken Cryer was a man he liked.

At this state, Bone refused to think about Jem Cryer,
whom he liked very much.

"Dr. Foster's on his way, sir. He phoned to say he
was almost here."

Oddly, for once, Bone did not look forward to Ferdy
Foster's caustic comments. The Home Office pathologist
had a line in jokes that helped your nerves as a rule; as
a rule the corpse was not known to you.

The police doctor, crouched by the body, turned
round and acknowledged Bone.

"Cause of death?"

Now this was the point: shot, strangled or stabbed?
How had this "Goodbye forever" been arranged?

"Difficult to say. Possibly accidental, as if he'd stumbled up there and fallen."

Bone, in the act of snapping on the transparent plastic
gloves handed him by Locker, paused. An accident? Ken
must have chosen to walk back from Herne Hall, lost
his way in the woods at night, and here—not far from
his own home, just over that tree-crowned hill—had he
simply fallen?

The police doctor, looking past Bone to see Ferdy
Foster arriving, stood aside. Bone came forward. He had
never been so unwilling. Cryer lay flat on his back now,
heavy lids closed as if in sleep, arms flung wide as if in
appeal to the justice of his fate. Evidently he had been
lying facedown when Hunter found him, as his face was
smudged and battered and gashed by the debris on
which he had landed. Curiously, in spite of the deep
lines on cheeks and brow, Cryer looked younger than
Bone remembered him, as if death had canceled some
of the years as it is said to do. The famous lock of hair

was stuck to the brow with grime and congealed blood. The mouth, which would sing no more songs in that slightly grating, melancholy voice, was open, and being visited by a couple of flies.

It was odd that he was wearing a bronze silk shirt which, for all its muddy, bloodstained condition, was showily expensive, and a leather jacket of the same shade of bronze. When he thought about it, Bone realized he had never seen Ken in anything but jeans and T-shirt. Leather jacket, yes, but nondescript, worn, white at the seams, nothing like this sumptuous rig. Cha had recently shown him a photograph in some glossy magazine: Ken on tour promoting his last album. He'd been wearing this flash bronze getup then. Had he really worn it last night when he rowed with Zephyr and took off into the gloaming? Bone bent suddenly to look at the dead face.

"Not a pretty picture, Robert." Ferdy's gravelly tones sounded over his head. "What made a rock star come to give his last performance in this arena?" He put down a mackintosh he carried over his arm and knelt there, snapping on his gloves. "Are you suggesting murder here?"

Bone sat back on his heels, hope rising.

"Not so much murder, I think. Perhaps forgery."

The Red Lion at Adleston was not a large inn. Pleasantly placed on the corner of Adleston village green and the road running through the village, it was not on the direct route to the coast and so not made hideous by lorries and coaches, and anyone who stayed at the Red Lion could be sure of a good night's sleep. Excellent food was to be had, as well as bar snacks, and Terri Greenwood was proud of her reputation as a cook. When she caught sight of one of the Lion's guests—so near September there were fewer than there had been in early August—coming in somewhat later than the advertised time for lunch, Terri did not hesitate to bustle forward, and she suggested a nice steak and kidney pie with a side order of chips and salad. She could even bring it outside where there was shade from the afternoon sun under one of the Red Lion's striped umbrellas.

She wondered if the guest were drunk. The refusal of food was abrupt enough to be downright rude, but what struck her was the glitter in eyes that seemed not to see her properly, and the intensity of expression. Later she wondered if it was drugs, and thought she'd just have a word with her husband about the occupant of Room Nine; they wanted no scandal, no brush with the police. Suppose they had a drug dealer in their midst? Even respectable little villages like Adleston didn't escape things these days, that wouldn't have been dreamt of a short time ago.

While Terri was reflecting on the decline of moral values in the countryside, the occupant of Room Nine was packing. Time to move on. Stay too long in any place and you ran a greater risk of attracting attention, of being remembered later.

It wouldn't be long before the big news broke. One had to be ready for anything.

In fact, thanks to John Hunter's having rung his wife directly after he rang the police, reporters from a local paper were already on their way to the quarry, enormously excited at the possibility of scooping the big evening papers. It was fair. Wasn't Ken Cryer a local hero? They were entitled to any gruesome shots of their own dead rock star before the world press and TV splashed it. One reporter had already put forward a banner headline for his editor's consideration, a steal from the title of the most famous Cryer album: Crying Shame.

Chapter
15

Things are never as straightforward as they seem. The pioneer band of reporters arriving at the quarry put up a display of indignation and reproach at the discovery of so little cooperation from the police. There had been as yet no formal identification. There was No Comment and they could come no closer. There was a police tent over Cryer's body, tantalizing them still further; they photographed that, and the groups of police, and the crumpled fence, and the farmer, who was being kept in conversation by the police so they could not yet get to him either. They had some rather good shots of Bone turning round and looking annoyed. The network was flashing rumor and he expected TV vans thundering from the local stations; a crew now arrived, one of whom was down at the end of the trampled path trying for a shot into the protective tent. Sergeant Shay stood casually in the way.

Even if national TV had not got in yet, Kent radio stations had picked up the titillating news. They carefully stated that there was as yet no confirmation that Ken Cryer, world-famous rock star, missing from his country manor home, had been found dead in a quarry close by, in suspicious circumstances.

Zephyr West, driving herself and Treasure back from London in her red sports car, was cutting up drivers on the M25 without even noticing that she did it. Her marvelous hair was swathed in lavender silk chiffon against the wind of her speed. She did not listen to the news on radio, for she was too busy singing along to Aretha Franklin on stereo tape, while Treasure glowered beside her, her own lank hair whipping her cheeks as a kind of mortification for the embarrassment her mother was causing her. She had no intention of wearing the replacement yellow frilled dress but she had not informed her mother of that.

Jem Cryer's neck was still surprisingly sore, and stiffening, even after Edwina's witch hazel compresses and icy drinks of the housekeeper's homemade lemonade. He was out in the grounds looking for his cat Buster. He still missed the gallant little terrier Fatstock Prices who, at the end of a remarkably active life, was buried under the cedar that shadowed his father's studio; he was feeling the need for companionship at a lower and more comforting level than the human. Edwina Marsh, too, missed the news about Ken because she was eating pie and chips with Ken's minders and anxiously canvassing their opinions on whether he would phone any minute to say he would soon be back.

Mrs. West, who had the radio on, did cause concern to Palmerston by dropping an exquisite teacup, one of a Worcester service and though it did not break it flooded the Aubusson, which had saved it, with Lapsang souchong. While he was mopping it up she told him the news.

"Never mind it, madam." Palmerston's consolation was as convincing as she needed it to be, and the more so for the measured tone in which it was delivered. "You must remember that the media often get things wrong. "No confirmation may mean they only hope it is true."

One who shared the media optimism was Dwight,

waiting to break the news to his ex-wife in case she had not heard it on the radio. Palmerston, on Mrs. West's order, was to endeavor to draw Zephyr aside as she came in and to explain matters to her as discreetly as possible, but he was no match for Dwight. As Zephyr's sports car scattered gravel into the flower bed in the center of the drive, Dwight shouldered past Palmerston and strode forward to open the car door and hand her out. Treasure scrambled from the far side with a face of deep suspicion.

"Honey, have you heard about your boyfriend?"

"Ken? He's back?" Zephyr, shaking her hair loose after its lavender silk confinement, glowed. She had known that no man could stay away from her longer than it took him to consider what he was missing. After a lovers' tiff there would be a beautiful lovers' reunion. Dwight continued to grip her hand in his broad one, preventing her dash for the house, and she looked at his face. "What's wrong? Where is he?"

If Dwight hankered to answer "in the morgue" he crushed it back, but he could not restrain a note of satisfaction in the grim: "He's met with an accident. The radio gave it out a while back."

"An *accident?*" Zephyr saw Ken hurtling down country lanes too fast, desperate to see her again. Her free hand flew to her mouth. "Don't say he's been killed?"

"Excuse me, sir." Palmerston had joined them, driven unthinkably to interrupt. "Madam, the news on the wireless expressly said that it had not been confirmed who the victim was. He had not yet been identified as Mr. Cryer."

"Oh my *God!*" Zephyr, in a manner her fans would have recognized, was weeping great tears that rolled down her cheeks to slide between the fingers still at her mouth. "Oh my God, I've killed him."

Wrenching herself from Dwight's grasp she pushed Palmerston aside and fled into the house. Treasure rounded the car, asking impatiently, "What's happened? Who's killed?" and Dwight, forestalling Palmerston, said with happy conviction, "Cryer's about to be buried, not married."

At about this time, DS Patricia Fredricks, dispatched by Bone, drove up to the Manor. Mel Rees at the monitor checked her credentials and switched the gate control while behind him in the room the videoscreen had just flashed up Fredricks' face, so like a friendly horse, above the warrant card she held out. Mel, Joe Tench the other minder, and Edwina sat staring at each other.

"I'd better go." Edwina put down a half-eaten chip as though it were poison, and hurried from the room. Mel and Joe were left with the same thought: if the police brought good news about Ken, why hadn't he himself rung?

Only a few minutes later the house phone buzzed and Edwina, in a voice that was rigidly controlled, informed them that she was on her way to provide identification for a body found in the quarry over the hill; the farmer who had found it thought it might be Ken. She added that no one was to say anything to Jem until she got back, nor put through any calls to his phone.

At the quarry, the police had made another discovery.

While Bone watched Ferdy Foster turn back the muddied and torn silk shirt on the battered chest, Locker had instituted a team search of the quarry. There was a definite problem about this because of the precipitate slope of the ground and the superfluity of obstacles; there could be no steady progress, knee to knee, elbow to elbow, patting with gloved hands at the area directly in front of each man.

"More like rock climbing than a search."

Someone added pungent words about the nettles. Someone discovered a heap of rusty tins. He called to the depressed farmer that he'd left it a bit late to clear all this out.

"I was only going to burn the mattresses," Hunter said.

Bone, bent next to Foster, pointed at the mess that

had perhaps been Cryer's chest, not one that could ever again expand to a song. "Could that be a gunshot wound?"

Ferdy turned treacle-brown eyes. "Wait for the post mortem, Robert. All I can tell you is that his ribs are stove in and a lung punctured. Presumably he did it on one of these handy saplings or debris and if there's a bullet waiting for me to fish it out, it too must wait. Shot or not, he'd have bled to death from this."

"Sir, sir!"

One of the searchers raised an arm. He held up a long object already safely bagged. "A gun, sir."

The line stopped. The finder made his difficult way along behind them to meet his senior officers, and held out the bag with much the air of a dog bringing a thrown stick back to his master. Bone and Locker examined it. Was this used to kill Cryer? Forensic would be able to tell; this was something to work on, and might answer part of their enormous question.

"Sir." One of the team called from the rim of the quarry above. He crouched to address Locker more directly. "There's press and TV at the tapes back here. They came up the hill by the wood track and one of them says there's a car among the trees on the far side. Do I go have a look-see?"

Ferdy Foster was standing up by now in the translucent gloom of the tent, stripping the gloves from his hands, and the body was about to be wrapped and put on the stretcher to be taken to the mortuary where, after a kindly tidying-up, it could be seen by Edwina Marsh for identification. The communications sergeant, talking into his radio, suddenly said, "Sir—Super—there's a word from Pat Fredricks—" and at the same time Edwina herself, Fredricks at her heels, came running along the field track, white-faced, determined. Edwina had the face of a Victorian china doll, with large starry eyes, small nose and rosebud mouth, and the redoubtable build of a Victorian matriarch which added to her look of being ready to face the worst. Bone was annoyed, because he had wished to spare her the sight of a man who was dear to her—perhaps had been her lover—in such a gruesome condition, but he guessed that she had insisted on coming at once to put her own mind at rest. He could not blame Pat Fredricks for giving way to her.

She came up with them and ducked into the tent and stood gazing down at the lined and bloodied face, the hair stuck to the forehead and the heavy lids closed to life forever. She bent and peered closer, her face nearly touching that empty one, while Bone, Foster and the police watched in silence. Remote voices came from beyond the quarry.

She hesitated for a moment and then, nerving herself, she put out a hand and pressed back an eyelid.

The next minute she spun swiftly round, and seized Bone's arm for support. She was actually laughing.

"It's not Ken. It looks like him. It's really very like. But it's not Ken."

Chapter

16

Bone's immediate, instantly suppressed and unprofessional instinct was to embrace Edwina on the spot. He managed to say calmly, "You are sure," his habitual question-as-statement. He did not for a moment suppose she was mistaken, knowing Ken as she did. An inner self, as he preserved his cool, was dancing a fandango and clicking its fingers. Although he was aware that they still had a luckless dead man here, he rejoiced.

Easy to say now that right from the beginning there had been something not wholly convincing about this man as Ken Cryer—he had not been able to put his finger on what it was, and he had given due weight to his own unwillingness to believe it, but he had used the term "forgery." The bashed state of face and body had not helped. Now here was the magnificent Edwina, promising him, with a smile of happiness inappropriate to the now nameless body being removed by the team, that he had been right all along.

"No way is that Ken. I was taken in for a minute—but he's younger! His *eyes* aren't the right color!" She stopped suddenly, and turned to watch the body bag being stretchered away. "But it's so strange . . . who *was* he? What was he doing here of all places—in those clothes?"

"That," said Bone a trifle bleakly, "we'd like to know."

Ferdy Foster stepped outside the tent into the hot sunlight that had made the inside steamy, encouraging the smell of general and particular decay; he said over his shoulder. "See you at the pm, shall I? Or is that Steve's pigeon? Now I'm not to cut up a rock star it won't come top of my list, you know."

He went off, humming *Voi che sapete* under his breath; Bone, leaving Locker to superintend the clearing up, ushered Edwina out toward the cars waiting in the field.

"Pat Fredricks will drive you back."

Edwina, no longer laughing, had now a glisten of tears in her eyes. She raised her hands and looked at them. "See how absurd! I'm all of a tremble. Coming here in the car I was seeing Ken dead in all sorts of ways and thinking how on earth I was to break it to Jem. Oh, it's such a relief."

Bone watched her go almost jauntily toward the car with Fredricks, her long, bright-flowered skirt swinging round her ankles. He was glad that she had evidently not allowed herself to consider that the real Ken had not yet surfaced and that there was no assurance that a fate as bitter as the one they'd just seen had not come to him in some other place.

His eye was caught by Locker slithering on the grassy slope down from the wood. Now he would hear about the car left there. Probably it was parked by some innocent persons out for a picnic.

He waited with his own news until Locker arrived, rather out of puff, flushed with heat and exertion.

"Can't be Cryer's car, sir. It's a Merc like the one he drives but Rees told me he left that one with them at Herne Hall the night he vanished. I had Donovan phone in the number to the station to check it out. This one's in perfect condition, not a mark on it, and not locked."

"I'm sure it's not Cryer's car." Bone gestured to the shrouded shape now being slid into the mortuary van. "That's not Cryer. Negative identification from Edwina Marsh and she should know."

Locker visibly brightened. "That's a mercy, sir." Then it struck him as it had struck Edwina. "So who the hell is it?"

Bone pulled his mouth down, watching the tent being dismantled and the search line making its painstaking way across the quarry. "Someone who not only looked like Cryer but who tried to look like Cryer, starting from a likeness he already had, wearing the sort of clothes Cryer wears on tours and perhaps, from what you say, driving the kind of car he used. Unlocked, you said."

"Keys in the ignition. No real stuff inside, no sign of occupancy, you might say. No mags or tissues or tapes in the hi-fi, no sweet papers." Locker stopped, aware he was using the inside of his own car as example, and shutting his mouth before he mentioned children's shoes and emergency potties. "None of the sort of mess people cart around. Ashtray empty. But just nearby were foil wrappings with crumbs inside and an empty thermos—smelled of coffee."

Bone considered. It was of course still on the cards that the car had been left rashly unlocked by someone who, after their picnic, had wandered off to admire the view; someone who was going to be surprised and annoyed on their return to find police picking over the contents. Yet he felt the strongest likelihood that the car was connected with this ringer for Cryer who had stumbled to his death just over the hill from it. A man imitating Cryer would duplicate his car.

As for the gun, and whether the man had been shot and, if he hadn't, what the gun was doing to the quarry, and whether this concerned the death threats Cryer had been getting, all was part of what had landed on his plate. Now at least, with a corpse to clinch the matter, it was an unnatural death, and therefore his business.

More than anything he wanted a good, strong cup of coffee.

Another who was feeling like a good strong cup of coffee, and was not about to get one, was Bone's wife Grizel. She sat, rather awkwardly because of her present size, on the kitchen bench and enviously watched her stepdaughter pour just-off-the-boil water into a mug. Cha stirred, and poured in milk, and then looked up and caught Grizel's expression.

"Would you like something else? Chamomile, something herbal? Hot milk?"

Grizel pouted horribly. "I'm only having a baby, I don't have to *be* one. And chamomile tea always makes me think of the rabbit in Beatrix Potter, tucked up in bed after being naughty. I've not had a chance to be naughty."

"I suppose it's only when you can't do things that you miss them. Chocolate biscuit? Do you want to dance and touch your toes, that sort of thing?"

"Being able to *see* my toes would be nice. No, I am not complaining," Grizel said quickly, patting the bump. "I'm grateful he's there and I'm looking forward to the sight of him."

"You actually know it's going to be a boy?"

"Yes, from the scan. Hamish."

"It was Kinloch yesterday."

"That was your father. He likes Kinloch only because it's my middle name."

Cha sipped her coffee, reflecting. "Hamish Bone. It's quite distinguished; probably grow up to be a brain surgeon. Sir Hamish Bone. Kinloch Bone, now, he'd be a racing driver. Kinloch Bone broke all records at Monte Carlo today—pictures of him on TV spraying everyone with champagne."

"Very wasteful and silly," said Grizel severely. "If he wants a bath he can just use asses' milk like Cleopatra."

"I always think she must have been miffy afterwards. I mean, milk goes sour straight off in that climate."

"Your father has a whim he's going to have a daughter he's going to call Utopia."

Cha tossed her ponytail. "If it's a girl she's going to have to learn to play an instrument jolly fast."

"Why? What instrument?"

"The second fiddle."

Cha burst out laughing at the same instant that the telephone rang. She put out a hand to stop Grizel getting up and skittered across the stone flags to pick the phone from the wall.

"Grue? What's up?" As she listened, her eyes opened wide in horror. "No! Ghastly! It *can't* be! Are they sure? Oh they *must* have got it wrong. Anyway, Dad will be there in a flash, he'll sort it out."

Chapter
17
·········

The chocolate looked delicious. Kelly had spent some time choosing them, taking into consideration both the kind of chocolates—eventually picking truffles covered in dark, milk and white chocolate—and also the picture on the box. The assistant was losing patience with this large young woman dawdling over box after box, asking her to take down those stacked on a high shelf so that she had to fetch the little stepladder. She felt like telling her customer shortly that the picture on the box didn't matter, the lumps of fat on those hips would be the same. The assistant, pulling her fuchsia jersey down smoothly over her own skinny hips, pushed across the oval box with the basket of kittens displayed on the lid.

Kelly lingered over this. One dark, tubby kitten with a bright blue bow had spilled out of the basket full of its siblings and had pounced on the tail of another that was wandering unsteadily across a turkey carpet in red and blue. The artist had been inspired to give this kitten blond and fluffy fur, and eyes large as saucers, matching the blue of the carpet. Whether he meant it or not, a touch of anguish and surprise had crept into this kitten's expression, a pink tongue showed and you could almost hear the squeal as the dark kitten's claws pierced its tail. Kelly smiled.

"I'll have this one," she said, opening her purse.

Back at the flat, she carefully peeled off the wrapping and examined the lid again. She put out a finger and stroked the painted fur of the blond kitten. It was really in pain.

Then she lifted the lid, took off the paper wadding and gloated. Sitting there, dark-brown, light-brown, creamy, the truffles, their surfaces swirled or tufted, in their crinkly cups, were a glorious, mouth-watering sight. Kelly instinctively put her hand out to one before she remembered.

There was work to be done.

Later, she carefully wrapped the box again, but not before she had said goodbye to the blond kitten in its suffering. She tied a bow round the whole package, a blue bow very much the color of the one round the neck of the dark, tubby kitten, the color of the carpet and of the blond kitten's eyes. The bow came from the drawer where she kept empty scent bottles, and hair clips; she had been saving it for some occasion though she had never known what until this moment.

When she heard the news on the radio she knew exactly what it meant.

Some time later, however, Locker did not know what his own news meant. He carried it into Bone's room, with heavy tread, and put it down on Bone's desk.

"We've traced the car in the woods, sir, but it's not clarified anything at all. It's a hire car from Pegler's Pimlico. When Shay first got on to them, the girl said the Merc was hired two days ago, Wednesday at eleven A.M. by Ken Cryer. She recognized him. He'd hired cars there before—"

"Wednesday morning? Cryer was in Kent Wednesday morning. And why hire cars when he owns a clutch of them?"

"Exactly. It seems he does, though." Locker obeyed Bone's sign and sat down opposite. He turned the piece of paper round and put a finger on the time. "The girl faxed this through, copy of their record. Then she sent this page. There was a bloke manning their desk the next evening, that's yesterday, and he hired out another car to Ken Cryer."

"Another car. Another car? Are we in a Marx Brothers movie? Do we have a fleet of them driven past by men in Harpo wigs?"

"The interesting thing is, the Wednesday Cryer paid in cash, yesterday evening's Cryer used Cryer's credit card."

Bone looked at the faxed pages, thinking. "Unless he nicked the credit card, the second Cryer is really Cryer; and it's not last night, Steve, it's two o'clock this morning. That would have given Ken time to, say, hitch a lift to London to this garage he knows and where he's known."

"Yes, sir. Has to be a hitched lift or from a friend; we checked all the local hire firms for record of him."

"I don't suppose he said where he was taking the car."

"He didn't say and they didn't ask. And they didn't ask about the Merc the day before—this one, Wednesday. She was surprised he was alone; seems he isn't often."

"So a look-alike rock star comes in for a look-alike Merc and pays cash, on the day before the real one walks out on his fiancée and then drops in at the same garage to hire the same sort of car . . ."

"His usual sort."

"And the look-alike is found dead and the real one's not found at all."

Locker was pinching the bridge of his nose as if to stimulate the brain. "You don't think this is some setup by Cryer? To confuse? As an escape route from this wedding? Say he hired this look-alike to cross our lines and make it harder to trace him?"

"And shot the poor ringer to cross our lines further? It all smells of fish, Steve, but that last bit's right out of character for Cryer and goes a long way too far even to get him out of Zephyr's hands. Jail for life isn't a viable alternative to marriage, no matter what he feels. But I don't think we can go much further until the pm. Any word from Dr. Foster as to when it will be?"

"His assistant said he couldn't make it any earlier than he'd thought could be managed. Four o'clock."

Bone supposed he would have digested lunch by then. Viewing people's entrails was not the world's most settling pastime; the hard lights, the white tiles, and the smells of formaldehyde, disinfectant, and worse, made him exceedingly queasy. He knew there was no need for him to attend, but his notorious liking for being in on aspects of cases that his rank enabled him to avoid ensured that he'd be there. Grizel knew of both his weaknesses and had already instructed him that he needn't be present at the birth of his son. "I don't want Hamish's first sight of his father to be the soles of his upturned shoes."

Later, Bone was pleased he'd got his lunch over early even though it only amounted to a round of cheese and pickle sandwich. Ferdy Foster was on saturnine top form.

"Your fake rock star couldn't have sung much even before his chest was stove in. Lungs show he didn't smoke—see, a beautiful color—but muscle tone is not a feature here: premature wasting all over his body. Wouldn't be surprised if he hadn't been anorexic at one time, probably late teens."

"Isn't that rare in boys?" Locker asked.

"It happens. You need only to hate yourself. How old is Ken Cryer, do you know?"

"I think I've been told," Cha was Bone's source, "that he's forty-two. Not as old as the Stones but no spring chicken."

Ferdy was busy at what Bone preferred not to see, but Locker gravely watched. "Well, this boyo was at least ten years younger, if not more. No bullet, though. Wanted me to find a bullet, didn't you?"

"We found a gun, so a bullet might be handy. We've

not had word from Ballistics to whether the gun was fired. The team's still combing the quarry, so a bullet may turn up there as it's not here. He died of a punctured lung, you said."

"Broken ribs did it for him as he fell. I'm not saying that was a sole cause. Do you expect a sole cause, Robert? What could be useful knowledge for you is that had he not bled to death internally, and it was a punctured pulmonary artery, Robert, be accurate, he'd have died in any case." Ferdy detached something, and looked at it with disapproval. "Massive kidney damage."

Bone, bracing himself, looked at what Ferdy, after weighing, had placed in a metal bowl. "Kidney damage. He was an alcoholic."

"That's liver, Robert, damaged liver; as a rule, unless you're rewriting my textbooks. Remind me not to swap jobs with you. This sort of damage I last saw in paracetamol poisoning; the other day, a seventeen-year-old who'd had a tiff with mother and decided to make Mummy sorry."

Bone was silent, looking down now at the ravaged form on the slab. Had this look-alike of Cryer, dressed like him, driving a car like his, had he come to look at Ken's home? Bone had been examining the map of operations and realized that the wooded hill where the car had been parked overlooked the Manor. Was he there to take his last farewell? What had brought him to suicide, if that's what this was?

Ferdy was speaking. "Last meal, prawn sandwiches. Coffee. And probably paracetamol. Let you know more definitely about that later."

"Collating with the picnic-crumbs and dregs analysis."

"Mm-yes."

Ferdy's assistant, a girl with thin blond hair, whose resemblance to a drowned Ophelia was heightened by the reflection from her green apron, took another bowl from him, carried it to a bench and buried herself with it. Ferdy was whistling under his breath as he examined one lank pallid dead hand.

"Can you give us any idea yet how long he's been dead?" Locker asked.

"Given the weather, warm for late summer, the kind of late summer we're used to in this country, and the place he was lying in, say a couple of days at the outside. Say late Wednesday. Flies' eggs not hatched, so no maggots. Rats, though. Rats, yes. You get them wherever there's rubbish." He laid the hand gently by the body's thigh. "If you're looking to get prints to match with your gun, forget it. Rats are partial to fingertips."

That evening Grizel complained of her husband's poor appetite. "Your son and I slaved over a hot stove at your favorite stew—and he was even nearer to the heat than I was—and that's all you can eat."

"After all," Cha chimed in, "it isn't Ken Cryer who's dead. You should be glad. There'd have been an almighty stink if he'd copped it, you'd have had the Chief Constable in your hair till you went bald and the Press and TV would have seriously gone to town."

"Gone to quarry." Bone fed a respectably large piece of meat surreptitiously to whichever of the cats was placing a paw on his shin. "The Press are quite pleased with the quarry, but cameramen are cross at having nothing but long shots."

"What they really need," said Cha judicially, "is spooky music as they do a slow zoom towards the tapes. Or of course a track from *Crying Shame*. Did they find out what Cryer thought about his spitting image lying dead on his doorstep?"

Bone ate a bit more of his stew and contributed another piece of meat to Ziggy, who had appeared with great suddenness on the bench at his elbow, still licking gravy off his whiskers. "You evidently aren't up to date. Friend Grue must be slipping. When they besieged Herne Hall to find out what Zephyr West thought of this business, she revealed that Ken was missing after a lovers' tiff. She was so afraid, she said, so dreadfully afraid that she'd driven him to desperation."

"Driven him to Timbuctu." Grizel removed Bone's plate, and Charlotte put the lid on the tureen and went to place it on the top of the tall fridge, accompanied hopefully by Ziggy. "The man's had enough and he's cleared out. No mystery about that."

"Maybe not," said Bone, remembering the car hired on Cryer's credit card, which he had clearly driven to somewhere, "but one of the papers is, I see, postulating the theory that someone was trying to impersonate Cryer in order to marry Zephyr West himself."

"Zephyr West! He'd need to have his head examined!" Cha was scraping rejected stew onto Ziggy's dish. She remembered, inconveniently, a TV scene of brains being examined in a pathology lab. Her father did attend postmortems. More subdued, she added, "I mean, a total bimbo, all hair and hysterics. Ken must be mad to say he'd marry her."

Grizel addressed her stepdaughter. "There's hardly a man to be found who'll not have seasons of lunacy. You'll find that out for yourself. Some get over them while they're young, and that's generally taken to be the acceptable time; some wait till they're old and people aren't so kind about it; some have such seasons all their lives. Ken Cryer would not be the first sensible man to go potty over big hair and a lovely face. And you'll not tell me, Cha, that if Archangel were to walk in that door this moment and suggest you marry him, that you'd hesitate."

Cha, who at seventeen still had a poster of Archangel, a rock star of surpassing beauty, dominating her bedroom, sat down all at once on the end of the settle, overwhelmed at the thought. Grizel smiled. Bone started to speak but a violent scuffle on the floor halted him. The Bruce, Grizel's cat, had come into the kitchen to find Ziggy eating, and a territorial dispute had erupted at Cha's feet. She lifted them both up, squalling.

"Give me something for The Bruce, Daddy, quick. I thought he was out in the garden."

Bone helped in the pacification of the cats—The

Bruce hastily fed from a tin under the envious side glances of the noshing Ziggy—and he thought of other rivals. How was Dwight Schlumberger taking the news that Ken Cryer wasn't, after all, conveniently dead?

And was it just possible that Schlumberger or an agent of his had been deceived by the look-alike and thought to get rid of Ken Cryer for good?

Chapter

18

·········

Emily Playfair was hoping, this Friday morning, that there would still be a copy of the *Radio Times* left at her newsagents in Saxhurst. She kept meaning to put it on her regular order for delivery, with *The Oldie,* but she liked to come into the shop on a Wednesday morning, when Mr. Hawkins had got around to sorting the copies he got on Tuesday, and browse among the cards and magazines before buying. She had been so busy all this week, what with visiting her friend Marion Wheatley who'd been confined to her house with a horrid go of arthritis and had to miss a meeting of the Saxhurst Crumblies' Club (known to social workers as the Senior Citizens' Circle), and of course there'd been the drama of her cat Arletty eating something that disagreed with her so violently that she'd thrown up all over the sofa and, more unluckily, the vicar and his tea. Emily later had to get the vet to another of her cats, Proudfoot, unable to eat or do anything but swear, on account of a fishbone lodged transversely in his palate, so transparent that Emily had not been able to distinguish it from the natural pattern on the roof of his mouth.

The way her luck had run that week it was surprising

that she did find a *Radio Times*. Mr. Hawkins said they were all gone, but looking along the shelves she saw one hidden behind another magazine. She picked it out and gazed with triumph at its cover, glad it had not been a picture of a comedian with his mouth wide open showing off all his crowned teeth. She had been forced to paste something over one such cover only a fortnight ago.

As she looked in her purse for the money she wondered if Marion would like a gardening magazine or if it would only tantalize her now she could do so little in the garden. She was sorting a twenty-pence coin from some tens when she felt a curious disturbance behind her.

Emily could not have described her perception except that it made her feel uncomfortable, as though a dark cloud had entered the shop, a cloud that made her fingers tingle, that gave her a sensation in her stomach of such unease that she almost wondered if she were going to imitate Arletty. She turned a little to look round.

There was the usual line to buy lottery tickets. It was only Friday morning and the line was local and small. On Saturdays people from villages all round came in for their chance to become millionaires. Mr. Hawkins was delighted at the extra profits the machine led to and, as he said, no one considered how high the odds were against a win when everyone knew of the farmer near Adleston who'd won just before Christmas last year and was now not tramping his fields in muddy wellies but basking on a Bahaman beach. If he could get lucky, so could anyone.

Emily knew at once what the disturbance was. The girl with the yellow plastic bow hair slides got her ticket and moved away to look at the cards in their rack near the door. Emily paid for her *Radio Times* and left the shop in a hurry, edging past the girl, glad to get out and breathe the clear air.

Why did she keep seeing a basket of kittens? The feeling of impending danger made her wonder if Skywalker had at last succeeded in falling off the curtains onto something that would injure him, the edge of a table, say, before he could turn in the air and land on his feet. She decided she could do without the rest of the shopping. She would go home at once.

She was glad she had, for when she reached the gate to her little front garden she recognized the car parked across the street and then the boy turning away disappointed from her front door. It was Jem Cryer, and his face lit up when he saw her.

"Are you busy or can I come in and talk? Things aren't so good at home."

"Of course you can. I was just going to make myself a nice cup of coffee and have some of those buns you like. Where's your friend?" Emily let herself in, fielding a rush of kittens.

"Treasure's stuck with her mother who's being so loving it's creepy and won't let her out of her sight."

Emily let herself into the kitchen with her nearly empty shopping basket, and filled the kettle from the filter jug. It was on the work surface which, as Jem noticed, was curiously dotted with jars and tins, with a row close to the edge. "To stop them jumping up," she explained, following his stare. "Arletty's done it in spite of the obstacles, but she knocked a tin down and she does hate a sudden noise; I think it may discourage her in the long run." Emily ducked to put her head in a low cupboard and reached for a cake tin painted with bright yellow roses. "One tries for hygiene, you see, but it isn't easy with—Skywalker? Is that Skywalker? Can you get him off my back, please?"

Jem set to unpicking the tiny needle-like claws while Emily stayed bent. He finally lifted Skywalker clear and put him on the floor. At once another kitten pounced from nowhere, rolled him over and set to work biting his ear. Skywalker embraced him with forepaws and made disemboweling movements with the hind ones.

"Don't you ever tread on them? I mean, they're sort of wall-to-wall."

Emily made coffee and put buns on a plate. "Oh, you

do have to watch out all the time, but it becomes second nature. And there aren't always kittens. I miss them when there's a clear floor. You get used to anything."

Jem groaned with theatrical fervor. "I'm not so sure. Not to Zephyr, ever. Look what she did to me." He pulled his shirt collar wide and turned to the window.

"My dear child! What did she think she was doing?"

"Strangling me. She might have succeeded if Mr. Bone hadn't hauled her off."

Emily clasped her hands. "Robert Bone is one of my favorite people. But there's more to this story. Come through to the sitting room and tell me."

Jem carefully trundled the trolley down the ramp of the passage and into the sitting room, Arletty, who had scented food, leading the way at a dignified trot. Emily came down the steps directly from the kitchen, and put up a leaf of the small gate-legged table in front of the sofa. As she transferred mugs and the plate of buns to the table, a tapping at the front door made them both look up and Emily go to answer.

Treasure stood on the brick path, with a bicycle, her lank hair ruffled. Emily welcomed her warmly.

"How nice to see you! Jem's here, as I'm sure you know. Prop the bike on the wall there. . . . It used to be all right to leave bikes outside the gate, but not any more, no place safe from crime these days." She ushered the girl along the flagged passage to where Jem was standing looking pleased.

"You got away!"

"Mom was pooped after the reporters had left and she went to lie down, and pop a pill I guess. Gran was coping, and Palmerston, with all the calls from people wanting to know if the wedding is off."

Emily, who had gone to the kitchen to make another mug of coffee, called, "The wedding off? What's happened?" She hurried back to them, hearing the lap of water in her head.

"My Pa has quit, slung his hook, done a runner."

Treasure grinned with a dazzle of metallic teeth. "Left

my Mom on the way to the altar, and serve her right. How's your neck?"

By now they had sat down on the blue and white sofa, mugs in hand, and Jem displayed his bruises to Treasure as he had to Emily. "Courtesy of Dracula. Wonder she didn't sink her teeth in while she was at it, she was mad enough. Does she beat you with coat hangers like Joan Crawford?"

Emily proffered the plate of buns, rather high up as Arletty had got on the sofa almost within reach. "I'm still waiting to hear about all this. I understand that your mother," she turned to Treasure, biting into a bun, "gave Jem that nasty bruise. Why?"

Treasure answered through bun. "He did something really cool. He knew what I felt about that totally horrible dress Mom'd had made for me and he just took some scissors and turned it into ribbons. Trouble is," she wiped sugar off her mouth, "trouble is, Mom whisked me off to London yesterday to her designer and ordered another just as god-awful. I'm gonna spill something over it the moment I get it on, like nail polish. Or I'll puke on it."

"Wouldn't show, not if it's that color again."

They collapsed, delighted, and Arletty swiftly gave a lick to the piece of bun in Treasure's hand and, offended at the sugar, decanted herself from the sofa and walked away.

"You know, I think I've missed quite a bit of local news recently because my radio's bust again. Proudfoot knocked it off a shelf."

"But don't you watch television?"

"Not a lot. "One Man and His Dog," the cats like to sneer at that, and some sitcoms. But I don't care for the news, it makes me feel helpless. All those things going wrong all over the world and I can't do anything about it." Emily looked at them sharply. "So what did I miss?"

Jem accepted another bun. "Well . . . it wasn't good and I'm glad I missed it too. Lunchtime local news gave out that a body that might be Dad's had been found in a quarry just over the hill from the Manor—"

"Hunter's quarry?" Emily spoke almost at random to block out the sound of the water lapping again.

"That's it. Of course it wasn't Dad at all, but some creep dressed up in stuff like his on-tour threads, but it gave poor Eddy a really sick time, she had to go and identify him—as it happens, *not*."

"And Mom thought Ken had killed himself because she'd quarreled with him, some hope."

"I beg yours!" Jem turned on her, indignant.

"I mean she wants the big romantic gesture and she never had anyone suicide yet."

Emily got up and deftly removed Skywalker from the back of Jem's collar. "It seems to me you've had an upsetting time. Have you any idea where your father might be?"

"Not the vaguest. But he's done this before, once when they wanted an album off him and he hadn't finished it; he hates to be hassled."

"And Mom's an ace hassler. Dad never noticed, so he was ideal for her. He's pretty mad, by the way," she addressed Jem, "that *your* dad isn't dead after all."

"So long as my dad stays missing, your dad can keep hoping. And *I* hope mine doesn't surface till the wedding day is over and your mother has gone back in a huff to the States."

Treasure had hold of Skywalker and was kissing the top of his head, while he made passes at her hair and kicked. "Don't I wish that too. I haven't told you yet, it's the pits. Mom's made up this terrible schmaltzy poem for me to say at the wedding, and if she makes me say it I'll murder her."

Though Emily knew exaggeration when she heard it, her awareness that the actual body of some poor man had been found in Hunter's quarry made her flinch at this. She was distracted by Skywalker, somersaulting in Treasure's hands and sending half a mug of coffee all over the trolley. As she dealt with this, Jem was asking

Treasure how she'd known he was here; she explained that she'd borrowed a bicycle from one of the women gardeners at Herne Hall and gone to the Manor, where Joe Tench told her where Jem had gone.

Emily put coffee-soaked tissues on the empty bun plate and shook her head abruptly against the sound of small waves beating on the shore.

Chapter

19

• • • • • • • • •

Kelly was in an excellent mood as her little Fiat bustled down the drive to Herne Hall. The weather was again delightful. She had the sunshine roof open as well as both windows and the warm breeze made her hair struggle against the barrettes which held it off her forehead. She drove slowly, savoring the moment and able, as there was no traffic to watch out for, to gaze round at the parkland, at the spreading oaks, their leaves already tipped with yellow by the approaching autumn; at the line of willows in the distance marking a stream, perhaps the stream that fed the lake, the famous Wedding Lake the tabloids had written up: "Cryer Makes a Splash"— how ridiculous, thought Kelly; as if it would have been Ken's idea!

She was looking forward, though, to hearing all the plans for the wedding. An unconscious smile curled her mouth as she slowed down to take the cattle grid. As the Fiat bumped over the bars and Kelly's tooth fillings seemed to jar in her head, a sudden thought came to her and she glanced anxiously at the expensive package, so carefully wrapped in gold-starred fuchsia paper and secured with blue ribbon, beside her on the passenger seat. Nothing must happen to those chocolates before they could be presented and enjoyed.

Palmerston had just served a light salad lunch to Mrs. West in her sitting room, and had informed her in answer to her questions that her daughter did not wish to have any lunch and that her granddaughter did not appear to be on the premises.

He had crossed the hall on his way to the kitchen and the staff lunch, and had opened the baize door to the staff quarters, when he heard the bell for the front door ring in the staff corridor. He hoped it would not be more reporters; the house was not at all equipped to keep these people away. The last lot had been very tiresome and one had even taken a flash photograph through the french windows of Mrs. West in her wheelchair, though of what possible interest that could be to anyone was a mystery to Palmerston. They had talked to the gardeners, or tried to, photographed the lake from every angle, even taken pictures of him at the door, though of course their real business at Herne Hall was to interview and photograph the beautiful Miss West.

She had posed against a pillar of the porch, against one of the urns where the scarlet geraniums and glossy dark ivy had proved a perfect background to her floaty dress in cream silk. To their vociferous disappointment she had, sweetly and absolutely, refused to walk half a mile or so to be photographed at the lakeside, but she answered most of the questions willingly.

Palmerston noted that, although Miss West had fervently claimed she was the cause of Mr. Cryer's supposed death, she now appeared serenely confident that he would return in time for the wedding, preparations for which were in full swing.

In the end, only the belligerent interruption of Dwight Schlumberger had sent the reporters packing, tantalized because they couldn't work out who he was or what was his footing here and they were not given the opportunity to find out.

Mr. Schlumberger, at this moment, was out looking at

some guard dogs to hire. Palmerston hoped they would not prove harder to handle than was the Press.

He opened the door and was relieved to see that neither Mr. Schlumberger nor any ferocious rottweilers would be needed to deal with the inoffensive stout young woman who stood, with a package in her arms, smiling.

"Would it be possible to speak to Zephyr West? I'm Mary Martin from her fan club." She had come closer, as though expecting him to step back and welcome her in. "We're getting out a special edition of the fanzine for the wedding and it would be lovely," she extended the smile so that the dimples in the round cheeks became little pits, "if Miss West would be terribly kind and answer some questions." She looked down at the package in her arms and Palmerston silently deplored the barrettes that hitched and flattened her hair, possibly chosen to go with the fuchsia wrapping paper. "There's a little present from the fan club, too, which I have to make." She looked up again, dimples fading. "Don't say she's not in."

"I will go and inquire, Miss Martin, whether Miss West is at liberty to see you."

Zephyr had not wanted lunch. She was restlessly aware she wanted something but she did not know what it might be. Palmerston, discreetly tapping at her door, informing her that Miss Martin from her fan club was desirous of seeing her and had brought a package she wished to present, revealed to Zephyr what it was she needed. The interviews she had given to the Press had not really satisfied her; some of the reporters had called out questions about Ken which she had smoothly ignored, but they'd been hurtful. These people had not been on her side at all. A fan would give her uncritical admiration, the support she needed to go on keeping her confidence at this difficult time.

"Show her into the blue morning room, Palmerston. I'll be down in a moment." As the door shut on Palmerston, Zephyr swung from her bed with more alacrity than she had felt for some time. She had been wondering if England had a debilitating climate, and if it was wise to spend much of the year here. Lucky that Ken was used to the States and could surely be induced to live there.

First, she examined herself in the big pier glass and then threw open the wardrobe doors to rattle through her hanging clothes and choose.

Kelly had been ushered into the small morning room off the hall and at first sat down on the sofa, a small sofa in an old-fashioned honeysuckle chintz of yellow and green on blue, that she thought was called Morris. She looked round while she waited. A gate-legged table in the window bay carried a silver thing like a tureen with a pot growing white flowers which Kelly thought very pretty. The picture over the carved mantel was less to her taste; a very gloomy wood with a perspective of trees and what appeared to be men in medieval costume hunting in it, they and their dogs after some wretched beast. One of them was dragging his horse back cruelly on its haunches. Kelly was very much against blood sports or abusing animals in any shape or form. She got up to have a closer look. The dogs, now, jumping in all directions away into the wood, they were nice, and it was *people* who took advantage of hunting dogs' natural instincts and used them; the dogs were not to blame.

She transferred her attention to the porcelain figures on the mantelshelf and examined each in turn, from the boy leaning against a sheaf of corn to the shepherdess with a ribboned crook and the dearest little lamb. Kelly was stroking the china wool with her forefinger when the door opened. Kelly turned, and saw her pause on the threshold, actress-fashion, for the eyes and the applause; and Kelly, clasping her hands under her chin, breathed, "Miss West! Oh, how wonderful!"

Zephyr accepted this tribute. She had considered her appearance with swift care in these ten minutes. The golden hair was ruffled, with glossy ringlets casually disposed on the shoulders, the expensive tan shown off by a cream silk shirt, a tiny caramel skirt; and the blue eyes enhanced by the scarf of sapphire chiffon flung artlessly round the slender neck. She stood a second longer without speaking, seeing her glory reflected in Kelly's eyes and then she broke the spell, smiled and came forward with her hands out.

"Palmerston said you're from my fan club. Do you know I wasn't even aware I had a fan club here in Britain? Didn't you ever write to me?"

"Well of *course* you have a fan club here. It's not been going for long. We're *thrilled* to have the chance to actually meet you like this." Gestured to the sofa again, where her shoulder bag and the splendidly wrapped package showed she had been sitting, she sat down and picked up the fuchsia object, holding it on her knee like a lapdog, and continued with the royal plural. "We could hardly believe you were actually over here, and we were so hoping you could give us some details, you know, specially for the fans, that we could put in the fanzine . . ."

"There's a fanzine too?" Zephyr sat in the small Osborne chair covered in buff velvet, low enough to necessitate crossing the long legs at a sideways angle, as though her coltish elegance could scarcely be accommodated by ordinary furniture.

"Yes, this will be the first proper edition, we only had a *letter* until now. We thought it would be gorgeous to inaugurate it with a real quotation from you. It is simply wonderful of you to give us this interview. We'd just love to hear about the wedding from your own lips."

Zephyr moistened the lips, lightly glossed for the occasion. "Well, I guess there isn't much left to tell you that won't be in the papers already. They're making a big deal over that nasty accident when they thought Ken was dead. They don't seem to understand that Ken and I are just doing what you traditionally do."

Kelly opened her eyes wide. "Traditionally?"

Zephyr waved an airy hand weighted with Ken's ring. "Sure. We don't believe the bride and groom should see

114

too much of each other just before the wedding, isn't that so? Till they marry, I mean. There's something about it being bad luck? Well, Ken and I are just extending that time a little." She leaned forward, sending waves of musk over Kelly. "It's kind of romantic, we're putting a little mystery between us."

Nothing in the glassy gray eyes into which Zephyr gazed betrayed Kelly's disbelief, but the plump hands with their tapering fingers rustled suddenly on the fuchsia wrapping. As if reminded, Kelly looked down at the package and then solemnly, almost ritually, held it out.

"A present from the fan club. With our very best wishes for your future."

Receiving presents was a specialty of Zephyr's. It had been one of her chief charms for Dwight who enjoyed showering his dependents with gifts in token of his wealth and generosity and who reveled in the resulting gratitude. Zephyr knew how to act gratitude. "Oh how sweet of you! What a darling thing to do!" She put the package on her knee and, feigning eagerness, pulled apart the blue bows while Kelly watched with eagerness that had no pretense. The fuchsia paper was discarded with a blithe hand and floated to the carpet. The chocolate box with its picture lay revealed. The tip of Kelly's tongue showed between her lips as she watched, much like the tongue of the fluffy blond kitten, victim of the black one. Zephyr exclaimed over the kittens, tracing the outline of one with a nail so long it would not have disgraced any Chinese mandarin who sought to show his complete freedom from manual labor. "Aren't they cunning! And what elegant candies!" She had lifted the lid and surveyed the neat rows of dark, milk and white-covered truffles sitting neatly in gold-paper cups. "Why, I do believe you've found my absolute favorites! How you do spoil me!"

Kelly dimpled. "We just wanted to show our appreciation by giving you the very best we could."

Zephyr impulsively offered the box. "Do have one."

"Oh *no*. They're all for you. We want you to have

115

every last one. They're for taking to bed with you while you watch a late-night movie—you know, to *binge* on, not to share with *anyone.*"

To appear to enjoy a present in the way the giver wants it enjoyed is very much part of the act. Zephyr, with a conspirator's smile, shut the box and nursed it on her knee. "Then that's just what I'll do. I'll have myself a real treat one night. It will have to be before the wedding or Ken might steal the whole lot!"

Kelly sat up straight, her gray eyes wide. "Oh no, those chocolates are just for you , Miss West. We wanted you to have them. The fans would be really put out to think of anyone else getting them—you will promise not to let anyone, won't you?"

Zephyr once more leaned forward, and placed a slender hand on her heart. "Honey, I promise. I'd never disappoint my fans. And that's a promise easy to keep." She gave one of what she knew to be her more dazzling smiles. "Trust me."

Kelly had not lived long enough to recognize a phrase that should trigger every alarm within earshot. She dimpled again, relaxing. Zephyr, having got her present, was beginning to feel that this interview should give her more. She prompted.

"You wanted to ask me about the wedding? What do you want to know?"

The girl paused, almost as if she was trying to think of something, then she rallied. "The dress! They particularly want to know about the dress. The papers say it's secret but we're your *fans.* You wouldn't mind a description for the fanzine, would you?"

Zephyr played with the end of the sapphire scarf, brushing it across her cheek like a caress, and veiling the sapphire eyes with what Kelly imagined must be false eyelashes, they were so long. "Your fanzine won't come out until after the wedding, will it? By then there'll be pictures everywhere."

"It'd be a special, special thing, to just a few fans, nobody would breathe a word. It would mean so much."

"You promise?"

Kelly in her turn pressed a hand to her heart. It copied Zephyr's gesture but the effect was far more pneumatic.

"Okay, why not?" Zephyr dropped the scarf and leaned forward, making a movement of the hand from bosom to waist. "Tight-fitting with a basque in white satin, sewn in silver and with pearls, you know," tiny movements of her spread fingers indicating the scatter of pearls, "and the sleeves long, of cream lace right to the wrists," a hand stroked down her arm, "and then," she stood up, the better to indicate the flow of the skirt, "it goes on, this time with lace over the satin, just masses of it and the pearls showing under the lace. What do you think?"

It did occur to Zephyr that the sartorial opinion of a girl upholstered in a white T-shirt and a drooping floral skirt, and wearing those criminal barrettes in her hair, was not going to be worth much, but she was not looking for an informed opinion but for admiration.

Kelly gave it. "You'll look a dream. Such a dream! All that lace—magic! And the pearls!" A cloud crossed her face. She pulled at her underlip with a forefinger, like a child doubtful if its words will be well received. "The pearls . . . you do know they're meant to represent tears?"

"*Tears?*"

"Yes. The right thing to wear at funerals. Didn't you know? Didn't anybody tell you?"

Zephyr stared at this fat girl pitying her. She saw that this interview had after all been ridiculous, a mistake, her kind impulse completely wasted. "No," she said brusquely. "I did not know. And it is superstitious nonsense." She turned toward the door. "I guess I'm feeling the strain of all this. Maybe we should cut this short right now. Look, thank the fans from me—" she waved at the chocolate box in the chair—"and do send me a copy of the fanzine. What is it called?"

"Go West." Kelly, rising with apologetic haste, followed Zephyr out into the hall. Palmerston, emerging from another door with Mrs. West's tray, put it down on the console table and came to open the front door. Kelly, on her way out, dodged back to call out to Zephyr, already on the stairs, "Thank you *so* much for seeing me. Enjoy the chocolates!"

Chapter
20
· · · · · · · · ·

It was Edwina Marsh who phoned the station and asked to speak to Bone. He picked up the phone—snatched it up—when he was told who was on the line.

"He's back." Her voice was jubilant. "He's back and he'd like to see you. He doesn't want to stir far because of the media. They haven't cottoned onto it yet that he's here."

"I can be there," said Bone, putting two files ruthlessly back in the In tray, "in half an hour."

In fact it was twenty minutes later that Bone sat down in the leather chair in Ken's study and looked at the man whose disappearance had given such eerie significance to recent events. He was not anxious to say to Cryer that the last time he had seen his face it had been on a dead man. Now he could study the famous features, neither obscured by blood and earth nor washed and pallid on the mortuary slab, he could better see the differences. The lines on Ken's face were deeper but less doleful, the face more muscular. Bone had not seen the color of the ringer's eyes, which had clinched the identification for Edwina, but Ken's gray gaze was fixed on Bone with some intensity now.

"What the hell has been going on?"

Bone smiled, but his voice had a touch of asperity. "A question that I might rather be asking you. Your exit into the night without a word created several problems."

Ken got himself out of the chair he had dropped into and went to look out of the window at the front drive, almost apprehensively. "The problems that are mine, I've come back to deal with. What I want to know more about is this guff about my being dead just over the hill. Archangel showed me the headlines in the tabloids and congratulated me."

"You've been with Mark Serafin in Scotland." Bone was not surprised that Cryer should seek refuge with another rock star, a friend who might understand better than anyone the scenario he had written himself into; Archangel had skillfully avoided marriage with an ongoing series of beauties—and the security system in his Scottish castle was reputed to be a challenge to even the S.A.S.

Ken turned, hands in pockets, to regard Bone. "Do you know, he claimed I'd somehow fixed this bloke's death. As a get-out plan."

From what Bone remembered of the beautiful Archangel, whom he'd met briefly once, the man might well be ruthless enough to contemplate such a scheme himself, though he had most likely been joking. To have arranged for someone to die, Ken would need to be utterly desperate to get out of marrying Zephyr West. Nor would it seem a workable plan in the long run. He said, "We haven't yet established the identity of your double in the quarry—"

"Was he shot? One paper mentioned a gun."

"He died of internal bleeding causing asphyxiation, from a puncture made by ribs in his fall; he'd have died anyway from a paracetamol overdose."

Ken stared. "You mean he killed himself, or meant to?"

"It seems like it."

"Why the gun, then? Was it his? A fallback method?"

"There's no theory about the rifle. We compared prints." Bone did not mention Ferdy Foster's tease about the rats; the unknown had thoughtfully fallen with the other hand partly underneath him, saving it from their attentions, as Ferdy very well knew. "He'd been carrying it. The same prints were on his wallet, his boots and on the car he'd hired and left in the woods up there."

"His wallet? No identification in his wallet?"

"Nothing in it but two tenners. No credit cards, no old envelopes, no family photographs, no addresses. He didn't mean to be identified." Bone recollected Locker's poignant exclamation as the last fold in the wallet had been explored and found empty. "All we know of him is that he looked like you, was wearing the sort of gear you wore on your last tour, hired a car where you hire one sometimes and died half a mile from the Manor."

Ken folded somewhat abruptly into the chair opposite Bone. "Bugger. How much did he look like me?"

"Superficially, very like. Enough to make quite a few think it was. I did. It gave your Miss Marsh a nasty moment. People who'd seen your photograph, rather than you, could be deceived. His face was messed up when I saw it first, and I tell you I wasn't happy. Hunter, the farmer who owns the quarry and found the body, was sure it was you and he's seen you in the village."

"What the hell was this freak *doing*? And the gun . . . what about the death threats?"

"It had crossed our minds," said Bone dryly. "There's a half-erased print on one of the threat letters, which they'll compare, but it won't be priority. And suppose he brought that gun along to kill you, he could not rationally have expected to find you in that quarry."

"Talk about walking backwards for Christmas . . . and if he was there to kill me, why the overdose . . . ?" Ken pushed his hands through his hair as though to stimulate the brain. "A loony."

"Were there any new threats waiting for you here?"

"I didn't ask. Edwina will know."

121

On cue, in came Edwina Marsh, in fir-green trousers, long purple T-shirt and a fir-green silk jacket. She bore a tray with two stoneware mugs of steaming coffee and a plate of chocolate biscuits. Ken took it from her and asked, "Any nasty messages since I left?"

"Not a thing." Edwina stood, her china-doll face alight with pleasure at Ken's return. She did not take her eyes from him. Bone wondered again how she felt about the marriage. Ken, in his fixation with Zephyr, was not likely to be considering her.

She directed a shrewd glance at Bone. "Was it the look-alike who sent them? It's a fair bet he was a fan as he was got up like Ken, and I've dealt with a good bit of mail lately on the lines of 'If he marries I'll kill myself.' Would a male fan think of killing Ken?"

"But why the hell should a *male* fan mind if I marry? Let alone want to kill me for it. And I'm not gay, everyone knows." Ken rumpled his hair again. "I could understand well enough if some of *Zephyr*'s fans want to get rid of me—luckily most of them are safely in the States."

"No American stamps," Edwina said. "So unless someone there got someone here to post them on, or had come over here."

"We've yet to see if that print we found on one matches your ringer."

"Do you know who he is yet?" Edwina's face was alive with curiosity.

"I was telling Ken he took care to be carrying no traces and no one's come forward to claim him so far."

"Have you tried the look-alike agencies? You know, they hire out people who look like celebs, to 'do' minor functions and to amuse people. Like that woman who's famous for resembling the Queen—"

"The Coronation Street version," said Ken, doing a slightly vulgar royal wave.

"That can't be the one I'm thinking of—she's quite good. But they hire them out as escorts too. People who'd like to be going out with a star can pay to live their dream."

Bone drank his coffee thoughtfully. "An idea. Excellent. I'll have them check it out. Thank you, Miss Marsh."

"Edwina, please. I've told you." She smiled at them both, and was adding something when a car squealed to a stop on the gravel and its door slammed. Ken started to his feet and shot to the window.

The car's driver had seen him, for a shriek of *"Ken! You're back!"* followed and there was a skitter of heels toward the front door. As Ken hurled himself from the room, Edwina made a face at Bone.

Chapter

21

·········

Palmerston was particularly fond of soft-centered rather than hard chocolates. He had once incurred a visit to the dentist as the result of an encounter between a filling and a rock-like caramel; he would have been pleased if Zephyr had passed on to him the box of truffles presented by her fan. He had discovered it in the sitting room after that eager, sadly unprepossessing young woman had left, and he took it upstairs to Miss West's bedroom, but she, as he afterward told the cook, had "turned up her nose" at it. The very idea of spoiling—not her appetite—her figure with such things was absurd, she never ate them. Yet she had not offered Palmerston the box, merely telling him to leave it on the bed. Going downstairs again, he did wonder if the rejection had been a little show for his benefit and she meant to sample them, if not gorge on them, later in her own time.

In the end it was Doreen from the village, who came in as daily help, who got the chocolates. She had been enraptured by the arrival of her employer's daughter from America, a real star who looked and dressed like one—Zephyr's clothes were minutely described to Do-

reen's attentive family in the evenings—and she was
suitably overwhelmed to be made such a present. She
had tapped at the door, hoping in fact that Zephyr
would not be there so she could go over the things on
the dressing table at her leisure, even open the wardrobe and feast her eyes on its contents, sniff the scent
that came from them in an almost visible cloud. But
Zephyr had called her in and given her the chocolates
at once. Doreen had displayed such rapture that Zephyr's choice of her over the correct, undemonstrative
Palmerston was justified, and with no idea that Zephyr
regarded her as an ambulatory dustbin, she clutched
the box to her unendowed bosom and gasped her way
out of the room.

Although she showed the box to Mr. Palmerston and
to the cook, who was especially taken with the kittens
on the lid, Doreen had no thought of offering it round.
The chocolates were in a sense sacred. They had to be
shown in their entirety to her family before anyone was
actually allowed to eat one.

As a result it was not until nine o'clock that night,
after a takeout curry followed by a solemn inspection of
the box, its various layers of padded paper and the truffles in their golden nests, that a ritual binge of them took
place and Doreen, her mother, her sister and brother-in-
law, their two children and Doreen's own little Jason,
were taken ill. Luckily for them, this family gathering,
for the effects were dissipated. Little Jason, who had
cornered more than his share, was sick over the settee
and the new living room carpet but his stomach had
reacted with such energy that he was better all the faster.
They all agreed, next day, that every now and then, you
could get unlucky with a curry.

Luck, or the lack of it, was much in mind not only
at Herne Hall but also at the Manor. Apart from relief
at Ken's demonstration, by turning up, that he was
undoubtedly alive, neither his son nor his secretary
was overjoyed because he was also demonstrating his
intention of marrying Zephyr after all. They had per-

haps cherished a hope that he had come back to tell her it was all off; such hope died once they had seen the pair lovingly entwined, mouth to mouth, in the doorway.

Bone, leaving, had to edge past this clinch. As he drove away he could see, in his rearview mirror, no change in their position. Absence had demonstrably made the hearts grow fonder. A touch of cynicism told him that not Ken's heart was concerned but another part of his body entirely.

Would Jem show his father the bruised neck? How would Ken react to that spirited attempt at strangulation? Just now it seemed that Zephyr had only to twine her arms round him to be forgiven anything.

Two other people besides Edwina and Jem who had cause to regret Ken's return were Dwight and Treasure Schlumberger. Zephyr telephoned Mrs. West as soon as she let go of her grip on Ken. Treasure, in a purple track suit, was reading a book on the sofa beside her grandmother, the second volume of the *Lord of the Rings*, and she was enjoying it very much. Nevertheless, when she heard that the wedding was still on she threw it across the room, startling Palmerston as he came in and causing a Meissen parrot to totter dangerously on a side table. She then rushed from the room—Palmerston stepping out of her way with unexpected agility—and fled from the house and down the steps from the garden to the lake, her face so ferocious that one of the gardeners thought better of calling a cheerful greeting as she pelted by.

Treasure found her father at the lake, sitting on a tree root and sketching on a pad. Dwight was no Cézanne and this amazed Treasure, who went up to him and looked over his shoulder. A crisscrossing of lines on the paper, though boldly executed, said nothing to her.

"What's that meant to be?"

"The wedding raft. And those marks are where I'm having them put the lights. Your mom will love it."

"So will Ken." Treasure, in a tight voice, passed on the bad news. "He's back, and he and Mom are still crazy for one another."

Dwight looked round with a grin. "Not a problem, honey," he said. "You and I, between us, can settle all that. We'll be a family again. I promise."

Chapter

22

·········

The day of the wedding, announced finally to the Press through loyal guests and the caterers, the marquee firm and the hired security squad, had known and been teased in vain at least a week earlier, dawned as fair as the best weather predictions could make it. Only Palmerston, drawing back Mrs. West's brocade curtains at seven o'clock, looked at the sky with a degree of doubt. His grandfather, head gardener at one of the great country houses up North, had passed down a piece of weather lore which he remembered now: if a day starts fair, it doesn't mean it has to continue in the same. That blue sky with its promise of glorious sunshine could well turn treacherous and let everyone down.

"A very fine morning, madam," he reported, settling the breakfast tray on the eiderdown across his employer's knees—Mrs. West despised duvets. It was a butler's business to see that all ran smoothly and, even if he could not command the weather, there was no need to hint at trouble ahead. On any day of this kind tension was bound to mount high; as it was Mrs. West's daughter getting married, Palmerston was confident that there would be spats, as he put it to himself, before the day was out.

The first spat came quite early, courtesy of Mrs. West's granddaughter and ex-son-in-law. Zephyr was still in her bath when Dwight and Treasure arrived to see her, and was enjoying the dreamy, steamy relaxation before the hassles of the day took over. She was timing herself nonetheless—skin tone being important—and when she heard knocking on her bedroom door she thought it was either the designer come too early with her assistant and the bride's and bridesmaid's dresses, or the hairdresser. Either way, she was not pleased and there was venom in her shriek of "Come in!" What was Palmerston about, not to keep them at bay until she signified that she was ready?

The next thing she saw was her daughter's face peering round the bathroom door, and it struck her at once that Treasure, even obscured by steam, was not looking her best. Her complexion was like dough, she was scowling, and it was fortunate there would be somebody to make something of that god-awful hair the poor girl certainly hadn't inherited from her. And as for the person responsible for her daughter's disappointing looks, why could she hear Dwight in the bedroom talking on that wretched mobile of his? He had been endlessly helpful—crazily so—in fixing all the details for this evening's vows down by the lake but, after all, fixing things was his passion and he had no business interrupting her privacy time. If he was going to ask her again to give up Ken and marry him instead, she had her answer ready.

"We have something really important to say. Daddy wants you to come out and listen."

Zephyr groaned theatrically, yanked out the bath plug with a pedicured big toe, and reached for the huge white fluffy bathrobe. As she stood up and stepped out, she saw a look in the eyes of Treasure, who still hung on the doorknob, which she read as envy. The child plainly couldn't wait to grow up and look like her, have this glorious body that drove men mad—though there was no guarantee that she would, and if she kept that face would any man want to get as far as the body? Zephyr cuddled into the soft toweling and followed Treasure into the bedroom.

It struck her that Dwight looked both serious and pleased, almost excited. Was he prepared to give up this stupid idea of marrying her again and to settle for rejoicing in her happiness although with another man? He looked unusually smart, too, already dressed in a suit, his buttonhole of a white rose in place. She had to smile at him. He truly had been doing his best to please.

How good his best was, she learnt in the next few minutes.

Palmerston, leading the designer and her assistant upstairs, with their long cardboard boxes scrolled with the designer's name—Palmerston first heard the noise. He had not previously had the misfortune to work for anyone who indulged in hysterics but he had no difficulty in identifying them now, nor in guessing who was having them.

As Felicia Pavane, the designer, reached the landing and crossing the blue carpet, passed the big arched window, the door they were approaching was violently flung open and Treasure dashed out, scarlet and weeping, collided with the long box already offered toward the door and sent it end over end above the banisters to land with a crack in the hall below, breaking something on one of the tables. Felicia Pavane had barely time to cry out and reach after the vanishing box before a bulky bearded man she had never seen before strode out after the bombshell bridesmaid, pushed past the sidestepping butler and thundered down the stairs just as Treasure's bedroom door slammed reverberantly shut.

Palmerston, following the assistant downstairs to retrieve the box, knew that his premonitions were quite correct. It was going to be a lively day.

Outside, on the new-mown great lawn that stretched away under the branches of the cedars toward the blue horizon of the hills, a team previously admitted by Security were with leisurely skill erecting the vast marquee destined to hold so many illustrious guests. The caterers were timed to come later in their refrigerator vans, bearing delicious smoked salmon, lobster mayonnaise, chicken mousse, peaches poached in wine, caramel ice cream pudding, and a variety of rice dishes and salads intended to please the palates of celebrities such as Archangel himself. For Archangel's helicopter the front lawn had been cleared, a marker pegged out, and local air control and police and security alerted.

Security was going to have its hands full.

At the Manor, although Ken's security was also preparing for a heavy day, things were proceeding more sedately. There were no hairdressers and no designers. Ken had accepted the necessity for a suit but he had the art of making the formal appear casual. A loosely knotted tie stood in for the golden cravat Zephyr had specified, and the way the jacket hung on his angular shoulders made the suit seem as much at home on him as did the carefully studied flamboyance of bronze leather and silk at his concerts. While he did not look as if he had actually slept in it, he certainly did not appear as if sleeping in it would give him any worry.

As for his face, it was not so relaxed. Ken made a point of sleeping well, but there was plenty to disturb him had insomnia been his bag. The bruises on his son's neck, so far from fading had intensified now to a rich intermingle of purple and ochre, a vivid reminder of his bride's potential for mayhem. Jem had suggested, po-faced, that he might wear a chiffon scarf to disguise this souvenir, if Edwina could find one of a decently macho design and color.

Ken was already feeling guilty for accepting rather readily Zephyr's lovely apologies and her plea that she had simply been carried away by despair that the wedding was to be less than perfect because of Jem's prank—so she called it—and he did not smile as Jem had hoped. He touched his son's neck and asked abruptly, "Does it hurt?"

Jem temporized with a grin. His neck was still too stiff for a headshake.

Ken said, "She didn't mean it, you know. She was very upset. It was a bloody silly thing to do."

He walked off, leaving Jem to wonder if the bloody silly thing had been his cutting up Treasure's appalling frock or Zephyr's nearly strangling him. He decided to turn up his shirt collar and look as casual as he could. No one would be looking at him, anyway. Zephyr's idea, of having him as a pageboy at Treasure's side, his father had vetoed when he first heard of it, but now had accepted. Everything always gave way to her.

Others were more confident of attracting attention. Kelly, for instance, dressed with care in the rather cramped hotel bedroom, where she kept stumbling into the bed on her way between wardrobe and mirror. The dress she had brought from London had benefited from a night on the hanger. She would not have to borrow an iron after all. She smoothed it out over her hips and gave a little twirl, watching herself in the mirror. It floated divinely. Who said you had to be slim to wear a dress like this?

It was with regret, though, that she abandoned the barrettes for her hair. She had washed it. It really needed holding back, it was so fine. Her mother always said she had hair like a baby's. Kelly sighed and consulted the photograph again. No barrettes if she was to get that drippy look. Well, she must carry them in her bag and could put them on for the ceremony—they went so well with the dress, glitter on tortoiseshell. They had real class and, though he liked simplicity, he would know at once these were for the special occasion. Today was her day of days.

Mrs. West had chosen silvery silk, and Felicia Pavane sent her assistant to help her dress. She had intended to go herself—after all, Mrs. West was paying for everything—but the bride was demanding so many last-minute tiny adjustments, was being, so she said, violently scored

by a scratchy inner seam, was ready to hit the strato-
sphere at a buckling of the lace nobody but she could
detect; Felicia thought it wiser to stay with her. Mrs.
West would probably thank her for it if she knew, and,
in any case, Mrs. West looked elegant whatever she
wore. She was the least of Felicia's problems.

A major one was the refusal of the bridesmaid to
emerge from her room for the hairdresser or for her
dress. Zephyr had at first, turning before the triple mirror, told them not to bother: Treasure would get over
her tantrum if no one paid any attention to her.

Felicia supposed that in that case Treasure's character
must be the diametric opposite of her mother's.

Time was getting short. The first guests were due
within the next two hours. If Treasure were to have that
hair made reasonably presentable, and to be coaxed into
her frills, operations should start at once. Felicia left
Zephyr crossly picking at some pearls on the gauze
hood, which she now felt would detract from the full
impact of the face beneath, and went to rap on Treasure's door herself; a little cool authority must come with
the request that she should submit to the occasion and
offer herself, a living sacrifice, at her mother's wedding.
Felicia had a well-buried sympathy with the child who
had sense enough to deplore the singular inappropri-
ateness of the dress her mother was forcing on her.

What Felicia was deceived about, as it happened, was
Treasure's bedroom door. After knocking on it, and calling out in tones that rapidly lost their cool authority and
took on a dark note of threat, she seized the handle and
wrestled with it. It was indubitably locked, just as it had
been when her assistant tried it; but Felicia could not
know that this time it was locked from the outside.

Chapter
23
· · · · · · · · ·

By four in the afternoon Archangel arrived. By then enough guests were already assembled in and around the marquee and on the vast back lawn, to turn up their faces to the clattering roar of the helicopter, and were well primed with the drinks of their choice to welcome the most distinguished guest of all; even Zephyr's producer, hitherto the lion of the party, gave way in spirit before this phenomenon. Archangel's albums sold far more profusely even than Ken Cryer's, his world tours drew greater crowds, his wealth ran into several millions more. Mark Serafin, to mention his actual name, was not a man with any need to feel superior and his presence here was not self-advertisement but real friendship. Ken had taken refuge in his castle in Scotland only a few days before, and had heard his advice then about avoiding marriage at all costs, especially to someone like Zephyr West. Ken had chosen to ignore that advice but Archangel had come to give his support.

He emerged from the helicopter, flanked by his bodyguard, smiling, wearing a suit of such pale gray that it looked like silver. All he lacked, said one jaundiced guest among those who had swarmed round to the terrace to observe, was a pair of wings to validate this descent from the heavens. Archangel's severe beauty, that so crazed his fans, increased this impression; though one of his bodyguards, a six-foot Native American called Mary Highmountain, dressed from head to foot in supple brown leather, gave a bizarre tinge to it.

Ken was there to greet him and Archangel said immediately, "Not going well, is it?"

"Don't ask." Ken led him into the house and the VIP reception room. "The bridemaid's missing and so is Jem. I think they're in a conspiracy. Lying low somewhere—Security says no one's left the perimeter."

Mark Serafin raised the symmetrical arcs of his eyebrows. "Has the bride killed anyone yet?"

Ken handed him a glass. "Any minute now. You can't really blame her."

Archangel, drinking, merely looked philosophical. He had seen people bewitched before this time; no point in saying a word until the spell had worn off. For Ken's sake he hoped his lawyers had sewn up the prenuptial agreement really hard because, if he could read the signs, this marriage was heading for the rocks before the couple had even come onboard.

Zephyr had at first refused to appear, simmering as she was at the disappearance of her daughter and Ken's son. It showed with clarity their opinion of the marriage. Her mother, however, with a few tart words, pointed out that the absence of the bride would give a far more mortifying impression. She made herself ready, then, for all the guests now shepherded onto the back lawn. Mrs. West's wheelchair arriving at its prearranged place was the signal to the band; a drumroll announced Zephyr's arrival at the french windows, where she paused for everyone to receive the full force of the effect and then, at last, she floated across the terrace and down the steps, a dream goddess in gauze shimmering over lace and satin, and the pearls shining like drops of dew. The famous hair was piled on her head except for two rich coiled ringlets descending either side on her breast, the hairdresser's perfect realization of Felicia Pavane's design. The lovely face radiated serene happiness.

This was no doubt partly due to Mrs. West's instructions that the morning papers were to be kept from her daughter, who had been told that a security problem had held up their delivery, for she would have seen that the amazing dress was less than a surprise to many. One of the tabloids had printed a sketch taking up most of the front page and accurate enough in general, showing the boned satin basque covered in lace, the flowing folds of lace in the skirt but not, strangely enough, the gauze cloak with its scatter of pearls and the hood wired to frame that beautiful face. Felicia Pavane was harboring this knowledge like a bosom viper and would conduct a bitter investigation among her staff. Mrs. West hoped that the day would pass without a display of her daughter's famous temper. She also hoped that once Zephyr was married to Ken, his easy calm would have an effect on her.

Mrs. West had not been in the least surprised when Palmerston came to tell her that Treasure could not be found. Considering her state of mind, and the dress she was supposed to wear, and Zephyr's poem she had been obliged to learn and was to recite, her granddaughter had done the sensible thing. How much worse had she thrown an active tantrum during the exchange of vows down by the lake. . . . Mrs. West would not put it beyond Zephyr to pitch her bridesmaid straight in.

A storm of applause greeted Zephyr's appearance. Guests hampered by wineglasses beat their wrists with one hand, jostling champagne onto the grass, or cheered instead. It was a theatrical occasion. The bride might not be adored by those who knew her best—or at all—but she was certainly worth looking at and, given her temperament, the day promised great entertainment. The rumor had circulated that her frump of a daughter had shredded the bride's dress, so a few were disappointed to see no tatters—though what swift repairs might be concealed among those folds of lace?

Zephyr was now in her element. She was not a very good actress—she lacked sympathy with people and so their motives and behavior were beyond her—but she was fantastically good at being Zephyr, a beautiful and popular star. Her role that day was to act Zephyr getting married to a famous rock star in the most romantic possible way. She was not about to spoil her perfect day with petty annoyance about the auxiliary roles of bridesmaid and boy attendant.

She ignored, with smiling charm, questions about Treasure, as she moved among the guests in a sea of compliments, able to turn from a questioner to speak to someone else without exciting too much curiosity. It became general belief that the plain little daughter was anxious to hide herself all she could, avoiding eyes that compared and pitied, and that she was lurking somewhere before the ceremony of the wedding vows forced her into the open. One or two wondered where Ken's son had got to, but he was even more vague in his response than Zephyr was, looking round with the reply that "he'll be here somewhere," and as adept at moving on.

Among the crowd, feeling awkward because he knew scarcely anyone there, was Bone. He had received a family invitation, as a friend of Ken's, and he excused his presence by the need to see that all went well at Herne Hall today; there were the death threats to consider, and the mysterious case of Ken's look-alike, his chest stove in, found just over the hill from the Manor only a few days ago. The media had loved it—the headline "Bell Tolls for Rock Ringer" being one of the best—and they pestered: when would the police get off their backsides and solve this mystery? The Chief also wanted to know. There were times when Bone wished Ken had not picked him to consult about the death threats, for a private investigator might have been able to concentrate on it more. Of course, once Hunter stumbled on a corpse in his quarry, never mind one looking like Ken's twin, the ball was always going to land in Bone's court.

He was considering all this and in a blue mood when, among the unfamiliar faces, one he knew and liked swam into view. Emily Playfair, smiling so that her eyes creased up almost to disappearing point, raised her glass to him. She was sporting a very fancy hat, a purple straw with a lavender tulle bow, under which her gray hair vigorously curled, and she was, as usual, set on enjoying herself. Bone made his way to her.

"You're having a good time, I see."

"Oh, am, am. Lovely food there in the marquee, have you found it? They're doing things very unconventionally, party first and then wedding."

"I gather it's party, wedding, more party."

"I'm all for that," said Emily. "And isn't she lovely? What a pity she's so sad."

"She's sad." Bone's bare statement was his inquiry. Emily nodded, dropping her voice so that he had to bend his head to hear.

"Oh yes. I don't know why, but she's not happy."

To Bone's eyes, Zephyr on her appearance had looked entirely radiant, yet he knew Emily's eyes often saw more than others did. It was a talent, gift, that had come to his rescue in the past and he willingly admitted it; after all, it was known in these days that police forces openly asked the help of psychics to do such things as find missing people. That sometimes the psychic saw inexactly or that sometimes the people were dead by the time they were found did not invalidate the process. Emily's sight came to her from no wish of her own and couldn't be called on in the usual sense, but she was sometimes attuned to Bone's riding concern and saw some connected thing.

She did not explain her impression of Zephyr's unhappiness but was now, perhaps, picking up Bone's train of thought about missing persons, asking about Jem and Treasure. "I was hoping to see them here, because I can tell her that Skywalker is ready to leave. I hope Mrs. West doesn't mind about curtains, though. Mine are all pulled threads. It's not his running up them, it's the falling off part that is ruinous. And Jem: he was asking about a companion to Buster. I've got the very thing in Skywalker's sister Douce, who won't mind being bossed by a territorial cat, if spaying doesn't alter her temperament." Emily fell silent and looked at Bone, pressing the rim of her glass against her lower lip. "They've taken off, haven't they?"

He nodded. Ken had told him when he arrived, but like Ken he was not too worried. If Security hadn't seen them leave, then they were lying low somewhere. He fervently hoped that they had not dreamed up some plan to ruin the ceremony. That lake was asking for trouble. "I don't think they'll have gone far. Jem's got sense, he wouldn't want to cause his father grief." Which is more, he thought, than I can guarantee for Treasure; she would not hesitate to distress her mother if she could.

Emily's eyes clouded. "Not far, but too far," she said cryptically, and then gave her head that characteristic little shake to clear it, and applied herself to the champagne. She spoke resolutely, as if she had decided not to show she was troubled. "I'm looking forward to this evening. It promises to be very romantic—lights, music, flowers, even poetry. That's a wonderful way to get married."

Bone shut his mouth on the answer that he would have preferred the couple to get married far more prosaically and for choice within four walls with Security lining every one of them. In this shifting mass of people, in the rising noise of conversation punctuated by brays and shrieks of laughter as if exotic birds had got loose in this very English landscape, he was conscious all the time of continual threat. Emily might be able to see more than others could. He had the sensation common to good policemen that he could feel what was not yet there. He wondered if that sensation was like the hairs stirring on one's nape, that had saved people in the past from getting a knife in the back.

Only it would be Ken, if those who had made the threat had managed to infiltrate this little do, who could be getting knifed. Or possibly shot. Bone gave up sipping his champagne, and drank it off.

As he drank he was aware of a cool sprinkle on the back of his hand, as if the wine had fizzed onto it, and a low murmur, bass beneath the noise of conversation, told him that Zephyr's wedding day was about to be marred by an English spattering of rain despite the forecasts. Emily, like several others, glanced up and held her handbag protectively over her hat. Tulle and straw respond badly to moisture.

All conversation changed note, there was a concerted move toward the marquee, women with high heels tottering, clutching their escorts' arms and urging hurry. A group that had been posing against the great stone urns spilling ivy and scarlet geraniums, broke up in haste and pelted across the terrace and into the house, a clergyman in a black cassock among them. Bone could see Zephyr nowhere: rain is even less friendly to satin than to tulle and straw. He wondered if the ceremony planned for the lakeside might after all have to be taken elsewhere. It would be more convenient for security. The massive forms of the hired security guards, and Ken's own minders, visible from time to time among the crowd, incongruously suited and often with a walkie-talkie cuddled to their ears, could now be seen ushering guests to the marquee. Bone thought, watching them, that there was a quite striking resemblance to sheepdogs—they had only to stand and people were deflected almost by their act of will. He recollected Cha watching sheepdog trials on TV and crying out at the running sheep, "Oh, look at their clever little knees," and he watched the knees of the hurrying women with a thoughtful smile.

He looked round for Cha as he too headed for the marquee. Ken had been very kind to include her in her father's invitation, and Bone found himself quite unable to refuse permission for her to skip school and come. Term had but just started, Cha was vehement that absolutely nothing was ever taught in the first days. "We just get our books and timetables and chat about what's on the agenda and make fun of the new teachers' clothes. It's *pathetic* how little we do."

And how could he prevent her from going to a party where Archangel was going to be? His splendid face had graced her wall since her early teens; one of her greatest thrills had been when her father met him on a case and brought back his autograph. To have stopped her from seeing the man himself in his beautiful flesh would have been, she claimed, the act of a monster. Bone had achieved monster status before, in various small collisions of aim and attitude, and preferred to give way where reason prompted. Domestic calm, with Grizel so near her time, in any case came first.

He was sorry Grizel had opted out. He missed her at his side, someone on his wavelength, but she was firm. "I'm not popping your son and heir at anybody's wedding. What if I brought the marquee down, thrashing about in sudden labor? No, I'll save drinking champagne for a better occasion, thank you."

This curious sense of danger was intensifying. He was extremely glad she had stayed away, and wished Cha was not here. She had met a couple of girls Jem went to school with, and whom she knew, and had been lost to view ever since. Had she managed to meet Archangel?

He was getting wet, at the tail of the herd entering the marquee. Emily had bustled ahead, sensibly not waiting, and as he came to the entrance and had to stand there while the sheepdogs induced the crowd to move on inside, he turned and caught sight of Dwight Schlumberger on the terrace outside the house, hands in the pockets of an unnaturally smart dark suit, rosebud in buttonhole, gray cravat with pearl pin, standing without moving, staring down toward the lake, his hair being plastered flat by the drizzle.

Chapter
24

....

Indoors, Palmerston was experiencing his own problems. Almost the chief function of a butler is to appear imperturbable at all times, no matter what is happening to perturb. His previous employers, Sir Valentine and Lady Herne, had presented problems which Palmerston had always contrived to surmount, and he had remained on excellent terms with Lady Herne during and after the sale of the Hall. He was on excellent terms with his present employer. It was his employer's daughter, following her routine of disorder, who quite casually overloaded the system.

Her living at the Manor with Mr. Cryer had been of inestimable convenience for all at Herne Hall, but her decision, very late in the day Palmerston considered, that propriety demanded the bride should live with mother, not lover, in the time preceding the wedding, had provided Palmerston with a loose cannon on deck. His training and instinct led him to protect Mrs. West against even her daughter but it was impossible to tell in advance what the wretched young woman would do to upset everyone, even on her wedding day. Especially on her wedding day.

His sympathy was entirely with Miss Treasure when her disappearance became known. He had been required to open her door with his master key and, when the room proved to be empty, rather wished he could imitate the bridesmaid in her vanishing act. However, he soldiered on, concentrating on seeing that Mrs. West was comfortable and at first taking upon himself the task of pushing her wheelchair about the lawn, trying to keep his dignity when shouldered aside by the hired security guards. Watching them now, from the long windows giving on to the terrace, hurrying Mrs. West through a veil of rain toward the house, he consoled himself with a small private joke: *Gorillas in the Mist.* Later he would tell Mrs. Baker the cook, perhaps, if Doreen was not there. Doreen was due for a severe ticking off on her return—two days absent and today of all days when all hands were needed, and not even a phone call. However, it must indeed be a crippling illness that kept her away on a day when she wanted above all to gawk—as he put it.

All this was going through his head as he glided to and fro, supervising the hired waitresses, serving drinks and canapés to the guests who had taken refuge in the house. He did not care for hired waiting staff in the house; he disliked having any staff of whom he had not had the training.

Just as he bent solicitously over Mrs. West with an offer of smoked salmon on a tiny biscuit and wearing a curl of lemon, not unlike some of the hats on view, the telephone rang.

"Excuse me, madam. I'll find out what that is."

He could hardly make out, even with the receiver pressed to his ear, what the gentleman was saying on the other end. He had a strong American accent, and a guest was screaming with laughter only a few feet from Palmerston. He put a hand over his free ear.

"I beg your pardon, sir? A transatlantic call? But I'm afraid Miss West is not available. She is getting married

143

today. . . . Oh, I see. Well, in that case, I shall see if I can find her but I'm afraid I may be some time."

As it happened, he was not. As Palmerston emerged into the hall, steeling himself to go through the shower to the marquee, or with a better thought about one of the security men in the house conveying a message on one of their telephones, Zephyr came out of her bedroom and appeared on the landing. Of course she had had to check that her appearance was still all it ought to be, and she had refreshed her makeup and, perhaps, her spirits. Doreen had told him, before he repressed her gossip, of the immense array of pillboxes in Miss West's bathroom, and Palmerston was not so naïve as to suppose they were all for her complexion.

It was possibly the first time he had been glad to see her.

He climbed the stairs toward her. "Madam, there is a gentleman on the telephone who wishes to speak to you. He says he is a producer speaking from Los Angeles and he particularly desires to wish you well today."

Zephyr, a cloudy vision in gauze against the landing window, put silver-taloned fingers to her mouth. "Oh! I'll take it in my room." She turned, gauze swinging out to brush the banisters, and was gone. Palmerston, with the utmost speed permissible in a butler, went to replace the receiver in the sitting room as soon as her voice came on the line. Already, he computed, it must have cost the gentleman in Los Angeles a few good dollars to hold the line even for that long. After the penury of his previous employers, when he had been forced to watch the Hall decay around him, Palmerston was not yet used to people who saw expense as a challenge rather than a disaster.

Someone tapped him on the shoulder and asked his opinion of the weather. A young lady whose skirt was barely visible beneath a lime-green silk jacket, and who had drunk more champagne than she had any need for, hung on his arm and begged him prettily to tell her

"What it's like outside," evidently under the impression that what the windows allowed her to see was a delusion.

But clearly God chose to answer her instead, as a ray of sunshine swept across the marquee, evoking a squeal of joy.

"Come *on!* The band's playing!"

Through the open windows came the thump of a drum and a long exciting wail from a saxophone. Out of compliment to the bridegroom they were playing his old-time hits, some of which those present had danced to on *Top of the Pops* when they were in their teens. "I'm Crying for You" brought the guests from the house to pick their way across damp lawn and join the throng under canvas.

Bone had inexplicably lost sight of Emily Playfair by the time he got inside the marquee. The purple straw with its lavender tulle bow was obscured by taller guests and wider hats, but he did get a sighting of Cha on the far side, past the dancing guests. She was standing talking to Archangel, or rather standing gazing at Archangel while he talked, gesticulating, laughing. Perhaps he was telling a joke, one that Bone was certain would go on record in his own household as the best joke ever told, the only foreseeable problem being that Cha might be too enraptured to hear the punch line.

Zephyr was not to be seen, nor was Ken. The band played at a pitch soft enough not to drown conversation, which in this place sounded like a hive of uneasy bees. The smell of canvas, flowers and women's scent was such that someone unhooked a yard of the side wall on fresh air and a view of hazy distance.

Ken was nowhere about. At the back of Bone's mind all the time was the specter of the man in the quarry, the not-Ken who had died so short a time and so short a number of miles away. With that little mystery haunting him, Bone could not be easy. He felt sure the death—suicide? murder?—was in some way connected with the ceremony to take place so romantically by the lake in the autumn twilight. If the dead man had been the source of the threats and, encouragingly, Edwina had reported there were no more since the body was found, it might be possible to relax; then he would have to ignore the danger warning, the restive sense that had rarely ever played him false.

He had just reached this gloomy conclusion when he found himself in the middle of an impassioned argument on the weather, conducted over his head by an extremely tall young man with a mid-Atlantic accent and another, less tall but making up for it by being already far drunker. The tall one maintained that the lakeside wedding would be rained off and have to take place squalidly in a wet tent, the second was convinced, to the point of belligerence, that the skies would clear and perfect bliss would reign. He now got his feet crossed and plunged toward Bone, grabbed his arm and begged him to support this view. The tall young man adverted to a complaint he had evidently made before, that his camera had been confiscated by the minions of a magazine on whom Zephyr had conferred sole rights of photography. They were not risking amateur shots being flogged behind their backs to the tabloids. Incorporating this grievance with perfect logic into his argument, he towered over Bone demanding that he subscribe to his disaster theory. Rescue came in the form of Security, smoothly parting the adversaries and extricating Bone. He knew one of the men and talked to him for a while, approving the fact that the man never looked at him but constantly scanned the scene.

The excluded section of the Press had done its best to get a glimpse of proceedings, but Security had been very efficient. Only those with invitation cards, checked on the list, were admitted; only those with passes, provided with their holders' photographs, of those working for the magazine, or for a sister magazine with a safely later publication date, could circulate with the guests.

To the frustration of the tabloid that had hired it, the helicopter which clattered overhead acquired only shots of the marquee roof and various guests like ants heading for their nest.

Kelly kept out of the way of those with magazine badges, so far as she could. Their turn would come later, she would give them all the photographs they could possibly dream of. She was careful not to drink too much either. It would be absurd if, after all this trouble and planning, she wasn't absolutely alert and ready to respond to all opportunities that might come her way. Ken was going to be proud of her.

Wherever he was. She had been so sure of catching his eye at once. After all, he had been waiting for her all his life, waiting for this moment. And now he was not here. She had been wandering the grounds, and had run into the marquee when the rain started—brushing back the curtains of hair that so irked her—confident of seeing Ken there attending to the guests; but unless he was hiding under one of the long tables covered with linen damask and set with all sorts of dishes, from rice salads to Black Forest gâteau—Kelly turned resolutely away—he wasn't there. Kelly pushed through among chattering groups, collecting annoyed glances and exclamations, minding nothing as she knocked elbows, spilled drinks, and kicked suede heels in her advance. She recognized Archangel. She had seen enough of his videos not to bother with his concerts even to compare him unfavorably with Ken; what were looks when you're talking genius? He made her eyes brighter now solely because Ken surely could not be far from such a celebrated guest, his friend as well. She was not sure of Archangel's influence after the marriage, though. She had read in the magazines of his cynicism and it might be as well if Ken didn't see so much of him. Ken would want to concentrate on his bride.

Time passed. Bone had a word with Cha as they found each other by the buffet and helped themselves to canapés. The air had cleared, evening sun shone outside. Kelly wondered when people would move toward the lake. She had heard the band launch into a definite intro after the soft background stuff they'd been playing for the dancing; she stood for a moment quite still, as "I'm Crying for You" rose above the chatting voices and the sound of feet.

Guests consulted their watches, reminded each other of the timetable briefing and that the stable block by the house had been fitted up as washrooms. A general exodus at last began, the women in particular feeling the need for repairs after the humidity of the marquee which had caused makeup to go critical and which wilted stiffened gauze. It had been assumed by now that the bride and groom, after their initial appearance, had been saving themselves for their climactic arrival by the lake.

Some members of the band shipped instruments and left the marquee, to trail down the shallow stepped slope to the lake. Dwight had specified a few violins, an oboe, a sax, a trumpet, and he had chosen the music, intending that all who heard Tchaikovsky's *Swan* theme were for the rest of their lives to associate it with the twilight of a perfect day and the wedding of the decade. The photographers for the favored magazine were already in place at the lakeside, setting up and finding their angles. The lanterns, as Dwight had dictated, hung not only on this side of the lake but were also strung in trees on the far side, along the public footpath where they already gleamed mysteriously among the leaves, deepening the shadows in the woods there; on this side, lighting up the garlands of white roses twined with ivy that had been wreathed from tree to tree among the silver birches, on the slope leading down to the lake and all round the little arena.

The effect of all this was to make the first guests reaching the slope gasp and exclaim. The weather had relented, and in any case the ground under the trees was all but dry. The clouds had rolled on to do any serious unloading elsewhere, leaving a sky of washed blue slowly turning to indigo—darker for the glow of the lanterns. It was a perfect evening for the wedding.

All it waited for was the bride.

Chapter
25
·········

Kelly, however, had moved across the lawn while it was not yet quite time for the down-to-the-lake migration which the programs and ushers had been mentioning. The sun behind clouds on the horizon was sending random shafts of light and one of these lit a small folly or gazebo on the rise beyond the lawns. Kelly paused to take the diamanté barrettes from her shoulder bag and slide them into her hair either side, freeing her face of that disguising hair. Now she looked herself.

She saw the movement inside the gazebo. Identifying that particular gesture from so many videos so constantly viewed, she ran forward up the slope. From the depleted band in the marquee came the distant, poignant sound of "Waiting for Love."

She ran. Emerging from the gazebo Ken came to meet her. She stumbled on the slippery damp grass, recovered and, beaming with joy, flung herself at him.

"It's me. I came. I heard all your messages and nothing could keep me from you. I'm here . . ."

Ken took her by the shoulders and held her off, to look at her. He was puzzled, with a polite half-smile.

"Who on earth—"

"Me. Kelly." She laughed. She felt her triumph like a wave of physical pleasure. So much surmounted—

He looked past her, frowning. Someone took her in an iron grip by the arms and jerked her backward.

"I'll look after her, guv. Sorry about this," a bass voice said overhead.

"It's all right. Don't hurt her—"

"Tell him, Ken. Tell him. You called me and I came to help you and—"

"Oh God." The authentic Ken, frowning, propelled her toward this stupid brute who held her. "I've not time for this." Kelly, no fool, went passive in her captor's grasp and his hands relaxed. She leapt forward, arms round Ken so that he would know who it was.

"Ken, I'm ready. 'Forget her, you know she was never the one' " she sang the line urgently into his face, his inexplicably cold face. It chilled her. He knew her, *of course* he knew her. "You've been waiting!"

The minder had got her again, by the wrists so that grotesquely for a moment he too was embracing Ken. He yanked her arms apart and got one wrist behind her back.

"But we're going to be married!" Frantic, she shouted at Ken as he backed away. There was the tousled hair that Alan had imitated so well; the eyes, in their real color, that seemed not to recognize her. That really did not recognize her.

"You go, guv. I'll take care of this."

And Ken turned away and set off at a loping run toward the birch trees that hid the lake.

"You're an eighteen-carat nutter, I'll give you that," said the minder, getting her other wrist behind her. The shoulder bag slipped off her shoulder and it trailed on the grass as he marched her off. Everything had gone wrong. How could it be like this? How could that creature still have him in her spell? It wasn't possible, none of it was possible, it could not be happening.

"You don't understand," she cried. "Ken wants me!"

"Oh yes," said the minder, forcing her inexorably

toward the house and the marquee from which people were spilling out toward the lake. "A pathetic lump like you when he has Zephyr? Get a life!"

Ken avoided the little crowd descending the shallow steps and went down through the trees, a trifle recklessly, and ducked under a garland. He had plunged into the dimmer light of the lake's hollow, and avoided a tall carved chair with the skill of one used to avoiding objects onstage when blinded by spotlights.

"Thought we'd lost you." Archangel did not appear disturbed at this. People were finding seats—folding chairs and stools. A woman took the carved chair and one of the organizing team swiftly found her a seat elsewhere. The music played so gently that the lapping of the water could clearly be heard, along with the low talk. Little lights strung in the trees became slowly bright, to a murmur of appreciation. Lanterns stood at the foot of trees here and there, and at both sides of the steps flared flambeaux.

Bone had just prevented a guest from getting a foot in the lake. He was thankful to see the number of watchful security men, some at the top of the bank against the sky, some on the public footpath along the far shore. They must have shut off public access after all and small blame to them.

Cha had found a place under a birch tree and was gazing at Ken and Archangel as a visionary might. Bone thought Ken looked edgy—more than edgy—and he was glancing at the little raft riding the water, and pulling at his cuffs. Beside him, Archangel's serene and perfect symmetry made Ken appear more frayed and lined than ever.

A cluster of men coming down the steps were carrying Mrs. West, whom they made comfortable in the carved chair. She held out a hand to Ken, who took it and bent to talk to her, but he still kept glancing at the raft, then up the slope of steps. Bone wondered if part of his anxiety was for his missing son.

It was becoming evident that the bride was late. Quiet talk became louder; a small hint of impatience entered. Heads turned as someone came down the steps, a bustling hurricane with mobile phone in hand, and crossed to Mrs. West. Dwight ignored Ken entirely, standing in front of him for a moment; then wheeled to speak to a security man and caught his foot on a lantern. He struck aside the man's rescuing hand and with a violent swing kicked the lantern into the lake, where it died with a small explosion.

Among the guests a couple of unseemly laughs were smothered. The little orchestra happened to have paused at this moment and were conferring. They struck up a tune they had played a few minutes before, and their leader stepped out of their niche to look up the slope. A woman was silhouetted at the top, but not in gauze and lace. Felicia Pavane came hurriedly down between the lanterns and the flambeaux, and as everyone hushed at seeing her agitation, some heard her stage-whisper to Mrs. West.

"I can't find Zephyr. I hoped she'd be down here. She seems to have completely vanished."

Dwight stamped forward, as comments and exclamations rose. Bone thought the bride's absence pleased him.

"Maybe she's changed her mind. Maybe she's not so set on this particular marriage after all. Come on and let's find her."

"Mr. Schlumberger, I promise you—we've searched the whole *house*, we all have. She's not there."

"Have you looked in the closets?"

*"Every*where."

With an eager snort about doing the job for oneself, Dwight forged through the throng and pounded up the steps.

It seemed to Bone, who had found a tree to lean on and hoped his coat would brush clean, that Zephyr would have a hard task disappearing in an area pullulating with security men. Had she really had second thoughts about marriage to the superlatively eligible Ken? What was she up to? A tinge of disgruntlement had crept into the guests' talk. Temperament and a desire for theater were all very fine . . . what about other people's comfort? An ironic contralto remarked with clarity, "I could have gone to the stable block after all." A light tenor responded that she might as well do that now, for even when Zephyr turned up, these vow-thingys would be bound to take forever. Ken was conferring with Mrs. West, Archangel, the clergyman and one of the organizers. He spoke to the bandleader and, as the music swelled into a medley from *Cats,* he ran after Dwight.

The dusk by the lake was now quite deep, intensified by the lights that made the sky darker. The tiny stars among the far shore's trees glittered and danced on the water, and conversation settled to a resigned, desultory note. A little breeze swung the garlands and brushed the lake into crazy patterns. Someone sneezed.

The band ended their medley with a plangent chord, and the security man who had been talking to Mrs. West pocketed his walkie-talkie and clapped his hands.

In the ensuing silence, Mrs. West said, " I think we'll all go back to the marquee and wait in comfort, and when my daughter's ready the ceremony can take place on the terrace."

She spoke as hostess; slowly the congregation became guests again and climbed the steps. Charlotte was hanging back, and under no delusion that it was her father she was waiting for when Archangel still stood beside Mrs. West, Bone decided all the same to join the tail of the procession.

He took a final look round the emptying shore across the water. Something attracted his eye in the shadows at the far end of the lake. It came again. The carved chair was being picked up bodily by a posse of heavies, and Archangel accompanied the group, behind him the hitherto invisible Mary Highmountain, her bronze face caught for a moment in the ray of a flambeau. Cha joined them casually.

Bone picked up a lantern and made his way past the area of garlands and stars, along the shore where there was quite a well-kept path. At the end he saw the boat-house, and caught again the momentary light between the boards. Approaching quietly along the path, he heard rustling and a whisper.

He found the side door without falling over weeds or stones. The water flapped hollowly inside the boathouse; an object made a light thud, followed by a whispered "You idiot!" Bone turned the door handle.

His lantern showed a tableau of Jem and Treasure, he in boxer shorts, she in bra and panties, frozen in shock, encircled by a comfortable picnic. From a rope slung across dangled a frilled yellow shirt, yellow trousers and a frilled yellow dress daubed and splashed with disfiguring stains.

Chapter

26

•••••••••

Treasure, folding her arms round herself, took the news of her mother's disappearance with so offhand an air that Bone believed it disturbed her. Jem, clumsily packing the detritus of their meal into a bag, said in slurred tones, "Looks like you're still clear of slushy poems and yellow frills, Trez."

"Mm-hm." She glanced up, unfocused, and Bone was not sure she had taken in what he said. He noticed splashes of mud on her arms and legs.

Jem asked, "So what's happened, Mr. Bone?" This time he enunciated with a care that showed.

"Everyone's gone up to the marquee to wait—the guests, that is. Everyone else is looking for Miss West."

"I bet, I bet Dad—Dad's organizing that," Treasure said, and this Bone could not deny.

"How did you get wet?" he asked.

"Oh, cooling the whatsits. The drinks," said Jem. He waved toward the bay of water lying under the doors and as far as the slipway they sat on. "We lost . . . a shandy can in the water."

Bone could smell wine, not shandy, but he said nothing, and he may have said it oppressively for there was

155

silence as he escorted the subdued pair to the marquee. Jem, in splashed trousers, Treasure in his frilled shirt like a mini-dress, attracted amused notice.

Mrs. West, in the carved chair just inside the entrance, surveyed her granddaughter, and observed, "I wonder what has become of the yellow frock. You had better go to bed and I shall talk to you later. Jem, you must find your father, in the house, and make your peace."

Bone felt grateful for her calm of mind. Jem dragged his feet on the way across the terrace until, seeing that Bone was following, he cried, "I'll find Dad. I will," as if he thought he was being convoyed under guard, and ran ahead.

The house was certainly being searched. When Bone joined them, security men and Dwight and Ken were coming down the attic stairs sweating from the stifle of empty servants' quarters under the roof. They invaded the bedrooms, while Felicia Pavane and her aides stood on the landing repeating in high voices that they'd *searched* there with a *fine-tooth* comb. There was a monotonous sound of wardrobe doors shutting. Bone found himself searching Dwight's room in wry obedience to its owner's despotic command. Neither the wardrobe, full of hanging fresh shirts, several suits, and a dozen pairs of shoes, nor the bathroom that smelled, as Dwight did, of Sardonyx for Men, nor the space beneath the bed (spotless) yielded a gauze-clad or any other kind of Zephyr. Ken's minder Mel Rees had come in and looked behind the long corded silk curtains. He shrugged the useful shoulders.

"It's like that airhead to pull this sort of caper."

"Something may have happened to her." Uneasiness was fretting at Bone and Mel looked up sharply.

"You reckon?—in the middle of all this security . . ."

Bone grimaced. "You're right, of course."

"Give up this kids' game, get back to the tent, make party noises, and she'll come in laughing like Tinker Bell."

"How is Ken taking it?"

"With any luck she's blown it with this stunt. They had another spat about the vows—" Mel stopped and shut his mouth. Ken was in the doorway, his hair more than usually over his eyes. He looked at Rees, and then turned to Bone while Rees industriously searched behind the long curtains again.

"Thanks for dealing with Jem. He's fairly canned. God, what a day. You and Grizel had a nice village wedding, didn't you? That's what I wanted." He spoke with savage exasperation.

"Ours wasn't without incident," Bone said.

"Grizel didn't run out on you, however. I suppose she's doing this to pay me for my trip to Scotland." He hunched his shoulders and turned away.

There was nothing to be said to this. Bone followed Ken out onto the landing; everyone was descending the stairs to spread out on the ground floor. On the hall's black and white marble, foreshortened to Bone's view from the landing, Dwight stood listening to Palmerston. Beside them, the head of the security firm, Peter Chapple, whom Bone had known when he was in the police, stood with his walkie-talkie, a hand over his free ear. Dwight's mobile phone tilted out from his coat pocket.

"We have searched the cellar, sir. In any case Miss West did not ever care to go there."

"She's holed up somewhere, I'm telling you. Just having second thoughts about this marriage." Dwight was elated.

Ken, beside Bone, began to speak and then shut up abruptly. They joined the pair in the hall.

"Are you starting in the grounds next?" asked Bone.

"Finish here first." Dwight's gesture grazed Palmerston's waistcoat and hit Chapple's arm. He stepped back, saying into his walkie-talkie, "Reception's bad in here. I'll be out on the terrace," and he strode toward the front door. One of his men, Harry Owen, whom Bone also knew, trying a room door, said "This is locked," and, without halting, Chapple took a key from his pocket and held it out, calling some order. Since he was passing

Bone at the time and heading away from Owen, Bone took the key to save Harry from chasing out of the front door after him and, with the curiosity very familiar to his own subordinates, went with him to the locked door.

The room was small, paneled in blue, and contained a plump, pretty young woman, sitting with her feet planted in front of her, heels in the carpet, toes up. She wore a multicolored chiffon dress, diamanté slides straining her soft hair back from her face, and she had been crying.

"Come on, love. I'm to see you off the premises."

She got up, picked a crushed-velvet poche on a shoulder cord from the floor, and came reluctantly forward.

"Who is she?" Bone asked, sotto voce.

"An intruder. She had some press pass. We checked and it doesn't belong to her. There'll be blood-for-breakfast over that."

In the hall, Ken called out something. Instantly the reluctant young woman, galvanized, put her head down and barged between the two men, and might have made it but that Harry grabbed her arm, she stumbled and wheeled round as in a wild dance, shouting, "Ken! KEN!"

"God!" Ken regarded the frolic with horror. "Where the *hell* has she sprung from? I thought you'd got rid of her."

Harry and a colleague got hold of the young woman by the arms and marched her, still yelling "Ken!" out through the service door. Ken headed for the library, where Bone found him pouring himself a triple whisky. He drank, and pointed with the glass-holding hand toward the kitchen quarters.

"That maniac turned up earlier, out of the blue, claiming I'd *called* her. She sang at me, would you believe it? She sang "Forget her." He drank. "God, this isn't in any conceivable way my day."

"It isn't, either, in any conceivable way my business, but if you're going to be taking vows, however delayed . . ." he indicated the glass, "isn't that . . . ?"

"Vows! I told her I was ready to love and cherish her . . . she wanted me to invent a whole rigmarole of schmaltz and when I said love-and-cherish only, she wrote it all out herself. I've written some romantic rubbish in my time but who expects a pop song to be real? I tell you that was another second-thoughts time . . . but you know how it is—she only has to be there and that's all that matters, all I can think of. And after all, this vowing is immaterial; I'll straighten my spine and try to read off this guff," he tapped his breast pocket "in the way she wants." He glanced at Bone as if to gauge how he was taking it. "I'm enough of an actor."

"I haven't got this sorted, you know." Bone watched Ken tilt the whisky down. If he really had to recite some starry-eyed drivel to please Zephyr, if and when she turned up, whisky was probably a helpful item. "I've never had to be cognizant of the law concerning marriage, but are these 'vows' legally binding? And what has the clergyman got to do with it?"

Ken's head came upright and he looked at Bone over the empty glass. His gaze was subtly off-center. "Should have told *you* at least. This 'marriage,'" his forefingers made quotation marks in spite of the glass, "is really the charade Dwight called it. Registrar, Maidstone, yesterday, dead secret. We're already married."

159

Chapter

27

•••••••••

"Excuse me, sir. You are Superintendent Bone?" Elderly, thin, in a gray dress that managed to suggest a uniform even with a silver neck-chain and a little jeweled pendant, she had arrived at Bone's side. When he admitted his identity, she said, "Mrs. West asks if you would be kind enough to come and see her."

Ken put down the glass. "I'll talk later. I must join this hunt-the-slipper."

Mrs. West was evidently upstairs and no longer in the marquee. The sound of the band came clearly, playing some innocuous music to eat to. From the landing window Bone saw the glowing canvas and a slew of empty hot-trolleys outside its service entrance. He heard the music, the clamor of voices, of knives and forks, a sudden guffaw. The guests were quite reassured about the state of affairs.

Mrs. West was in a reclining chair. She had a small medicine glass in her hand and sipped from it. She was pale, a cream-like pallor, and for the first time gave the impression of being an invalid.

"Mr. Bone—it's kind of you to spare the time. Have you managed to have something to eat?"

Bone had forgotten such matters. He made a vague acquiescent sound and took the chair Mrs. West's maid placed for him.

"Thank you, Lexie."

The woman moved a little electric bell further forward on Mrs. West's side table, gave an officious tweak to the nosegay there in its tiny vase, and took herself off.

"I thought I could manage out there—" she indicated the marque. "One of the family should; but . . ." She sipped her medicine. "It's too bad of Zephyr. She's impulsive. She prides herself on following her impulse. It's absurd to worry about her with the place so thick with bodyguards. They say she's not in the house, but I really don't know how she could contrive to get out of it without being seen. You know what the security arrangements are."

"They're very good, Mrs. West. It's a highly competent firm. I've known Peter Chapple for years."

There was a sound of breaking glass and a raucous yell from the marquee.

"Oh, it's a pity at least Dwight isn't there." She smiled suddenly. "He is *ex* family. Can you see anything, Mr. Bone?"

Knowing he couldn't, but out of courtesy, Bone went to the window. The canvas obdurately hid events; there was laughter now, however. He came back. "I think it's all right." He was arrested by the sight of a portrait photograph in a silver frame on the desk that stood by the window. "Is this Zephyr when she was younger?"

He picked it up and almost dropped it because the picture next to it came too. He had thought they were separate, but they were hinged together, two girls very much alike, in their early teens. The one he had taken for Zephyr was not, he saw now, and it intrigued him that she did have an odd resemblance to Treasure—a quality of disturbance; unhappy eyes for all the conventional smile.

"That's Storm." Mrs. West's voice had lost expression.

161

"She died. She was killed, in fact, which I didn't tell you."

Bone, who had normally an iron control of his face, let his shock show. She paused a moment and went on: "They were wrongly named, those girls. Storm was a quieter girl, though very determined, much more of a zephyr. My mother-in-law named them, and of course she knew nothing of their characters at the time. Mr. Bone, where do you think Zephyr is? Why haven't they found her?"

This was making Bone, too, uneasy. He managed to keep his voice casual as he asked, "Do you want me to join the search?"

"I'm sure they're being very thorough. I suppose I am really worried by something else. It's quite needless to consider it but I can't help thinking about it all the same. It's probably nothing to do with all this . . ."

Bone waited in attentive silence, regarding her. She didn't withstand it long. She finished the medicine and, nursing the little glass, began to speak.

"The man who killed Storm is out of prison. It seems they let them out after half their sentence or something, on license. What does that actually mean? It seems strange that they can do that with someone who's killed a person."

Bone tried to answer dispassionately. The disappearance of Zephyr escalated in importance of a sudden. "The parole board enquire exhaustively. They must have agreed that he was no longer a threat to society. What sort of man was he?"

"A quiet man. People say they're the worst, which is probably nonsense." She let her head drop back on the headrest, and went on in the same tired, almost toneless voice. It was not an aspect of her he had seen until now. "I liked him very much. He was a university don. Unlikely, isn't it? Rawdon Chase. *There's* another peculiar name. He said his father was sold on Thackeray, whom I can't read at all, and named him after someone in *Vanity Fair*. Isn't it strange what one remembers?

"He was in love with Zephyr. She was over here filming some scenes at his college, and he fell for her. He turned up at our house—my husband was alive then, we had a place near Oxford—and I asked him to lunch, as one does, and we all took to him. Perhaps we shouldn't have had him to stay so much but I didn't take it seriously—people were always falling in love with Zephyr. He had one of these prematurely gaunt faces—rather like Ken, in fact—and thick dark hair, rather unruly; he could talk, you know. He was interesting. Dwight was in America, telephoning every day, or rather every night. We had to get a telephone installed in Zephyr's room because he never would understand that the household went to bed by eleven. What *does* 'license' mean, exactly?"

"It means that he's out on parole. He's not free to do as he pleases. He has to live under restrictions and report to his parole officer, and this officer can call at any time to check on him, and so on."

"I don't know if St. Benet's will let him back again; he's a research fellow, an historian. They may think he's safe too."

"What happened?" Bone put the double photographs on the desk, facing Mrs. West. She looked across at them, and spoke almost coolly, in her old sardonic tone.

"He said Storm harassed him. He said in court she wouldn't let him alone. She used to seek him out, even going to his rooms in Oxford. She jeered at him because Zephyr wouldn't sleep with him, and called him names because he wouldn't sleep with someone else who was willing. She kept—offering herself, he said.

"Finally there was a scene—Zephyr was there—Storm threw herself at him and he shook her so violently he broke her neck. Zephyr said he had sworn he would."

Chapter

28

·········

Bone did not spend time telling Mrs. West how appalling this must have been for her. After all, she knew. He was silent for a moment, and then he said smoothly, "I'll keep this in mind, but I don't suppose it's relevant. The most likely scenario is that Zephyr is playing a game"—*silly buggers* suppressed—"and the worst is that she's sprained an ankle and is waiting somewhere for help."

Mrs. West said, with a definite return of strength to her voice, "Either scenario would be perfectly characteristic of her. Well, I'm ready to attend to my guests again. That rescue remedy always works." She pressed the bell. Bone took the hand she held out to him and found, such was her manner, that he was almost bowing over it. As he left, he thought *I'll be kissing it next,* and nearly collided with Lexie in the doorway.

Peter Chapple was on the front terrace still, with his radio. He had put out the terrace lights and was watching the movements of flares and big torches in the grounds. He was listening to a report and to Bone's face of inquiry he shook his head. Then he switched off and said, "Damn the silly cow."

Bone, with an obscure thought of Rawdon Chase, said, "Have there been any intruders besides the crackpot girl?"

"Would you believe she had a press pass? We're checking it out. No, no one's reported any extraneous persons. Of course with miles of perimeter like here, you can't be a hundred percent sure, but I've had men roaming all evening and no one's been picked up."

"Right. I'm just going to see how my daughter's getting on at the shindig and, if she's enjoying herself still, I'll go down to the lake. Incidentally," he said with a grin, "your boys missed intruders in the boathouse. Treasure Schlumberger and Jem Cryer were holed up there."

"So I heard. My lads said it was locked when they inspected it."

"From inside, I suspect. They'd got it unlocked when I happened by—probably forgot to lock it again after nipping out for a pee. They'd decided to skip the wedding and have their own party. A pair of monkeys . . . Those woods will be a devil to search."

"Should be a doddle—a woman in white." Chapple's voice was resigned. "My people found an empty champagne bottle, still with dregs, in the boathouse just now. Kids!"

That would, Bone thought as he went round the corner of the house on the terrace toward the marquee throbbing with dance rhythm, certainly account for the state they were in.

Bone had only to stand in the doorway to know that Charlotte was enjoying herself still. She was dancing with Archangel. Both of them looked happy. Bone hoped Cha was not tiring her vulnerable right leg, but modern dancing . . . Bone watched her ecstatic face. She might be favoring her leg, she might have forgotten it and everything else, watching her partner. Archangel had taken off his coat, he was in shirtsleeves, moving precisely, adroitly, smiling a little, watching her. Incredible good looks can be downright offensive in a man but Archan-

165

gel's ability to seem unself-conscious about them made it bearable. All the same, his face set him apart as if he belonged to a separate race.

Bone saw the delinquent attendants of the bride slumped on the floor in a corner, in jeans and T-shirts now. Jem watched the dancers with muzzy concentration. Treasure appeared to be dozing; she should have obeyed Mrs. West and gone to sleep it off. Champagne taking its toll, Bone thought. These truant attendants of the bride made him think of Zephyr and the dark presentiment came back. He thought to walk a little way onto the lawn, stand in the dark and see if he had any hunches.

He had not got far when a powerful torch from the terrace swung and found him. He flung up a hand to shield his eyes, but the beam switched off. Chapple had identified the rover. A moment later, the light came on again, but to illuminate the step from the terrace down to the grass. Chapple called out, following its beam down. "Super?" And coming closer he said, "My lads have found signs of an intruder across the lake. Coming for a look-see?"

The flambeaux and lanterns still burnt along the sides of the shallow steps into the hollow, and the fairy-lights flickered among the incongruous garlands. The flashlights of Chapple's men were directed across the dark stretch of water to where two more figures stood, one of them thigh-deep, examining the reeds under the bank, and flashing their own lights at the path above and into the scrubby dwarf alders and weeds. Chapple called on his phone and one of them answered. He said to Bone, "Someone's made a way through those reeds and alders. There's dried mud on the path. Why the hell didn't they see it earlier?"

"No reason for them to look so close," Bone said.

"Jee-sus!" Dwight came hurrying down after Bone, elbowed past him and took a jump onto the raft, which had drifted sideways a little on its moorings. His feet thumped over the planks until he stood on the far edge, gazing across. "What's that? What the hell——? Signs of——You mean she's been abducted?"

"Or gone on her own," Chapple said.

The raft swung a little, making Dwight do a step-dance to keep his footing. He looked down. Then he knelt, and reached into the water. Then he flung himself down full length.

"Give me a light here," he demanded. "There's something . . . that damn cloak thing of hers."

Bone stepped onto the raft and knelt beside Dwight. His arrival had made the raft swing and also perhaps dislodged what Dwight was pulling at. Chapple came with his torch. Into sight under the water moved a pale swathed shape, turning over as it came, and rising. Twisted around with sodden gauze, smudged with silt and weed, Zephyr West had finally shown up.

Chapter
29
•••••••••

In this moment, Bone ceased to be a guest and became the most important person present. Peter Chapple acknowledged it by ordering a freeze on all his men's activities and turning to Bone to say, "What d'you want done, guv?"—a reversion to his former policeman's way of addressing him. Dwight acknowledged nothing. He was up to his shoulders in the water, leaning far out. Bone called, "Get her out. Give a hand," and knelt by Schlumberger.

Two of Chapple's men dumped their radios and torches on the shore and waded in. The water beyond the raft was waist deep and they took hold of Zephyr's body and heaved it toward the raft. Dwight got up on all fours and shuffled back a foot or two, and his phone slid from his pocket, hit the raft and swiveled off it like a live thing to fall into the water. He made a grab at it but the automatic movement was transmuted into the more urgent one of receiving Zephyr. The men put her on the raft's edge. Her face, pallid and with eyes open, was obscured by the wet folds of gauze. Schlumberger took her in his arms and cradled her while water flooded over him.

Bone said to Chapple, "Start resuscitation. See if there's a doctor in the marquee. Say there's been an accident. Send someone discreet to call HQ. We need the team, which includes policewomen. And no one must leave—the guests must stay on site. I'm going to the house. Mrs. West must be told; an announcement made . . . and the daughter, Treasure, get her out of the marquee to go to her grandmother. Where's Ken Cryer?"

Chapple said, "I'll put out a call for him."

"I expect I'll find him in the house." Bone thought: Cha; and I must phone Grizel.

"We'll keep this place sealed off till your men arrive," Chapple said. "We've already trampled all over every square inch of it."

Bone could only shrug at this. He glanced at the shrouded figure in Dwight's arms. For a moment nothing but the lapping of water could be heard. He said to Chapple, "You know the drill. Lucky you're here."

Also looking at his men working on Zephyr's body, Chapple returned, "Not all that successful, were we?"

Dwight caught this, and as Bone made his way up the steps he heard him launch into a diatribe against Chapple, his firm, their stupidity and their responsibility.

Bone halted and called, "Mr. Schlumberger. Come up to the house, please."

"I'm not leaving her."

"You better, sir," said Chapple. "He's the police."

Bone left it with Chapple; he knew Dwight would be up at the house shortly.

As he followed the path toward the lights and music, he thought: I knew it; I knew it, from the moment she didn't appear; wish I'd been wrong.

Palmerston was crossing the hall with a tray. He paused when he saw Bone, put the tray down on a console table and came toward him with a face of solicitous inquiry. "Can I be of assistance, sir?"

"Is Mrs. West still in her room?"

"No, sir. She went to the marquee—"

But Mrs. West was being wheeled into the hall from

the garden by Harry Owen. She sat straight, upright, in the chair, and her eyes and brow showed her apprehension. "Mr. Chapple says you want to speak to me. What's happened, Mr. Bone?"

"Can we go—"

"What's happened?"

Bone went to the door of the small blue room where the strange young woman had been incarcerated. He looked in, found the room empty and stood back, opening the door wide. Harry Owens conducted Mrs. West in and left her there with Bone. She said, "You've found her, haven't you?"

"Yes."

She put her hands together and pressed them hard. He said, "She was in the lake. We don't know how it happened yet."

Mrs. West sat so still that only the slight rise and fall of the gray silk over her heart showed that she lived. Then she lifted her head a little and said, "I saw Treasure in the marquee. I must tell her. I must tell her myself."

"I believe she has been told to come in." Bone opened the door and looked out. Treasure, sullen and flushed, was demanding her grandmother.

"In here," Bone said. She turned, stumbled slightly on the Kirghiz rug, veered uncertainly toward the door, located it and went in.

"They said you wanted me."

Bone, as he shut himself out, noticed that her truculence was not extended to her grandmother. Her voice was tentative.

"May I ask, Mr. Bone . . . ?" Palmerston was at his elbow.

"Yes, Miss West's been found. She was in the lake."

Palmerston looked at him, and must have seen from his face what the situation was, for he asked nothing but only bent his head; the telephone ringing at that moment he went to answer it. Bone heard his own name and went to take the call; the duty sergeant reported that a team was on its way.

He set off for the marquee and met Emily coming anxiously in. She was carrying her hat, and her hair was tousled, as if she had run her fingers through it. Bone paused beside her.

"What's happened?" She echoed Mrs. West. "I have such an oppressive feeling . . ."

Bone spoke gently. "Zephyr West has been found in the lake. We have been trying to resuscitate her."

She looked up at him. "So that was it," she said. He supposed she meant her feeling of oppression. "You'll tell me, Robert, if I can be useful."

He touched her arm and said, "Thanks," and went on to make his announcement in the marquee. He could not expect such self-command and responsiveness from anyone else; clearly Emily had been forewarned by her particular, erratic visitations—so often, as now, an affliction to her.

The guests were partying still. There had been a consensus that Zephyr West was simply overplaying a bit of mystery; Bone arrived on a scene of dancing, talk, eating at the buffet; wedding hats had been discarded, the band thrashed out a dance beat. One of Chapple's unmistakable crew had been watching the entrance, and jerked his head toward the band in interrogation. Bone nodded, the man spoke to the band leader and the music stopped. After a moment of confusion and some laughter, the company gradually fell silent and turned toward Bone. He had announced death a score of times, to families, spouses, colleagues. It never got easier.

"I don't have good news," he said. "Zephyr West has been found in the lake. She had been under the water for some little time. We don't as yet know what happened."

Faces registered shock, horror, titillation. Questions and talk broke out. He raised his voice over it and said the usual things about waiting to give their names and addresses to the police, who were arriving.

"Is she *dead?*"

"Police! Was she murdered?"

"If she *is* dead, when the cause of death is not known, the police investigate. It's routine."

Someone gave a hysterical laugh, and stopped or was shut up. They began a slow surge toward the door. Bone moved through them toward Mary Highmountain, who true to her name could be seen above the throng. He heard snatches of talk: "Appalling" . . . "Not surprised actually" . . . "Good God, I mean" . . . "*What* a wedding party" . . . "Certainly upstaged the lot" . . . "Can't *wait* to tell Boodie!" (*Boodie?* Bone thought) . . . "Poor Zeph . . ." "Do you think he pushed her in?" . . . "Where did you put the car?" Bone knew that Mary would be next to Archangel and that Cha was likely to be there too. Remembering Ken's weird fan, he hoped she had not been too much in the way, or importunate.

She was sitting on the edge of the orchestra platform, near her idol but not obtrusively close. He thought, *Damn, she's tired,* and wondered if he had a professionally social obligation to a celebrity or if he could follow his need to attend to her. Archangel, however, was speaking to Mary—"I'll hang around to see if Ken needs a shoulder or a drinking partner; if he doesn't, we'll blow," and he followed the crowd.

The band packed up their instruments. Bone put out a hand to Cha, and she pulled on it a little as she stood up.

"I'll arrange a lift home for you, chick. Was it a good party till now?"

She nodded. "Till now. And it's awful but I feel mad at her. Zephyr, I mean. You'll be stuck here till all hours and she spoilt it all. Sorry. I shouldn't say."

"Say what you like. I don't hold a brief for Zephyr

172

West. I very much fear your sentiment will be rather general."

"Did—did someone drown her?"

"We don't know."

But, remembering the arch of pallid neck as the doctor-guest labored over the heart that had ceased to beat, he thought: "It's more that we don't know who."

Chapter 30

•••••••••

In the house they found crosscurrents of guests: Palmerston, implacable, deferential, backed by Peter Chapple, barring access to Mrs. West in the blue sitting room for those who thought they should commiserate, and accepting their messages; people coming from the stables with belated realization that they ought to commiserate, personal friends who had left coats and wedding hats in the library; and some were being admitted to the blue sitting room—Archangel, Edwina Marsh, and Jem. Bone asked Palmerston where there was a private telephone, and hearing there was one in the little office place beyond the sitting room, he took Cha with him and found, to his relief, Emily Playfair, standing and putting on her hat.

"Emily—"

"Good! From that tone of voice I deduce that I can be useful."

Bone smiled. His face felt as if he had not done this for some time. "Are you going home now? Then is it too much—"

"Go round by Hawkwell and take Charlotte home? Of course. I'd be very pleased to do that."

Emily looked at Bone's face and added, "I do like company when I'm driving, so I can thank *you.*" She thought, how anxious one can be about one's child. . . . She rather wanted to know if Zephyr had been wrapped in all that gauze, but Robert had enough on his mind as it was. She patted his hand and said, "I will look after her."

He found the telephone in the "office place" that had once been Lady Herne's workroom. As he was tapping out his home number to phone Grizel, he wondered if he had thanked Emily. He had no recollection of it—his relief at settling one problem seemed to lead him straight to dealing with the next. He was haunted by that torchlit streaming-wet shrouded face, by the useless work of resuscitation among the wedding lanterns. God, say Ken hadn't—Bone refused to complete the thought— and was it connected to that pseudo-Ken dead in the quarry? And there was the Oxford don, perhaps not satisfied with the death of one sister and popping back for more. . . .

Grizel heard his voice with enormous relief. She had been considering, as she walked to and fro on the slight slope of the kitchen's brick floor, ringing Herne Hall to see if he could be got hold of. Her body was still echoing to the extraordinary sensation that had brought her to a standstill in the middle of arranging the store cupboard.

"I shouldn't think I'll be too late," he was saying. "Steve or someone should be here any minute. Emily Playfair is going to bring Cha home, so they'll be with you shortly."

She played back the words he'd begun with, and said, "Zephyr West? Or, poor Ken! On their wedding day! You can," she went on, telling herself about being a policeman's wife, and summoning the determined resolutions she had privately made, and hoping she wasn't going to regret this desperately, "tell me all when you do come."

He said sharply, "Are you all right?" and at this temptation she replied as sharply, "Of course I am." Robert knew her tones of voice, and Robert had intuition. "I'd shout for you soon enough if I wasn't."

So, she thought as she rang off, is it more feminist to tough it out on my own—*ouf.*

She hung onto the table.

When it was over, and it was brief, she checked on her watch. Nothing was to be expected but more of the same for some hours. She rang her midwife at the hospital and felt, with a good deal of trepidation, that she was in for it now. She told herself Robert would be back before it happened, anyway; an old panacea of hers when things got hairy, "by this time next week it will be over," didn't help.

Bone's doubts had been aroused by her voice, but her brisk reassurance banished them, the more effectively for his need to think of this case.

Emily and Cha were gone from the sitting room. He went out to the hall, empty now and very quiet. He thought: murder, or suicide; it can't be accident. Those are the options. We know who was present for the wedding, the ceremony of vows, that is. Zephyr West was not the universal idol she seemed to assume she was. There was her attack on Jem—just how had she reconciled Ken to that?

Perhaps she hadn't. But still he'd married her.

Felicia Pavane came through from the stables with a small, stout, badly dressed woman he had earlier seen bossing the photographer. One of Chapple's men was with them and now pointed his walkie-talkie at Bone, and left.

"Are you really the person in charge?" demanded the small woman incredulously.

"I'm waiting for the police team. I'm Superintendent Bone, Kent police."

"I am Julia Stenn-Boughton, of *Gracious Living,* covering this wedding. I'd like to know where we stand."

"Ah!" Bone, who saw use in this, dug up his charm

176

act. He was not to know that it worked the better for an air of slight awkwardness occasioned by his knowledge that it was an act. "I'm sorry to have neglected you. This shocking event has put your journal in a quandary, I can see. But it would be necessary for publication of anything you want to print to wait for the outcome of the investigation—"

Julia Stenn-Boughton hadn't reached her position by being slow on the uptake: "In case we've got pictures of a murderer. Yes, I had considered a "Fatal Festivity" number, if you can believe it, because, and *this* you can believe, it'd sell. So, yes?"

"So we would like to see all the pictures you have."

Mrs. Stenn-Boughton eliminated one of her chins by poking the top one out at Bone. *"We* would like an exclusive interview with the Superintendent conducting the investigation."

"I'm not conducting it," Bone said thankfully, seeing a way out of this requirement, "and we're far from sure what sort of an investigation we have in hand."

Mrs. Stenn-Boughton put her head on one side, sniffed and said, "Of course we expect it's accidental—"

"Of course," said Felicia.

"—but anyone who's had dealings with Zephyr may entertain doubts. Who is, then, conducting the investigation?"

Bone appreciated her remark but could not afford to rise to it. He said, "The police team will be here. The Press Officer—"

"Not good enough." Mrs. Stenn-Boughton created a third chin by tucking the top one into her neck. "We want *you.*"

"While I'm very flattered, I promise you we have an immensely photogenic young Press Officer. Think about it, Mrs. Stenn-Boughton." He gave her a social smile and headed for the front door. It would be possible to get the photographs anyway, but to obtain them on an amiable basis would be quicker. He knew what Charlotte thought of his being-interviewed technique: he looked, she said, like the stone from which blood was being extracted.

Where was Ken?

His absence was making Bone increasingly concerned. From the porch he could see a white glare in the woods above where the lake lay. Someone had organized floodlighting.

The blue revolving lights of police cars showed across the park where the approach drive must be. The lights shone off the park trees when the cars swung out of sight and almost at once were illuminating the circular grass plot in the center of the drive sweep before the house. One drew up with a scattering of gravel, small stones rattling about Bone's feet, and disgorged two officers, Tyrell and Shay. He left Sergeant Shay in charge at the Hall and took Tyrell and his radio along the flambeau-lit path toward the glowing hollow where the lake was. Chapple's men had got a floodlight on a line from the house, and this and their torches shone on the sodden tangled heap on the shore that was Zephyr West. They had stopped their attempts at resuscitation. The doctor—a wedding guest—had his coat on again and was tucking the tail of his shirt into his trousers waistband, looking down at the body where Dwight still knelt. Evidently even Chapple had failed to shift *him*. More torches were coming past the boathouse along that path, and someone ran forward now, for a moment seeming huge as the torchlight threw his shadow ahead, then emerging into the lights, thin, disheveled, wet about the feet and sleeves, his eyes fixed toward Zephyr's body so that he stumbled. He stood staring down, and breathed "No!"

Dwight heard this. He sprang up and without preamble seized a handful of Ken's shirt front and roared, "You goddam murderer!" into his face.

Ken swore, twisted away and struck at Dwight with his forearm as if to brush him violently aside; he was still looking at Zephyr, his face contorted, and trying to reach her. Dwight jerked him away and roared again, with the augmented fury of one who has been hit across the nose. One of Ken's shirt buttons broke free and flew in an arc to land on Zephyr's cheek. Chapple's men rallied to stop the struggle as it swayed to and fro, but were foiled by both men toppling out of their clutches and crashing resoundingly into the shallows.

They hauled them out separately. Dwight still stamped and roared, accusing Ken to his face and to the world at large. Ken stood, rigid, glowering at Zephyr's body.

"Up to the top." Bone gestured to the steps, and Chapple's men turned Dwight in that direction. Ken, Tyrell gripping his arm, jibbed slightly but went to the stairfoot walking sideways, still looking at Zephyr's body.

Dwight found he was being maneuvered past Bone. He dug in his heels and yelled at him, "You letting that killer walk off? No arrest? What sort of police force do you have here?"

"You'd do better to be quiet," Bone said.

"Look, there's the woman I'm crazy about, you get that? She's lying there, he killed her sure as if you saw blood on his hands—he's a goddam murderer!"

Ken, oblivious to this, turned and said, "Robert, what—"

"Robert?" roared Schlumberger. "Robert? That's how it is? Now I get it, he walks because he's your buddy and I get manhandled! I'm not about to be the patsy here—"

Bone said curtly, "Stop that. No one's being favored."

At this moment there was an influx of uniformed figures down the stairway, followed by a plainclothes group. Bone saw with relief the burly form of Detective-Inspector Steve Locker. After them, detachedly picking his way, came the tall long-legged shape of the pathologist.

Dwight, perhaps on account of Bone's rebuke but more likely because of the interruption, became a little subdued. He moved off, attended but not touched by Chapple's men, and watched from the steps as Smethurst, the police surgeon, crouched by Zephyr and after a moment stepped back, having a word with the doctor-guest. The light of torches and flambeaux was now wiped by the white light of the flood, which in its turn was punctuated by flash.

The pathologist stood beside Bone, waiting. Ferdy Foster liked to make examinations and collect his samples himself; he had all the freedom of not being a police employee, but his independence of mind, beyond that, was all his own and he had a strong line in disconcertion. His harsh drawl sounded in Bone's ear.

"Ah," peering past the deliberate movements of the police team, "how nice—gift-wrapped this time."

Chapter

31

·········

After Dr. Foster had done his preliminary work, Zephyr West was more relentlessly wrapped—shut in a body bag—and carried away as if she were any body. Ferdy, crossing the grass to the house beside Bone, paused as Dwight on the terrace got off another diatribe against Ken, who supported himself on a flower-spilling urn and watched Zephyr's going.

"Who are those two, Robert? Not matey."

"Zephyr's exes; at least the American's her ex, Ken is her widower."

"This looks not like a nuptial."

They halted. Ken, his dander once more roused, had shouted back, six inches from Dwight's face, with all the power of lungs developed during his early years of bawling lyrics over manky sound systems in provincial gigs. The words were not distinguishable but they had the unlooked-for effect of allowing Ken to turn on his heel and walk away from a momentarily deafened Dwight.

Ferdy was chuckling as he walked on. He strode toward the marquee with a purpose Bone did not recognize until they came up to it and found the caterers busy removing the remaining food. Ferdy stood surveying the dishes carried out past him and intercepted one. He abstracted from it a pâté croquette and, offering the plate to Bone, ate as he looked round. "Have you any favorite for the role of murderer?"

"At this stage, Ferdy? You haven't even told me if she was dead when she went into the water."

"Certainly I haven't. I ask only for theory, on a totally insufficient basis."

Bone felt, at that moment, curiously remote from it all. He walked out of the marquee and stood looking up at the sky. Stars hung in the black infinite. Ferdy, in comradely fashion tilting his head back too, observed, "If one of those flared up and went nova before our eyes, we would know it happened centuries ago. When a little TV star goes out, it is instant. Poor pretty thing."

"I never saw her on TV."

"She wasn't very good, as it happens, but she had vitality; which is quite ironic, m'm?" He touched Bone on the shoulder, "See you at the morgue," and was gone.

PC Shona Wilkinson was coming in search of Bone, and he left the night and the sky and went into the house, where he was directed to the small office room that had been Lady Herne's workroom, and found Locker and DS Pat Fredricks. The olive velvet curtains were now closed; there was a desk-table with a telephone, and a leather swivel chair and several straight ones with tapestry seats, and armchairs by the hearth.

"Hallo, sir. We've got the old coach house for an incident room and Mrs. West thought this'd do for us as well. It has this independent phone—seems it was intended for Mr. Schlumberger's office when he comes to see his daughter on access visits, but he's never used it."

"He may wish he had. His mobile went into the lake and I can't imagine him without it. What's the situation?" He sat down in one of the armchairs and realized at once that he hadn't sat down for ages and that an easy chair was a dangerous relaxation. He got up and sat on the arm of it.

Locker said immediately, "Would you rather sit here, sir?" indicating the leather chair in which he had been about to spread himself. Bone declined, and Locker, who knew him, did not waste time insisting but sat down. "Well, I said I'd talk to Mrs. West in the morning. Her maid Miss Alexander let us know the lady's much more exhausted than she seems. And Cryer wants to send Jem home, so we could talk to the boy now."

"I don't know how newts got their reputation for being pissed, but Jem could give them points at the present time. And I don't know if we can interview Jem with his father as guardian adult; Ken has to be "on the list." I hope he and Schlumberger are being kept apart. They threw each other in the lake."

"So Tyrell told me. He's looking after Cryer and young Jem in the conservatory. The poor kid Treasure's in her room and I hear she's locked herself in again, but Palmerston says he has the master key if necessary. Mr. Schlumberger's having a hot bath and changing his clothes."

"And Cryer?"

"He's in somebody's toweling bathrobe. One of his heavies has gone to the Manor for dry clothes. We have the names and addresses of everybody else, bar an intruder who seems to have got in on a press pass."

"The fat girl fixated on Ken."

"Harry Owens says he saw her off earlier. He tried to get her name and phone number—to pass on to Ken, he told her, but it didn't work, she'd clammed up; Ken had only wanted her off the premises. Tyrell got her car's registration and thought he'd been smart but it's registered to the girl whose press pass she'd got hold of. We're after her, but no luck so far."

"How did she get hold of the press pass and the car?"

"Not yet ascertained," Locker admitted.

"Let's hope we don't need to know," said Bone cheerfully. "We must talk to Treasure Schlumberger, but she's as tight as Jem. Another pleasure reserved."

"Her father told Pat here that he is going to be present if anyone grills his daughter."

"Grills?"

"Grills," Fredricks confirmed. "Damn well going to be there if any cop grills his daughter."

"Think you could rustle up a hard spotlight and a couple of nightsticks? Mustn't disappoint him."

"Oh, I expect I could, sir. Incidentally, Treasure's been throwing up. I heard her in her bathroom, poor girl. She said she *didn't* want any help and she *wasn't* coming out."

"Leave her till morning," Bone said. "I'm not prepared to trouble a sick child who's just lost her mother, whether or not she's sobered up."

"Miss Alexander says that Mrs. West had hardly told her about her mother when she hurtled out of the room and upstairs and locked herself in straightaway. Mrs. West was upset enough before."

"Shall we see if this protective father has finished his hot bath?"

Locker nodded to Pat, who went out to see. While she was away the phone rang—their base in Tunbridge Wells was calling to check the number.

"How nice," said Bone as Locker affirmed this. "The Chief can call us. . . . Hallo, Mr. Schlumberger."

Dwight invaded the room, accompanied by Sardonyx for Men to a degree that made Locker cough. Pat came after him, pinching her nose. She caught Bone's eye and went blank.

"My daughter is certainly not able to be questioned." Dwight had also been using a strong disinfectant mouthwash and, given the green silt of the lake, this was a wise precaution.

"Of course not," Bone said. "She's in shock. You must be feeling it yourself. Won't you sit here?"

Dwight had been ready to challenge. He became wary, looking under bristling eyebrows at Locker and at Bone as he sat down. When Fredricks crossed to her place his eyes followed her figure and his expression changed.

Then he seemed to remember himself, and events, and frowned again . . .

"Well then. What do you people want?"

Attack as a means of defense, Bone thought. He became vague. "Preliminary inquiries, Mr. Schlumberger. We have to establish a picture, overall. You won't mind," he added firmly, "if we record the interview."

"Sure, but it's a hell of a time to have to do this."

"This is Detective-Inspector Locker, in charge of the case; Detective-Sergeant Fredricks."

Dwight nodded. "I want to get one thing straight before we go on: my daughter has just lost her mother and she is deeply traumatized. I'm not having her interviewed."

"We understand that—for the moment," Bone said.

Schlumberger placed his hands on his thighs, elbows out, in the attitude of one ready for anything. He had put on a clean linen jacket, and at his side the pocket sagged, marsupially, bereft of its mobile-phone joey. Locker spoke.

"Can you give us an account of the afternoon, Mr. Schlumberger—where you went and whom you talked to?"

Dwight gazed at the floor. After a moment he raised his head. "That's a tall order, Inspector. I was just about everywhere and I talked to just about everybody. You'll understand that what with my mother-in-law's disability, though she very wonderfully surmounts it, the duty of host devolved upon me."

Bone thought this little speech had been given more than once to guests in the course of the day.

"Perhaps you can tell me what was the last time you saw Miss West."

"The last time I saw her—alive," his hands tightened on his thighs, and his voice thickened, "was when Treasure and I talked to her, trying to get her not to marry Cryer. I don't mind telling you I still thought I could persuade her to marry me. She told me it wasn't possible. She said she was married to Cryer already at a registry office and that was legal. So all this stuff by the lake was just a charade. I hadn't understood that. I won't deny it was a blow to hear Zeph had been legally married as of yesterday. I had a license"—he put his hand to his inside pocket and withdrew it, shaking his head— "for us to marry today. Of course it was in the jacket when Cryer threw me in the lake and it's pulp by now I guess. There's a difference in law that I hadn't grasped either. I took it the ceremony by the lake was the one with official status, with the priest, but I was all out there. I had organized the whole reception with the idea we would remarry . . . then when she didn't show, I thought she might have reconsidered, you know? I began to be hopeful she'd had second thoughts."

He lowered his head abruptly. "Well, I still think she may have done just that. She knew I was right for her. She was no pussycat. She needed a man like me to manage her. As I see it, she told Ken Cryer it was off, and he couldn't hack it."

Unexpectedly he put a hand to his face and brushed a thumb under one eye and then the other.

"He killed her," he said. "That's what I believe. I don't have any proof. That's your concern. For what it's worth I believe Cryer killed her. Jesus. I can't think about it . . ."

Bone looked at Locker, who was waiting for Dwight to calm himself, but he was not yet calm when he came to his feet and went on, "You want to know what I was doing all day, ask around. I didn't see Zephyr after we talked, with Treasure that time. I can't see I'm any use to your inquiries right now and I need some space."

"You'll be here, Mr. Schlumberger," Bone said. "We have no reason to keep you at the moment."

"I'm not going anyplace," Dwight said, and seemed to belie this by making for the door. "Goodnight."

When the door had shut Bone got up and stretched.

"He has accused Cryer from the start. Cryer seems to have had ambivalent feelings about the whole thing," said Locker, "what with taking off for wherever-it-was just before the day."

"Scotland," Bone murmured absently. "What I saw was a man physically spellbound—how else would anyone get away with attacking Jem as she did? And he knew well enough Jem disliked her. D'you know, when she brought things for the house, ornaments, flowers, what have you, Jem carted them off to her room? If Charlotte had felt like that about Grizel, we'd never have married."

"I expect she thought she could win Jem over, in the long run."

"Perhaps," Pat Fredricks suggested—and both men turned their heads sharply as if they had forgotten there was a third sentient being in the room, "Zephyr West didn't expect the marriage to last long enough for it to matter. She was married to someone else for a year or so after she divorced Treasure's father."

As they were considering this, the door opened to admit PC Shay.

"Excuse me, sir. Joe Tench is here to know if you can see Ken Cryer. They want to get back to the Manor."

Bone said, "We'd better see Cryer. After all, according to Schlumberger . . ."

"*Oh* yes." Locker nodded portentously. He gestured to Shay, who went out. When the door had shut, he added, " 'Enter a murderer,' is it?"

Ken was a friend, but "Don't rule it out," said Bone.

Chapter
32
•••••••••

The room felt enclosed, and when Fredricks suggested opening a window both men agreed. She disappeared for a moment behind the olive velvet. Bone looked at his watch, didn't take in the time, and pulled back one of the curtains on the emerging Fredricks. He saw himself reflected in the glass of a French door against the lighted room. The air outside was heavy and still. Far off, the horizon momentarily showed up against a flicker of light. The railway must go past there, thought Bone. What line would that be? Then he heard the thunder.

The inner door opened, pulling a faint breeze past Bone's face. He turned, expecting Ken, and saw Palmerston, attentive in the doorway.

"I wondered if you might like coffee and perhaps some supper, Mr. Bone. We have been able to supply the police setting up their work in the coach house—"

"So they got it before we did?" Locker asked, genially enough but piqued.

Palmerston faintly smiled. "I was experiencing some difficulty of access to this room."

"Shay kept even coffee away from us!" Bone broke

into a laugh. "Mr. Palmerston, supper and coffee will be welcome. Thank you very much."

Palmerston demurely withdrew.

"I'll have a word or two with Shay," Locker mused. The idea of nearly missing a supper disquieted him.

Bone shut the french window on the night just as the electric lights wavered and the horizon briefly showed up again.

"If the electricity cuts out the VDU's will go down," Fredricks remarked. "I'll check if the generator's come."

"You ordered one up?"

"Yes, sir. I didn't know what the wiring might be like here, and as well, there was the forecast of a storm."

Bone gave no more than an approving nod, but Fredricks was perfectly aware that her efficiency had been appreciated, and smiled to herself as she went out on the terrace with her radio.

Ken appeared no more than usually the worse for wear. At its best his face looked slept in, or perhaps like a face that had stayed up too many nights. Now he was gaunt, and dark round the eyes.

"Sit where you like, Ken. Sorry we have to bother you at a time like this."

"I've never had a time like this." Ken took up the conventional phrase. "I suppose there are times like this and you've seen plenty of them. I still can't believe . . . And what was Zeph doing down by the lake? Why did she go there?"

"We'd like to know."

Ken's voice cracked as he said, "She must have been in the water all the time we were looking." He took hold of the back of an armchair as if to anchor himself.

Fredricks slipped in and sat down beside the recorder with her notebook.

"Where did you go during the search?"

"Where . . . ? I went up to the gazebo. We used to sit there and I'd gone there earlier but that mad girl found me. I went there again because I thought Zeph might be hiding there—playing one of her games, you know—because I'd legged it off north. So I was looking in places in the grounds where she might expect me to find her, places where we used to go when she first came over from America, before she moved in with me."

"Did you come across other people searching?" Locker asked.

"No. Because I went further, perhaps. There's a hollow yew tree with a table and seats, right up on the hill. Then I went down the stream to another place we knew. I thought she was expecting me to find her so I was going all over the place. God! I mean it seemed so *like* her to mess around like that. By the time I came across Chapple's lot down by the stream I was sick and tired of trekking about in the dark. Bloody furious at the whole thing . . ." He stopped and rubbed his face. "And then Dwight going for me. There she was on the ground, and Dwight giving out with all that shit . . ."

The phone buzzed. Fredricks answered, made a note, and rang off.

Bone said, "How did you get on with Miss West? What was the relationship like?" It was a genuine question, not asked out of curiosity or needling. Ken stared at him.

"Well, not all wine and roses. You know that. Zeph has a murderous temper, but she's so much more alive than— Oh God!" He rubbed his hands down his face. "I mean *was*. She *was* so much more alive. It's unreal. Yes, from time to time I didn't know if I could take it. I admit that." He shot an odd look at them. "Dwight told me he was going to get her back and I told him 'Dream on' though I knew life with her wasn't going to be easy. You know I keep thinking it's a mistake and she'll walk in." He stopped, rubbed his face again and stared at the carpet. Then he looked up. "But how did it take so long before anyone found her? The lake had lights all round. I'd have thought she'd be seen right away in all that white. I suppose she drowned because of the dress, she could swim like a mermaid. I suppose that dress and the cloak got round her and tangled her . . ."

The lights dimmed, flicked off and on, the curtains went brilliant white at the edges and an enormous crack of thunder rendered everyone deaf and shaken. It felt as if the house had been struck, so violent was the noise. Bone thought a tremor had gone through the floor.

Fredricks' hands were flat on the desk. She and Locker both looked white; Bone supposed he did too.

Ken came round the chair he had been gripping and sat down.

Shay opened the door, checked on them and shut it again. Bone was not entirely sure, in that moment, that Shay was justified in thinking all was well.

Locker grunted. "That was a stunner. Let's hope there's no more of the same."

"Let's hope it's moved on," said Bone.

"Have I said all you want?" Ken asked abruptly. "I'd like to go home. This is like hanging round in . . . I don't know. Everything's shattered."

Bone consulted Locker with a glance.

"Oh, I think so, Mr. Cryer. For the moment."

"Then you get on home. Don't take off for anywhere without consulting us, though."

"I needed time to think!" Ken was defensive. "I said to Archangel the magnitude of the undertaking had just stricken me. He got me to see I'd run out of option time. So I came back and went through with it."

"You weren't looking forward to married life."

"I didn't see how it would work out. Being crazy about someone isn't—you know—reliable. I thought it wouldn't last." He stared at Bone. "Didn't expect it to be this short." He paused. Nobody commented, and he got up and went out. The door shut. Locker murmured, "Exit mourning husband."

"My bet is that *she* proposed to *him,*" Fredricks said. The phone rang and she picked it up. She looked puzzled, put a finger on the privacy button and said to Bone, "It's Miss Playfair, for you. How did she get this number?"

"She's psychic," Bone said, taking the receiver as Fredricks opened the line again. "Hallo, Emily?"

"I'm speaking from the hospital." Her voice came through against an echoing background of footsteps and a distant ringing phone. "Grizel said you shouldn't be disturbed because it could take a long time yet. She's started with the baby."

192

Chapter

33

....

Driving the car himself would have been a helpful distraction, but Bone could see the risk of having a distracted driver belting down these lanes at night. Powers' hand dipped and undipped the headlights continually; he kept a good speed without the urgency Bone felt.

The darkened countryside was invisible under the low heavy cloud. Every so often a ripple of light went through the cloud or shimmered briefly to earth. Rain slashed at the car; for a long minute Powers had to slow to a crawl, wipers on storm speed, as water seemed to sheet from the sky. Bone became horribly aware of the loom of headlights from behind; his body readied itself for impact, but the car in the rear slowed. Then trees and hedges and the shape of the road became visible once more. Powers picked up speed.

Bone shut his eyes in a short-lived attempt to relax. He had determined not to urge Powers on or to harass him with inquires about how far they still were. His silence recoiled on him. He saw Grizel's face in pain. Over and over he hurried down hospital corridors, met a nurse to whom he gave a face familiar from Charlotte's birth . . . Across this vision lay images of the lake, the lapping waters and the flares and torches, Chapple, Dwight and others, the faces of the night.

They emerged from the lanes on to a bypass. Powers' foot went down. There wasn't much traffic. Then they were back in the narrow roads.

Thank God he had asked Emily to take Charlotte home. She would be company for Cha; or would they let her be with Grizel? Emily had seen so many things in the past. Had she seen anything about Grizel—and not told him?

Grizel: a loved and, to English ears—a faintly ridiculous name. He found he had been inwardly repeating it like a mantra.

It was not the hospital where Cha had been born, or her small brother; that flashback, all but subliminal, visited Bone, the unbelievable moment of collision, the car tossed aside, the moment Petra and the baby died. He took a breath, made himself see the present time, Powers drawing up in a parking slot, turning off ignition, opening the door.

Bone briefly gripped Powers' arm, and fled into the hospital doors that opened as he came.

Charlotte was waiting at Reception, her pale face lighting up when she saw him. She took his hand and led him toward the lifts. She was saying that Grizel was all right, and the depth of her concern showed in her speech, tangled with faulty consonants, legacy of that crash. They emerged into the bright lights and subdued sounds and a reek of air-freshener. There was a woman behind a counter, to whom Charlotte spoke—"My fa'er"—and who nodded them in. There was a corridor, shiny-floored; an open door, a room with a bed on which Grizel was sitting, in a hospital robe. Emily was there, but he saw Grizel, white, nervous, her eyes huge. She pushed herself up to standing—should she do that?—and they hugged in the sideways stance that had become so familiar, additionally hampered now by a monitor line attached to one of her fingers.

"Not yet," she said. "And I've stopped having contractions. Isn't it a swizz?"

Anticlimax carries its own shock. Bone, sitting beside Grizel on the bed, holding her hand, was dazed. All was yet to come, put off until an unknown time, impending. A curt soprano in the corridor said, "The husband's here," to which someone replied, "Oh good." Nothing happened. Grizel murmured her infamous little joke: "My hubby the bobby," and Bone had not the energy to protest.

"They say that even if it doesn't start up again they want to keep me here," Grizel said. "Emily and Charlotte are worn out. They must go home."

"Will your cats be all right if Cha comes home with me?" Emily asked. "I'd love it if she would."

"If there's any more thunder, The Bruce will be under some large piece of furniture," Grizel observed. She had her left hand on her abdomen as if testing for tremors.

"Ziggy will have been doing his dance. Thunderstorms get in his fur and he goes bonkers. Hope he hasn't broken anything." Charlotte articulated with care. "I fed them when Grizel was getting ready."

"I'll ring Mrs. Poulter to look in and feed them in the morning," Bone said. "You go with Emily, pet."

He stayed beside Grizel for a while after they had left—Charlotte unwilling to leave but so obviously tired that he was very grateful to Emily. Grizel got into bed and he saw her settled, with a pillow under the once more quiescent child. A nurse looked in and listened to its heartbeat. She handed the stethoscope to Bone, and he listened, enchanted, to the busy thrumming. When she had gone he said, "These miracles. And you're both all right."

"Of course we are. If it wasn't for Emily you'd not have been aware of these goings-on at all and you'd have been no worse off."

"Thank God for Emily." He smoothed down Grizel's short blond hair. "Grizel: another time, have me called."

"Cha told me about this dreadful thing happening. Poor Ken! He must be in a state. How is he taking it?"

"We've just been talking to him. Yes, he's upset."

"Upset!" She was scornful at what must be an understatement. Then, quick as ever, she caught the meaning of "We've been talking . . ." and said incredulously, "He *can't* be suspected."

"Take it from your hubby," he said. "Everybody is suspected. We've been talking to people and waiting for Ferdy Foster's evidence."

"Why does it seem more dreadful when someone young and beautiful dies? The old and plain deserve as much pity."

"They don't get it. Human nature." He settled into the chair, rested an arm on the bed to hold her hand, and said *"Try to get some rest."*

She looked at him, and made a hideous face.

He left some hours later. Grizel did not wake, nor did his arm at first. The ward sister, or whatever their title was these days, was reassuring about the baby. They would monitor mother and child, all was routine, nothing unusual. He made his way down the stairs, unreassured and rather sad.

Powers was sympathetic in an impersonal way, which Bone appreciated. Early light was creeping over the civic gardens as they drove, with a mist over the ponds. The roads were still puddled, trees dripped, the hedges glittered with wet. Bone ran the window down to get cold air on his face. He felt far too anxious to doze. Mist showed the course of a stream down a hillside meadow.

He woke as Powers drove across the cattle grid at the Herne Hall park entrance. After a moment the Hall came in sight, its eighteenth-century classical lines among the spreading lawns and oak trees soothing to Bone's eyes. A clutter of vans, a truck, and white cars with the blue top-knot did what they could to uglify the stable yard. Bone decanted himself stiffly, looked in at the coach house to tell Action that he was back, and strolled along the terrace to the open French door to meet a wonderful smell of coffee and to hear Locker's voice going over a report.

Locker looked up, the desk lamp lighting half his face, the dawn lighting the other. He saw at once that Bone had no news, and was puzzled. He asked, "How is Mrs. Bone?"

"They're keeping her in for obbo," Bone automatically used the professional slang for observation. "Nothing's immediately happening. I left this number with her." Bone had, in fact, written it on her arm near the wrist. Fredricks held out a mug of coffee and he smiled at her gratefully. "So, Steve, the news?"

"I've got statements here from the caterers and the house staff and guests. So far nothing shows up. . . ."

The door opened. PC Higg, looking the worse for wear, leaned in and said, "Mr. Palmerston'd like to see you, guv." Suddenly finding, halfway through, that the Super was with Locker, he divided the sentence between them. Bone nodded and crossed the room to take his earlier place on the arm of the easy chair. Coffee, harsh and strong, reassured him. Palmerston, spruce in gray linen jacket and black tie, smelled of soap. His thin gray hair looked darker than usual and Bone realized it was damp.

"You're up very early, Mr. Palmerston. Are you always about at this hour?"

"No, Mr. Bone. I woke remembering something I had forgotten about. I hope it's of no importance, but I thought it best to tell you immediately."

He was one of the few men Bone had ever met who could stand with their hands by their sides, without gesture, and look natural doing it.

"What was it, then?" Locker asked. Bone saw in his tired face the urge to say, "Spit it out, man."

"Yesterday afternoon there was a telephone call, from America, for Miss West. So unusual for such a thing to slip my memory, but there was a certain amount of confusion yesterday and I must suppose I was distracted. I apologize most sincerely."

"Don't disturb yourself about it." Bone thought "a certain amount of confusion" was a masterpiece of description of yesterday afternoon and evening. "Can you tell us more? What time did this call come?"

Palmerston thought. "It was just as the shower began. It cleared soon after. The gentleman said he was a producer and was speaking from Los Angeles. He particularly wished to speak to Miss West. I explained that she was not available since it was her wedding day, but he was very pressing and I said finally that I would see if Miss West would speak to him. I was on my way when Miss West came from her bedroom onto the landing and when I informed her of the call she said she would take it in her room. When I had ascertained that she was speaking on the line, I replaced the receiver downstairs."

"What was the caller's name?"

"I am ashamed to say I did not even ask for his name. I really cannot understand it."

"Did Miss West say anything about the call?"

"Not to me, sir. Indeed . . ." He stood looking thoughtfully past Locker into the parkland, "I do not recollect seeing Miss West after that time."

"Was Miss West about to come downstairs when the call came?"

"That was my impression, sir."

"Thank you, Mr. Palmerston. Any detail may be of importance."

"Thank you, sir. Is it too early to suggest breakfast?"

Not only Locker's weary face prompted Bone to say that it wasn't at all too early. He realized that he was ravenous.

"It would be more than welcome," he said. "Thank you."

What sort of breakfast would the hospital provide for Grizel? In a couple of hours Cha would be having breakfast amid Emily Playfair's cats.

When Palmerston had gone, Bone picked up a ballpoint and wrote on the back of his own hand *Mrs.*

Poulter. He had promised Cha to ring her to feed their own cats that morning. His responsibilities covered, he went to the garden door to look out. It was daylight already, a subdued very early daylight, the oaks like gray cut-outs against paler mist, dew on the small terrace plants and on the urns' geraniums, a light air scarcely stirring.

"What have we got?" he asked Locker.

Fredricks rubbed her eyes with both palms and arranged notes and the folded printouts.

"If the rain had just begun when that American call came for Miss West, it looks as though Palmerston was the last to see her. That leaves us with: how, and why, did she get down to the lake?"

"She got down there with no one seeing her, or no one who admits to seeing her. If she talked to someone there it suggests an agreed meeting—that she went there to talk to them."

Locker said, "It may be an outside possibility, but could the call from Los Angeles have arranged for her to meet someone? It's what you call fantasy country, sir, but she seems to have disappeared right after it."

"Entertain all possibilities," Bone replied. "That one is particularly far-fetched."

"Then we've got Motive," Locker said. "Dwight Schlumberger wanted to marry her again. Had he any foundation for thinking she would? He seems to have arranged all the business yesterday with a view to it being him who'd marry her."

"He then finds she's already legally married to Cryer. He strikes me as being the type who'd get on quietly with his own business until she was free to marry once more; but yet . . ."

"And Ken Cryer," Locker was saying. "He couldn't make up his mind if he could stand it."

There was a silence. Fredricks cleared her throat and said, "The children. They were so near in the boathouse. They both had the same motive as their parents, and both had their own personal reasons for dislike. And, well, children aren't rational."

Bone experienced a sense of distaste or recoil. There was a silence. He said, "A matter of degree, of course. Murder is irrational; children are just less rational than adults on the whole. Their view of the world can be—less informed? I don't know. Yes, there's the children."

Chapter
34

········

"Would they have the strength to drown her?"

"Combined, they might . . . Neither of them is puny, come to think of it. *I'm* irrational in disliking the thought." But he disliked it strongly. True, he was far too experienced to be gullible about the innocence of children or about their inefficiency at deception. There were, too, famous recent cases of children killing, cases that no one had wanted to believe in, cases in which children had united to kill. Simply, he hoped that his reading of Jem was correct—that Jem would have been deeply and unconcealably disturbed if he had been party to Zephyr's death. Bone would not have gone bail for Treasure yet he balked at the idea that she could have killed her mother.

"They were drunk," Locker remarked.

"It can't be ruled out."

A draft once more hit his face as the inner door opened. Higg admitted Palmerston with a trolley. There was a smell of bacon. There was a rich and wicked smell of fried bread. Bone, salivating like Pavlov's dog, came in and shut the garden door.

"That's very welcome indeed," he said. As he drew a

chair to the desk he looked at his watch. Too early y⟨
to ring Mrs. Poulter, but hospitals wake at unconscion⟨
ble hours. Soon he could check on Grizel.

A little later, at a more conventional breakfast tim⟨
Kelly was enjoying a "Full English" in the pub's loung⟨
The grille was down over the bar, giving a somewh⟨
dour appearance to that end of the room, but she w⟨
in a sunlit window bay overlooking a brick-paved ya⟨
with tubs of little bushes and a prostrate sleeping Labr⟨
dor. She was aware all of a sudden that she was smilin⟨
And why not, indeed? Things had turned out so we⟨
The morning paper lay on the table by the teapot: "N⟨
Wed But Dead—Cryer's Bride Drowns." Ken, incred⟨
bly, was free. This was a nice place she had found la⟨
night; she would stay longer. While she was at Her⟨
Hall she had found Ken's private number from the litt⟨
book by the telephone.

She speared a slice of fried potato, loaded it wi⟨
bacon, fried tomato and sausage, and opened h⟨
mouth wide.

The watcher from the woods, eating a stale sandwi⟨
in his car parked at the top of the long and windin⟨
entrance drive to a House For Sale, listened to the radi⟨
Zephyr West, star of TV, on the day she was to marr⟨
Ken Cryer the rock scar, had been found drowned . .⟨
He listened, not moving.

At the Manor, Ken had not slept. He had declin⟨
breakfast, only looking in on the dining room, findin⟨
Jem picking at scrambled egg, telling him he must ea⟨
and then going out to walk the grounds.

Edwina Marsh came into the dining room. This mor⟨
ing she wore a long Chinese silk shirt in a green th⟨
did nothing for her pallor. She poured herself tea, an⟨
leaned an arm on the table and seemed mesmerized b⟨
the steam from her cup drifting lazily up in the sunligh⟨

"You all right?" Jem inquired.

"Mm-hm. Oh yes. It's so unbelievable . . ."

"I think I should be feeling much better about it tha⟨

I do." He put the plate of egg firmly away from him and went on, "She was awful. I mean seriously awful. I suppose I shouldn't say so now. She just took Dad over. I'd never ever have thought he'd be like that after she tried to kill me over the dress. He said she didn't mean it. Didn't mean it! I was *there,* I knew she meant it all right. And now she's dead and I'm not sorry. I'm just not at all sorry. I'm glad. I feel good about it. I don't care."

Edwina's round, china-doll face showed strain. She picked up the mail and shuffled through it and put it down. "I've had to take the phone out. If you want to make a call, plug it in. The vultures are on the line. Ken's line in his studio is all right but it's only a matter of time before someone gets hold of that number too."

"Shit. Treasure might call."

"They've got Ken's studio number at Herne Hall. She might ring that. I'll field it and call you."

"It's dodgy with Trez. I mean, it's her mother. Was. Here am I thinking—whoever did it needs a medal—"

"Whoever . . . ? Jem—isn't it being taken as an accident?"

Jem hesitated. "Trez didn't think so last night."

Edwina had gone even paler. She got up, took the pile of letters and said, "I'll be in my office."

Treasure and her grandmother were busy with croissants, apricot jam, and coffee. Mrs. West ate and drank with a deliberate determination. Treasure, walking about, equally determined to ignore headache and queasiness, scattered pastry crumbs over the carpet, her T-shirt and jeans. They did not talk. Mrs. West could not, and Treasure was lost in disturbed thoughts. A loud clattering roar disturbed their quiet, and Treasure went to the window and stared upward. Her eyes followed the helicopter. She saw its open side and the long snout of the telephoto lens. She came and sat down. She put her hands between her knees and hunched her shoulders.

"Is it the police?"

"No. It's circling the lake. And police ones say "Police" on the side. Someone was up by the gazebo first thing with a camera. Horrible beasts. Don't go near windows, Gran."

"No," said Mrs. West. "I don't think I shall. It's a pity we haven't those security men still here, if the house is going to be under siege."

"The police are still here."

"They can't keep helicopters away. . . . I want Palmerston to have the day off, but I don't know if the girl, what's her name—"

"Doreen."

"If she's here or not."

Treasure shrugged. "It's no good him having the day off, he can't go anywhere because of the cameras and things and anyway he wouldn't do it. I'll take the breakfast trolley and save him coming for it."

"You're a kind, thoughtful girl, Treasure."

Treasure's grimace was made more hideous by the metalware on her teeth. "You don't know what I'm really like, Gran."

In the hall she met her father, nursing his right hand. "I just socked a reporter. What's the law here, do you know? Can he sue me?"

"I bet he can. Why'd you do it?"

"I ordered him off—this is private property and he knew it. You know what he said?"

"He said you couldn't make him."

"He said, 'Drop dead, pops.' " Schlumberger cuddled his hand. "Stop by my room on your way back, honey. I need something on this."

"Run cold water on it in the sink," she advised, and wheeled the trolley on. After a few paces she stopped, looked round and said, "Great work, pops."

Something in her face made him stride after her and take her by the shoulder. She turned abruptly toward him, flung her arms round him and, burying her face on his chest, burst into painful, all but silent sobs. His arms came round her in turn and he held her, his head bent over hers, muttering, "Honey."

Palmerston, coming to fetch the trolley, withdrew

again into the staff quarters and softly shut the door. In the quiet, the telephone could be heard in the room the police were using.

Fredricks swung round from the VDU and answered it. She put it on hold and said, "It's about the man in the quarry—the Cryer double. A Mr. and Mrs. Wilson are at HQ. They've identified him as their son."

Chapter
35

• • • • • • • • •

Bone left the Zephyr West inquiry in Locker's hands. Mrs. West had sent her maid to say she could see the police when they should want her.

Bone, going back through the morning sunlight, having phoned Mrs. Poulter and the hospital, dozed off in the car and dreamt confusedly of the lake, with the wedding party waiting and then, as dreams manage it, empty chairs and Ken's look-alike lying on the shore. As is the way with dreams, too, neither lake nor body were as he had seen them but he recognized them as what he had seen. He woke, heavy-eyed, as the car drew up at the Station.

He washed, and put on the fresh shirt he kept in his desk, and went to find the Wilsons. They sat over empty teacups and plates and sandwich wrappers in the interview room that had been decorated for the bereaved, for victims, and children; the yellow painted walls with a flowery frieze, the watercolors of indeterminate countryside, looked faded. The chairs' upholstered backs and seats were frayed and stained, the carpet worn bare in patches. An enterprise in obedience to a directive about responding to public needs had foundered for lack of funds.

Mr. Wilson was tall, bony, balding a little, his wife thin, in a denim skirt and a cotton sweater, soft, blue, looking new. She was gray-haired with a dutch-boy cut too young for the color, and pale blue eyes. They both looked awkward, sad, bewildered and strained.

"I'm sorry you had to wait," Bone said; introduced himself, shook hands and sat facing them as they took their places again. "This is distressing for you. Do you feel able to answer a few of our questions? It will be a great help to us."

It was almost as much a formula as the statement of arrest. Mrs. Wilson's hands clasped a tissue on the table before her, though she did not seem to have been weeping. Her husband ran fingers inside his collar to ease it—collar and tie not often worn, Bone thought, but donned for this crisis. Bone had been briefed by the police-woman who had been looking after the Wilsons: "You saw the television picture—?"

"I said, 'That's Alan. It's Alan.' I said that right away."

"We couldn't be sure. The picture didn't look right."

Getting a photograph of a dead face to look as it might have looked in life was a cheerless skill. Rick Sheffield, their photo expert, had done wonders but no one could deny that it didn't look right.

"But it's Alan. They let us see him."

Mr. Wilson said, "We can't tell you what he'd be doing here. We didn't see a lot of him, not lately."

"We don't even know where he was living. He was with a girlfriend for a while, but they didn't get on."

"We don't know that, love," Mr. Wilson objected diffidently. "He didn't say so."

"I could tell. We never met her. Alan would never give us a phone number or an address where he was staying."

"I said to him, it's not fair on your mother, she worries."

"It's not as if he was strong."

Bone recalled Ferdy Foster's mention of "muscle wastage." He said, "He'd been ill."

"Yes. How did you know? He was ill in bed for a long time when he was a boy—"

"In his teens," said Mr. Wilson, "but he wasn't ever what you'd call tough."

"He had a bad chest when he was little. I used to have a night-light burning under a holder of balsam. He took up singing for his chest. That was at the convalescent home. He had a lovely voice."

"Spoiled it with all the pop singing, though."

"He wanted to be a pop singer. We bought him a guitar, he really wanted to play a guitar."

"If he'd stuck at it he might have got somewhere."

"That's not quite fair. You couldn't stand him practicing—Jack couldn't stand him practicing. I said, how is he to learn?"

Wilson sighed. "It's all water under the bridge, now. It might've been easier for him if he hadn't looked like that Cryer. People only wanted him to play Cryer songs. When he was in bed ill, he used to write songs, not bad some of them. I saw on a fly-poster he was singing at a pub gig over in Battersea, I saw the name he used, so I went there. I didn't tell him, I knew he wouldn't like it, so I stayed at the back. And he did Cryer's songs, nothing but Cryer's songs. I was so disappointed."

"Jack really was disappointed."

There was a little silence. Bone was about to inquire as to Alan Wilson's friends, when Mrs. Wilson said tentatively, "What—what actually—what happened? We saw his picture on the South East news—they said he had been mistaken for Ken Cryer."

"A farmer found him in an old marlpit—a quarry. Alan seems to have strayed through a broken fence and fallen into the quarry."

"But how did he come to be there?"

"It seems he'd hired a car."

"Hired a car!" She was impressed by this. Her husband went more to the point.

"Why there, though? I mean, out in the middle of the country? Why did he come down to Kent?"

Bone said, "We don't know. But it's not far from Ken Cryer's house. At first he was taken for Cryer."

"Oh, he was always being taken for him." She was proud of this. "He could look really like him."

"But why walk over a fence? Was it nighttime?"

This had haunted Bone: the strange figure, got up in Ken's gear, wandering to the brink of that pit full of garbage, carrying the gun.

"He may have been confused. He'd been taking painkillers."

"Painkillers!" they both exclaimed. She pursued it. "He did get pains in his legs and his back," but she sounded doubtful, as if this did not account for "confused."

"We don't yet know enough," Bone said.

"Did he come to see Ken Cryer?"

"Cryer doesn't know anything about him, Mr. Wilson."

"You'd think he'd know about someone so like him." Mr. Wilson was piqued.

"There are quite a few people who look like the famous. Cryer knew he had 'doubles' who imitated him at parties or entertainments. There's a TV show which features doubles—of Presley or Marilyn Monroe or Sting, anyone well-known."

Jack Wilson's mouth had tightened. Oddly, at this moment Bone saw a likeness to Ken. He turned impatiently in his chair as if he would have got up, and broke out with, "Just one of a bloody mob of doubles!"

"Jack—"

"I know, I know! Sure, but he could have been . . . He was clever, you'd think he could have got somewhere, but he'd all sorts of stupid ideas in his head. Mother found a whole pile of scrapbooks—"

"I wish I hadn't looked! The one I looked at was full

of pictures and things cut from magazines and papers, it was all set out as if it was a real book, so neatly. But he found me looking, you see, and after that he moved out into a bed-sitter although I promised him . . ."

"He wouldn't be turned from it."

"What was the scrapbook about?"

"There was a picture of a big concert, I remember, and a band, quite a lot of pictures of that, and Ken Cryer."

Jack Wilson said bitterly, "He could have done his own songs! He could have been—you know how you expect—we expected—"

She put her hand on his, in a curiously stiff way, as if she were unaccustomed to such a gesture.

Bone thought to Grizel, of his unknown child, of his own tentative expectations. There was a pause. Jack Wilson said, "Sorry. I'm sorry," to his wife.

Bone had to go on.

"Did Alan ever say to you that he had a gun?"

"He belonged to a gun club at one time, as soon as he was old enough. I suppose he went on with that, because he was quite a shot. I daresay he was sorry when they shut the clubs down."

"He won a junior trophy, Jack, remember—" She turned to Bone. "He won a junior trophy."

Bone said, "You don't know where he could have got a gun."

They looked at each other, baffled.

"We don't know what he was doing recently. We don't know his friends. We didn't even know his girl-friend's name. He never brought anyone to see us when he came."

"Not that he came that often."

"Did he seem depressed at any time?"

"He never seemed anything else."

"Jack!"

"We didn't know what he was doing. He wasn't happy about his life but he wouldn't talk about it. Not a word. I said to him: if you've got in with the wrong crowd, we'll do all we can for you. But he laughed and said not to worry. And after all what was he in with? A crowd of pretense celebrities living off other people's backs. I said: you've got a good education, what are you doing with it?"

"He did miss a lot of school, but he had a tutor. The council sent tutors. He was bright, they said so. They told us he was a bright boy."

"Bloody waste, that's what . . . So he had a gun? What kind was it?"

"A rifle. Quite a high-powered thing."

"But he didn't kill himself!" She started half up from her chair at this terrible thought.

"No, he didn't kill himself." Bone's denial was specious, in view of the paracetomol, but it was truthful enough. She accepted it. Jack Wilson leaned his forearms on the table and looked at Bone.

"What did kill him?"

Mrs. Wilson chided softly, "The fall, Jack. He said it was the fall."

"Did he hit his head, then?"

"He fell on some debris that was lying there. We haven't got the full pathology report." And if Bone wimped out about the deep injury to the chest it's on account of these two sad people.

"The sergeant downstairs said we could arrange the—the funeral after the coroner's inquest."

"We'll let you know about that, about where it's to be and so on."

"Thank you. You've been really kind." Mrs. Wilson took her handbag from her lap and put it on the table, a signal of departure. "If that's all you wanted to know, do you think we could see him again for just a minute?"

Bone turned to Vigo, mute all this time beside the door.

"I'll go and see, sir," she said, and vanished.

"Then we want to go home." Mrs. Wilson got to her feet.

"Do you have your own transport?"

"We came in my van," Jack Wilson said. "I'm a carpenter."

"Take it slowly on the way back," Bone said.

"Jack's a careful driver!"

"It can be difficult to concentrate when you have something weighing on your mind."

They stood, waiting for Vigo, uncertain. Jack Wilson put a hand out to touch his wife's back, tentatively as if he too had forgotten how to make such a gesture.

"If you should come across any information at all about what Alan was doing or about any of his associates, you will let us know."

"We've been out of touch with him," Mrs. Wilson said.

"Other way round. He was the one out of touch. I never wanted to be out of touch. It wasn't our doing."

"What name," Bone belatedly asked, "did he use professionally?"

"Grant, he called himself. Alan Grant. Why didn't he sing his own songs? They were as good as Cryer's any day. And I'd like to know why he didn't use his own name."

Bone produced a soothing scrap of knowledge Charlotte had once vouchsafed about stage names. "A single syllable is bolder on the posters. It can be printed larger. I daresay that was his reason."

Wilson answered with a grunt. Vigo came in at this moment. They could see their son once more. Bone inferred that the young man's body was still in its carefully arranged presentation room and not in its drawer in the morgue.

"You make sure Mr. and Mrs. Wilson have our number, Vigo."

"Sir."

They were gone.

Bone read over the notes he had taken, added "Grant" and brooded. He was haunted by the image of Jack Wilson, standing incognito in the crowd at the pub gig, in the shadows amid the noise, listening disappointed to his son.

Chapter

36

·········

He rang Fredricks with the name of Alan Wilson or Grant. "Pass this on to whoever's doing the trawl through look-alike agencies."

"It's Harker, sir. Will do."

"I'll be here doing triage on the paperwork; there may be urgencies in the middle of all the bumf."

He rang the hospital. Grizel was comfortable, they said. Labor had not recommenced. Bone reflected on the difference between medical ideas of comfort and those of the lay public. He very much doubted that a woman in the latest stage of pregnancy, having had a foretaste of labor and with the prospect of it before her, would call her condition comfortable. It was, he thought, an inept term for No Immediate Crisis.

He had to cope with a phone call from the Chief, who had a curious conviction that by demanding results in a loud voice he helped to obtain them. He had to tick off Sergeant Harris (known, it appeared, as Harass among the women) for out-of-line comments and suggestions. Bone had been called to account for sexism by Charlotte's mother years before; it had surprised him, believing as he did in the equality of the sexes, to find

213

how innate, how casual, his assumptions were. He still, unregenerately, thought that women overreacted to male teasing, but all the same he gave Harris a gypsy's warning.

Having dealt with other urgencies he set off for Herne Hall through a sudden rainstorm. The police at the gates made way for his car through the press of the Press; a thousand grasshoppers stridulated as the cameras focused on him and lights blazed. Bone promised a press conference during the morning and, watching for the pleasant view of Herne Hall to appear as his car followed the drive, wondered what there would be to tell.

Locker had finished the search of Zephyr's rooms, at the Manor and here—there was a box of fan letters but no other correspondence, people used phones and faxes now. There was jewelry, real and faux thrown together in a drawer, surprisingly until Miss Alexander—Lexie—explained Zephyr's theory that a thief would believe it all fake and leave it alone.

Zephyr's studio rang to say they were sending a PR man, "Which," as Locker said, "we could well do without."

Zephyr's clothes and makeup had been looked over and an array of pharmaceuticals had gone for examination by Forensic. The pathologist was conducting the postmortem, which Locker was setting out to attend, in an hour's time. "He wasn't pleased," Locker reported. "He doesn't see why a minor media star should jump the line."

Bone was visited by a macabre vision of Zephyr in her body bag, as in a sack race, jumping ahead of a line of similar corpses. He remarked, "I can hear Ferdy Foster saying that. Has anyone given out word that the death may not be an accident?"

"Not that I've heard. All personnel have been warned, and the media are calling it a mystery still."

"When are you taking your rest time?"

"After the postmortem, sir."

214

"Which will be in the P.M." Bone trotted out the perennial pun and Locker obligingly groaned.

"Mrs. Stenn-Boughton has sent photographs of the guests and so on—all sorts of roughs in case anything's useful. There were fan letters in Miss West's room, not very many considering, but I suppose most of her fans are in the States."

"That's where the studio's PR man will come in useful."

"Palmerston said there was a visit from the head of a fan club two days ago. He thought Miss West must have given her an invitation, because she was here last night."

"Has that phone call from the American producer been traced?"

"No, sir; and Miss West's studio says her producer didn't ring. I'm waiting for word from Telecom on the call trace."

"Don't hold your breath," Bone advised. "They'll have to sift through thousands of numbers."

"Their computers should have shown it up but they say they've no record of an overseas call to this number yesterday."

"Perhaps this producer said if she'd waited he'd have married her himself and given her the star part in his next film. In any case, whatever he said could hardly have made Zephyr rush to the lake, hit her head and hurl herself in."

"We're left with the theory that she went there to meet someone she knew."

Bone, still avoiding the tempting armchair, propped his shoulders on the gray paneling. He felt detached, drawn out for lack of sleep. The little room, with its charming Regency fireplace and rococo sconces, oppressed him. "Dwight Schlumberger, Ken Cryer, Treasure, for starters."

"Edwina Marsh," said Fredricks. She turned pages in her notebook and read out, "Statement of Mel Rees, Jem's minder: 'None of us was in favor of the lady much, on account of she was high-handed and that vicious temper. We all thought Ken might have taken her going for Jem more seriously, Edwina thought she could have killed him. And I'd say Zephyr wouldn't stand having Edwina around much, after they was married.' "

Bone hesitated, was aware of his reluctance, and spoke. "I had an impression that Edwina Marsh and Cryer were intimate." *Intimate,* he thought. The official term saved him from saying they were lovers. "I'm interested to know what Ferdy makes of the marks on Zephyr West's neck. If they're not strangulation, we're left with the abrasions to the head that Dr. Smethurst found on his first examination by the lake."

"If she hit her head really hard and stunned herself and reeled into the water . . ."

"Hit the *back* of her head? She'd have to be walking backwards for Christmas. Daylight search this morning— has any sign been found on the raft? Shreds of that gauze hood? If she fell backwards there'd be traces."

Locker pursed his lips. "Or she was hit by someone."

"That's why we must keep the option open on Intent To Kill. Let's see the team in case of info or ideas. We have to do a press conference."

"We've not got anything to tell them, sir."

"I do a good line of noncommittal obfuscation," Bone said.

Still there was no news from the hospital. Grizel lying there on the pillow, his phone number on her hand, haunted Bone's mind. Her short blond crop had been tousled, making her look more than usually unfledged.

He asked Pat Fredricks to ring Emily Playfair, and to relay the word that Mrs. Poulter had undertaken cat care until further notice. Fredricks let herself into the team conference late and nodded to him. Charlotte was all right.

The team had little to say.

"The big question is, why did she go down to the lake? She wouldn't go alone to rehearse the ceremony, and we are told she wouldn't be at all likely to go down

216

to check arrangements for herself—completely uncharacteristic. Granted, people do what is uncharacteristic."

The coach house was quite unlike Bone's memory of
it when the Hernes had lived here. It had matting on
the bricks, the walls and barrel vaults of the ceiling were
covered in coral colorwash. An exercise bike had been
moved out of the way; a trapeze was looped back against
the wall. Bone could not bring himself to imagine Mrs.
West using these, and so perhaps they were for Treasure;
then it came to him that Dwight could well be given to
workouts. Or, it came to him happily, Palmerston.

"Cryer thinks she may have been playing games—because he got cold feet and took off for parts North."

There was a short silence. Finally Shona Wilkinson
remarked, "No one can disprove it."

"The fact is that her being down by the lake at all
seems to surprise everybody—the dress designer, Mrs.
West's maid Lexie who'd been helping Zephyr to get
ready, Mrs. West herself, the butler, her husbands, her
daughter."

"*Someone* can't be surprised: whoever got her to go
there. If she didn't simply take a fancy to rehearse her
show, someone lured her there. To state the obvious."

"There's no threats to her among the fan letters. A
few of them don't like her getting married but they're
not violent."

"Ken Cryer's had threats," Bone said, "but they
threaten him, not her. They don't even hint at removing
his bride."

"Is that connected with the dead ringer in the quarry
with the gun, sir?"

"Alan Wilson alias Alan Grant; it's possible." Bone
reflected that if Alan Wilson had intended to kill Ken,
then he'd taken identifying with him a bit far. "We're
looking at it. Has no one come up with anything useful?" He glanced at the Press Officer, who was indeed
photogenic, being tall, dark and very pretty. "Jean, we're
in for a hell of a press call at this rate. Are we calling
it accidental?"

Over at the Manor, the media outside the gates were suffering their occupational boredom. They had watched the delivery of newspapers and post and had heard it collected by minders or staff from the mailbox inside the gates; they had made a half joking effort to bribe the driver of a delivery van—"Bindle of Saxhurst" the writing on its side proclaimed in flourishing cursive—to smuggle a photographer in with the groceries; and they had been driven back to their cars by sudden rain. There they sat morosely, eating buns and pies bought at the village bakery, listening to their car radios, and watching their windshield blur. No pulse rates were raised by the sight of a gardener in a dingy beige rain jacket with the storm flap fastened and the hood drawstring drawn up round the face like a polar explorer not prepared to yield an inch to the cold. There was rain on his back, and he rode an elderly bicycle, a wooden box crammed with plants battered by the rain corded to the carrier, giving instant job identification. No one stopped chewing to get out in the rain to question him. The chances of his being Ken Cryer's sole confidant over his wife's death were not rated very high. One of the reporters said feelingly that if you got to be a millionaire it meant you didn't have to mow the lawns any more. The gates opened and the man went in.

Mowing lawns was evidently out of the question in this weather and no one was surprised when the gardener, after less than twenty minutes, still with his hood drawn up and his head down against the rain now driving against him, pedaled vigorously out of the gates as if glad to be going home. Barkworth of the *Ray* cursed as he dropped the major half of his pie on the car floor, giving it an instant fur coat.

"Wonder if he gets a full morning's pay for that?" He watched as the Manor gates swung relentlessly shut, scattering their own extra shower from every surface. If Ken Cryer were halfway decent he'd have all the Press into the dry and give them hot coffee and even a juicy interview.

Ken Cryer, as it happened, was halfway to the village. No one on the way recognized him except an old biddy in a plastic hood, dragging a tartan shopping trolley over the Council's new, specially designed uneven pavement. He had once given her an autographed album for a raffle at a summer fete and she still thought of him as "that nice man," forgiving him his songs as a harmless eccentricity. Ten minutes later two others recognized him simultaneously.

It was some time since Ken had been on a bicycle. He was finding it tiring and he was aware of being sore. Exhilaration at getting free of the Manor and the jailers at the gate had worn off. Here he was on the outskirts of Saxhurst and ready to rest, and the man he had thought of visiting lived on the far side of the village, up the hill. Seeing Emily Playfair wave to him and make hospitable gestures toward her door, where she stood in her garden with a bouquet of kittens on one arm, he braked thankfully and swerved toward the white picket gate in the hedge.

It was a narrow lane with barely room for two cars to pass, but the small yellow Fiat just ahead stopped abruptly in the middle of the road, making no attempt to park, even up on the curb—though Emily and her neighbors waged war on those who did; it left no room for prams or wheelchairs. But only one thought was in Kelly's mind as she struggled to open the car door and squirm out.

Ken had come looking for her and she had nearly missed him.

Chapter
37
·········

Emily was delighted to see Ken, the strong features framed by that incongruous hood. She guessed that a man more used to limos twenty feet long must be hard-driven to take to this disguise. She had seen the papers—Lady in the Lake. Pop Star's Bride Drowns. Why Did She Die?—and it was hardly safe for the poor man to show his face abroad. He must be in dire need of hot coffee, and some of the little biscuits she had baked that morning. She beamed at him as he lifted the bike up the brick steps, through the gate, and leaned it against the inside of the hedge. Skywalker and his sister Nan Tucket, borne outdoors for an airing as the rain stopped, stared over her arm as Ken came up the path.

They only started to struggle as a stranger came into view. Emily could see the roof of the yellow Fiat in the road and now here was a large young woman in caramel clinging trousers and tunic whom Emily recognized at once bursting through the gate and charging up the path. Ken, smiling and about to speak, had nearly reached Emily when he saw her astonished gaze go past him, and turned.

"I'm here, Ken! You found me!" The girl held her

arms wide as she came and Ken, panicking, sidestepped. The grass was wet, the brick path slippery. Kelly's weight landed enthusiastically against him and they fell, Kelly on top.

Emily, trying to control her armful of kittens—for the lane was dangerous—watched helplessly as Kelly swiftly pulled the hood's drawstring free and covered Ken's face with kisses, babbling, "You don't have to hide, my darling. The secret is safe with me, safe forever . . . Nothing stands in our way."

Ken, half winded, his arms pinned beneath, tried to escape, wriggling like any kitten, and in the end it was the kittens who saved him. Emily, stooping to pull at Kelly's arm, could no longer contain them, Skywalker landed on Kelly's back, Nan Tucket on her hair which had shed one barrette and presented an interesting playground.

Kelly, with Skywalker promenading her spine and, as he slid on the silky tunic, taking hold, squealed and would have sat back on her heels but that Nan Tucket had found the barrette glittering through the swathe of hair on the grass and nailed it down. Ken took his chance, squirmed free of the shrieking, swiping Kelly, rolled away and sprang to his feet.

Emily did not miss her chance either. Nimbly and ruthlessly scooping up both kittens, Nan Tucket with a tuft of Kelly's hair and provoking fresh screams, she pushed open her front door and jerked her head at Ken who was through it like a shot. Once they were both inside Emily slammed the door shut just as Kelly managed to get up, muddied and by now crying.

"She can't get in, can she?"

Emily heard Ken's desperation, and made soothing noises as she decanted the kittens onto the floor and watched them scamper off in search of siblings to persecute.

"No, no, there's no way she can get in. The front windows are always shut because of the traffic in the lane. A kitten was run over last summer. Do you know

221

her well?" She led Ken into the sitting room, where
Arletty had jumped to the sill beside Makepeace and
now both cats, as though trained in a chorus line, ducked
together and elongated their necks to peer sideways at
the front door.

"Know her well? I don't know her at all but, my God,
she seems to think she's my wife! She's totally lost it.
She did this before—"

Kelly had found the letter box and was shouting
through it.

"Ken! Darling, you don't have to worry! Everything
is all right now, we're safe!"

"Safe!" Ken looked round the room as if he feared
Kelly could still infiltrate, perhaps down the chimney like
Father Christmas. "How the hell am I going to get
away?"

"There's a back door from the kitchen," offered
Emily, "and a lane beyond the garden, but your bicycle's
in the front and you won't have a hope of getting it
before she gets you. She has a car, too, which gives her
an advantage."

This opinion was not entirely justified. In addition to
renewed battering at the door, which greatly offended
the cats, there now came a persistent hooting from a car
in the lane. Someone had had the misfortune to come
across the abandoned yellow Fiat and that person didn't
sound pleased.

Ken had an idea. With a hasty, "May I?" he gestured
at the phone and, striding to its corner on the desk, he
began to press buttons. At this moment Kelly appeared
at the window, hands splayed, face pressed to the glass
in an effort to cut out reflections and see inside. Arletty
deserted the sill on the instant. Makepeace blinked.

"My petunias!" Emily cried indignantly. "She's treading on my petunias!"

Not for long, though. The fanfare in the road had
ceased and, suddenly, Kelly was snatched back from the
window to the sound of shouting.

"It's General Snell!" Emily hugged herself. "He'll give her what for."

The what for provided by the General was so loud that even Ken on the telephone could hear some of the words. Kelly was being arraigned at military decibels for disgraceful selfishness, for hogging the road like—here the General was lost for a simile and, taking in Kelly's weight, ended unforgivably, "like a *hog.*" She was to come and remove her car at once or he would fetch the police.

It might have been the porcine comparison that, so to speak, tipped the scale. Kelly, deprived, frustrated, dragged over the petunias by an angry stranger whose vibrating white mustache resembled frosting on the fire of his face, snapped. She had no handbag to swing, but she put beef into her punch. The General was waving his arms, a poor stance for steady balance. He went down like a felled tree.

Emily, going to the window to look out over the attentive head of Makepeace, saw once more a body on her lawn. Kelly, beyond, had dashed open the gate and disappeared into her car. Perhaps she thought it wise, after two assaults and Saxhurst's most striking example of road rage to date, to avoid the scene. General Snell had managed to get onto all fours, head raised like some uncouth dog about to bark, when the Fiat coughed into action and buzzed off up the lane. Emily had half expected the crazed fan to smash the General's windshield as she made for her car.

Emily's instinct was to run out and help the General, ply him with tea, and calm him down if it could be done; her first duty was to the guest she already had, whose privacy must be respected. Although General Snell was wholly unlikely to rush to any reporters with the story, Emily felt sure Ken was not up to meeting a military man on the boil. Moreover the General was insatiably inquisitive and a terrible gossip. He would want to know why a large, pretty, violent young woman had abandoned her car in the middle of the lane, come to dance on Emily's petunias, and land a punishing blow on one who remonstrated.

Ken, who might well be aware that a popular view of his wife's death involved a passionate quarrel with him on the borders of the romantic lake, did not deserve the General. As she tiptoed up the three steps to the kitchen and beckoned Ken to follow her, they heard the General apply himself, more circumspectly than Kelly, to the knocker.

"What a *bloody* day," breathed Ken, accepting the biscuit Emily pressed into his hand from the baking tray above the cooker. "I rang Joe to fetch me. He says he knows the track at the top of your garden." The knocker gained in force, and he drew back against the roller towel on the wall. "Hasn't she gone yet?"

Emily began to explain, though she herself would have been glad of an explanation. She did wonder what was the secret supposed to be safe with Ken's demented fan. Generals were not alone in their curiosity.

Chapter
38
....

"Superintendent Cottard from Oxford on the line for you, sir."

Bone took up the phone and pressed the button that connected him. Vigo ceased to fiddle with the printout they had been discussing—guest lists—and sat with her narrow hands obscuring what she pretended to read, alert, hopeful of a lead. Amazingly, it was.

Bone had done Colin Cottard a favor as long as three years ago, but here it was in return.

"Your Lady in the Lake, Robert. The whisper says you're looking for one who may have dunked her."

"I am."

"It may be of use to you to know we've a bloke on license who's gone missing, not reported to his probation officer for seven days."

Bone put *Oxford* and *on license* together with Mrs. West's story, and his hand tightened on the receiver. All he said was, "This could be of use?" Locker raised his head.

"Bloke that's missing had been doing a stretch for manslaughter. Broke the neck belonging to the sister of your Lady in the Lake some years back. Not a lucky family." Colin Cottard laughed heartily. "But the nub of the matter is that your film star bride was a witness to the sister's death. I thought at the time there was something between her and the killer, but as it happens, what she said to the police who arrived at the scene clinched the sentencing although he pleaded guilty."

Bone was silent a moment. He thought of the photographs in Mrs. West's room, the girl he had taken for Zephyr until he looked closer. He put warmth into his voice as he answered. "Could be very useful; very useful indeed, Colin. Can you have the details faxed to me?"

"My pleasure. And if you find our wandering boy, we'd like him back."

"You'll be the first to know."

Bone put the phone down and Vigo leaned forward. "Useful, sir?"

"Another candidate for the removal of Zephyr West. And," he added thoughtfully, with pity, "about the only person who can tell us about him may well be Mrs. West."

She had not been well. Bone was scarcely surprised to hear it, but she insisted that she was well enough to see him.

Herne Hall, as Powers drove him up to the gates, was still under siege. Hopeful reporters at the gate brightened at the sight of him and clustered forward to shout, "Any news, Super?" He disliked being recognized but he was fair game now he had appeared on the lunchtime news for his five seconds of sound bite, after Zephyr's face and form had been presented in various clips from the American TV series shown over here. Cha had missed this, but her friend Grue had phoned her to say that her father had said nothing as nicely as possible.

He said more of the same now, while disappointed cameras took him doing it. He would, he lied, keep them fully informed; he got back in the car and Powers drove him on across the parkland. In the distance he caught the yellow flicker of police tapes cordoning off the lake.

226

He had read somewhere—was it in Bill Bryson?—of a roadside notice in the States: "Get your Dead Skunk here." For the media at the park gates it was "Get your Dead Bride here." They would hang on until they could have the murderer as a bonus.

Palmerston had the front door open and stood, gravely welcoming, in the shadow of the columned porch. With all Nature's usual failure to sympathize with events, it had become a particularly fine day and the geraniums spilling from the stone urns either side of the porch shone as brilliantly as splashes of blood. Palmerston withdrew into the hall, where the light made him look sepulchral and Bone, hearing his own footsteps on the stone and the hollow slam of the car door behind him, felt he was walking into a nightmare. How to speak to a woman whose two children had both been killed?

He must keep what he did say short and to the point. Lexie shut her mouth hard and shook her head when he asked how Mrs. West was. She might have been about to tell him something when Mrs. West called from the downstairs sitting room where he had first met her, in a voice husky but not feeble.

"Is that Mr. Bone? Do come in."

He had expected her to be in her bedroom, resting, but she had opted for coming down. She sat, as before, in her wheelchair. The sleek gray bob was immaculately groomed, the face pale but subtly made up in the way that, as Grizel had once explained to Bone, deceives one that the effect is wholly natural. Her dress this time was deep indigo blue, not black, as though she refused mourning, refused the convention that claimed sympathy. As Bone came toward her, she smiled and extended a hand on which the square-cut diamond slewed on a thin finger.

"How can I help you? Or have you come with news? Lexie, ask Palmerston if we can have some coffee. Now, sit down, Mr. Bone. I must tell you that if you want to talk to my granddaughter, she is in bed with a headache and I don't think she should be disturbed."

"I'm sorry to hear that," but headaches, Bone told himself, don't last forever; Treasure had questions to answer. "But I've in fact come to tell you something and ask you something."

He was silent for a moment, rehearsing again how to put his information, and she spoke first, in a constrained tone. "You were waiting, I understand, for the postmortem." She had paused all but imperceptibly before the last words.

Bone cleared his throat. "Yes; and we have some results." Delicate pressure had induced Ferdy to work into the small hours. As Government pathologist he was not responsible to the police, but he could be cooperative when he chose. "It looks very much as if we have to give up the idea of Miss West's death being an accident. It appears most likely that she was held under water after striking her head on the raft." He omitted to mention that Zephyr might have been half conscious at this time, and had most likely been knocked to the planking with some force.

Mrs. West examined her diamond as if she had been asked to assess its value. "And so she drowned. How can you be sure of things like this?"

"It's very difficult to be sure of anything, but there are bruises that make such a scenario very likely. Her neck is also bruised. More tests are being run." There would be people in plastic gloves, with test tubes, pipettes, tweezers. One did not tell her mother about that. What he had said was bad enough. She looked at him now, with those wearily hooded eyes of a blue denser than Zephyr's.

"Who could have done a thing like that? She had no *enemies*."

The emphasis might be justified because Zephyr didn't seem to have many friends either; enough people to populate a wedding reception, enough to show off to, but no one, so far as Bone could tell, passionately concerned about her survival.

"Rawdon Chase, Mrs. West. What more can you tell me about him?"

The eyes opened wide for an instant, vivid blue, startled. "Rawdon? You explained to me what being out on license meant. You think he could have come here? That he . . ."

Palmerston arrived, coffee cups chiming gently on the trolley he maneuvered to stand alongside her chair. He waited a moment to see if anything else was required, before subtracting himself from the room.

She poured coffee as if she had not spoken, and Bone took his cup, a fragile thing painted with gold fleurs-de-lys, and answered with a question.

"What sort of man was Rawdon Chase?" He used the past tense without thinking. It can be that a man who has been in prison, for even a short time, is never the same man when he comes out. "Did you see much of him?"

"I don't think I can say more about him than I said before. He used to come often to the house we—my husband and I—had near Oxford. To see Zephyr, I'm afraid. She was married to Dwight at the time; he was going to and from America, as he does, and Zephyr was staying with us because she was making a film with the background of one of the colleges. Rawdon was a professor, of medieval history I think it was, at the college they were using and he just happened, as far as I could make out, to be crossing the quad when they were filming Zephyr." She paused. "Zephyr could have that effect on some men."

Bone recalled Ken Cryer's face when Zephyr made her entrance at the Manor, the first time Bone had seen her: a look both bemused and avid. It was a bad move to excite that kind of hunger in some people if you did not intend to satisfy it. His imagination presented him with a stereotype of a professor, tall, thin, and scatty-looking, with pince-nez perched askew on the bridge of his nose. Would such a man drown the woman he loved? And what of the woman he had already killed?

"Your daughter Storm"—what an ill-omened name to give a girl—"was she staying with you then too?"

"That was when it all happened. She was my husband's favorite and used to come home to be pampered. She had one or two failed relationships and a marriage and she'd just sold her flat in London after a breakup. She and Zephyr did *not* get on." Mrs. West put down her cup in its little gilded saucer; her hand was not steady. "Storm was envious of Zephyr's film career. She felt she was just as beautiful and clever." She sighed, and turned her eyes again toward Bone. "They fought as children and they never stopped trying to get the better of each other."

"How did Rawdon Chase come into this?"

She sighed again, looked at the biscuit she was holding as if its purpose was concealed from her, and put it back on her plate. "Storm wanted him, I supposed, because he wanted Zephyr. . . . If he'd been a toy they'd have pulled him apart between them."

Bone saw the professor as a doll, pince-nez stitched to his nose, head jerking as his arms were dragged asunder. How on earth did Storm get killed by this passive object? He had read the pm report faxed by Cottard; Storm Linnane had died quite simply from having her neck snapped. A previous injury had weakened the vertebrae—there was a fracture already that might have proved fatal without warning at any stress.

Rawdon Chase had got off with manslaughter, mainly on that account. If you shake someone violently with intent to damage, you cannot know it will kill them. The inquest established that Chase had not been told of Storm's condition . . . The degree of violence had become the point. Premeditation could then have entered into it.

"So the quarrel which caused Mrs. Linnane's death was really over which of them Rawdon Chase preferred?"

Mrs. West gave an abrupt, voiceless laugh. "No doubt about that. Rawdon was crazed about Zephyr and had no eyes for Storm. It was Storm who made the running, Storm throwing herself at him—literally, I understand—that finally made him do what he did."

Bone imagined Storm, a clone of Zephyr, all big hair, cleavage and long legs, clinging like a limpet to a man who didn't want her; and apparently in front of Zephyr, whom he did want. What could be the magic difference that turned him off one and on to the other? Why, for that matter, did people want to marry one of a pair of identical twins, not the other?

But it did look as if Rawdon Chase, who had killed Zephyr's sister for her importunity, was not the most likely candidate for Zephyr's murder, if he so much adored her.

On the other hand, he gets out of prison and hears she's on the point of marrying again. Perhaps, if he had heard she was divorced from Dwight, he might have had hopes of marrying her himself. Such hopes must be remote, Bone thought. Zephyr was not one to risk her reputation by marrying the man who had killed her sister, whether or not it was out of love for her. That wouldn't look quite so well in the gossip columns as marrying a famous rock star.

"What did Miss West herself feel about Rawdon Chase?" Bone did not suppose Zephyr had felt anything apart from gratified vanity, but the question had to be asked. She might have disliked him, discouraged him, though it sounded as if he'd visited often enough to suggest she hadn't; she might have given Chase grounds for resentment. Even imagined slights can fester during the interminable years of a prison sentence. Chase would have time to replay every nuance of remembered tone and words.

"Zephyr enjoyed his company. She told me so. She wasn't used to the kind of man he was, highly educated, amusing, full of stories about the past. I think she was fascinated by him."

"Fascinated."

"Oh yes, they spent a lot of time together when she

231

wasn't filming. He showed her the colleges. He gave us an entertaining tour of his own college—I was still on my feet then. He took her on the river . . . Dwight wouldn't have liked it at all. Even Treasure, who was about eight then, followed Rawdon about. He was very nice to her, he didn't tease."

Bone was busily revising his picture of Chase, whipping off the pince-nez, fixing a charming smile on the gaunt face . . . what about its expression when he broke Storm's neck?

"But not nice to Mrs. Linnane?" He was careful with the question, but Mrs. West had accepted the subject and continued to examine it.

"I don't think he relished the way she went after him. He was quite a shy man and Storm refused to see how she was putting him off." Bone imagined that Storm must have gone for Chase much as Zephyr went for Ken; but Ken could not be called, in that sense, a shy man. "I think he was drawn to Zephyr's air of mystery."

Mystery. Bone reflected that, originally, Zephyr's mystery had been a cloak drawn over not very much; hardly a personality worth exploring. Now, Zephyr had by her death created a mystery far more tantalizing than any lure she had cast for the professor of medieval history.

"More coffee, Mr. Bone?"

He had set down his cup; at his refusal, Mrs. West took her hand from the coffee pot and turned to look out of the long window, at the distant oaks spreading their branches over the parkland, untouched by centuries of human problems, their leaves shining under the autumn sun.

Her voice was infinitely sad as she went on. "You know, I'm sure every parent does, you wonder what you did wrong that your children grow up to invite trouble. To be beautiful is a trouble in itself. . . . Rawdon pleaded guilty to killing Storm, but he was much provoked. And Zephyr . . . from what you tell me, it looks as if she brought her death on herself too."

Bone could not reassure her. He took his leave, and

as he left he looked over toward the lake cradled in its trees, and thought how useful it would be if inanimate things could be questioned—or even creatures, such as in Rawdon Chase's medieval times were prosecuted and executed for causing disasters. All he needed to do was to get a fish from the lake as witness, or make the raft tell him who had pushed the bride underneath it.

Of course, that was exactly what Forensic was trying to do.

Chapter
39
•••••••••

Bone wondered, not for the first time, whether if hospitals painted their walls in cheerful colors rather than seaweed green and drab, and if they hung pictures around, as they did in the children's section, and sprayed the place with a proper good scent instead of cheapessence disinfectant, would people simply adjust their associations, start to feel sick and apprehensive when they saw and smelled the substitutes. Tiling, in particular, reminded him of morgues and postmortems, a part of his professional life he preferred to forget when visiting his wife.

Nor could he forget his own long stay in hospital, along with Charlotte, those years ago after the car crash that had killed Petra and their baby son. When Mrs. West spoke of every parent wondering, when disaster struck, what they had done wrong, he thought he would have been glad if his little son had grown up at all; at least he was no more to blame than for an unlucky choice of time, for being on the road when that drunken fool had come swerving . . .

But you still could blame yourself for that. Bone gave himself a mental shake and a scolding for this line of thought, making the ward receptionist experience a twinge of sympathy for Mrs. Bone, married to such a severe-looking type, a policeman into the bargain. She wouldn't like to be arrested by *him,* and she reckoned any child of his was in for a tough time . . . Oh yes, a friend was already with Mrs. Bone but he could go right in.

The friend was Emily Playfair. She and Grizel, when Bone walked in, were in fits of laughter and Bone thought he had rarely seen Grizel more beautiful, her blond hair on feathered end, the little pink bed jacket reflecting rosy light into her face. How had he managed to be so lucky? He smiled at Emily and bent to kiss Grizel.

"You've been prescribed jokes, have you? Or are you trying to hurry up the baby with bouncing it around like this?"

Grizel held his hand in her warm one. "Emily's been cheering me up, Robert. Something so hilarious happened to her yesterday. Ken Cryer came to call—"

"Ken Cryer." Bone's professional interest awoke. What would make Ken emerge from his fastness at the Manor and brave the encamped media in order to see Emily Playfair? True, her presence alone made one cheerful, but with his bride so lately dead, kittens would hardly have prime place in Ken's mind.

"Yes indeed." Emily took up the tale. "I was standing on my doorstep just after the rain. I'd come to see if the rain had flattened my petunias and I was giving a breath of fresh air to a couple of kittens; there was Ken on a bicycle coming down the lane, looking in real need of a cup of tea. So, he got off his bike and right away a little car stopped square in the middle of the lane and a rather burly young woman I'd seen before, leapt out, rushed after Ken and tried to kiss him in the middle of my front garden."

"She knocked poor Ken flat." Grizel squeezed Bone's hand. "Squandered him on the path—"

"And I dropped the kittens on her while she was kissing him, and while she was recovering from that, and I tell you they were really interested in her, Ken disentangled himself and I got kittens and Ken indoors."

"Then she had a good try at breaking the door in, hammering—"

"Flattening my poor petunias to look in at the window—"

"It's common assault, isn't it, Robert? The young woman must be mad. I know Ken's tasty but—"

"Did you see her car? What kind was it?"

"Always the copper," Grizel said, with a resigned gesture to Emily.

"You know I can't see that part of the lane, it dips below my hedge, but it's yellow, and General Snell says it's one of those funny little Fiats, the old sort, not the latest kind. General Snell almost ran into it."

"This part's even funnier, Robert."

"The General is quite rabid about people who block the lane, so he charged up the path to tell her off, shouting as he came, and she hauled round and clocked him one. Bang went a second man on my path . . . The cats were in the window. They loved it." Emily twinkled at the memory. "It was that girl at the wedding party. I'd seen her last week in the newsagents. She must be staying somewhere near."

Bone did not say that his men, at that moment, were making inquiries about Ken's large fan all round the neighborhood. He noted: yellow Fiat. Whoever she was, she might yield useful clues as to what Ken had been doing that afternoon during the crucial time when Zephyr disappeared from the house and went inexplicably down to the lake. As it seemed she had been waiting her chance to corner Ken alone, it was likely she had monitored his every step. Of course it would be necessary to give her no inkling that she might be putting her adored in danger with her account of what he did, or they might get assaulted themselves; there was also every chance that she might be in a position to clear him, but

Bone smiled at the vision of Locker being handbagged round the room, and Emily wagged her finger at him.

"You are laughing at the misfortunes of others, Robert; you must see such a lot of them, far more than we do." The thought made her serious, and she went on, "A terrible thing, that poor girl's death. I knew something was going to happen, but I couldn't imagine when or where, or what. I only knew it had to do with water."

She shuddered a little, and Bone looked at her with both pity and frustration; pity at the nightmare quality these glimpses could have, frustration because of the use it could be were she able to envisage things at will. Bone wondered if it wasn't perhaps like the early stages of any science and could become more manageable. However, he thought that in spite of her cordial and happy manner, in another age, living alone with her cats, Emily would have been in danger of being thought a witch.

She was getting to her feet now, gathering her scarf, purse and jacket. "I'll be off, my dear. I'll come tomorrow, same time, unless the baby comes before me. I'm looking forward to seeing his face, a blend of the two of you will be worth seeing." She leaned to kiss Grizel, a waft of lavender reaching Bone on the other side. "Think pretty thoughts and he'll arrive with curly hair."

When she had gone Grizel said, "I notice she is in no doubt that you're to have a son, Robert, though I hadn't told her. So she can see nice things as well as nasty."

"Tell me that when Kinloch's fifteen and thinks his dad's a pig. When he gives up shoplifting for joyriding."

Grizel pinched his finger painfully. "Seriously, how is the case going? You don't look as if it was a breeze."

Bone examined a spray of flowers in a small vase by the bed, which told him his daughter had been in—honeysuckle from over the porch, some Japanese anemone, the daisy flowers of feverfew and a sprig of thyme from beside the path. He said, "I came here to find how *you* are." He surveyed the wires attaching his wife to the monitor. "You look a bit like an object from Star Trek; are they thinking of beaming him up?"

He remembered listening through the stethoscope and he could still hear in his mind the extraordinary sound of the infant heartbeat, magnified to a swift, almost ferocious little wow-wow noise as if it could scarcely wait to be out and dealing with air itself. A cesarean had been mentioned in view of Grizel's slight build, but she was anxious to have the baby normally if she could.

"No. They're all holding their fingers crossed, including Kinloch." Was there a hint of apprehension in those clear green eyes looking up at him? "You're not to worry about missing the birth, you know. I'll have lots of people to hang on to. You'll just have to face it, Robert: while I'm getting on with producing life, your business is with tracking down those who have the gall to take it away."

Bone stood up to go, not relinquishing her hand. "Try to—"

" 'Take things easy.' I score." She leveled a finger at him, one up in the game he and Charlotte played. He smiled and, kissing her hand, gave it back to her.

It was true—he reflected as he drove out of the hospital gates, skirting two elderly women who stared at him as if he had deliberately set out to run them down—that most advice was not possible to take. He could no more stop worrying about Grizel than he could stop breathing. The best he could do was to push another worry to the front of his mind.

The two people he most wanted to interview were not at hand: the enigmatic Rawdon Chase, and Ken's bulky besotted fan. By now Cottard had sent the fax on Chase, including the "mug shot," and Bone had congratulated himself on his visualizing. Chase did have a gaunt face, and normally wore spectacles; but he had also a thick mane of dark hair, and the face was not that of a passive creature but strongly lined, with a beak of a nose and a thin, humorous mouth. A man, Bone judged, capable of passion, possibly of calculated violence. Of course that was what he had gone to jail for, but Bone felt dissatisfied with both the official version of what he was said to have done, and the account given by Mrs. West. If Chase had snapped Storm's neck to stop her molesting him, why had he been sent down for so long? Even if he'd been unlucky with his judge, it still seemed over the odds for what was practically an accident.

Something must have emerged at the trial which made him out as a more sinister figure; whatever it was might also account for violence that could hold a struggling, half-conscious woman down under the water until her lungs filled with it. Bone was still pondering this, wondering if he was going to need a transcript of the trial or at least notes, when he came in sight of the Press encamped outside the Manor. It was better weather and the sun had tempted them out of their cars to sit on the bank opposite the gates, playing cards and eating ice cream. Now that, Bone thought, watching them scramble to their feet as his car was recognized, would make a fine change for vultures short of a bit of carrion to pick over: swoop on the ice cream, my fine-feathered friends.

A police motorcycle was in the bay of the gates, the rider astride. He oared it to the side as Bone's car came in, bringing it to Bone's window and so spoiling the vultures' chance. The gates were opened by someone monitoring in the Manor, Powers drove through, and Bone had escaped all but the inevitable cameras. As the car whirled over the gravel to the door, Bone spared a thought for those useless shots of a blank Superintendent; one or two of them would nevertheless appear captioned "Police Report No Progress." The case had become a focus for attention, thanks rather to Ken's rock star status than to the less familiar and not native glamour of the victim. The usual indignation was being voiced in the tabloids over the police failure to haul out the murderer instantly from the ranks of wedding guests. A reference to Archangel just failed to suggest openly that he had helicoptered in with the express purpose of drowning the lovely bride of his rival in pure jealousy. That Archangel could literally lay his hands on a hundred girls as beautiful as Zephyr West—could, indeed,

command almost anyone with an idly beckoning hand—
had sidestepped marriage skillfully for years—had no
relevance. But no one had gone a millimeter further
than a hint at this fantasy. Archangel's lawyers were the
Jaws of the legal world.

Ken was in. His recent bid for a piece of personal
space on the gardener's bicycle, from which he'd had to
be rescued by Joe in the limo, had not been a venture
he wanted to repeat. The Manor was once more his refuge, even in siege, from the media; also a sanctuary from
the Fan From Hell. He was sitting with Edwina in his
Victorian study when Joe ushered Bone and Powers in.
His face lightened and he sprang up.

"News, Robert?"

"Nothing pleasant. I'm sorry. We have the results of
the pm."

Bone saw the anxiety in both faces. They both knew
the importance of this news and, deliberately, Bone left
it to Ken to ask.

"It wasn't an accident, then? She didn't just slip?"

"She slipped all right." Bone ignored the leather chair
Ken invited him to. "But the slip was probably forced
on her; the damage was to the back of the head."

"But one can slip and land on one's back. I've done
it, on a floor Mrs. Rudyard polished into a ski slope."

Edwina, Bone noticed, was watching Ken. He went
on, "The blow to the head would not have been fatal if
someone hadn't taken advantage of it."

Edwina's china-blue eyes, Ken's gray ones, were
turned to him now. He had to bear in mind that for one
of them, perhaps both, the rest of his news might not
be new.

"She was held under water until she drowned."

Edwina put her hands to her mouth, Ken turned
abruptly and flung away to the window. When he spoke,
his voice was muffled.

"Oh God, poor Zeph."

A comment that could as truthfully be made by her
murderer as by her bridegroom. Bone tried to look at

this dispassionately. Quite a few murderers he had come across, in fact, had told him that after the act was done they felt instant remorse and regret. Whether that was a mitigating factor was for God to know. Conceivably, serial killers also felt sorry every single time. What he had to remember was that Ken might not be acting this grief.

Ken turned from the window, in shadow against it.

"What do you want from us? Who do you think did that?"

Bone shook his head. "You know I can't tell you. Nor is even a guess possible until we know more. That's why I'm here. I need to see Jem, with your permission, and you may wish to be present."

Ken said instantly, "I don't want you badgering Jem. He's upset enough already. Damn it to hell, you may be used to murders but he's only fourteen and the whole business has shaken him up till he's in a really nervous state. If you go at him he may say anything, something totally untrue just to get you off his back."

Bone said, "You know me better than that. And your son was as near as anybody to where your wife was killed. He may have seen or heard something; he may have seen the murderer."

"Do you think that?" Ken gripped the back of his chair hard and Edwina had gone spectacularly pale.

"Please bring him to Herne Hall. You can be present, Ken, and look after him."

Chapter

40

. . . .

Jem had been found by Edwina inducing his cat to chase a twig in long grass in the garden. He did not seem happy at the idea of an interview; a silent and rather hostile pair sat before the recorder, united, father and son, Bone felt, against him. He hoped he would not lose a friend over this dislikable business; he hoped, too, he was not going to lose a friend to life imprisonment through these investigations.

Fredricks, unobtrusive as usual, sat at the end of the desk. Jem glanced at her, frowning, and shifted; he sat up straight, hands tense on the desk's edge, rather as if he waited for an exam paper to be put facedown in front of him.

Bone, after the preliminaries about recording, began in as friendly and low-key a tone as he could. Ken was in a fidget.

"We'd like to hear, in as much detail as you can, what you did on the afternoon Miss West died."

"Honestly, I don't see I can be any help. I was in the boathouse when it happened."

Bone did not ask how Jem knew when it happened.

Instead, he inquired, "When did you go to the boat-house? Was it your idea?"

Jem nervously grinned. "Oh no. Treasure thought of that. She'd sussed out a good place, it was perfect because no one would look there once Security had checked it. They'd locked it after they checked but she knew where the keys were hung. Silly of them, she said, to put them back but they had."

"The idea of the boathouse was for you both to get out of the ceremony by the lake."

Bone waited for the statement to be confirmed or rejected, as Jem, shifting again, glanced at his father.

"Yes. Well. Both of us thought what we had to do and wear was really the pits. Trez said she'd never, ever recite the poem her mother had written about love lighting up the sky and stuff. And the clothes, hers in particular, well. They'd put her dress box outside her door and she took it out and put it on, just for the hell of it. Our only way out was the vanishing act."

"How did you vanish?"

"I'd thought we'd just wander off through the crowds. There were masses of people all over the place. But Trez said it had to be the cellar way or someone'd be sure to see us and tell. And when it rained everyone crammed into the marquee or the house anyway and we'd have been a bit visible careering over the grass in all our gear."

"The cellar way. Please explain exactly."

"Well, it's an old house, you see, not as old as this but old. Trez found out about the cellars when she was exploring, the first time she came to stay with her grandmother here. I bet Mrs. West hadn't seen down there or she'd never have let her—the backstairs are horror movie, no handrail and it's all dark and fusty at that end, not like the proper wine cellar Palmerston looks after. Trez had a torch of course, though she said there's lights. The passage at the end of the cellar comes out in a weird little pit with steps up to no door, under bushes, just where the trees round the lake begin. Perfect."

Bone supposed this was the Hall's old ice house. He said, "What time did you go there? When did you reach the boathouse?"

"We weren't wearing watches." Jem glanced at his father. "I lost mine last week and Dad said I could buy my own from now on."

"His third this year," Ken said somberly. "He drops them like confetti," and as if this reminded him of his ill-starred wedding, or at least the trappings of it, he frowned and folded his arms. If people were properly instructed in body language, Bone reflected, they'd be more careful about assuming defensive positions.

Jem warmed to his story. "And Trez was made to take hers off because her mother was making her wear yucky wrist things with flowers round and long ribbons." He drew his mouth down. "So we didn't know the time."

"Did you go to the boathouse after the rain had stopped?"

"Ye-es. The trees sort of rained on us on the way. Trez said some of this evil poem on the raft, doing faces and things to it, and then we went to the boathouse."

"Did you see anyone on the way?"

Jem hesitated. "I thought I saw Dad for a sec before we went down to the lake. In the distance, going quite fast."

Ken laughed abruptly. "You might have seen me. I was on the lam like you. Trying to get time to think."

Just a little late to start thinking, as he was actually legally married to Zephyr already. Panicking more likely, thought Bone. And it was possible that going through the lovey-dovey scene she had devised at the lakeside would prove a bigger obstacle to Ken than the quick ceremony at the Registrar's office. Nevertheless it was interesting that the only person Jem had seen before the bride turned up drowned had been the reluctant groom.

"So, the boathouse. What did you do first?"

"First thing we got out of our awful gear and hung it on the line—you saw it—and when we were eating we chucked stuff at it. Trez said, before all this, to get food, and that was easy, I went to the caterers in the tent and they gave me a bag of stuff, seeing I was the groom's son and I'd put on my page outfit on purpose and boys are supposed to be always hungry. And we nicked a bottle from the cellars on the way through."

Bone nodded slowly, swiveling a pencil on the desk. "There was a crack in the boathouse wall. I saw your light through it—did either of you see out through it? Anyone down by the water?"

"I never got the chance. We meant to watch the whole thing and have a really good laugh, but Trez was sitting where she could see, and when I tried she pushed me and we both went in the water."

"Was this soon after you got there, or had you been there for a while?"

"I'm not sure. I mean, hard to tell."

"Had she seen something?"

Jem did not reply at once, and his father turned to look at him.

"I don't think so."

It sounded lame and he did not look up. If Treasure had seen anything, she had evidently instructed Jem not to say. Bone did not comment. It was for Treasure herself to answer that question, and better that Jem, if he managed to see her before Bone did, could report that there had been no curiosity about it. That way, sudden probing on the subject would carry more of a shock.

"If you saw nothing, did you hear anything?"

Jem considered. "Well, we heard the band, and the people coming down, and talking, of course. Not what they said, just talking noise. We'd got very wet and we had to dry off somehow, there was an awful old dog towel there and some paper napkins the caterers wrapped things in, and we were too busy mucking about to pay much attention; we were in stitches with having to be quiet."

Bone supposed the state of being "in stitches" owed much to the bottle of champagne. Unlikely that even had they heard a heavenly choir it would have sobered them up. After all it didn't seem that Jem had much to contribute to clearing the mystery of his stepmother's death.

Unless, of course, he and Treasure had got drunk *after* she died.

Important to remember that this skinny boy before him, with eyes demurely cast downward or raised candidly to his, had been nearly strangled by that same stepmother. He might well dread a future of some years with Zephyr before he could leave home—or they divorced— some years with a creature who had so beguiled his father that the shocking incident seemed to have gone almost unnoticed.

Impossible also to believe that children of the age of Jem and Treasure could not murder. Too many had done it. Treasure besides had evidently a deep grudge against her mother. It might be quite deep enough for her to plot a revenge, in which Jem would have been willing enough to join; a revenge that could easily have gone further than they intended. Such a scenario made Jem's very candor suspect.

"Can we go? Jem's told you all he knows. They played a silly prank and that's all there is to it."

Bone turned his gaze on Ken, who had pushed back his chair.

"For the moment, yes."

As he glanced at his watch and gave the time, and Fredricks switched off the tape, he thought: now is not the time to push it, but this silly prank could perhaps have led to something fatal.

246

Chapter

41

·········

Locker, in the incident room, sat monumental and
gloomy. Before him lay some papers, a cardboard box
open on flaky crumbs, and a mug with dregs of coffee.

"Any news, sir?"

"You take the words from my mouth. I've drawn a
blank with Jem Cryer—Pat Fredricks has the tape—but
I fancy that's because Treasure Schlumberger has sewn
up his lips for him. And Treasure is in bed with a headache, according to her grandmother; quite incapable of
helping the police in their inquiries."

"Young madam," grunted Locker. "Her hangover's
lasting conveniently long. At her age you scarcely feel
it."

Bone sat down, relishing the cool of the airy brick
vault over his head. He noticed, in a high corner opposite the window, a hanging pocket of mud. In summer
they must have left the window open for the swallows
that nested there. Birds don't have to worry about murderers—then he remembered cuckoos and magpies, who
year after year got away with it.

"Come on, Steve. They had a bottle of champagne
between them; that's a hangover to last more than a

morning, though Jem didn't seem to be suffering. But you're right. I don't think she wants to talk to us."

Locker sighed heavily and pushed his mug away. "You don't think they did it, sir?"

"I don't at all want to think so, but it's possible. They had something of a motive. They had opportunity. It could have been partly an accident." Yet, he thought, Jem had shown absolutely no consciousness of a secret of that magnitude.

"Begun as an accident, you mean, sir? If she killed her mother," said Locker, flattening the cardboard box with his fist and shying it into the bin in the corner beneath the swallows' nest, "she could be having one hell of a headache."

"True. Well, we'll get her up from bed when we have to. In the meantime, what's the team doing? Anything? No sign of the fan who floored the General at Miss Playfair's?"

Locker's gloom gave way. "Wish I'd seen that. The General was in at Saxhurst station, apparently wanting to lay a charge of assault. Got across the desk sergeant and near as a touch assaulted *him*. . . . I reckon that young lady'll be around wherever Cryer is. I sent a man to scout round outside the Manor in case. With that security I don't see her getting inside the walls."

"Hold the thought, Steve. We don't even know it wasn't she who sent the death threats."

"Why'd she want to kill Cryer if she's so crazy for him?"

"The threats said, 'Marry and you die.' That's significant, surely. And don't forget the 'each man kills the thing he loves' idea." Seeing Locker's face wrinkle with incomprehension, Bone translated, "Suppose she's so obsessed with him she only wants to connect with him in some way, regardless. The bloke who shot John Lennon admired him as a hero."

Locker wagged his head. "Killing someone is making them notice you, for sure. And she knocked him flat with no thought of if she'd hurt him, it seems . . . What do you reckon on her going for Zephyr West, then? If she believes Cryer's rightfully hers it's a bit of a facer to find he's marrying another woman. And she was near the lake, too, as near as Cryer, making for the gazebo."

"I don't rule her out, Steve. She appears to be potty enough for anything. All the same, her certainty that Cryer returns her love and is but biding his time before carrying her off to bliss, argues that she might not see any need to get rid of a rival. Might not even see Zephyr as a rival."

"Get away, sir! Wouldn't anyone be jealous of those film star looks? When Cherry saw her in the news, she said, 'I'd kill for hair and legs like that.' This girl could have killed because she *didn't* have them."

"She may be mad enough to think they don't matter. If it's a clinical case of erotomania she may well think Cryer prefers her looks to Zephyr's, or that she has something more important than looks—a kindred soul. Or perhaps she doesn't see herself as she really is—the way anorexics don't. Yes, Fredricks?"

"Something came through, sir. On Rawdon Chase. Someone, a Mrs.—Greenwood," Fredricks checked the message, "of the Red Lion in Adleston, thought she recognized the photo, she thinks he might be the man who stayed Wednesday and Thursday nights last week."

Zephyr had died on Friday so, if the man was Rawdon Chase, he hadn't chosen to go back that night. Was it possible he'd taken off with a second murder on his conscience? Bone's impatience to meet this elusive figure was increasing. Had he some monstrous grudge against the West sisters? Mrs. West had been positive that Chase had been in love with Zephyr, but he'd reminded Locker of the platitude, that each man kills the thing he loves. Suppose Cryer's besotted fan had in fact sent death threats, the same lethal impulse might operate in Chase against the woman who had helped to wreck his life. Even quiet academics might have reserves of rage not entirely sublimated by carving each other up in print.

"Did this—" Bone too consulted the message Fredricks had given him—"Mrs. Greenwood get any idea how the man spent his time while he was at the Red Lion?"

"Like coming back soaking wet with a bit of wedding veil in his fist?" prompted Locker, unexpectedly frivolous. He had lost his gloom at this first scent of the hunt.

Fredricks turned her serious equine face to him. "She said she didn't really notice much about him—quiet, polite; she didn't think he looked very well. Her theory was, she told her husband, he'd just had bad news and had to leave in a hurry. She wondered if his girlfriend had ditched him."

"Or *he'd* ditched *her* in the lake." Locker was rubbing his hands. "What home address did he give at registering?"

Fredricks pointed to the paper, which Bone swiveled for Locker to read. "No use, though, sir. We checked and the road doesn't go with the postcode. No one there had heard of a Rawdon Chase when I rang, or anyone of his description. You see he registered as Roland Chart."

Locker nodded. "Funny how it's almost a rule, that people who take false names tend to choose their own initials."

Bone said, "In the old days I suppose things like cigarette cases and handkerchiefs might be monogrammed; then initials would be a giveaway. That's what I've read. Personally, I think it's just easier to remember a false name with your own initials."

"So. No trace there. What about his college? Were they going to take him back?"

"We tried there, sir. It's still their vacation for ages yet, I was told. We got put on to different people, including the Bursar, who was very short with us, and said he would tell us nothing at all on the phone and it was entirely the business of the college whom they employed."

Bone said, "There's his probation officer."

"I'll get on to him as soon as possible—"

"We did ring him, sir, but he was out on a case. We

left a message on the machine for him to ring here when he did come in."

"Good. Well, Chase could have holed up anywhere. We should have more luck with the girl who can't leave Cryer alone. She must be floating around in the neighborhood and we want her." Bone smiled involuntarily at the idea of that large young woman floating, like some captive balloon, straining toward a Cryer forever pelting into the distance.

"When we've finished with Treasure Schlumberger we'll have to have another chat with Dwight. I'm told he wants to know why we haven't arrested Cryer, but he's entitled to be surprised we haven't arrested *him*. That reminds me, Steve: news from Forensic?"

Locker snorted. "The usual. Armstrong's song about being overworked and underpaid and understaffed, with a backing of urgent cases dating to last Easter, I don't think. I dropped the news that the Chief was keen on getting results on a case that's attracting such publicity, and he actually said he'd hurry the team up."

"Wonderful. Well, we can expect them to come along with Schlumberger's hair and fibers from his suit, all over our victim. She'll be covered in beard hairs too. What we need is something to indicate whether he put her there in the first case."

"If he did, hugging her like that was quite a way to cover his traces."

"You've said it. I still want to know why he was so confident the wedding with Cryer was not going to come off."

"Because there wasn't going to be a bride?"

"The Schlumbergers have a few questions to answer."

Locker peered into the dregs of his coffee mug as if he were considering a refill. "It's not that we haven't the work to do, sir. It's that not a lot of suspects are lining up to be interviewed."

"Pat, see if Treasure Schlumberger's well enough to talk. If Mrs. West says no, bring Treasure's father."

"Sir." She went out. Locker, when Bone looked round at him, wore a diffident air.

"Mrs. Bone, sir. How is she?"

Underneath all this—the talk of motive and means, the various considerations—there moved the undercurrent, a very strong current indeed, towing Bone's thoughts continually toward that hospital bed, toward Grizel and their unborn child. Locker knew him well enough to sense his abstraction, and he spoke briskly to cover his desire to be there, not here.

"She's fine. We might even crack this case before the baby decides to show up."

Locker's face, but not his mouth, said: chance would be a fine thing.

Chapter
42
· · · · · · · · ·

Mrs. West, Fredricks reported, had started to tell her that Treasure was still in bed, therefore unwell and not able to bear questioning, when she caught sight of her granddaughter strolling fully dressed in the garden; with slight acerbity she asked Lexie to fetch her. Treasure, brought in, had admitted her headache was better, had glowered a bit at the thought of talking to the police but had acceded to Mrs. West's suggestion that the sooner she did it, the sooner it would be over. She did *not* want to be interviewed with her father sitting in.

"She made such a face, sir! Mrs. West suggested then that she herself might be what she called "the obligatory adult" and there was no fuss from the girl over that."

"And Schlumberger?"

"I found him by the lake, sir, looking at the water."

Bone and Locker exchanged glances. For some murderers, as they knew, the scene of the crime exerted a fascination that led them back, over and over, although Dwight Schlumberger's solid, unromantic figure did not lend itself to this idea.

Fredricks coughed. She said, "He'd been crying."

Bone raised his eyebrows but did not comment.

Zephyr West might be truly mourned by her ex-husband who, in his odd way, had put up with her tantrums and her willfulness, even to have admired or at least appreciated them. If Schlumberger had indeed killed Zephyr in some frantic rage at seeing her out of his clutches, he could be suffering regrets more bitter than if he were innocent.

"Did you tell him his daughter was going to be interviewed?"

Pat Fredricks became a demure horse. "I didn't think it necessary, sir. Mr. Schlumberger said he had to make a few calls and he'd be available in about twenty minutes and would come to this room. So I just thanked him."

"Excellent. Within about twenty minutes we hope to be able to get some sense out of his daughter. We certainly won't trouble Mrs. West to come here, we'll take the interview in her sitting room if you'll ask her, Pat, if she is willing."

Mrs. West was waiting for them, elegant as usual in a silk dress of gunmetal gray with a black chiffon scarf at her throat and drop pearls at her ears. She was not in her wheelchair but in a straight chair of dark green velvet, a somber background for her pallor. She greeted them with a smile; in direct contrast was the subdued glare they received from Treasure, lounging on the base of her spine on the sofa, legs stuck aggressively out before her as if, given the choice, she might jump up and aim a kick at the visitors. Her black T-shirt had a row of white asterisks across the front, inviting the substitution of a swear word. The interview with Miss Schlumberger did not look to be an easy ride.

She was, however, faintly impressed when Fredricks set up the recorder. She even checked the time on her own watch when Fredricks stated it on the preliminary note. Bone remembered that neither Treasure nor Jem knew the time when they made their party in the boathouse. Well, there were other questions besides that.

"The evening of your mother's wedding day—"

" 'Twasn't her wedding day. She'd got married already."

Not a good start; she said it as if the news had come as an unpleasant surprise. Bone recalled Dwight's story of the confrontation—that he and Treasure had gone to Zephyr on the morning of the reception and attempted to get her to change her mind at this last minute. How could they have thought that, however subject she might be to whims, she would decide for a less glamorous man—especially one she'd tried before? There was more to that little session than had been revealed, Bone was sure.

"The evening you and Jem went to the boathouse, did you see anyone through the crack in the door that gives a view of the lake and the raft?"

Treasure's momentary widening of the eyes showed that she had not expected so direct an approach.

"Anyone? No. Who should I see?"

"That's for you to tell us, I think. Did you see your mother?"

"No." The denial was swift, as though it had been waiting to be made. "No. She wasn't there."

Bone told himself: That sounds remarkably as if someone else perhaps *was*. Treasure had balled her fists in her jeans pockets and was staring at him defiantly.

"Then who was?"

"I told you. Nobody. I didn't see anyone."

Bone considered; then he said, "You'd had a row with your mother that morning."

One of his statements, and it appeared this was not to get a denial, probably because the aftermath, Treasure storming out in tears and locking herself in her room, had been seen by too many people. She shrugged.

"Mom was having fights with everyone. She always did."

Neat to put the onus on Zephyr, but Bone acknowledged it to be true. If Zephyr didn't get her way, the weather for everyone around was due to be stormy.

The word put him in mind of the dead sister, Treasure's aunt, for whose manslaughter Rawdon Chase had gone to jail. On impulse he asked: "Rawdon Chase. What did you think of him?"

Treasure was jolted upright, her hands flew from her pockets to grip the sofa cushions either side. Mrs. West, Bone noticed peripherally, moved a little, her own hands coming together on her lap.

"Why? Why d'you want to know? He's in jail."

She turned to her grandmother as if in appeal and Bone cut in with, "He was released two weeks ago and has failed to keep in touch with his probation officer. It's possible he has been here."

Treasure looked round the room as if challenging Chase to emerge from the curtains or from behind the tallboy. *"Here?* Oh come *on,* why would he? How could he know Mom was going to marry?"

Bone suppressed: he's been out two weeks, and it was in all the papers and on the news. Treasure must suppose prisoners were cut off from the world. He asked quickly, "Do you think he'd have minded if he knew?" He didn't add, *her being married to your father didn't bother him before.*

Treasure, still sitting up straight, kicked her heels against the sofa. "Mind? Of course he'd *mind.* He was bats about Mom. He'd have done anything for her. Anything." She stopped abruptly, almost as if she'd said too much. "But he couldn't have been there that day—when we were in the boathouse—because of all the security. How could he?"

Bone did not answer. There was no security so perfect that it could not be penetrated; if it were, presidents and heads of state would never be assassinated. If Rawdon Chase had evaded security that day, it would be useful to know how. Treasure was looking triumphant, her head up, her hands relaxed on the cushions. Why? What had she said? She had pointed out that Chase couldn't have been there, that she couldn't have seen him.

It immediately convinced Bone that she had.

Chapter

43

·········

"Just what is going on here?"

It was Dwight, thrusting his way into the room past a politely expostulating Lexie. He stood in the doorway, staring at them and swinging his lowered head like a buffalo reconnoitering before a charge. Treasure rolled her eyes to heaven in mute appeal for a thunderbolt to remove embarrassment, and Mrs. West permitted herself a frown.

He strode forward.

"I go down to the coach house where I had been told you would be and I find a room full of idiots who say you're in the house and will I wait. I will not wait. I told your girl here I would see you in twenty minutes and that time is up. I come here and find you interrogating my daughter without my permission and without my being here while you do it. Now I warn you," Dwight's face was a dangerous red above his grizzled beard and Bone wondered if Schlumberger's blood pressure had been checked recently, "I warn you that I am going to make a complaint about this."

"Mr. Schlumberger," Bone's voice cut through, "you are free to make any complaint you wish, and Detective-

Sergeant Fredricks will give you the details of where such a complaint may be entered, but your daughter has had her grandmother's presence throughout this interview, which fully meets—"

"I am the one who should have been here, and I demand that tape"—he gestured at the recorder so violently that Fredricks, who had been registering the interview's suspension in a low voice before switching off, flinched—"be erased. Wiped. Do you hear?"

Bone refrained from saying that, had he been deaf, the message would still have got through. He also refrained from smiling, as he was tempted to do, in case he lost this possible suspect to a stroke. Dwight, standing there with even his beard bristling, was a comic figure but no rule said that a comic figure couldn't be a murderer. Now that Treasure had been effectively shut up, it was time to grill papa.

"I am sorry you feel like this, Mr. Schlumberger, but I am sure you will understand—"

"Understand? *Understand?* What *you* have to understand—"

"Dwight."

The single word from Mrs. West could in no way be compared to the crack of a whip, being both mild and calm, but its effect was no less. It took Dwight off the boil and reduced him to simmer. Treasure, conversely, exploded. She sprang from the sofa and confronted her father, the metal on her teeth flashing in the sun.

"You're *hopeless,* Dad. You had your chance with Mom and I did all I could to help. I'm not going to give away any more secrets. You're on your own."

She stamped out, passing a baffled Dwight and leaving Bone with an intense curiosity to know what secrets Treasure had given away so far. Yet more interesting would be the secrets she had declared she would now keep.

Was it not Rawdon Chase but her own father Treasure had seen through the crack in the boathouse doors? Her father drowning her mother? That would be a secret she'd keep, well worth getting her to divulge if it could conceivably be done. Treasure's present mood did not in the least encourage optimism, even without the obstacle of Dwight's insistence on being present.

Well, the alternative was before them: questioning Dwight. With luck his daughter's temper would have put him on edge sufficiently to make him less guarded. It might even be enough to help them get at this secret with which she had challenged him.

"If you're ready, Mr. Schlumberger," Bone injected a peremptory note into his voice on the principle that those used to giving orders often respond to them, "we can conduct the interview in the coach house and not give Mrs. West any further trouble."

Fredricks was picking up the recorder in a businesslike way, while Dwight paused as if considering whether it would be advantageous to cause further trouble. It was Mrs. West who settled the matter, firmly, in that voice of such husky clarity that one would think she and not her daughter were the actress.

"What a good idea—to get it over."

Dwight luckily saw wisdom in this and went with Bone and Fredricks, making no further trouble. His replacement phone sounded and he grunted something dismissive into it as he went. He was ready, if not willing, to give them his time.

His time seemed all he was ready to give. Bone's attempt to pin down his movements during the time when Zephyr was attacked met with impatient answers. No, he had not seen Zephyr; no, he had no theory on how she could have reached the lake unseen; no, he had seen no one near the lake except security men he had himself hired and whom he recognized. Except for one person.

"Cryer was roving about on his own, looking kind of mad. Now, why don't you"—Dwight leaned forward, jutting his beard at Bone—"why don't you ask him what *he* was doing? He starts off his marriage by having a fight with Zeph. Ask anyone who saw them come back the evening before. That was when they'd been to the

259

Registry office. I've inquired and I know. Then nothing more likely than he has another fight with her on the raft and throws her in the lake to drown. Poor Zeph." Unexpectedly Dwight's eyes, dark and bloodshot, filled with tears. "When I had that raft fixed up so she could have just what she wanted, how could I ever think to find her under it?" He stopped, dashed away the tears with a broad hand, and added harshly, "I mean to see him in hell before I finish. If you don't get him I will."

Over lunch, taken in a pub, Bone retold this to Locker, who had been making inroads in a rack of lamb and who said, "There you are. He does for his ex when he finds she's really gone and married again, and then vows to do for his rival. Plenty of violence there." He leaned forward suddenly to prevent a drip of sauce from landing on his chest.

Bone stole one of Locker's chips and ate it thoughtfully. "Seems to me we have too many folk with delusions to deal with. There's Schlumberger, who has the delusion his wife would be prepared to marry him again instead of Cryer, and plans the event for her down to the last detail—"

"Which might include popping her under a raft—" Steve went over the rack to see if any meat was left, "when he found his delusion didn't work. And I suppose another delusion belongs to that barmy fan of Cryer's who believes he's going to marry her. Pity they couldn't have got together and worked it out—Schlumberger to get his ex, fan to get Cryer. Everyone happy. Except Cryer, of course."

Bone, finishing his spaghetti Bolognese, was wondering what Grizel was having to eat in hospital and it took him a few seconds to play back what Locker had just said.

"Clérimbault-Archer."

"Pardon?"

Bone laughed. "The syndrome. Falling in love with people who don't love you back and being convinced that they do. You don't even have to have met them."

"Not so unusual as all that," objected Locker, chasing sauce round the plate with the last few potato chips. "There was a bloke after Cherry before I married her who wouldn't take no for an answer because he was dead sure she was secretly mad about him." With regret he pushed away the wreck of lamb. "Suppose he thought she was punishing herself by marrying me."

"What happened to him?"

"Went to South America, I heard. Cherry was glad, said he spooked her. And he always called her by her proper name, that she hates; said it was her name 'just for him.'"

Since this name was "Selina" which, suggesting to Bone someone tall and willowy, could not have suited Cherry less, he agreed that this was an extra persecution.

"There's no appealing to reason with these people. Erotomania's another word for it—accent on mania. Lots of adolescents go through a mild stage of it when they fall for pop stars. There was a time Cha would have killed for Archangel."

"But she didn't think he would marry her."

"Don't ask me what she imagined, Steve. I'm just glad to have no idea. The point I'm making—let me relieve you of that chip—is that you cannot predict how far someone with an obsession will go, because their mindset, as the shrinks say, isn't normal."

Steve was now tackling his sticky toffee pudding with concentrated relish, the happier in that it was safe from his Super, who preferred fruit. "Then you think the fan might've killed Zephyr for being in her way?"

"As I've said, this girl might be so far off the planet as to fancy Zephyr was a mere stopgap till she herself came along. Though, if she thought Zephyr was being a nuisance to Cryer—"

"Didn't most of the death threats to him come from London?"

"Posted all over London. Yes, they did. Fredricks got in touch with Battersea, the address the fan gave Harry Owens, but the postcode doesn't go with the road, her name isn't on the post office list; she could be a short-stay tenant anywhere. They're working on it. But she's clever. There's this whole story of the fan club and the press pass. How did it go?"

"The girl at her hotel, Mara Smith, was from *Gracious Hostess,* an associated magazine with Mrs. Stenn-Boughton's. This mad fan suddenly latched on to her—it was certainly the same young woman she described—and when she was talking after dinner on Tuesday, the woman, Katy she called herself, said she had a genuine description of the wedding dress. Mara phoned the description to a friend on the *Blaze*—we saw it next morning. She got money for it. But she couldn't find her press pass next day and wasn't allowed in."

"What name was it our mad fan used at the hotel?"

"Katy Hepburn."

"Perhaps that's her mirage of herself. Slender and dynamic. We have to get hold of her, Steve. If she can pull off a little stunt like that, to get near Ken Cryer, and put a General, however retired, on his back on Miss Playfair's lawn, she can push a bride off a raft. . . ."

Suddenly through the steady roar of the lunching pub they heard the trilling of Locker's mobile and he fished it out from an inner pocket and bent his head to listen.

"Sorry—just a minute, I'll have to go outside."

A minute later he appeared at the window, beckoning and holding the phone up. Bone went out, and while Locker returned to polish off his pudding, he stood in the comparative quiet of the car park, listening. The voice that came through was Mrs. West's, husky but not as composed as usual.

"Treasure's missing, Mr. Bone. She told me she was going on a picnic with Jem Cryer in the Manor grounds and of course I gave permission. She took the food about an hour ago and went off, and I thought no more about it until Palmerston took a call from Jem just now asking to speak to Treasure. He said they'd never arranged a picnic and he'd no idea where she could be. I'm worried. I thought you should know."

"Yes indeed, Mrs. West." Bone signaled to Locker, who prudently spooned up the last of his pudding. "We'll start a search at once."

Treasure missing. Last time it had been Jem's task to collect food, when they intended to hole up in the boathouse. She had provided the wine. Could she have decided to go and sulk there again?

He hoped she did not mean to go further. If it had been Rawdon Chase whom she saw through the crack, and if he really had a grudge against Zephyr and had assuaged it by holding her under water, might the grudge extend to the rest of the family? To her daughter? To her mother? If Chase was a psychopath who had broken the neck of one sister and drowned the other, he might still be prowling unsatisfied. Years in prison did very little for the sense of perspective.

Now there were three people he urgently needed to find.

Locker emerged from the pub at a leisurely pace, mopping his mouth with a paper napkin.

"Come on, Steve," Bone said. "Quick sticks."

There had been no one in the village street except one elderly woman dragging a shopping trolley, her head down to observe in advance such obstacles as an ill-laid paving slab or the pale yellow depressed Labrador tied to a stanchion outside the post-office-cum-general store. The street was as clear as it was ever going to be.

Luckily, the telephone booth was tucked away in between the entrance to the Scouts' wooden meeting hut and the driveway to a house, and shaded by a copper beech. Yet once he had got safely inside without attracting more than an indifferent glance from the Labrador, he'd stood with his back to the street so that no one, unless they came up and peered round the side of the booth, could get a glimpse of his face. He was not paranoid. He knew perfectly well he was being looked for, and though no one in this somnolent place might be alert enough to recognize him, he took no chances. He had no idea if his picture had been on TV; to see it in the newspaper had been bad enough.

But this chance he must take. He dialed and, as he put the notebook back in his pocket he caught sight of himself in the fly-spotted booth mirror and frowned. It was a risk, yet he must make his point. With his past, he might not be able to convince anyone but he could still be lucky.

He had not finished with that family. They owed him.

Chapter
44
···········

When Bone and Locker returned to Herne Hall, Palmerston had the door open before Bone was out of the car. Although he was too professional to show emotion, he gave Bone the impression that he was disturbed. He backed into the cool marble-flagged hall with less than his usual grace, almost hitting one of the half-tables with its Chinese bowl of coral begonias.

"It seems I was the last to see Miss Treasure, sir. Apart from Doreen in the kitchen, that is, who found her in the larder and gave her buns and fruit for her picnic."

"What was she doing when you saw her?"

"She was on the telephone, sir. A gentleman rang not long after you left and asked to speak to Mrs. West. I was about to go and ascertain whether she would take the call—although as I told him I doubted if she would, as he declined to give his name—when Miss Treasure, who was out here in the hall, came into the room and took the phone from me. I thought she must have been expecting a call and she gave me no time to explain."

"Did it seem to be a call she was expecting?"

Palmerston looked gravely reproachful, and Bone deduced that butlers do not listen to private telephone calls. He added, however, "Miss Treasure gave her name, and although I did not catch the reply, she answered, 'I know who you are. I remember you perfectly.' And do you know, sir," Palmerston bent his head confidentially, "as I went out, it almost seemed to me that I remembered the gentleman's voice myself. American, very similar in accent and even in words to the gentleman who telephoned from Hollywood asking for Miss Zephyr the other day."

Bone thought instantly: Rawdon Chase. Mrs. West had said he was American. He didn't have to be calling from Hollywood; it had been merely a magic word likely to bring Zephyr to the phone. If he was Chase, had he made a tryst that caused Zephyr to disappear and, later, literally, to surface at the lake? God knows what impulse had made Zephyr, in all her wedding finery (and once more, how had no one seen her?) go to meet a man just out of prison where he had been serving a sentence for killing her sister. Could she have been silly enough to think herself perfectly safe?

And now Treasure. What kind of charm, of persuasiveness, could this man have to con a family who had every reason to steer clear of him? Treasure of course was in just the mood to do something stupid. He thought briefly of Cha, whose current boyfriend was an out-of-work actor, at twenty-five far too old for her seventeen, too beautiful to be true in any sense of the word, with wavy gold-brown hair to the shoulders, a merry smile and a tendency to refer to himself, complacently, as "dippy." Her previous one, even more bizarre than this, had taken off for parts unknown, Cha refused to say where. Teenagers were driven by such unpredictable inner forces that one could only hope, but not expect, to stop them before they came to harm. For Treasure Schlumberger's safety, however, he was at the moment responsible. He turned to Locker, looming behind him.

"Get on to the Action Officer, Steve. See who can be rustled up for another search of the grounds."

"If you will excuse me, sir." Palmerston hovered by the baize door of the kitchen quarters. "Miss Treasure may have borrowed Tracey Jackson's bicycle again—one of the gardeners."

Bone knew that this was the first day the gardeners had been allowed beyond the kitchen gardens into the general grounds of the Hall since the reception. The only area still cordoned off was the area by the lake. There would certainly be plenty of damage for the gardeners to repair, after hundreds of guests had spiked the grass with their heels, flattened it with the floor of the marquee, left cigarette ends, tissues and cutlery among the flowers; then police had trampled everywhere in their line searches. The necessity for another search of the grounds might be less urgent if Treasure had taken a bicycle. The odds were they should be combing the district round about rather than the grounds. Locker would take care of that.

Something else struck him. He strode after Palmerston to the baize door and pushed it open.

"Where is Mr. Schlumberger?"

Palmerston turned back and came toward Bone courteously as he answered. "He has taken the car, sir, to go round Saxhurst and the local lanes to see if he can spot Miss Treasure. He thinks she may have gone for a spin to get away from things."

"Thank you." The baize door swept shut with a polite sigh.

A world of possibilities was contained in that word "things": the presence of the police everywhere, the probability of another interview with them and therefore the need to go over the horror of her mother's death, terrible whether or not she had anything to do with it. Neither the silent grief of her grandmother nor the aggressive activity of her father would make "things" easier to bear. Ken Cryer, feeling himself a prisoner at the Manor, had made his attempt to break free using, oddly enough, exactly the same means of transport, a gardener's bicycle. Perhaps Jem had mentioned to Ken Treasure's previous borrowing.

Bone was left in the Hall with Mrs. West's maid Lexie who had appeared from her sitting room.

"Mrs. West will not bother you at the moment, Superintendent, but she would be glad to speak to you at some point when you are less engaged."

The message seemed to be: get on with it and come back with results. What must Mrs. West be feeling, with two daughters killed, perhaps by the same man, and now her granddaughter missing with that person still at large?

"Please tell her I shall come immediately there's any news."

A fine rain had blown in as they took the shortcut to the incident room across the back of the house. It was a slight shower, but enough to make the distant purr of a lawn mower stop like a suddenly displeased cat.

Bone was visited by a hope that if Treasure had in all innocence set off to cycle away her frustrations, the sprinkling of rain might bring her home. It was also possible that Rawdon Chase had not been found locally because he had the sense, guilty or not, to get as far from the scene as he could.

There was news, when they arrived at the coach house, heads and shoulders spangled with rain, of Rawdon Chase—or someone who might be him.

"A car, sir." Fredricks was quite flushed with excitement. "They've found a car just beyond Saxhurst. Keys in the ignition, one door not shut, as if he'd simply given up and got out."

"Was he out of petrol? Not near a filling station?"

"I don't think they'd checked, sir. But he could be anywhere on foot unless he risks public transport."

On foot, anywhere. Saxhurst was not so far from Herne Hall, but would he risk the police presence here of which he must be aware? Bone put up a hand to dry his face as a drop of rainwater fell on the paper Fredricks held out. Treasure was away on her bicycle, not strolling on the grounds. Suppose he had flagged her down on some lonely lane—on the other side of Saxhurst?

"What makes them suppose this car belongs to Chase?"

"It's the registration number the landlady gave us, and it's an Oxford lettering. They found this, sir, in the boot."

This, produced by Rawlings and laid before Bone and Locker, turned out to be plastic-bagged clothing like something made ready for the washing machine. Separated into components, it offered a muddy T-shirt and boxer shorts, both stiff as if they had been wet and left to dry, both heavily creased. There was a stain on the leg of the shorts, very like blood. Bone peered at it through the plastic bag.

"So that, Steve, is how he got across the lake."

Chapter
45
·········

The incident room fell silent as Locker addressed it; people stood awkwardly, holding pieces of paper, files, a polystyrene cup; or sat at their keyboards, while the screens before them glowed. A phone rang. Someone snatched it up and muttered into it.

"What I would like to know," Locker said slowly and heavily, "is, who it was who went ape and searched the car without waiting to see if the owner was around or coming back to it?"

After a pause, Rawlings plaintively spoke. "I don't see how I was to know whose car it was or why I had to wait."

"We have a murderer at large," growled Locker. "You had the registration number for the excellent reason that it belongs to a suspect. There could have been a body, not a T-shirt, in that boot. The owner might have come back and by keeping observation you just might have managed to apprehend him though on present showing I doubt it."

Bone, learnedly not interfering, recalled a case where indeed there had been a body in the boot. Had Rawlings been with the team then, would he have been more circumspect now?

Fredricks was hurrying from the small office, once more the bearer of news. To Rawlings' relief, Locker paused to hear although it was to Bone she spoke. "Sir, London on the line. Superintendent Merton. Something's come through about the Wilson case." Seeing Bone's momentarily blank look, she added, "The lookalike, sir. Alan Grant."

Bone refrained, before this audience, from smiting himself on the forehead. It took a drowned bride and a missing teenager to make him forget that bizarre scene in the quarry, the body that so mercifully was not Cryer. He still had a gut feeling of a connection between that pathetic object carrying a gun so near the Manor, those death threats Ken had been getting, and Ken's bride. The only thing Alan Wilson/Grant had done to rule himself out as a suspect was to be found dead before she was.

The small office had once been a tack room; it had a telephone, a table, a chair meant for Locker and a couple of plastic stacking chairs; they had moved out of Schlumberger's study to be near the incident room. Bone picked up the phone and gave his name.

"Robert—no joy over one aspect: we sent a man round to the address for Alan Grant that the Select-a-Star agency gave, but he'd left six months ago, no forwarding address."

"So, no news then." Bone shook his head at Locker filling the doorway.

"We got back to the agency." Bill Merton was spinning it out a bit. "And the best they could do, I'm telling you, was to dig out the number of a client who kept hiring him. Appears he got sacked on her account because he was giving her freebies when he should have been bringing in commission. She'd become his girlfriend. Their rules are strict about that, stands to reason, it loses them commission. And they weren't keen on him at best—picky about what jobs he wanted, turning up late, refusing to get tinted contact lenses to look more like Cryer. 'No attention to detail' was their complaint.''

"And the girl?"

"We went to that address too."

"Good of you, Bill."

"No, no," Merton said insincerely, and laughed. "You'll scratch my back someday. The girl wasn't in. Away on holiday, the people downstairs said; yes, she had a boyfriend who looked like a pop star and played music too loud, but they had given up making a fuss because she got so stroppy. We showed a photo of Cryer and they agreed that was the one."

"You have been a considerable help. Did you get a description of her?"

"I'll have it faxed through for you. Shortish, brown shoulder-length hair worn straight but with clips both sides. Not bad looking but rather large. Name of Kelly Hunt."

Bone, staring at the listening Locker, saw him catch something from his own expression and lean forward. "That was very helpful indeed, I can tell you."

"Pleasure, Robert. Regards to Disgusted."

This was an old joke. Merton affected to believe that the mythical writer to newspapers, "Disgusted, of Tunbridge Wells," was kept actively corresponding by the antics of the local police.

Ringing off, Bone said, "Our link, Steve! The look-alike and Cryer's fan could be in cahoots."

A plastic chair creaked as Locker dumped himself on it, staring.

"She used to hire him, most likely as a substitute when she couldn't get the real thing, and then hooked him as a permanency. Don't put on that face, Steve—some men prefer a bit of Rubens rather than Twiggy and I seem to remember she's pretty as well as podgy. We'll have to do some dredging as soon as we get hold of the wretched girl. Why has no one clapped eyes on that bright yellow Fiat she drives? Don't tell me Rawlings has had it towed away."

Wounded, Locker got up from his chair with stern resolve. "I'll put a bomb under them. Anyone would think we were in the middle of impenetrable jungle instead of a few villages and a country town to search. Might she not have gone back to London, sir?"

"She hasn't married Cryer yet, remember. Obviously we ought to use him as bait, set him up someplace and see if she comes running."

"She came running to Miss Playfair's," said Locker thoughtfully. "You could have something there, sir."

There was a knock, and Rawlings, still aggrieved rather than abashed, stood there. "The butler, sir, wants a word. Says it's important." For Rawlings, butlers were not part of the real world and he spoke with faint incredulity.

Bone, wondering if Palmerston had remembered more about the telephone call which had almost certainly been from Rawdon Chase, asked, "Where is he? Don't keep him waiting. Of course I'll see him."

"Sir." With the air of one asked to summon a dinosaur, Rawlings vanished, and in a moment Palmerston, unflurried but in some way urgent in bearing, took his place.

"I am sorry to disturb you, sir, but I thought you would wish to be aware of what happened in the cellars just now."

"The cellars." Bone's imagination supplied him with a scene from *Young Frankenstein*—cobwebs, looming shadows, menace, but from whom?

"Doreen." Palmerston's voice conveyed that this was not a name he cared for, nor did he like what he had to say. "Doreen is a good worker and Madam likes her, but I'm afraid I have had my suspicions for some time that bottles of wine have been removed from their racks in the far cellar. On occasion cook sends Doreen to the freezer at the foot of the cellar stairs. Today when she did so I pretended to be occupied elsewhere."

Locker made a winding-up movement and Bone lifted

his hand. To hurry Palmerston might do worse than offend his dignity, it might deter him from cooperation.

"I had just opened the cellar door when I heard a scream." Palmerston scanned his audience, now wholly in his grip, Bone in fact having visions of Treasure strangled by Rawdon Chase, though reason told him Palmerston would not be calmly narrating such an event. "It was Doreen, sir, in the entrance to the far cellar, having hysterics with a bottle in her hands. I took it from her"— Bone saw that a responsible butler must remove a bottle of his employer's wine from a girl having hysterics— "and she told me she had seen a ghost."

"A ghost. You have a ghost at Herne Hall?"

"Not in the cellar, sir. Doreen was under the impression that she had seen Miss West. In her bridal clothes."

Bone exchanged a glance with Locker. Not Young Frankenstein, evidently, but Miss Havisham; though if Zephyr West ever turned up from the spirit world the very last place she would want to be seen in was the cellars. Helpful, of course, if she'd arrived with a tip about her killer.

Palmerston was shaking his head. "Naturally I told her not to be ridiculous, but then I myself heard something in the far cellar. A rat, I thought. I went to see. The passage leads past several cellars and actually leads to the old icehouse in the grounds, above the lake."

Bone and Locker stiffened like pointers.

"There was no one to be seen, though I didn't go right to the end, but I found something." He held out an object that swung glittering from his fingers. "Miss Treasure's bracelet. She constantly wears it and I'm sure she had it this morning. I called her name but there was no reply. Considering the circumstances, I believed I should inform you at once."

If Treasure were in the cellars and did not reply, perhaps she was being prevented. Bracelets can come off in a struggle. If Rawdon Chase could evade security when everyone was on the lookout for him, might he be, now, in Herne Hall itself?

Chapter
46

••••••••••

The naked light bulb in the first cellar cast huge shadows, which Bone lit up with a sweep of the torch he carried. Rawlings was with him, and Fredricks in case Treasure was there, needing feminine comfort. Locker had swiftly organized a posse and gone straight out past the Hall to the icehouse—now that a turf mound among shrubs had been identified. He sent men to search, again, the area of woodland in the uncomfortable proximity of the lake. Others he led up the passage to meet Bone in the cellars.

It was cold in the cellars, penetratingly cold despite the warmth outside. The smell was of damp and stone, reminiscent of a church. The first cellar had a vast chest freezer, squatting like a polar bear against a wall, and racks of stores such as the kitchens required; the next held racks for wine, so extensive that it was plain how much wine such a household had once consumed. A modest store of bottles inhabited one rack nearest the door, glittering under a film of dust. Treasure was not lurking there.

Through a stone archway—bone had not realized the extent of the underground of Herne Hall. It had been built at a time when such a basement had to provide all the storage of a great house; this last room contained cupboards, and Bone found that one held large tins, Kilner jars of preserved fruit, king-sized storage pots, sheaves of candles.

Locker's torchlight preceded Locker in the far doorway. He said, "There's a bicycle out there under the bushes, a woman's bike."

"So Treasure may really be here . . . !" Bone, more swiftly, went on opening cupboards. He had no real expectation of finding Rawdon Chase glaring at him from inside one, so shelves of innocent tins were no disappointment, but he would have liked to find Treasure crouched there sullenly.

Suddenly electric light startled them all. Shay was wrestling with a door in the corner, whose wooden panels the light showed to be battered. "Sir, this one's locked."

They heard steps coming through the cellars. It was Palmerston, who had evidently switched on the lights. Unable to keep up with the stampede he had set off, he had finally arrived to see the results. Bone greeted him with a question.

"Are there any more cupboards where people could hide? Except for this one which is locked?"

Palmerston surveyed the storeroom. "If you will excuse me, sir, that door has no lock. It is the door to the backstairs and, if it will not open, it must be bolted inside."

Bone strode forward to examine it. "The backstairs. Where do they lead?"

"Right up through the house, sir, from cellars to attics, with access to each floor. They are not used now. We use the matching stairs at the far end. That door has two heavy bolts, top and bottom."

Generations of servants since this house was built must have run or toiled up these stairs, with jugs of drink, hods of coal, and trays. Bone thought solely of the murderer who might have shot the bolt on them, a murderer pushing Treasure ahead of him up these stairs. He strode off toward the other stairs. "The attics, Steve; search the house as we go."

Rawdon Chase might be aiming at a greater target even than Treasure. If his resentment was against the whole family—and Bone had come across killers quite meticulous in ridding the world of every member of a family—usually their own—to pay back a grudge, it would not prove difficult to overcome a woman in a wheelchair, and Lexie would be but a frail obstacle. Bone was halfway to the ground floor by now. He heard Locker assign people to guard the door they had just found.

Bone hoped his fears were unjustified, that the whole business would turn out to be Treasure leading them a dance. She had hidden before. She had plenty to hide from, with what had happened recently in her life. Yet why in her grandmother's house? The bracelet Palmerston had found might simply be a cry for help, dropped as a deliberate clue.

The kitchen held only the cook comforting Doreen, who at sight of the police sent her teacup flying and cowered, moaning. Passages, hall, Mrs. West's sitting room, the dining room, blue sitting room, conservatory, library, Schlumberger's office, morning room, all were empty. Last time, they had been searched for an errant bride, and hiding places still yielded nothing. Bone took the main stairs two at a time, to the first floor and Mrs. West's rooms. Lexie was inclined to protest at any disturbance, but Mrs. West called out, "Is that you, Mr. Bone? Any news?" She lay on a chaise longue at the foot of her bed, and for all her composure looked worn and anxious.

"We're searching the house in case your granddaughter is here." No mention of Chase until and if they found him.

"She hasn't come in here." Mrs. West struggled to sit up and Lexie was quick to help her. "Why do you think she's in the house? If she is, we needn't worry."

This was positively not the time to tell her how much she needed to worry. Bone managed a smile, scanned the room briefly and left. Locker met him at the stairhead.

"We checked the lift Mrs. West uses. It only runs from here to the ground floor. Rawlings and Fredricks have covered this floor. There's only the attics. Wilkinson and Higgins are in that far cellar guarding the bolted stair door . . ."

The game of hide-and-seek must be getting close to its goal. They started up the backstairs, from a paneling door outside Zephyr West's room in a corner of the landing. Bone motioned with his hand for them to keep the sound down. It was still possible that if anyone were in the attics, pursuit had not yet been realized. Suppose Treasure were a hostage, anyone who held her must not be alarmed.

The attics, as Palmerston had said, ran the whole length of the house. A corridor with a slanting ceiling went ahead, a long vista lit by small windows that each faced a door on the opposite side. The rooms as they began to search smelled warm, musty—the dormitories of the staff in days gone by. Here were two iron bedsteads and a view of the park impeded by a parapet beyond the small window, here an iron bedstead with a mattress rolled up covered with sheets of newspaper. Elderly washstands held jugs and bowls; a table in another room stood on three legs, the fourth laid apologetically on top. There were no visible cobwebs, no mouse droppings, these attics must be regularly cleaned; there was a haze of dust over everything and a sensation of breathing it as they went on. Bone was aware of the roof just overhead, the slope of it visible in the corridor and along the front of every room. These rooms would be stifling in summer and perishing cold in winter. Only one room had a small iron fireplace. The dust was not thick enough to show footprints—he had checked that before they began. Could he be completely mistaken in believing there was someone here? What had they to go on in believing it?—That the cellar door had been bolted inside.

They came to a bigger room, again with an iron grate and a big bed piled with plastic-wrapped blankets and quilts, and with an iron structure above that must have supported a tester. The bedhead and foot were of wood, carved with a certain sweep and grandeur matching the carved armoire against the wall, both articles of furniture exiled here as too old-fashioned and large to grace any of the rooms below.

Bone turned to Locker, pointed, and nodded. With ponderous care Locker crossed the linoleum and seized the tarnished brass of the armoire's door handle—Bone, every sense sharpened, saw it was a lion's head in the second before Locker's hand descended.

The door was wrenched open.

No anticlimax. They had found what they were looking for. They had not found it in any manner Bone had imagined. Treasure stood just inside, and so did Rawdon Chase, the strong saturnine features resembling the photograph. He was clasping Treasure in his arms but the wholly baffling thing was that she was also clasping him. Treasure Schlumberger had her arms tightly round the waist, and her head on the chest, of the man who had killed her aunt and, possibly, her mother.

Chapter

47

·········

"He didn't do it."

Treasure had raised her head to glare at them. She was shaking, either with fury or from the fear of being pursued. Rawdon Chase looked, if anything, embarrassed at being caught in a cupboard embracing a teenager. He dropped his arms but Treasure continued to hug him defiantly.

"You had better come with us, Mr. Chase."

He disengaged her arms firmly, stepped from the wardrobe and put out a hand to help her, but she jumped down, ignoring it. She faced Bone, flushed with rage. There was a sudden strong resemblance to her father. "You're just being stupid. He's been through enough without your persecuting him."

Bone, filled with relief that the search was over, Chase found and Treasure unharmed, could not help smiling at her, which enraged her further. Fredricks, out in the passage, was on her radio reporting the capture, and, Locker advancing on Chase, Treasure gave vent to her feelings by shoving him in the midriff with both hands, and much the same effect as a butterfly shoving a buffalo.

"Leave him alone! Why don't you give him a chance to tell you what really happened?"

"In fact that's exactly what we're going to do. I suggest that you go and tell your grandmother that you are all right. I don't think you realize how worried she has been about you."

"I told her we were going on a picnic."

"Yes, but Jem rang up. Believe me, she is very worried."

"Only because you think Rawdon's a murderer and he *isn't*. He's absolutely innocent of everything."

We should all be so lucky, thought Bone. If he's so innocent how did he go to prison in the first place? Why did he plead guilty? And, in particular, what was he up to in the neighborhood when Zephyr drowned? Nostalgia was hardly the answer. Nothing explained his turning up at Herne Hall in this furtive fashion. Rawdon Chase was in arrears with a great deal of explaining and it looked as though Treasure was set on doing it for him.

Best to let her talk about it rather than assault the police and glower. When they got her story they would see how Chase's version tallied. Of course the two had spent time together, in or out of cupboards, enough to align their facts or their fictions. At the back of Bone's mind was the unpleasant idea that although Treasure might not have killed her mother, she showed no aversion to protecting the man who possibly had. Was it not her father, or Jem's, but Chase, whom she had seen through that peephole in the boathouse door?

"This way, Mr. Chase."

Locker was not a man to be argued with physically, nor did Chase, unlike Treasure, seem inclined to put up any resistance. On the contrary, he looked relieved. His features, now that Bone had a chance to study them, were melancholic as well as strongly marked. Bone had an unusually deep stir of curiosity to know about this man. How, for a start, had he managed to get Treasure so passionately on his side?

The small party made its way down the main stairs.

Bone wanted to deliver Treasure to her grandmother but he did not want Mrs. West to know she was harboring Chase. He sent Fredricks to inform her that her granddaughter had been found, was safe, and would be coming to see her.

They ran into trouble as they crossed the hall.

Trouble came from the front door, mobile phone to his ear. If a large florid man can look haggard, the pouches under his eyes and his air of burning frustration made him so. The frustration, though, melted into astonishment and then to rage as he saw what was before him.

"What in hell are *you* doing here?" It was not a question to which he expected an answer and indeed Chase had said nothing so far. Dwight turned to Treasure, his face dangerously flushed. "Was he messing with you? Did he touch you? I'll kill him if he touched you!"

Treasure's reply to this was to fling herself at her father, somewhat as she had at Locker, and pummel him on the chest which, as he was not built quite like Locker, made him stagger.

"Everybody's being stupid about him, you don't understand." She was crying by now and Bone could not be surprised. The tension of being hunted, all that she had been through, a girl of fourteen whose mother had been killed only days ago, it was a wonder that counselors of all kinds had not been unleashed upon her to stir up her grief.

One thing Bone needed, at that moment, was Dwight Schlumberger.

"If you will come with us, sir, we'd appreciate it."

Dwight, having got both Treasure's wrists in one hand as she wept, and applying his large multicolored handkerchief to her cheeks, looked at Bone with suspicion. Through all this, Rawdon Chase had been standing, attentive and polite, with the look of a professor at a tea party waiting to be introduced. Gold-rimmed spectacles, which Bone took in for the first time, added to this effect. If he were a killer, he was a very cool customer, but Bone had met some as cool.

"What do you want *me* to do?" Dwight had by now gathered Treasure to him, and she snuggled into his shoulder, his beard rumpling her hair. All at once she was a child and not a ferocious young woman. Dwight jerked his beard at Chase. "I'd like to know what that bastard is doing out of jail, and what he's doing round here. Any questions about him I'd be glad to answer."

At this moment Palmerston manifested himself, holding open the green baize door that separated the house from the kitchens, checking to see if he was wanted. It gave Bone the thought that they must make an odd group, with Treasure quietly sobbing in her father's arms and a total stranger standing by with Locker crowding him. Palmerston evinced as much surprise and concern as a butler may permit himself but was ready, at Bone's reassuring nod, to vanish again. Curiously enough, his appearance had the effect of provoking Dwight.

"Let's get out of here, someplace we can talk. Why don't we go to my room?"

The biggest objection was that from now on things had to proceed on more formal lines. Fresh in Bone's mind was the memory of the crumpled dried-out boxer shorts, stained with what might be lake mud and with weed and smears of blood, found in the car traceable to Chase. He gave another nod to Locker, who had been anticipating it and who turned to Chase.

"Rawdon Chase, I arrest you—"

Locker had barely time for the words before Treasure went off like a steam whistle. Bone had supposed she might and hoped to provoke something useful, a word or so that might help him to the right line in the coming interrogation. What he had not expected was that Treasure, wrenching herself from her father's embrace, should rush to confront him. He almost flinched. Red-eyed, tooth-braces showing in a snarl, she was not the loveliest sight.

"I *tell* you he couldn't have done it! *Why* don't you leave him alone?"

"You saw him at the lake with your mother." Bone was not going to lose this opportunity.

"Yes—but he was just *talking* to her." She turned to Chase, who incredibly, still played the role of ironic spectator in this drama. "You never meant to hurt her, did you? You said you left her there."

"What the hell's this? Did *you* murder my wife?"

Locker was instantly between Dwight and Chase.

"I think," said Bone, raising his voice a little, "that we had better go to the incident room. Mr. Schlumberger, I would be grateful if you would follow and hold yourself in readiness for when we can hear your daughter's story. Sergeant Fredricks here will look after you."

The touch of pomposity worked. Dwight, whether or not he was happy to hold himself in readiness, appeared at least to hold himself in check. There was no unseemly tussle on the black and white marble flags of the hall. Treasure, too, had been sobered by Bone's manner; it was a tone he had adopted successfully with Cha in past confrontations and he told himself that sticky moments with stroppy teenagers demanded a very steady touch when you were putting on authority, or you risked the slammed door and the forty-eight-hour sulk. Above all, he needed Treasure's cooperation if he was to nail Chase, now that she had admitted having seen him at the lakeside with Zephyr.

They reached the incident room in silence, crossing the cobbles with a varied sound of footsteps while in the distance a lawnmower buzzed like some demented bee. Rawdon Chase, who had shown no emotion at being arrested, still had the air of a detached observer. His thick dark hair was untidy but the thick dark eyebrows did not frown. If he had strangled Zephyr's sister in a fit of temper she must have been far more maddening than even Zephyr could be.

The incident room greeted their entrance in an awed and sudden hush. Here was magic indeed. Send out all available men to scour the countryside and you net an empty car and a pair of muddy boxer shorts. Send out the Super himself and he comes in ushering a meek suspect.

He did not prove as meek as he looked.

"Rawdon Crawley Chase," Bone read from the folder Hooley had put on the desk. They were again in the little tack room, with more of the plastic chairs. "You have recently failed to keep your appointments with Mr. Bagot, your probation officer, after your release on license from Pritchard Prison a fortnight ago." Rawdon Chase nodded and then, as Bone gestured at the recorder, said, "Yes."

"What was your reason for failing to keep these appointments?"

"I had to discover something." The voice was deep and the accent transatlantic.

"Something."

Chase smiled. It gave a hint of why Mrs. West had once liked him. "I came to see if a promise would be kept."

Bone was aware of a rising impatience, and of Locker shifting as he listened. With this sort of answer it would be evening before they got anywhere. Yet it was self-defeating to rush things.

"Zephyr West made you a promise." It was a fair guess, if he had swum the lake to talk to her.

Chase looked directly at him, the light glinting on the frames of his glasses. He spoke with more emotion now.

"Zephyr had promised to marry me when I came out of jail."

He could hardly, Bone thought, have been thrilled to the marrow at finding Zephyr in the act of marrying someone else—no, of course *having* married Ken Cryer the day before. If he was speaking the truth.

"Why would she do that, Mr. Chase? You had been in prison for killing her sister."

Chase nodded again, and his tone was brusque. "Yes, yes, but I didn't do it. She knew that."

Bone raised his eyebrows. Go slowly, he told himself; one step at a time. "If she knew you did not kill her sister, why did she let you go to prison for it?"

"Because *she* did. Zephyr killed Storm herself."

Chapter

48

··········

In the silence that followed, the murmur of voices next door in the incident room, the soft clack of computer keys, the muted shrill of a telephone, came clearly. Locker, after a second or two, produced a snort, of either amazement or disbelief. Bone continued his steady observation of Chase. The man had spoken with perfect calm; with conviction. If Zephyr had not killed her sister, Chase believed she had.

"How did she kill her?"

"She shook her till she snapped her neck. The way I was supposed to have done."

"Why did you claim to have done it?"

Chase shrugged. "You might say I was crazy. Well, I *was* crazy. Zephyr had that effect on people. On men. In those days I had only to look at her and if she'd asked me to jump out the window I think I'd have done it."

What came to Bone's mind was Ken Cryer, his face when Zephyr had arrived at Herne Hall and Bone had first met her. Perhaps, if it hadn't been for the blessing of Grizel and her sanity, he might have had the misfortune to kill for a woman like that. This thought strengthened his constant subliminal awareness of Grizel, smiling

287

at him from her hospital bed, stranded there by her size and by what was happening to her. That was where, incongruously, he wanted to be, now, holding her hand, comforting her, not sitting here listening to the tale of how a selfish woman had ruined a man's life.

"She asked you to say you'd killed her sister, in return for a promise to marry you when you came out of prison. You believed her."

Chase frowned for the first time, his face severe behind the glasses. "People may not have thought she was much of an actress but she was a brilliant actress off-screen. Of course I believed her. *You* would have believed her."

Locker, seemingly emerging from trance, leaned forward. "You are saying you let yourself go to jail for manslaughter for the sake of marrying Zephyr West?"

Chase turned his head toward Locker, with something approaching distaste.

"I just said that. If you cannot understand my motive you may possibly never have been in love."

Bone, knowing that Locker was hardly going to claim a passionate past, intervened.

"Mr. Chase, what we are trying to understand here are the facts of the situation. Can you describe to us exactly what happened on," he consulted the file again, "the seventeenth of August, 1992, at Parleston House, just outside Oxford?"

"There's nothing to tell." Chase looked over at the file almost benevolently. "Everything's exactly as you'll have it there, except that where you have me attacking Storm, put Zephyr instead. She had one of her rages, not unusual."

"You stated at the trial," said Bone, scanning the printout in front to him, "that you were in love with Storm, not with her sister, and that her rejection of you caused you to attack her as you did."

Chase laughed, a harsh sound, and it came to Bone that he resembled a crow, with his deeply lined face, beak of a nose, thick dark hair and eyebrows, and this caw of a laugh.

"You don't know what a joke that was. Storm was jealous of Zephyr, furiously jealous. She could not stand men fancying Zephyr above her. She didn't have"—he broke off and spread his hands helplessly—"whatever it was that Zephyr had. Sex appeal, I suppose. Storm was the one making passes. Zephyr found Storm clamped against me and she was not pleased. Oh, it was okay Storm wanting me when she'd got me herself, but she drew the line at her trying to get me away. I think the phrase is: she flipped."

"Wasn't all this," Locker put in repressively, "while Miss West was still married to Mr. Schlumberger?"

Chase tilted his head forward to look at Locker over the top of his glasses. "I was not aware you were here to make moral judgments. I supposed the legal aspect was your province. Dwight Schlumberger was in the States at that time."

So that made it all right, did it, thought Bone; he did not suppose the existence of a husband affected Chase. When you're under a spell things like husbands are nebulous, disposable at the wave of a wand; nor did he imagine that Zephyr, happy in this odd conquest, would have been in a rush to remind Chase of Dwight.

Chase was explaining further. "She told me she was considering a divorce. Schlumberger meant nothing to her."

Bone had a maverick urge to say: he's sitting in the next room, why don't you try that out on him, you might just get your glasses broken. Schlumberger had meant something to Zephyr: somebody to cater for her every whim and pay for them heartily too. It was a wonder she had ever divorced him.

Get to the point. "You spoke to Miss West," it was ironic referring to her as a single woman, "by the lake toward evening of August the twenty-third. How did you get her to meet you?"

Again, Chase's sardonic caw. "I knew she'd be too

busy to come to the phone for anything less than a Hollywood producer so I said I was one. It got her all right. Then I told her I was out and I had to talk with her." He paused and looked at his hands. "I had written to her from jail—carefully—but she'd never written back. Of course I was imbecilic. I almost knew what she was going to say but I had to hear it from her."

"She told you that she was married already."

"She told me she had gotten tired of waiting for me, she had her own life to live." Chase's smile twisted wryly. "I'd had mine, too. Inside, waiting to get out, waiting my reward."

"Had you thought," Bone's voice was carefully neutral, "that she might think it would look strange if she were to marry the man who was believed to have killed her sister?" In fact, the question had little point, for Zephyr had taken away this clever man's logic and left him with only hope and desire; which have little to do with reason.

"Ah yes, she said that. 'What would people say?' It's what she said, right at the start, when we found Storm was dead. 'What would people say?' It would be the end for her. She begged me to take the blame. I was the one she could trust to save her."

The bitterness was open now, without cover of academic detachment. Six years of his life this man had spent waiting to claim his prize: the beautiful creature who owed him, for whom he was making the sacrifice of his freedom, enduring the restrictions, every moment circumscribed—his career on hold if not ended. He comes out, finds she has, the day before—that must have been bitter indeed—married, not the perpetually busy, long-suffering Schlumberger again but Cryer, as rich, and also famous, fascinating, who could hardly be represented as a stopgap. Bone saw the scene, Zephyr in all the glory of that wedding dress, gauze and pearls arched above the teased-out splendor of blond locks, those huge blue eyes raised—how? Pleadingly? Or had she simply told him how impossible was his expectation, made him

realize, brutally, how crazy he had been to waste his life
for her? Either way, it was cogent reason for murder.

"You were angry when she told you she was married?" Bone thought he was stating the obvious, but
Chase shook his head, a brief negation.

"Not angry. I can't tell what I felt. Disappointed.
Numb. I'd been expecting it."

Locker put in again, "Expecting she was married?"

Chase addressed his answer to Bone. "I was expecting
her to say what she did. God knows I had plenty of time
to think, inside. You go over everything you've said and
done, everything other people have said and done. You
may invent scenarios of what you said and they said, but
you come back to the facts. You get a historic perspective on things. For the first few years"—he adjusted his
glasses higher on the beak of his nose—"for the first few
years I was full of hope. She was waiting for me, with
gratitude. Then you know, I came to thinking. Why
should she trouble?" The laugh this time was desolate.
"I'd taken the rap for her, I'd performed my function
in her life. She would have no further use for me. I have
no money to speak of; St. Benet's is not likely to take
me back on the faculty; and certainly no prospects. I'd
never kidded myself she was in love with me." He
paused and then continued as if talking to himself.
"Blackmail. That was the only way to get hold of her.
Threaten to tell what had really happened. While I
watched all the preparations for the ceremony going
on—"

"You watched."

"I had a place in the trees opposite. I watched with
binoculars. I planned what I'd say to her."

He fell silent and, after a moment, Bone picked up.
"You said it when you swam across the lake."

"Oh yes. I must have looked stupid standing there
wringing wet. She laughed. She covered her mouth with
her hand but she was laughing. Who would believe you,
she said. I'd confessed, I'd done my time. People would
think I'd worked up a grudge in jail and was taking it

out on her. I'd killed one sister and was aiming to shoot down the other."

There was a longer silence. Locker this time let it alone. It seemed that Rawdon Chase had come to the end of what he had to say. Bone, now, had to put the inevitable formal question.

"Rawdon Crawley Chase, did you, on the afternoon of August the twenty-third of this year, kill Zephyr West?"

Chase pushed up his glasses and spoke with pedantic clarity.

"No. I did not."

Chapter
49
....

The day was beautiful, fresh, with the sun shining through chestnut leaves that already were gold and tawny with approaching autumn. Yet Kelly, bowling along the road in her little yellow Fiat, felt much less cheerful than she usually did.

She had been frustrated everywhere. All that consoled her was that Ken must be feeling it too. If she was being kept from him, he was being kept from her. She leaned and pushed the cassette player's button, smiling in anticipation.

It was one of her favorite tapes, and today it had a special message for her. Ken had used some orchestral instruments on this one. She had bothered to find out that those were oboes sadly wailing in the background, soon to be overtaken by a rather sinister drum and that noise a bit like squeaky shoes going softly over a wooden floor. Ken's voice was low, intense. She shivered and tightened her grip on the wheel.

Don't kiss Despair . . . Spit out his tongue.
Hear all I've sung . . .

293

She did, she did. She had to keep trying. Perhaps this was all a test for her. Once more she swung off the road into the track she knew well from all those expeditions with Alan. How often they would come down here, one of Ken's tapes playing as now, the picnic box in the back with their favorite sandwiches and the thermos of coffee, to be enjoyed when they'd had their fun, what they came for. Poor Alan, looking at him had always been a let-down, afterward.

She was smiling at the memory when, turning the bend toward the top of the hill, she was forced to tramp hard on the brake.

There was a chain across the way, from tree to tree.

She flung open the door and got out to stare at it, hands on hips. Who could have put it there, and why? She looked up the hill at the trees on its crest, and thought she saw odd movements up there. It was not quite the dazzle of sun on leaves shifting in the breeze. She made out colors, blue and white, police tapes marking off an area they had been investigating. Turning, she ran back to the car and switched off the player and the ignition. This was to do with Alan. She had no connection with Alan, nothing to do with him . . .

It made her think further. There sat the little yellow Fiat, conspicuous in the dappled sunshine. The police would be looking for anyone who could help them in their inquiries, as it was politely put. Anybody who had been at the wedding reception and was still about. She mustn't be found. She was the one who must protect Ken.

Her mission was to offer him comfort, a refuge from all that had gone wrong in his life and she was here—let her remember this—because he had asked her to come. She must keep her spirits high. He would want her to.

And, after all, it was a fine day! As she picked her way down the lane, or track, she was glad the grass at the edge was hardly wet at all after that rain earlier, it would have wrecked her shoes. Everything arranged itself! She was carrying her overnight bag with her purse in it and, of course, the tape she had rescued from the car. At the bend she turned to look at it, sitting as if baffled in front of the chain. A shame to say goodbye like that, but there were things more important than cars. And Ken would certainly give her a car.

Humming "Hear all I've sung," she walked away.

If Kelly could have seen Ken at that instant, she might have faltered in her cheerful mood. He was, as she might have pictured him, at the grand piano in the big sitting room, but he sat sideways and his hands were not on the keys but on the waist—the far from slim waist, Kelly might have been encouraged by that—of his secretary Edwina Marsh, who bent over him, her hands on his shoulders, her hair in a sweep that obscured both their faces. Had Ken been at death's door, Edwina's mouth-to-mouth resuscitation might well have caused a dejected Death to slam that door shut. Edwina, generously built, had generous kisses to give.

"My God," said Ken finally, emerging from under the bell of hair with his own ruffled, and rather in want of breath. "I begin to feel I can get back to sanity. Can we possibly, really, have escaped from that nightmare?"

Edwina, gazing down at him with her little china doll smile, fondly, put a finger on his lips. "It may not be over yet. They still think you may have done it."

"They could never prove I had." He put his head forward to rest on her bosom. Muffled, he said, "They don't even know how glad I am she's dead. It's a dangerous thing to admit even to you."

Edwina cupped the back of his head in her hand, and there was a silence. She said, "Could anyone at all have seen you while you were walking about that day? Everyone was in the tent when it rained. What about that fan who jumped you in the gazebo? She could be a witness."

"You seriously think anyone would believe a word she said? She lives in la-la land." He raised his head; his arm slipped as he made to pull Edwina closer and struck a few jarring notes on the keyboard. It made them laugh and tighten their embrace.

Jem, wandering the grounds of the Manor not far off, thought it was his father getting annoyed with whatever he was trying to compose—how lucky to have something to do, something to distract him at a time like this. Bored with his computer, unable to raise any of his friends—the worst of going to school in the North, few of his friends lived near—he had no way of passing the time but to worry over the idea that sooner or later the police were going to question him again over what he or Treasure had seen or done that awful day. He badly needed to find out what Treasure wanted to say, but where was she? The phone call he'd made only increased his worry. If she'd said she was going off on a picnic with him, where was she? Why hadn't she warned him what she was going to say? It was stupid because he'd shot her story down without meaning to—and at first he'd thought she would turn up here at any minute.

That was an hour ago. More.

The only idea that came to him was to ring Miss Playfair. Maybe the rain had put Treasure off a genuine picnic and she'd gone instead to have another look at the kittens. He wouldn't mind doing that. Better than mooching around here.

Emily Playfair was at home and no, Treasure wasn't there but it would be delightful if Jem came to see the kittens and probably Treasure would show up before long. Emily had just baked a walnut cake and was looking for someone to help her with it.

Jem immediately found Mel, who was free to drive him to Miss Playfair's cottage, and left a message saying where he had gone. Ken was very tough about such things, and indeed about manners in general or Jem could have permitted himself the satisfaction of making a hideous face at the few reporters still at the gates. Instead he gave them, as the car slid by, a regally courteous wave that would not have disgraced the Queen Mother.

* * *

Bone leaned back in his chair and considered his options. Perhaps he hadn't expected to get a full and fluent confession from Rawdon Chase, but the man had appeared so cooperative, so calmly willing to tell all, that it had not seemed impossible; after all that easy journey—had he refused to answer a single question?—they had landed up with a jar at the buffers. Full stop. Rawdon Chase denied killing Zephyr West, in spite of having enough reasons to have made Bone want to drown her himself.

"I think," he said eventually, "we need to go over exactly what you did that day."

Chase proved perfectly willing for that. He confirmed that he had been staying at the Red Lion in Adleston, whose proprietors had later helpfully identified him from the photo faxed from Oxford. He had paid up and left on the morning of the reception. He explained how he had already explored the woods that led down to the lake on the far side and had watched the near shore through binoculars.

"I saw Zephyr the night before. Beautiful as ever. Dancing by herself in the twilight." He shook his head. "I almost changed my mind then."

"Changed your mind. How?" Bone's question was quick and brought an involuntary hesitation from Chase as though some wrong step had been made in a maneuver which until that point had been faultlessly executed.

"I meant . . . I had been thinking the whole thing was hopeless. She'd never intended to marry me, she had been ready to promise anything when Storm died. I'd come to terms with it, so to speak, with the waste it had been and then—seeing her dancing—it all came back. She was so very beautiful."

"You changed your mind." Bone did not let go.

The reel on the recorder made several revolutions before Chase replied.

"I'd intended all along to shame her, force her to tell me what I knew, that I'd wasted my life for her. Seeing her like that, I wanted to believe I was wrong." He was used to academic exposition and gave the impression of marshaling his thoughts. "Yet—" he shook his head as if throwing off a spell, and gave his harsh laugh, "she was dancing for happiness. Not because I'd got out of jail—I'd written to tell her but I don't suppose she read my letters—but because she'd netted the man she wanted. How could I compete with some mega-rich rock star? How could she marry the man who'd 'killed her sister?' "

It was a plausible line of thought, but Bone was still wondering whether Chase's purpose, so nearly changed by seeing the beauty that had once enchanted him, had originally been to kill her for the waste of his life he spoke of so bitterly. Had he almost decided he would not kill her?

"Tell me what happened after you left the Red Lion . . ."

"I parked the car down the drive of an empty house, one with a For Sale sign—along the road here and I called Zephyr from the call box at the head of Chapel Lane. I asked her to meet me at the lake. There'd been a rain shower and of course," he smiled slightly, "she was worried about messing her clothes in the wet, or being seen—and then she remembered some passage through the cellars, she said, would keep her feet dry most of the way and no one would see her."

"You swam the lake. No one from Security bothered you?"

"The rain seemed to clear the place of everyone. And I guess Security was concentrating on the reception area, for I saw no one although I was certainly looking. I left my clothes up among the trees. I think she found it romantic my swimming across to her, Leander swimming the Hellespont to Hero, though I don't imagine she'd have had the least idea about *them.*" Chase, seeing no intelligent response in the faces of Bone and Locker either, went on. "Just an old Greek story. There's no more to say. I told her what I thought of her and swam back."

"You did not drown her?"

"I did not even touch her. I tell you I did not kill her. Whatever she'd done to me, I could not have harmed her."

And at that he stuck.

Bone sat back and let Locker take Chase through the details again, with only the addition that when he had swum back he had dried himself on his T-shirt, put on the rest of his clothes and walked up through the woods.

Bone broke in. "Did you look back at any time?"

Zephyr must have met her death within the next quarter hour or so. If Rawdon Chase were not her killer then he had an opportunity of seeing who was. If they had not got a murderer, had they a witness?

"No. I didn't look back. I'd finished with her forever."

He was telling the truth there, either way. And how much of the rest of his story was true?

Dig for Treasure, thought Bone.

299

Chapter
50
· · · · · · · · · ·

Chase was escorted out, and Treasure escorted in. Dwight had a protective arm round her, advertising to the police that he would monitor her interests and they had better remember it. Oddly enough, Treasure did not shrug off her father's arm. She looked suddenly very young and tired. The professional in Bone hoped that she was tired of lying or at least of suppressing the truth. He was convinced that she must have seen or heard something or she would not be cagey.

She was anxious to tell, but not what they most needed to hear. She wanted to clear Rawdon Chase of her aunt's murder all those years ago.

"I saw all of it happen. Nobody knew I was there." She sat leaning forward, her fingertips on the edge of the desk. "There was Granpa's sort of study or writing room, a little place with this desk in it that had a square place for your legs." Her hands sketched a cuboid hollow.

"A kneehole desk," Dwight suggested.

"Right, a kneehole desk. I used to go and sit in the kneehole and read, I could go there and not be interrupted the whole time. Nobody knew I was there that

day either. Mom was ramping around upstairs in a mood
about her hair or something and I had *Black Beauty* and
I went and hid. There was a door into the library that
didn't shut and so when the maid showed Rawdon in I
could see him sit down and look at the newspaper and
the maid I guess went to tell Mom he'd arrived. Then
he got up but it wasn't Mom, it was Storm and she said
for him to sit down, and he did, and she went and fiddled
with the flowers on the table right next to him. Rawdon
had sent them and Mom had arranged them, she loved
arranging flowers and things—" a spasm crossed Treasure's face at the thought "—and Storm would forever
be rearranging anything she did so's to be different."

Dwight was nodding, and Bone wondered how much
he knew of this event, if Treasure had just told him or
if this was news to him or, disconcerting thought, that
he'd known all along that Chase was innocent and col-
luded with Zephyr in pretending otherwise, for her sake.
Locker was stirring impatiently but Bone's just-lifted
hand kept him quiet; they were justified in finding out
as much as they could about Chase, in case he had a
motive here for killing the woman he adored. Along
with this, Treasure was in the flow.

"Well then, I was reading and I heard Rawdon say
something, like 'No, look,' and I did look and Storm was
sitting on his knee. She said like he was wasting his time
running after Mom who was married to someone rich
she wouldn't give up, and she was touching his face—"
Treasure's forefinger traced a line—"and he stood up
and he was telling her 'No' and she just clammed on to
him and he was pulling back and then there was a
screech and Mom came rushing in. She got Storm by the
hair and Storm clawed her hand off and they were yelling and Storm said something I didn't catch and Mom
totally flipped. She got Storm by the neck and shook
her." Treasure stopped and shuddered. "There was a
sort of click. I heard a click. And Mom let go. Storm
went—she dropped. Like a doll. She lay there on the

rug and Mom started having hysterics. I scrooged way back in the desk."

Dwight put his broad hand on hers, and she went on, in a small voice, "Mom said, 'Oh *God* oh *God* oh *God*' and Rawdon was doing something, he must have been feeling for a pulse, I guess, and Mom was saying, 'She's *dead* she's *dead.*' She would know; Storm had this accident when she was my age. She fell off a horse and injured her vertebrae—vertebrae, right?—in her neck. She was supposed to wear a collar at night and take care all the time though she didn't. Mom knew she never should have shaken her."

Didn't put her off shaking Jem Cryer, Bone thought. For all she knew that might have been just as dangerous. He noticed that Dwight was not surprised by this story.

"When I looked, Rawdon was trying mouth-to-mouth and I couldn't see what Mom was doing but she was kind of moaning and he told her to get an ambulance and she picked up the phone but she put it down and was saying her life was ruined, everyone would say she'd done it on purpose and it was terrible and she was sobbing—and Rawdon said he'd say he had done it, that it was an accident. Mom just snapped onto that."

Dwight was nodding his head again, as if this was a deal he could approve of, one he would have faxed himself if he could. But if a doting lover had not been at hand, would he have made such a sacrifice for Zephyr himself? Bone doubted it. Dwight liked power. He was not a man for romantic sacrifice.

"Please try to recollect, as far as you can, exactly what Rawdon Chase said." Could they rely on the memory of a child who must have been eight or so at the time, confused and distressed into the bargain? But Treasure's manner was quite positive.

"He said he'd say she was coming on to him and he'd pushed her off, shaken her off and must have broken her neck."

"Didn't they get an ambulance?" Locker burst out, unable to hold his peace.

302

"Sure! Mom said she wasn't getting any answer and it turned out she'd been dialing nine one one like you do in the States for emergency, not nine nine nine the way you do here. Rawdon told her and the ambulance came almost right away."

"The bargain with your mother." Bone brought them back to the point. "He was going to take the blame. What about her side of it?"

"Right, so she was crying and saying she'd do anything for him, anything if he'd say he'd killed Storm, and he was wonderful and a hero and all of that sort, and he came back right away with 'Marry me' and she said she would. She said if he went to jail she'd wait for him, but of course he would never get sent to jail because she'd say it was an accident."

Here they were at what Bone really wanted to know.

"He did get sent to jail. Do you know why?"

"Sure." Her voice, which had been high and hurried and childish as if she inhabited that child's personality of acute memory, became teenage and cynical. "When the ambulance men turned up and Rawdon said to them it was all his fault, Mom went straight into acting mode and she shrieked, 'You hated her! You always said you'd kill her!' "

"Why do you think she said that?"

Treasure shrugged. "I guess she just said it to be dramatic. Some lines from the series she was making, could be. Rawdon looked—oh—surprised?"

As well he might, thought Bone. And if that was repeated to the police there would have to be a trial, and if Zephyr stuck to her piece of drama before the judge, it was no longer puzzling that Chase had gone down for so long. It was only to be wondered at why the poor devil fancied that, having so immediately and spectacularly broken one promise, she would keep the other.

It was necessary, now that Treasure had got this off her chest, to guide her back to the matter at hand: what, precisely, she had seen or heard on that fatal afternoon. The problem here was that she had clearly made herself the champion of Rawdon Chase and might bend the truth to favor him. They had been together during the recent search for them, and could have concocted a story. The approach must be cautious.

"You said, just now in the hall, that you saw Rawdon Chase talking to your mother when you looked through the crack in the boathouse door, and that he told you he did not harm her. You did not see him leave or swim back across the lake."

Treasure moved her shoulders and frowned, disturbed at this résumé of what she had said in the agitation of his arrest. This was the first Dwight had heard of Chase's being there at so vital, or fatal, a time and he sat up, glaring. Treasure said, "Sure I did. He was talking to her and then he swam back across the lake. That's what he did."

"Did you see him do it?"

Treasure hit the table with both hands. "Why don't you *believe* him? He did, he told me he did. If he says so, he did."

"Did you see him?"

Treasure's answer was to burst into tears, and Dwight was at once on his feet. "This is harassment. I demand this interview be stopped right now."

"Of course," said Bone. "We've no intention of causing distress." He nodded to Fredricks, who leaned over to give the time of the interview's conclusion and switch off. Treasure looked at Bone from brimming eyes over her hands pressed to her face.

"Thank you, Treasure. You've been very helpful."

And so she had. Thanks to her partisan espousal of Chase's cause they knew now that he was probably innocent of the death for which he had served time. They also knew that she had seen him talking to her mother perhaps only moments before she drowned and that he had the strongest possible motive for drowning her.

"So what have we got?" Bone faced the incident room, leaning his hips against a table, a blank screen

304

behind him on which he had nothing to project. Some of the team were having a belated lunch. Tyrell, as Bone's gaze lighted on him, stopped chewing as if in respect, giving the Super his full attention, one cheek bulging. Bone was conscious of a pang of hunger. Locker must be suffering severely. Useless for Tyrell to focus on him. "Carry on with the nosh. I'm sorry to say we have nothing concrete. Rawdon Chase denies killing Zephyr West although he admits to arranging a rendez-vous at the lake and he had therefore opportunity as well as motive."

"Motive, sir?" It was Tyrell, emphasizing his attention although he spoke through sandwich.

"There is the possibility that he did not kill Storm West, our victim's sister, but that Zephyr West did, and that Chase made a deal with her that she'd marry him when he came out of jail if he'd take the blame for her."

There was a silence, and a change in the expression of the faces turned toward him. Someone shook his head. Someone else muttered a sibilant "Shit" under his breath. Chase was qualifying as a suspect worthy of being hauled in by their Super.

"What evidence, sir?"

"Yes, well. Unless we can establish it's the victim's blood on the boxer shorts left in Chase's car, there so far is nothing. The pm showed a graze on her wrist, probably from a struggle that scraped her arm against the raft."

"The shorts are with Forensic, sir, but they said—"

"That they're too busy to process them yet."

Everyone dutifully laughed.

"We have no witnesses either way, of course. Treasure Schlumberger insists that she only saw Chase talking to her mother and I'd say, since a lie would apparently get him off the hook, that she's sticking to the truth very honestly. Stalemate."

While Bone was speaking a phone rang and Fredricks had snatched it up and stood listening. Now, still holding the receiver, she signaled.

"Pat?"

"It's Rawlings, sir. He's found the yellow Fiat."

Amid a murmur of amused comment at Rawlings' power of finding cars, Bone took the phone. "Have you got the girl?"

"No, sir." Rawlings' tone was dismal. It was his fate to come upon abandoned cars. Bone wondered if it had been Rawlings who found that first, hired, car left by Alan Wilson on the hill before he wandered down to die in the quarry and give everyone a bad time until he was known not to be Cryer. "I'm sorry, sir. Should I wait until she comes back? It's where Mr. Hunter put the chain across, where we asked him to shut off the lane. The car's almost against the chain. Looked like she didn't want to reverse out. Perhaps she isn't too good at reversing." The tone almost ventured to be facetious.

Bone permitted the joke. "That's always possible. Is there anything useful in the car?"

"Mostly sweet papers, sir. Mars bar wrappers, that sort of thing. No personal belongings, at a quick look. I didn't hang about, sir, in case she came back; I've withdrawn to an observation point."

"Well done. She may have gone off on foot. Maintain obbo." He repressed the wild wish to add, keep this up and you may find an abandoned murderer.

He looked at the faces in the room. There was a buzz of hopeful talk as the Action Allocator despatched a plainclothes couple to go to Rawlings' find and wander innocently up the hill. The fan in the Fiat might have come to see where her friend Alan Grant died.

"Could be the girl's a witness . . ."

"Saw her beloved Ken dunk his bride in the water."

"Keep her short of Mars bars and she'll crack and talk."

Chapter
51
·········

While the incident room was speculating on her future, Kelly was busy with her present. This had suddenly offered a glittering opportunity.

She had taken a bus, caught at a stop about half a mile down the main road from the lane, into Saxhurst where she meant to buy food and perhaps to find a bed-and-breakfast where she could stay until Ken found her. The fare stage was just before Saxhurst and she was walking past Mouse Corner when she saw a limo, black and sleek, turn up Mill Lane by the cottages, and she recognized the boy beside the driver. Ken's son.

Emily had finished icing the walnut cake and, leaving it on an upturned plate on the kitchen dresser, she cast a final routine glance round to make sure she had contrived to exclude every cat and kitten from the kitchen. Skywalker in particular, she searched the curtains for; once, when she had been entertaining the General to tea, he had gallantly come into the kitchen to carry the tray for her and Skywalker had tested his battle nerve by dropping from the curtain rail onto his head. There had been no replacing those beautiful cups and saucers from her grandmother's tea service.

The front doorbell rang as she completed her check and, smiling in anticipation, she went out and shut the door quickly as Arletty made to slip past into the kitchen. Cats may not care for sweet things, are indeed said not to be able to taste them, but Arletty was an inveterate experimenter and did not draw the line at icing.

Jem waved to Mel who had turned back to the limo when Emily opened the door; all was safe at the front. It naturally did not occur to her that she might well have checked for intruders at the back. She had lost some petunias to Kelly in the front garden a few days ago, and would have been nervous to see her treading purposefully through the back garden now.

Anything belonging to Ken had a compelling magnetic power over Kelly, drawing her closer irresistibly before she had time to think, but now her resourceful brain was evolving a plan. Any minute now, she thought, the limo would leave the front lane where parking was so difficult, and come round to the grassy little alley at the back, where no other cars came, to wait for Jem there. She must get out of sight, therefore. A little arch, covered in honeysuckle, protected a white-painted iron table with two chairs on the small terrace outside the back door, and Kelly edged into it. She was not to know she could have saved the trouble, for Mel had taken the limo into Saxhurst in search of some excellent cinnamon buns homebaked at the High Street bread shop.

Emily feared that kittens underfoot would prove a hazard to Jem, not trained in her skill at lifting them softly out of her way with her toes as she carried the tray, so she refused his help and went into the kitchen to make the tea. Through the glass upper panel of the back door, Kelly had observed the walnut cake, but she ducked back under the honeysuckle when she saw the inner door opening. Emily was humming happily to herself—she had been hearing that lapping water, on and off, all day and was glad of the distraction of a visitor. She had unlocked the back door when Jem phoned, as she thought he might like tea in the garden.

She poured boiling water into the fat black teapot, and was putting its lid on when she heard a sound behind her and turned, half expecting that Makepeace had at last perfected his technique of reaching up to drag at door handles—he could open all the latched doors in the house—and she vaguely wondered how he had managed a round handle. She had no time to turn fully before a great blow on the back of the head made her see first a sparkling darkness and then a brief vivid glimpse of the floor tiles as she descended into unconsciousness.

Jem, on the sitting room sofa, heard a ringing thump and a disorganized tumbling sound and he called, "Are you all right?" Although there was no answer, he heard movement about the kitchen, opening and shutting drawers and, reassured, he sat back. Arletty jumped off his lap and went to stare at the kitchen door, the end of her tail twitching. Jem supposed that tea must be very near.

Tea did not come. Jem thought he heard moaning mingled with that sound of someone moving about the kitchen. Had Emily hurt herself after all? He got up and sped to open the kitchen door.

He stood there for a moment, disbelieving. Emily lay on the floor tiles, with a hand to her head, making the moaning he had heard, and a large young woman in black leggings and a blue and pink flowered top stood over her, not offering any help. Was she a neighbor or the cleaning woman? What had happened?

"Are you all right?" he said again; the young woman was in his way, he could not reach Emily and he hovered, not sure what to do, feeling useless.

"I'm all right, I think," said Emily with a quaver. "I don't know what happened." She struggled to sit up, and managed it, holding her head.

"Don't touch her." The young woman stopped Jem in his lunge forward. She had gone down on one knee by Emily.

"She's hurt her neck?" Jem knew people shouldn't be moved if the neck was hurt, it could damage the spine, she could be paralyzed, she should have a collar—the paramedics on television put them on people even before they moved them to stretchers. The young woman, however, was helping Emily up, pulling her roughly to her feet although she tottered and clung to the edge of the drainingboard for support. She was white and looked confused. Jem was somehow more upset to see her normally tidy gray bob all tousled and on end.

"I honest think she should have an ambulance. I'll phone." Jem was turning to go into the sitting room when a gasp from Emily stopped him. She was staring at the young woman who gripped her arm.

"Who are you? What are you doing here?"

Jem thought, Oh God, she's not remembering people. The young woman ignored her but spoke, quite ferociously, to Jem.

"Where's your father?"

Briefly he thought of the famous picture of Roundhead soldiers and a small Cavalier boy: when did you last see your father? If the boy told, his father would die. Jem now felt, along with the distressing strangeness of Emily looking so ill, that this woman was a threat.

"What's Dad got to do with it? He's not a doctor?"

"Tell your father to come here at once. Ring him. Now."

To his astonishment—he did not at first register horror—he saw that she had a knife in her small plump hand, a cake knife with a curved point and serrated edge, and she was holding it to Emily's neck, the tip just under her ear. Emily, not daring to move, was peering down at it. Her mouth was slightly open and her underlip quivered.

Jem knew in a flash that this was the crazy fan his father had told about. He'd laughed with Edwina. But she was actually, really, mad.

"What for?"

"He must come here. He'll come. He only needs to know where I am."

She was propelling Emily, who was definitely not steady on her feet and walking awkwardly because of the knife at her throat, toward the sitting room. Jem retreated before her.

There wasn't any choice. He picked up the phone.

Bone surveyed the wall map in the incident room, where someone had helpfully circled in red the spot where the yellow Fiat had turned up. Locker pointed over his shoulder to a cryptic map sign on the road north of the lane.

"Bus stop there. Buses run to Saxhurst, Adlingsden, Ashford, Tunbridge Wells. She could be anywhere."

"That's what I like about you, Steve, always accentuating the positive. One thing we know, however. She's not going to be far from Cryer, unless she's given up on him as a bad job."

"Come to her senses, you mean. If she can find them."

Bone turned away from the map, abruptly. "We have a nutter on the loose and I'm not, as they say, comfortable with that. Not in any way. Cryer's death threats stopped since we found Alan Wilson dead. Now we know that Alan Wilson was the nutter's boyfriend, for an obvious reason. The odds are he did a self-destruct—again we don't know why unless Cryer's marriage made him look at his own life and not like the sight, his girlfriend falling a little short of Zephyr West for a start. But suppose he didn't plan on killing himself. Keep in mind, he could have been after Cryer. He had the weapon."

Locker had planted himself, hands in pockets, staring at the floor matting. He raised his head now.

"So? You think she stopped him from killing Cryer? Stick paracetamol in his coffee. Could she be sure he'd drink it?"

"Where had he left the hire car? In the woods where there's a short walk to a view of the Manor, and the spot had signs of past use. Suppose they'd made a habit of watching their beloved from afar? Drinking their coffee and doting. Cryer might not appear in the grounds at all but they could have all the fun of hoping he would. And sometimes he might."

Locker's face showed what he thought of people who chose to waste their lives this way.

"Steve, Wilson had a gun. It was a Winchester and with a range certainly as far as the Manor grounds.

Wilson could shoot. His parents say so. A good shot could take out someone walking there."

"He meant to do it?"

"Unless his girlfriend prevented him."

Locker sucked his cheeks. He came to the point, though.

"She's dangerous, sir."

Bone had been thinking this for some time, an unease at the back of his mind, present there just as his separate anxieties about Grizel and the baby never left him. He nodded.

"We'd best warn Cryer. He might be able to give us a sighting of her. He seems to be her magnet."

And a sighting was, after all, what Ken Cryer offered. Almost on cue, Fredricks came with a knock at the door and urgently interrupted.

"Sir. Ken Cryer just rang; message for you. He's on his way to Miss Playfair's. His son is there and rang him a minute ago—that fan is there and demands to see him. She's got a knife and is threatening to kill Miss Playfair if he doesn't come at once."

"God, sir, you'd got it. Pat, call off the squad in Hunter's wood, get them to Willow Cottage, Mill Lane, Saxhurst. No blues, no twos, no show. We have a hostage situation." Locker was bent toward the map. "There's a lane at the back—or a grass track. One vehicle is to go there."

Bone looked at the map. Too late to circle in red, there were the cottages, and the one holding a boy, an elderly woman, both friends of his, at the mercy of a woman whose obsession left her with no feeling for anyone but Cryer; those feelings might turn from love to hatred at a wrong word from him.

Chapter
52
·········

Ken in the limo leaned forward to the limit of his seat belt; Joe was speeding when he could. He had skimmed the ankles of a woman crossing the road not far from the Manor, blasted the horn at a dawdling car, sworn and hit the steering wheel and violently reversed after coming on a stalled furniture van blocking a narrow road that was a shortcut to Saxhurst. Joe was going as fast as he could without hitting anything.

"What the blazes is Mel doing? Why isn't he at the cottage?"

"I got him on the mobile. He was in Saxhurst buying buns."

"Bugger buns. I want him to get that madwoman before she hurts Jem."

"He's on his way. Get *on*, you bloody fool!" This was not to Ken but to a woman who had pushed a baby buggy out into the road while chatting to a friend on the pavement, as if no traffic existed. Short of infanticide they had to wait until she had crossed. Ken had time to wonder what he was going to do when he reached Emily's; Jem had said "She's got a knife" in a voice that shook slightly. God! If the lunatic hurt Jem he'd tear her apart. Time she got a life that wasn't make-believe.

Joe drove up with a screech of brakes in Mill Lane. He picked up the phone to check where Mel was—had he got to the back lane as planned? Was he out of sight? Ken insisted *he* would get the knife off the woman, she was not to suppose they were there. If Mel came blundering down the back garden they could cause Emily Playfair's death. Joe had not been minder to Ken for so many years without grasping the essential detachment of fans from reality, and this one was almost over the horizon.

Ken opened the white picket gate and ran up the path, past where he had floundered on the grass in the embrace of the woman now waiting. Emily and her kittens had saved him then; now, coming to her rescue, he had to be the sacrifice. As long as Jem didn't try heroics— he'd told him to keep it cool.

It was Jem who opened the door and Ken froze between impulses to snatch him and rush back to the car, or push him out and slam the door; but Jem had drawn back up the narrow hall and Ken, following, looked into the sitting room and saw Emily, in her cozy fireside chair, pressed against the back of it, a knife at her throat, her face white under the disordered gray hair.

"Ken! Darling, I'm here! You told me to come and I did!"

She's got it all arsy-versy, thought Ken, in turmoil. I'm the one who was told to come, I never asked *you.*

How avid she looked, fatter than he remembered, in a floral chiffon thing that snagged on her hips, her eyes glittering as she smiled at him with such rapture. Oddly enough, she'd be pretty if she wasn't so frightful. He held out his hand.

"Give me the knife."

He wasn't ready for the rush she made, overwhelming him, pinning his arms to his sides, his mouth crushed by her lips. She still held the knife and he was aware of it behind his back. How to get things straight, to call Joe and Mel in, hand her over to the police . . . Robert would have brought them, they must be near. He tried to get free of her, jerking his head back as he felt her tongue in his mouth.

"No. Listen. You have to stop this. Get real—"

She clung to him, smiling, flushed, amazed.

"But you don't have to pretend any more, darling. Don't you see it's all right now? We're together. And you needn't worry—I'll never tell them."

It's just possible, flashed through Ken's mind, that I'm the one who's mad. He tried to put her from him but found, as he had the day before, that there was nothing wrong with her muscles. Best to play it cool, as he'd told Jem, soothe her and hope to Heaven that someone turned up soon. *Where* was Robert and his posse? He temporized.

"We must talk about all this, yes. About what you're going to do."

Again she resisted his efforts to ease her arms from their encircling clasp. She was dimpling, as if he'd made a joke. "What *we're* going to do, darling. And what's to talk about? I know it's soon after her death, but people will understand. They'll see what we are to each other. And we don't need a lot of fuss, a reception and all that stuff. I know you so well! I know you like simplicity, honesty, no pretense. That's why I'm here. You told me so much in your songs. We can be married privately anywhere and, if you want, go abroad right away to give people time to get over the surprise."

Ken thought: I'd need a lifetime to get over that surprise. He had not realized her fantasy extended to marriage. Groupies who followed him on tour, fought their way to the front row at gigs so that he came to know their faces like those of his own band; who threw flowers, and panties with phone numbers scrawled on them— these girls were mostly practical. They might have their dreams but they didn't expect marriage. Should he pretend to go along with this until the police arrived? He glanced at Emily, crumpled in the armchair. Where had the police got to?

Not far away, but acting on strict instructions, like Joe and Mel, to keep out of sight. Emily's neighbors, returning from shopping, dead-heading roses in a front garden, or gazing from their windows, were riveted to see several police cars in what seemed like a line away down the sunken lane. Could Emily be involved in that terrible business at Herne Hall? Were the police here to arrest her?

Ken was trying reason now, with little hope. The woman gazed into his face with such devotion. She looked so happy that he might have been touched—if she had not the knife; its point brushed the hair at the back of his neck. Keeping his voice matter-of-fact, he said, "You don't need that. After all, I'm here," and he held up his hand for it.

"Yes, of course, darling."

He took the knife and didn't know what to do with it. She still half-embraced him, and Jem as luck would have it had bent his head over Emily who moaned at that moment, and did not see his father's offer of the knife. Ken tossed it into the bank of ash on the hearth, where it disappeared in a little avalanche and a false smoke of ashes, making Jem and Emily start. He felt more at ease as he looked into her rapt face.

"We really can't get married. You have to love someone to marry them"—or at least to desire them, his honesty told him—"you only think you love me. You don't know me—"

"Of course I do! Of course I know you! I've done everything you told me in your songs, every single thing you asked. I listened over and over and I'm not wrong, I *know*." Her face was distorting. Damn, was she going to cry? Slowly, she released him. He saw, past her, Jem squirrel the knife from the ash and dodge back to Emily.

A ginger cat emerged from somewhere and, running low, made for the kitchen. The tension in the room had almost cleared it of cats; those left, even the kittens, had gone into hiding. The woman still gazed into his face. The whites of her eyes showed all round the iris. "You wanted her to die," she stated confidently. "I knew. You just wanted peace."

He had been trying to avoid facing this for days and he knew it would haunt him all his life. But was she saying he had told her to kill Zephyr? Had this creature, with her grotesque love, killed Zephyr? If that's what she was saying, just as well the police hadn't arrived yet and heard her. Was that a noise in the kitchen?

Ken turned and in that moment she had slipped across to the hearth with surprising agility, felt for the knife in the ashes and, unable to find it, snatched up the long poker from Emily's fire irons. Then she faced him.

"Have you been making a fool of me? Getting me to do it all for nothing? Are you telling me you don't love me?" The voice, no longer babyish, caressing, had gone shrill. Ken stepped back. "After I did what you told me you say you don't love me!"

"What the hell do you mean? I never told you anything! What did you do?"

But he knew. He felt cold and wished with all his heart Jem and Emily were out of here. This woman was a killer, her face red, her eyes wide, the poker raised.

"You know what I did! Now you want to get rid of me! But you can't do it. You're mine."

She charged. Ken brought up his arm, heard the crack of bone as the poker came down, and felt pain like fire burn into him, turning him faint, making him stagger. Jem shouted and rushed forward as she raised the poker for another blow at Ken's bent head, but she side-stepped, knocking askew a little table with a vase on it and, more importantly, a cat under it. Makepeace, too old and thwart-natured to go far, had hidden near Emily but now burst out, haring across Kelly's path as she lunged again.

She stumbled, and Jem clamped both hands round her wrist. His effort at a Chinese burn made her release the poker, which span against the mantelshelf shattering a

small Doulton figurine of a rustic couple and then joined
the shards on the bricks and wood ash of the hearth.
Emily cried out. Ken was still doubled up holding his
arm, Kelly on her knees before him while Jem, trying to
drag her away, found in his turn how strong she was;
and the kitchen door swung back and Bone, just ahead
of Mel, surveyed the scene. In a moment it completely
altered.

Mel took two strides and seized Kelly by the shoulders, allowing Jem to snatch up the poker and back with
it out of her reach. Bone registered this and turned to
Emily, with that knife in mind.

"I'm all right, I'm not hurt, it's poor Ken who's hurt."
Her voice was feeble, almost lost because Kelly broke
out screaming as she twisted and kicked in Mel's grip.
Bone, leaving Emily, went to help and got a kick on the
shin that disabled him for several seconds. He shouted
above the yelling scrum of Mel and Kelly that shifted
dangerously between Emily's chair and Ken's bowed
figure.

"Jem! The front door—call them in!"

Jem wasn't slow. He slung the front door open just as
Kelly squirmed from under Mel and, gripping Ken by
the ankle, brought him down with an agonized roar into
the melee. Bone's team, two of whom had been
crouched on the reviving petunias, poured inside and
into the room, headed by Locker and Fredricks, and
found themselves forced into the problem of sorting out
Kelly from the threshing mass before them. Ken howled
again as his arm hit the floor when Kelly rolled over
on him.

"Cryer's hurt. Get him out of it," Bone shouted. For
all he knew Kelly had used the knife. She might still
have it—he looked about for blood. She didn't seem to
need a knife, though, for she shifted in the scrum and
Mel swore. Kelly was suddenly silent, for she had her
teeth in his hand.

"Bitch! Get her off me!"

It was Emily who made the move. Perhaps driven by

a human desire to get her own back, she picked up a heavy *Gardening A to Z* tome from beside the hearth and brought it down with a resounding thwack, not on Kelly's head which might have sunk her teeth deeper in Mel's hand, but on her rump raised in the struggle. The shock opened her mouth again and enabled Locker to catch hold of her right arm and twist it behind her back. Shay got hold of the other and the handcuffs ready, but Kelly had spirit in her yet.

"Help me, Ken! Help me! I only killed her because you told me to! Don't let them do this!" and, eeling away from Shay, dragging Locker with her, she knelt on a piece of broken Doulton porcelain and let out a shriek of astonishing force. The next second Rawlings and Shay had wrestled the left arm across her back to meet the one Locker still held, and snapped the handcuffs shut. She was heaved and maneuvered, yelling "Ken! Ken!" in a surprisingly imperious tone, and finally was tripped and thrown, and carried out facedown among six officers, still crying "Ken!" in a choking voice that dwindled down the path.

The battle was over. The casualties had still to be counted.

Chapter
53
·········

Looking out of the car window as they lined up before a roundabout, Bone caught sight of one of the roadside objects that always delighted him and Cha, a shared joke they greeted whenever they passed it in the car. Outside the car park of an inn stood the life-size figure of a chef, white coat and tall white hat conspicuous, jovial face smiling, arms held out with elbows bent as if he offered food—arms only. The hands had long been trophies for some discriminating vandal. Cha stated that they had been converted into doorknobs or perhaps table ornaments. To her disappointment, the stumps visible inside the cuffs had not been embellished with gore but painted white. This had led them to speculate that the mutilation might demonstrate the splendid hygiene obtaining in the kitchen, a symbol of the claim "untouched by human hand."

Mel, nursing his temporary dressing, followed Bone's gaze and groaned in sympathy.

"Bring him in too, we should. Looks like *she's* been this way."

In fact, Kelly was on her way to the police station in Tunbridge Wells, where Locker would have the unenviable task of interrogating her. Three victims, Emily with possible concussion and head wound, Ken with what the ambulance men diagnosed as a fractured ulna and laid tenderly in a channel splint, and Mel with a badly bitten hand, were headed for Casualty at the Madison, where Grizel happened to be in the maternity unit. Bone had seen it as necessary to accompany the three.

A stir was caused in Casualty by the arrival of Ken Cryer, and Bone was not surprised to see the triage nurse suddenly accompanied by others, while more personnel than was usual found themselves something to do around Reception. An injured rock star was not their luck every day. Ken, with ruffled hair and with face showing pain, was not Bone's idea of glamour, but the eyes of everyone in Casualty were turned toward him as he was wheeled off to X-ray. One man with a bloodied rag tied round his head cheered himself by humming loudly a tune Bone actually recognized because Cha, by playing it all day for two weeks when it came out three years ago, had imprinted it on his memory. It was the title track of the album "For Crying Out Loud" and the man clearly savored its relevance.

Mel, less privileged, was left to wait for his tetanus booster and what he feared would be stitches, while Bone had the satisfaction of seeing Emily put into a cubicle, helped by a sympathetic nurse, while a doctor examined the wound on her head and looked in her eyes with a light.

"I'd like to keep you in tonight for observation," he said, probing in her hair again, "it'll depend on the bed status."

Bone saw Emily's alarm.

"I'll see to it that someone attends to the cats, Emily, if you're kept in. What about keys?"

"Mrs. Little has a key, next door. Or you could take mine," she said anxiously.

He touched her hand. "I'll see to it."

"Don't worry about me, Robert. It's your wife you

should be thinking about. You go off and see her and give her my love. My love to the baby too."

As he closed the cubicle curtains, he thought: does Emily know something I don't or is she talking of the future? It wouldn't be the first time she'd latched onto an event that concerned him; he set her off in some way. Was it possible . . . ?

Joe Tench was talking to Mel. Everyone seemed to be getting looked after. Bone turned through the inner doors and headed at speed for the maternity wing.

"Mr. Bone! Nurse Carter said she'd seen you here. We have been trying to get in touch—your wife would like to see you."

"You'd better like it, Robert. I'm not taking it back at any price."

Bone looked at his son, who was turning his head to and fro and squeezing up his eyes as if the world was too much to bear in its loudness and newness. He thought, of course—impossible not to—about his first son, whom he had held like this, Petra's son. He made a prayer so strong he seemed to feel it physically, that Grizel's son should have a better fortune. Cha at his side leaned to touch the minute, soft finger, with a sound of awe.

He laid the baby back in Grizel's arms. She was pale, yet dark-shadowed round the eyes, and she looked triumphant.

"We'll keep it," he said. "Kinloch the Brave."

"I was the brave one round here, Robert, I'd have you remember. I refused to let them call you to come here and listen to my yelling. They were all for making you suffer but you were on a case and suffering enough already. Kinloch was to be the reward."

"Oh, if he's the prize," Bone said, pressing his hand gallantly to his heart, "any of *my* suffering was well worth it. Every bit."

"It's about time you told me of the bits. I've not heard much news recently. Cha said when she came that you'd arrested someone, a man just out of jail. She'd seen it on the news and she thought you and Locker were looking several sandwiches short of a full picnic." Grizel brushed her lips to the surprised fuzz on the baby's head.

"It's not surprising we looked half-witted, not on this case. Besides, you know the notices on the roads: Police Slow. We do it to fool the criminals into thinking they've got away with it."

"And have they?" demanded Charlotte. "The man you arrested was an Oxford lecturer in History, they said on the news—and you want me to go to University!"

She was in high spirits at having a brother once more. Bone remembered how she had constituted herself a special guardian of her first brother, for the few months of his life, and he watched her now, bending over the baby in Grizel's arms.

"It looks as though we may have been mistaken over the Oxford don, as it happens. He seems to be not only not guilty of the death of Zephyr West, but not even guilty of killing her sister, which is what he went to prison for in the first place."

"Her *sister?*" Grizel furled the baby closer. "Poor Mrs. West."

"Who did it, then? Have you got the right person yet?"

"Not a lot of doubt about that, I believe. The reason I turned up here so opportunely—as no one had thought to let me know the important news"—Bone touched the baby's petal cheek with the back of a finger—"is that I came in with a few of the people she also had a shot at removing."

"*She?* A woman killed Zephyr West?"

"Doesn't take a lot of strength to hold a woman under water when she's already had her head bashed on a wooden raft. Anyway the young woman proved today she's not short on strength."

"*Who?*" Charlotte took him by the lapels. "Who is she? Daddy, I hope you realize you are infuriating."

Bone nodded over her shoulder at his wife and son.

"I'm far from sure this is the sort of thing Kinloch should be hearing first crack out of the box."

"As the box in question," Grizel said with dignity, "I think it might be my decision. And I want to hear who it is. Do you mean to leave me here wondering while you waltz off and tell your daughter?"

Bone opened his mouth, and shut it again as a nurse appeared in the doorway.

"We must allow your wife to have a good rest now," she announced brightly, employing the royal plural to enforce cooperation. Grizel gave a pleasant smile.

"They're on their way, but I must have a word with my husband first."

A good teacher does not acquire the note of quiet authority for nothing, and the nurse hesitated, returned Grizel's smile and went out, saying, "Just one minute, then, we mustn't tire you out."

Cha drew Bone to the bed by his sleeve, and whispered, "Now hurry. Put us out of our misery. Who was it?"

"You know I can't possibly say for certain. We may not have a case, there's a lot of work to be done yet. What I can tell you is of a young woman who spent this afternoon breaking Ken Cryer's arm, biting one of his minders severely on the hand and knocking Emily Playfair on the head."

"Emily! Is she all right?"

"Is Ken all right?"

"Emily is a bit shaken, I should say. They're keeping her in for observation." He looked down into her anxious green eyes with concern. "I shouldn't be telling you this. It's upsetting."

"It's a very great deal more upsetting, Robert, if I don't know what's going on. What on earth happened! The young woman's a fine termagant from the sound of her."

At this point, the baby joined the audience by turning its face blindly toward Bone and using its fists with urgent vagueness. Bone laughed.

"Is *Ken* all right?"

"I'm sorry, Cha—a broken arm isn't to be sneezed at and he'll be very uncomfortable indeed. But you must keep the story under your hat, or the baby's bonnet if he had one: a fan of Ken's seems to have taken his marriage far too personally and run amuck. A whole hamper short of a picnic, I'd say. She's under arrest at present."

"That's all right then." Charlotte reached over and coaxed a finger into Kinloch's fist. His fingers closed again over hers, and she looked at Grizel with a delighted smile. Bone was aware of sudden, enormous happiness.

"Time's up, I'm afraid!" The nurse had returned. "Say goodnight to Mummy and Baby."

It was strange, thought Bone, kissing Grizel and brushing his son's forehead with his lips, how some people managed to speak in capitals. Cha, adding her embrace, shot a mischievous glance at her father as they prepared to leave, and uttered, with sickly sentimentality, one of their scoring phrases:

"Try to get some rest."

Bone, smiling, riposted with the almost equally popular, "Take it easy."

The nurse thought it decidedly odd that Mrs. Bone should shake her fist at her departing loved ones.

Chapter
54
··········

At Herne Hall in the incident room there was elation mingled with disappointment. Events at Emily Playfair's cottage had been retold by Locker on his way to headquarters with Kelly and, though everyone was relieved at this second arrest, which seemed most promising—for anyone who had accomplished the mayhem described by their Inspector could surely have drowned Zephyr West with no trouble at all—it meant that things here must now be packed up, and Herne Hall had been a most refreshing venue. For one thing, Palmerston had, on Mrs. West's orders, kept them supplied with excellent sandwiches and coffee; for another, Rawlings, apart from his aptitude for discovering abandoned cars, had found the leisure to strike up a flirtation with one of the female gardeners, who looked extremely fetching in breeches.

At Locker's instructions they had already been in touch with Rawdon Chase's probation officer and with the Oxford police. Breaking the terms of his license meant an automatic return to jail but he could expect, in view of Treasure's testimony, a re-trial. This, if he were proved innocent, might get him not only his freedom but also perhaps his job back: Oxford was still the home of lost causes and a professor who had the quixotry to spend time in prison for a murder he had not committed should fit very well into the scheme of things there. He would not be able to claim police compensation, as he had pleaded guilty, and it was to be hoped that, since he had served a sentence, he would not be charged with wasting police time and resources. Fredricks, vocally partisan about this, was promptly joshed for having fallen for him.

But before he was taken to Tunbridge Wells to await a prison escort, Mrs. West sent to ask if she might see him. Everything had been explained to her by her granddaughter and she was anxious to see, and perhaps apologize to, the man whose life her daughter had ruined. Locker, applied to by radio, gave permission, and Rawlings took him to Mrs. West's sitting room. Not much was said and Rawlings, who had positioned himself tactfully by the window looking out, was rewarded with a fine view of the urns on the terrace and the gardener Chloe bending over each in turn. She had just wheeled her barrow of tools, debris and planting-out boxes away when an odd sound made Rawlings turn and discover Chase and Mrs. West with their arms round each other, both in tears.

It was the first time Mrs. West had cried since Zephyr's death, and she wept now from shame as well as grief.

"I'm glad Treasure told me the true story. You must try to forgive her."

Rawdon, knowing she meant Zephyr, nodded as he stood back and fingered tears away under his glasses. "I've done that. Now you have to try."

Treasure was not at this meeting. She was strolling with her father under the sweeping boughs of the great cedar, where Rawlings might have seen them had he been less fascinated by the gardener's rear. For once. Dwight was not on the phone, had even left his mobile in the house. He was giving his full attention to his daughter and her plans.

"I want to live here. With Grandmother. I like it here."

There was a touch of defiance about this. Another girl might have preferred never to see the place again, a place one might suppose to be haunted with terrible memories, but Treasure was not that girl. She was a realist, and had a streak of toughness in her that her father proudly recognized.

"That's okay by me, honey, but I want you to visit on your vacations. L.A., New York, I'm thinking of getting a beach place in Miami. Your mother wanted that."

"Not Miami, Dad. New England?"

"What you like."

They strolled in silence for a while, Treasure kicking at moss with her sandals. He glanced back at the house.

"I feel badly about that guy Chase. But it's like your mother said, after you'd come to tell me and we tried to make her give up marrying Cryer, she was in the clear once he'd said he was guilty. She'd suckered him into it and he went along with it all the way."

"She didn't have to say he'd threatened to kill Storm before. *That* stopped it looking like an accident, that really put him in the shit."

"For all you know, honey, he had said it. There were times *I* wanted to kill Storm. She was not a comfortable lady."

"Well." Treasure stopped, to thump her foot down and bare the array of braces. "I'm going to go to court and say what I saw. It's no way fair that Rawdon should be treated as he has been. We owe it to him to put things right."

Dwight had stopped too, and was patting his pockets a little desolately, perhaps feeling the lack of his phone, his umbilical link with power and the world that obediently made his money for him. Instead, he produced a cheroot, lit it and blew smoke up into the branches of the cedar.

SUSANNAH STACEY

"If you want to do that, I'll hire a lawyer for you. I know Ablesteen over here, he'll get you one of the best." He drew again, exhaled and surveyed her through smoke. "You know, honey, you might want to take up law one day. It's a hard grind, I'm told, but it pays well and you have the mind for it."

Treasure had a vision of herself, hair in a sleek bob, smart executive suit, defending some poor downtrodden guy whose life was in her hands. No ringlets, no nonsense. And her father thought she had a mind. She smiled brilliantly, and plucked the cheroot from his lips to take a puff while he laughed.

"Sure I'll visit," said Treasure Schlumberger. "When I can spare the time."

Ken Cryer had never, he thought, been so grateful, even after exhausting world tours, to get home. The Press contingent outside the Manor, alerted by someone at the hospital, had increased threefold and dashed forward. All the limo's windows were a mosaic of lenses and its interior white with flash. Not one of the shouted questions could be heard. Joe, who had taken Jem home already and had come to fetch the hospital contingent, eased the car through the scrum as the gates opened; a cameraman lost his balance and fell against the foot of the wall, never ceasing to click away even at forty-five degrees. Ken gave him a commiserating wave as the limo slid to safety.

Edwina waited in the stone-flagged porch, and kissed him over the strapped arm, wagged her head sympathetically at Mel's flourished bandage, and led Ken, preceded by a backward-walking Jem with an imaginary camcorder, to the sitting room.

"Drinks, I thought, first, and then Mrs. Rudyard has made your favorite hot-pot."

Ken, who had been known to yearn for sausages and mash in Thailand, sighed and sank into one of the scarlet corduroy sofas while his son handed him a tall gin-and-lime, ice jostling against the rim. Last time Mrs. Rudyard

330

served up hot-pot, Zeph had laughed long and beautifully. "When we're married," she'd said, "I'll just have to take you in hand."

He owed that crazy fan for more than a broken arm.

Crazy, he thought. And *I* was crazy. It appalls me that Zeph's dead. Did I really want her dead? Did that girl latch on to— Oh no. I couldn't have wanted that. I never could. I'm to blame for not getting out when I knew it couldn't work. But my God, if she'd really killed her sister, perhaps she'd have killed me.

"Are you ravenous? I am." Cha was rooting about in the refrigerator, finding cold chicken and mayonnaise to make herself a sandwich, and ham and cream-of-horseradish, which Bone had a passion to put with anything, however unsuitable.

He sat on the cushioned settle in the kitchen, letting things happen round him and stroking the lithe gray back of Ziggy, who had jumped on the settle beside him and insinuated himself under the table to lie on Bone's knees and look up at him with purring faith in food to come. It brought back the scene in Emily's cottage half an hour earlier.

"How on earth does she manage with all those cats? I opened tins until my hand hurt."

Cha arranged her provisions on the table and sat opposite him, buttering bread. "Oh, but those kittens were *adorable*. I thought perhaps—"

"*No.*" All Bone's weariness, the tensions of the past few days, came out in that negative, and Cha looked up, startled. "No kittens. A baby's going to be quite enough."

"Well, I suppose at least babies don't climb curtains and drop on you from above." Cha pushed across to him a monster sandwich, frilled with lettuce. "What a mess poor Emily's place was in. I'm glad her neighbor had a key too and didn't mind coming in to finish clearing up before she gets back." She bit happily into her sandwich. "That fan of Ken's must be totally off the wall to have done all that damage." She spoke with more than usual impediment. "What I can't understand is why she broke Ken's arm if she was so mad about him."

"I shall not launch on an explanation about love." Bone too spoke through his sandwich, discovering that he was, like Cha, ravenous after all. "Warning and advice are useless, in my experience. You can't tell what's going to happen, with love. You can be lucky, like me. Or things can go badly wrong for no reason anyone can see."

"Should you go by instinct? I mean, you do, in your work, don't you?" Cha was looking at him quite seriously and he wondered if what he said would make a difference to her future. Was she thinking about committing with that unreliable-looking young man so proud of being "dippy"?

"I suppose I do." Bone considered the case that had just finished. What had his instinct been? Not to trust anyone, perhaps. "The trouble is, it's hard to be sure. I've instinctively liked some murderers, for instance. You can sometimes tell, I suppose, when something isn't right. . . . But, when it's love, that feeling may come a bit too late." He was thinking of Ken Cryer and his drowned bride. If Zephyr had not been murdered that day, her husband might well have regretted before long.

Chat rattled her tumbler of fruit juice on the table.

"What are we thinking of? We should be drinking to Kinloch. Haven't we got any champagne?"

Bone got up, sliding Ziggy to the floor, and went to look. The future was full of promise, after all.